Mixed Signals

*Also by Liz Curtis Higgs
in Large Print:*

Bad Girls of the Bible
Really Bad Girls of the Bible

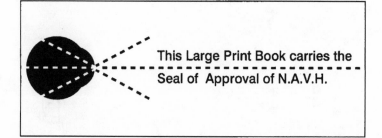

This Large Print Book carries the
Seal of Approval of N.A.V.H.

Mixed Signals

Liz Curtis Higgs

Thorndike Press • Waterville, Maine

This is a work of fiction. The characters, incidents, and dialogues are products of the author's imagination and are not to be construed as real. Any resemblance to actual events or persons, living or dead, is entirely coincidental.

Published in 2006 by arrangement with Multnomah Publishers, Inc.

Thorndike Press® Large Print Christian Romance.

The tree indicium is a trademark of Thorndike Press.

The text of this Large Print edition is unabridged.
Other aspects of the book may vary from the original edition.

Set in 16 pt. Plantin.

Printed in the United States on permanent paper.

Library of Congress Cataloging-in-Publication Data

Higgs, Liz Curtis.
    Mixed signals / by Liz Curtis Higgs.
        p. cm. — (Thorndike Press large print Christian romance)
      ISBN 0-7862-8748-9 (lg. print : hc : alk. paper)
      1. Large type books. I. Title. II. Thorndike Press large print Christian romance series.
PS3558.I36235M59 2006
   813'.54—dc22
                                    2006008688

In memory of my father,
who told me years ago
that my future would be in radio.
Bless you, Daddy, for being right.
As always.

Let your speech always be with grace, seasoned, as it were, with salt, so that you may know how you should respond to each person.

Colossians 4:6

Acknowledgments

It may not take a village to write a book . . . it just looks that way!

First, love and heartfelt thanks to my dear husband, Bill Higgs, my costar in our own radio romance. Bless you for giving me a reason to celebrate every broadcast day.

And double hugs to my children, Matthew and Lillian, who tiptoed around me while I was writing. I love you with every inch of my abundant body, kids.

A tip of the headphones to my far-flung radio peers from years past, at WQXA-FM, WKTK-FM, WFBQ-FM, WWWW-FM, WQMF-FM, WAKY-AM, and my last and best broadcasting home, 84WHAS-AM Louisville. Thanks for sharing the air with me, dear friends. (I promise, *none* of you was the inspiration for Frank the Crank!) A special nod to Joe Fedele at WVEZ-FM, Tommy McCarthy at WOGL-FM, and Randall Bloomquist at WBT-AM for their assistance.

A big howdy and thanks to my new friends at Multnomah Publishers, especially my precious editor and friend, Karen Ball, and all those in Sisters, Oregon, who've helped my prayers come true.

Where would I be without my friends in fiction? Francine Rivers, Lisa Tawn Bergren, Carolyn Pizzuti, Robin Lee Hatcher, Annie Jones, Angela Elwell Hunt, Terri Blackstock, Robin Jones Gunn, Debbie Macomber, all my LoveKnot sisters, and my first fiction buddy, Jack Cavanaugh. Bless you, bless you, one and all, for looking at my early writing efforts. From my point of view, you are the best in the business. I can't thank you enough for your generous gifts of encouragement and expertise.

A huge hug to fabulous fiction writer and online soul sister, Diane Noble, whose support, prayers, and daily accountability made this book happen. Love you, dear heart!

Cherished friend and literary agent, Sara Fortenberry, managed to laugh and cry at the same time when I read her a passage from *Mixed Signals* over the phone. Bless you for your boundless encouragement. Belle finally rang true because of you!

Gloria Looney, amazing office assistant, was the perfect first reader, keeping me going with her generous words of praise.

Mother-in-law Superior, Mary Lee Higgs, did a grand job as Head Grammarian.

Leesa Gagel served as my helpful proofreader.

Gayle Roper, talented writer and respected teacher, hauled the first draft to Canada with her, then continued to offer valuable suggestions. What a blessing you are!

Thanks to Lori and Tim Shahen at the Lovill House Inn in Boone, not only for your exceptional hospitality, but also for recommending Abingdon as "the perfect setting for a novel." You were so right.

Finally, my deepest gratitude to all the wonderful residents of Abingdon, Virginia, who spent time with me on the phone and in person, answering questions and offering ideas. Many of these folks were generous enough to read the manuscript as well . . . now *that's* a labor of love! Special thanks go to Marsha Miller at the Barter Theatre, Rebecca Boyd at the Martha Washington Inn, Joan Hilbert at the Abingdon United Methodist Church, Emily Umbarger at the Washington County Library, Martha Weisfeld at the *Abingdon Virginian*, Lesa Morrison at the Virginia Highlands Christian Fellowship, Rick and Mary Jayne Stevens at the Silversmith Inn, April Eskridge at the Abingdon Convention and Visitors Center, Craig Sutherland and Larissa at WABN-FM, Betty Cardwell at the Anchor Book Shop, Bonnie Clevinger of Balloon Virginia, and Don Hilton.

I always save the best for last; don't you?

That means my most heartfelt hugs go to *you,* my courageous readers, who've bravely moved into this fiction adventure with me. You, as always, are the reason I write.

Glossary of Radio Terms

stick — tower that supports the antenna

cans — headphones worn by air personalities

make good — re-air a commercial that aired incorrectly

spot break or *stop set* — short break in the programming for commercials and chitchat

liner card — printed promotional announcement posted in studio for personalities to read periodically on the air

hot clock — clock face showing how each hour is divided up into music segments and spot breaks

intro — the instrumental introduction to a song before the vocals

post — the first note of the vocals

hook — the most memorable part of a hit song

carts — tape cartridges for recording and playback

pipes — complimentary term for a DJ's voice

traffic — the department at a station that handles commercial schedules and logs *pot* — slang for potentiometer, the volume control on the studio or production board

day parts — specific periods during the broadcast day, usually divided into the following:
morning drive (6:00 a.m.–10:00 a.m.)
middays (10:00 a.m.–3:00 p.m.)
afternoon drive (3:00 p.m.–7:00 p.m.)
evenings (7:00 p.m.–12:00 a.m.)
overnights (12:00 a.m.–6:00 a.m.)

One

*Failure is the opportunity to begin again
more intelligently.*

Henry Ford

Rainy days and Mondays never got Belle
O'Brien down. Not when her radio listeners were waiting. "Hold On, I'm
Coming," she sang out with off-key
abandon. Sam and Dave had nothing on
her, she decided, grinning, as she tucked
her jeans inside her short leather boots.

She tamed her unruly hair into a thick
braid that reached her waist, and darted
out the apartment door. A chilly, mid-
October downpour waited to greet her.
Overnight, the rain had carelessly washed
the leaves out of the maple trees lining
Lake Shore Drive, plastering them across
the pavement like small scarlet hands.

Belle was still humming when she spun
the wheel of her Pontiac toward the station. Still humming when she tossed the
keys toward Max, the parking lot attendant, and made a wet dash for the glass
front doors of her radio station.

The doors with the famous call letters
mounted above them.

Yup. There they were. *W . . . WT . . . WTI . . . W-what?*

Her humming abruptly stopped as her heart lurched toward her boots, then snapped back with a sickening thud. *Not again. Not this time.*

Numb to the core, she stepped inside the reception area. Her umbrella was hanging open. So was her mouth.

"Belle!" Her general manager emerged from a huddle of men in suits and moved toward her. "You're just in time. We've . . . made some major changes here."

She gulped. "Starting with the call letters?"

"Right." His smile was strained. "Welcome to WTIE, Chicago's All-Sports TIE-breaker."

Sports? Help, Lord! "I don't do sports," she croaked.

"You do now." He reassured her with a wink. "Come meet your new program director, Snap Davis."

She watched the circle of suits move toward her, all smiling, all talking at once. Her mouth had gone dry — past wool, past cotton, clear to the linen setting.

"There she is, gentlemen." One of the strangers clenched his cigar in a churlish grin. "The Belle of the Ball."

"The *what?* You have the wrong announcer, Skip . . . ah . . . Slap . . . er . . .”

His tobacco-stained smile broadened. “Call me Coach.”

“Great.” She fought for breath, struggling to get her bearings. Her eyes drifted to the walls covered with thirty years of bold signatures scrawled there by every musical act that had hit the Windy City, from Sam the Sham to Manfred Mann.

Wait. She blinked. *They didn't! They couldn't!*

But they had. Her heart sank another foot as she took in the newly painted walls, now a solid navy latex. All those signatures, all that history, all *her* history.

Slam-dunked out of existence.

The suits guided her toward a row of shiny lockers, one of which prominently displayed her name in block letters. *BELLE.* She did as expected and yanked open the narrow metal door, only to find the shelves stuffed with sports paraphernalia: a Chicago Bulls jersey, a Cubbies cap, two Bears coffee mugs, a Blackhawks hockey puck, and two tickets to a White Sox game.

The loathsome new call letters were printed on everything.

She shuddered at the sight and slapped the door shut, turning to find her new boss regarding her with amusement. “You've planned this for months, haven't you?”

"Smart girl." Her cigar-chewing coach looked infinitely pleased with himself. "Only took us six hours and a ton of manpower to make the switch last night. None of your golden oldie pals were right for the new format. But we've found the perfect spot for you, sweetheart."

"But where — where is everybody?" She knew. Of course she knew. Hadn't she been down this road before?

"Nothing to worry your pretty head about, Belle. The rest of the staff received a generous severance check."

"And the contents of their desk in a box, I suppose."

He shrugged. "Ten years in broadcasting, isn't that right, Miss O'Brien? You've been around. You know how it works. Frankly, if you weren't a woman —"

One of the suits delivered a sharp elbow to his ribs.

"A talented woman, that is, you'd be looking for work along with the rest of them. As it is, Belle, we're delighted to keep you on the payroll as WTIE's official announcer. Commercial spots, sports scores, station IDs, all yours, ready to record."

Great.

Why, oh why, on this of all mornings, hadn't she listened to the station on the way to work? Instead of walking in clue-

16

less, she could have steered onto 94 South and kept driving.

The production director chimed in. "Yeah, we're looking for a sexy, breathy sound, Belle. Higher-pitched than your normal on-air voice. Kind of like . . . like . . ."

Her stomach tightened, desperation setting in. "Like Betty Boop?"

"That's it!" the suits sang out in unison. *Boop-oop-a-doop.*

She knew what she *wanted* to do. What every fiber of her being insisted that she *deserved* to do. Tell Mr. Slap Happy to stuff his cigar in his cauliflower ear. Bulk-erase every inch of tape in the wretched place. Plant that hockey puck between her general manager's chattering, chicken-livered lips.

That's what she wanted to do. And more.

But what she did — what she *had* to do — was choke down the huge lump in her throat and accept the inevitable.

She had no choice. Single, living alone in an expensive city, she needed the money. They wanted Betty Boop? They got her.

All week long, she marched into the recording booth, put aside her pride, and squealed like a teenager on helium.

All night long, she sobbed herself to sleep. *Five stations in ten years, Lord!* Her life

17

was like a broken record. The Shirelles singing, "Will You Still Love Me Tomorrow? — tomorrow? — tomorrow?"

Five times she'd stuffed everything she owned into a moving van and headed for a new horizon — Kingsport, Richmond, Atlanta, Philadelphia, then, two years ago, Chicago.

Five times she'd prayed this would be the one. Home.

Five times she'd had her dreams trampled by new management, new formats, and men very obviously from Mars who had no idea how oldies radio worked.

Finally, Friday afternoon, after a depressing hour of heavy breathing and squeaking in the production studio, she pulled on her green wool coat and started toward the front door, her feet and spirits dragging.

"Belle." She turned to see the receptionist signaling her. "Line three is for you. Pick it up in Snap's office if you like. He's already left for the Sox game."

She ducked into his crowded corner office, wrinkling her nose at the stale cigar smell that permeated the air, and perched on the edge of his chair. Clearing her throat as if an imaginary On Air light had blinked to attention, she cradled the receiver against her ear and punched the third button. "Hello, this is Belle."

18

"Sorry about the format switch, babe." The male voice was warm, familiar, empathetic.

"Patrick!" She tightened her grip on the phone. "You heard about it, then?"

"Everybody heard about it, Belle. It was in all the trades today. Front page of *Radio & Records.* And *above* the fold, no less. Big story with a photo of the staff."

Her throat suddenly felt drier than melba toast. "The staff? Before or after?"

"Before." His voice softened. "You looked great, kid. Major-market material. Have I ever told you how proud I am of you?"

Patrick Reese, her first boss in broadcasting, always knew the right thing to say. She felt herself relax for the first time in days. "We haven't talked since you moved to San Diego. How's that working out?"

His masculine hoot was all the answer she needed.

"Guess it's my turn to say sorry, Patrick. What happened?"

"The owner insisted we'd score big in the ratings with around-the-clock Christmas music. In July."

She grinned. *Good old radio.* "So where are you now?"

"Abingdon, Virginia."

Faint images of a small town tucked in the southwest corner of Virginia drifted through her mind. "I've been there." Her memories swirled into focus. "A bunch of us from Appalachian State took a carload there one summer for the Virginia Highlands Festival. Very historic, as I remember. Quaint." She chuckled. "Not exactly a radio town."

"Precisely why I'm here, woman."

"Let me guess." She sighed, so weary she could hardly think. "You have a job offer I can't possibly refuse."

"More than that."

She sensed him pausing for effect, imagined him leaning back, leather loafers propped up on a secondhand desk, the sleeves of his striped sport shirt rolled up to the elbows showing off his tanned, muscular arms. Casual. Confident. In control.

"I have the one thing you've always longed for, kid."

"Is that a fact?" *And don't call me kid,* she wanted to say. He was only a dozen years older than she. Forty-four to her thirty-two. *Kid?* Buddy, those days were long gone.

Wait. She frowned. What "one thing" had she always longed for?

Surely he wasn't aware of that silly crush she'd had on him all those years ago? She *had* been a kid then, green as April grass in the Carolinas. They'd kept in touch over the years, simply because they were

20

friends. Right? Just friends?

There was one way to find out. "W-what thing have I longed for, exactly?"

"Acting."

"Acting what?" *Foolish,* she chided herself.

"Belle, I'm talking about theater. Acting on stage. You know, drama? You majored in it, remember?"

"Oh, *that!*" Relieved, she grinned into the phone. "Of course I remember. Truth is, I haven't tramped the boards since you lured me away to WTFM."

"I can fix that. Abingdon has a restored playhouse —"

"Barter Theatre!" *Of course.* The State Theatre of Virginia. "Patricia Neal played that stage."

"And Gregory Peck and Ned Beatty and . . . Belle O'Brien?"

"Hmm. It *does* have a nice ring to it. What shows are they doing this season?"

"Aha! So you might be interested in Abingdon and WPER."

"WPER, huh? Who's the owner?"

"Uhh . . . I am." He cleared his throat. "WPER stands for Patrick Edward —"

"Reese!" She chimed in with him, laughing.

He groaned. "I know, I know, it's an ego thing." The man sounded genuinely embarrassed. "The call letters were available

21

so I couldn't resist. Forgive me?"

A warm sensation skipped along her spine. She'd forgotten how much she loved sparring with him. "At least I won't have to worry about whether or not the owner likes me."

His tone was more subdued. "No, you won't have to worry about that at all."

Was it her imagination, or was the ground shifting?

"Uh, Patrick, I . . . I really do need to think about . . . things. When do you need an answer?"

His manner was all business now. "The station goes on the air the third of November. I'll need you here by the first." He launched into a description of the format, the hours, the staff he'd lined up, barreling along with his persuasive salesman patter.

After five nonstop minutes, she jumped in. "Slow down, mister! I've heard this song-and-dance before." She swallowed, determined to make him see what this career was costing her. "Don't you get it? I have a car with Illinois tags and a Pennsylvania driver's license and a North Carolina savings account with exactly twenty-nine dollars in it."

A week's worth of frustration came rushing out of her, sweeping her along in its emotional wake. The tears she'd wept alone at home now showed up in Snap's corner office, unbidden. "Patrick, I'm thirty-two years old and I have *nothing*. N-not a house, not a husband, not a child, not even a decent dining room set." She sniffed, looking wildly about her for a tissue. "I have friends all over the country, but not one person I could call at four in the morning."

"You could call *me*."

"W-what?" With her eyes and nose running, she stared at the edge of her wool scarf, desperation growing.

"You could call me. At four in the morning." The phone line hummed between them. "I'm single, too, remember, kid?"

"You probably snore and wouldn't hear the phone ring," Belle muttered, pouncing on an ancient tissue tucked down in her coat pocket. With her tears quickly dried and voice steadied, she begrudgingly offered an apology. "I'm sorry to sound like a shrew. I'm absolutely —"

"Exhausted. I know, babe, and I'm sorry to pressure you after a week like this." The sympathy sounded genuine. Patrick *was* her mentor, after all, her confidant.

There had never been anything more between them. She was certain there wouldn't be now.

"Look, I'll get back to you," she promised vaguely, then hung up the phone before she realized she didn't have his number. *Should I have asked for it?*

She couldn't deny his offer was tempting. Oldies music, the midday show, small town, smaller egos, no more competition for ratings, the thrill of a brand-new station, the chance to pursue theater.

The chance to work with Patrick again.

"Oh, Lord . . ." She sighed into the smoky air around her. "I don't know whether to sing a chorus of 'You've Made Me So Very Happy' or 'The Sun Ain't Gonna Shine Anymore.' "

Patrick dropped the receiver in its cradle with a sigh of satisfaction and exchanged glances with his engineer, standing across from him in the production studio.

"Is she coming?"

"Absolutely."

David Cahill, radio engineer, construction crew, and all-around handyman, rested his lanky frame in the doorway, arms folded across his chest, one shoulder propped on the salvaged door frame he'd installed and painted only days earlier. He regarded his boss, bemused. "Are you sure that's what she said?"

Patrick shrugged. "She may need some time to adjust to the idea of small-market radio again." Patrick nodded at the felt-topped turntables, one of the many scratch-and-dent specials he'd dragged up to their third-floor studios. Someday it'd be digital equipment, he'd promised David. Today it was electronic leftovers.

"I'll warn you, David, these turntables will make her nervous."

"Why? Hasn't she ever played vinyl records on the air?"

"She's played 'em, all right. At WTFM in Kingsport, she was interviewing a world-class pianist who was in town to perform a benefit concert for the Bach Society. Belle cued up his latest album to the famous 'Minute Waltz.' You know the song?"

David nodded.

"As soon as the first note hit the air, this highbrow lowlife flung himself across the console, calling her every name in the book. Poor Belle had forgotten to change the turntable setting, so instead of 33 1/3 RPM, the album was moving along at a zippy 45 RPM."

"Ahh." David grinned. "More of a '*Half-*Minute Waltz,' eh?"

"Right. 'The Chipmunks Go Classical.' It was hysterical."

"Did *she* think so?"

"Eventually." Patrick smiled, recalling her crimson cheeks. "Belle is an ambitious gal who doesn't cut herself a lot of slack. Always wanted to make it big. Sure enough, she did."

"Then what happened?"

Patrick sighed. "I'll let her tell you about that when she gets here. And she *will* get here, trust me. I taught Belle everything she knows about this business. I'm the one who convinced her the jingle singers couldn't handle 'Belinda Oberholtzer' and changed her on-air name to 'Belle O'Brien.' "

"O'Brien? Sounds Irish."

"She's redheaded and stubborn enough to hail from County Clare, I can assure you of that." An image of Belle suddenly came to Patrick's mind — small hands on hips, eyes snapping at him, freckled face scrunched up in dramatic disagreement about one thing or another. *Probably a song she refused to play on her show.*

He smiled at the vivid memory. "O'Brien's her name now, legally and professionally. Since I gave Belle her first radio job in Kingsport, I figure she owes me."

But not for Kingsport. For Richmond. For the job that took her away from me.

Patrick felt his smile fade and his chest constrict. Mailing that demo tape of Belle to WRVQ in Richmond eight years ago was the hardest thing he'd ever done. It had cost him dearly, and not only in rating points. He'd sent it anonymously, knowing WRVQ would hear her talent in the first

26

sixty seconds and make her an offer she could not — must not — refuse.

And all because he'd made the cardinal mistake of falling in love with her. His own employee, his own protégé, and he'd almost ruined everything. By letting her go, he'd spared her from ever having to choose between him and fame.

She'd thank him, if she knew.

"Does Belle know?"

Patrick came out of his reverie with a guilty start. "Know what?"

"Know what a jerry-built, shoestring-budget kind of operation this is?" David was grinning as he said it, apparently meaning no offense. "You've got stuff here manufactured in three different decades, wired into a board with only eight channels. This isn't exactly Chicago."

"Yeah, but the price was right." More than once, he'd happened upon a perfectly good piece of radio gear propped against someone's trash can. King of the Road Kill, his last staff had called him. So he got a kick out of finding treasures hiding in people's junk piles. So what?

Besides, he had to cut corners somewhere or he couldn't afford to hire Belle. "Mark my words, she'll take the job." *Say yes, woman. I need you here.*

He slipped out of the studio and moved down the hall to his private office, tossing his raincoat over a set of deer antlers he'd dragged around the country with him, station to station. The antlers made a great coat rack and a better conversation piece, right along with the nine-foot marlin mounted and hanging behind his desk. He loved to tell people he'd harpooned it off the coast of Mexico, but usually ended up telling the truth: He'd found it sticking out of a Dumpster in Slidell, Louisiana.

David stuck his head in the post office and found it buzzing with late-afternoon activity. People came and went with packages and plastic tubs full of letters while he ducked in the side door and headed for his box — the smallest, cheapest one in the place.

He'd be happy if just one piece of mail was waiting for him. One particular piece. He pushed the hair off his forehead, stalling. *Please, Lord.* He shoved his key in the lock, hesitating. *I haven't asked for much. Let it be there.*

Swinging open the metal door, he felt his whole body tense. On top of the small stack of mail was an envelope with a handwritten address, neatly printed. He slipped his hand in the narrow box and pulled out the fistful of letters and postcards, forcing himself to shuffle through the rest of it — bills, mostly, and advertisements.

Nothing that couldn't wait.

He opened the long, white envelope last . . . the one with a return address that was permanently etched on his memory, written in handwriting he immediately recognized, even before he saw the name.

Sherry Robison.

His hands, tanned by the sun and torn up by nails and boards, were shaking. He told himself it was caffeine, but he knew better.

A single sheet of paper was inside, a short note written by the same hand, with small, carefully formed letters in plain blue ink. He scanned the words that told him nothing new.

Until he got to the postscript. *I understand what you're asking for and it's only fair. I'll send it soon, I promise.*

Soon?

Soon beat never, but not by much.

Two

Friendship or love — one must choose.

René Crevel

The bells of Abingdon United Methodist Church chimed a joyous melody into the crisp November air as Patrick pulled his '71 Eldorado up to the curb on Church Street. He pointed the blue behemoth with the coffinlike hood in the direction of Norah's brick Victorian on the corner of Main Street, where the third floor was ready and waiting for a new tenant — Belle O'Brien.

He checked his watch. Almost noon. Norah promised to call him on the cell phone when Belle arrived, but he'd gotten antsy waiting around his apartment all morning.

Now he felt like a stalker.

Even *he* didn't know what he was doing there early, sitting and waiting for her like some lovesick adolescent. *Ridiculous.* It was eight years ago, a lifetime ago. Then, as now, he'd hired Belle because she was the best person for the job, period. Any personal feelings for her had faded away to nothing but a warm memory.

30

Keep telling yourself that, buddy.

Clearly the Chicago deal had been rough on her — it had shown in the strained sound of her voice on the phone, in the cynical bent of her words — but she'd get over it. Like him, Belle was a survivor. One with talent. And brains. And huge amber eyes in a small, heart-shaped face . . . and a low voice that wrapped itself around listeners' hearts and wouldn't let go.

Funny thing was, Belle didn't have a clue about any of that. Personal appearances put her over the edge. Listeners gawking at her, saying inane things like "I thought you'd look different."

The fools.

He'd been in radio long enough to understand the problem only too well. No matter how beautiful she was — and she *was* beautiful — when Belle sensed that her five feet, two inches of Carolina casual didn't meet her audiences' expectations, her spirits sank, taking her confidence with it.

That, by jig, won't happen in this town. He'd see to it she was crowned the Belle of Abingdon in six months. Less.

The doors of the church swung open, launching a buoyant wave of townsfolk streaming along the sidewalk past his car. He'd been in Abingdon just over six weeks, long enough to recognize a few faces, not

31

long enough to nod as if he knew them. That'd happen soon. He was in Virginia to stay, no question. Belle wasn't the only one weary of being jerked around from one city to another.

A thirty-something guy with a high-voltage smile was walking toward Patrick's car, evidently on a mission. Patrick rolled down the window and put on his best public relations smile. Everyone in town was a potential WPER listener.

"Matthew Howard," the younger man offered, thrusting out his hand with puppylike exuberance. "I'm the new associate pastor. Were you waiting for someone?"

"Not exactly." *Then what exactly are you doing, Reese?*

"Well, don't be shy. Next Sunday, why not come in and join us?"

Given enough time, Patrick could think of several reasons why not, though none popped into his head at the moment.

"Appreciate the invitation, Reverend Howard." He returned the man's handshake. "I'm Patrick Reese, the owner of WPER, a brand-new radio station in town that's going on the air Tuesday."

"Oh, sure!" The pastor's eyebrows shot up toward his neatly trimmed, wavy brown hair. " 'Oldies 95,' isn't it?"

Patrick's smile widened. "That's us. Hope you'll tune in, Reverend." After all, the guy was smack dab in the middle of the station's target demographics — eighteen to fifty-four.

Unless, of course, the pastor's favorite music was hymns.

"Tell you what, Mr. Reese. I'll listen to WPER if you'll come listen to *me* sometime soon." Matthew winked then turned away to shake hands with an elderly man waiting behind him.

Pretty good salesman. Patrick watched him work the crowd still flowing past his Cadillac convertible. Belle might decide to attend church here. Handy enough, right across the street from her apartment. When they'd worked together in Kingsport, she'd often talked about going to services.

He was a Christmas and Easter man himself. Twice a year, just to keep his name in the hat. Maybe in a few weeks, he'd give Abingdon UMC his business for the holidays.

His attention abruptly shifted toward Main Street as a Pontiac slowed to a crawl in front of Norah's place, then turned on Church. When the car slid into the space reserved for Norah's tenant, Patrick sat up with a start.

Belle.

Though he couldn't see clearly from half a block away, he kept his eyes trained on the car nonetheless. A small, red-haired

33

woman in a dark green coat and blue jeans slipped out and headed for Norah's back door.

Yeah, she'd always looked good in green.

He took a deep breath, letting it out with a noisy hiss. *Showtime.*

Staring at his cell phone propped on the passenger seat, Patrick willed it to ring. *C'mon, Norah, I feel like a fool sitting and waiting. She's here now, so call me. Please?*

Belle searched for a doorbell until she gave up and tapped firmly on the back porch door. This was definitely the right address, since the house fit Patrick's description to a T. Her eyes drank in the weathered brick exterior — 1871, he'd said — and freshly painted white trim. Three full stories and a tin roof with two promising chimneys. *A fireplace? Hope so.*

She'd already fallen in love with Abingdon. Driving in on East Main, she'd nearly had a fender bender twice while trying to take in all the historic buildings on both sides. Antique stores, gift shops, restaurants, and one quaint residence after another were crowded along the narrow, hilly street. It had been a struggle, but she'd pulled her attention back to concentrate on the house numbers. *Plenty of time to explore later.*

And explore she would. Abingdon was the quintessential small town, population 7,003.

Soon to be 7,004.

Patrick had pushed all her buttons to make her say yes to this place, pleading one minute, needling her the next. "What are you afraid of?" he'd demanded. That was the question that'd made her so mad she finally said yes.

"I'm not afraid of anything!"

Liar. She was knee deep in fears. Afraid to see Patrick and risk falling in love with him. Afraid the station would fold after six months and leave her jobless again. Afraid that after dreaming of doing professional theater for so many years, she'd embarrass herself with an amateurish audition.

Afraid of being single forever in a sleepy Virginia town.

Though she had to admit, it was a *nice* sleepy town.

At Court and Main she'd snatched a quick glance at the building that housed WPER and liked what she saw. She'd continued the four short blocks to Norah's, expecting the eye-pleasing architecture to dissolve into twentieth-century mediocrity, but it never happened.

No wonder Patrick raved about this place.

All at once, the back door opened with

the tinkle of tiny bells and Belle was greeted by two unmistakable scents: fresh bread baking and Shalimar perfume. Both were quickly followed by a tall, slender woman in a fluttery silk jacket of rose and black. Her large silver earrings and necklace, though striking, didn't overpower the woman's dramatic features, now decorated with a wide, welcoming smile and silver hair cut in a flattering, chin-length style.

"You must be Belle!" The ageless beauty threw open the door further and stepped back. "I'm Norah Silver-Smyth." Her voice was husky and musical, laced with laughter. "And you're just in time. The soup has simmered all morning and our bread will be done any moment. Here, let me take your pretty coat."

Belle slipped off her green wool coat, suddenly feeling too casual in her long sweater, jeans, and boots. Why didn't Patrick warn her they'd be lunching with a fashion plate? Then again, Patrick probably hadn't noticed Norah's pricey wardrobe, so enamored was he with outlet store bargains.

"I'm afraid I've dressed for travel rather than for dinner."

Norah lifted her brows in a graceful arch. "My dear, if I looked like that in straight-legged jeans, you'd have to cut them off my dead body."

The woman laughed again and Belle was instantly put at ease. *Well, well. A real person.*

Her hostess waved in the direction of the pots, pans, and baskets dangling dangerously low from dark oak beams that ran the length of the room. "This place needs a Watch Your Head sign, doesn't it?"

"Not for me." Belle couldn't hold back a smile.

"Ah, lucky you, then. Patrick conked his head on that lethal frying pan once."

Belle looked up, remembering only too well how her first boss had towered over her. The memory sent a tingle of anticipation down her spine. *Won't be long now.*

Norah gestured toward an inviting doorway and flashed a sly grin. "I only let people I *like* use the kitchen entrance. Come have a seat in the dining room." She winked. "It's safer there."

And it was even more impressive. Belle's gaze took in a heady mix of muted plaids, large florals, polished cherry, and solid oak. A warm, sophisticated style one wouldn't find in any magazine, but style nonetheless. "Your house is amazing, Norah."

"You're too kind." Norah followed her into the dining room, where high ceilings, pale yellow walls, and dark oak floors served as a neutral backdrop for a host of vibrantly hued quilts and a rich Persian floor rug in an exotic pattern.

In the hands of an amateur, the eclectic ensemble might have jarred the senses. Clearly, Norah Silver-Smyth was not an amateur.

"Ohh." Belle sighed. "This is lovely." She gazed out the tall dining room windows that stretched floor to ceiling, offering an enticing view of a deep, wraparound porch that would surely call her name on lazy summer evenings. "I hope the apartment upstairs is half this nice."

"Shall we find out?" Norah disappeared back into the kitchen for an instant and returned, shaking a ring of keys. "Right this way, Belle. Forgive me for being so chummy, but Patrick has told me a great deal about you."

Belle felt her cheeks heating up. "I can imagine what he said. Promise me you believe only half of it."

"On the contrary, I chose to believe every word." Norah led her into a front hallway and gave her another dazzling smile. "I know all about your growing up in North Carolina and attending ASU and your passion for theater, not to mention the radio career that's taken you across five states." She slipped a silver key into a solid door, opened it to reveal a long, curving flight of steps, then turned to regard Belle

38

with a look that hinted at understanding, even sympathy. "I also know about Chicago."

Belle laughed and shook her head. "Does everybody know?"

"No, bless your heart." Norah tipped her head slightly. "One way or another, we've all been there, Belle. You're in much better hands now." She started up the steps. "Come see your new digs."

Belle trailed behind her. "How do you know Patrick?"

"We met at a Washington County Chamber of Commerce mixer. One of those parties where you stand around and smile for two hours, stuffing business cards in strangers' canapés. Patrick mentioned he'd hired a woman who'd need an apartment. I'd recently received notice that my tenant was moving, and . . . you know the rest."

Belle's curiosity was aroused. "When was that, exactly?"

"Ah, let's see. Two weeks ago."

The scoundrel. She hadn't come close to a decision until last Monday.

Belle followed her landlady up the enclosed staircase, mulling over the best way to get back at Patrick for telling Norah so much — and her so little. It would've been helpful if he'd said something other than "Nice lady, silver hair, great house."

Talk about an understatement.

Norah continued talking over her shoulder. "My last tenant, Deidre, lived up here for a dozen years. An exceedingly quiet sort. She held court in the Virginia Room at our public library on Oak Hill Street, three blocks away. Ate alone up here, night after night." Norah turned to give her a broad wink. "Promise me you won't be *that* solitary?"

Belle laughed. "I've never been accused of being a loner."

They climbed the last few carpeted steps to an open area with rooms that beckoned on either side and a window before them that was nearly the size of Norah's huge front door, one floor below. "Hold it, this *is* a door." Belle stepped forward to admire the view. "Was there a porch out there once?"

"Undoubtedly. These vintage properties have had more additions and subtractions than you can count. This was the house I was born in. When I was . . . well, single again and my mother became ill, I came back here to care for her, God rest her soul."

"She passed away, then?"

Norah nodded. "I think Mother would like the changes around here, though. The shop downstairs and this apartment. She'd certainly approve of my new tenant." Her smile was genuine, making Belle feel more welcome than ever.

"That's my church, by the way." Norah pointed across the street. "Almost as old as this place."

Belle nodded, about to explore the apartment further, when a familiar sight stopped her in her tracks. She squinted out the window in disbelief. "Is it my imagination or is that Patrick's rusty old Cadillac parked next to the curb?" It was a car like no other. Painted bright blue, it approached the dimensions of a small house on wheels. The *Blue Boat,* he'd affectionately named it in Kingsport. The thing had to be falling apart by now.

"I believe you're right." Norah nodded, looking over her shoulder. "One of the most outlandish cars I've ever laid eyes on. Can't imagine why he's sitting out there instead of ringing my front doorbell. He knows he's expected for lunch." The two of them exchanged a conspiratorial glance. "What do you think, Belle? Shall I call him?" Norah reached in the voluminous folds of her silk jacket, pulled out a slender cellular phone, and punched in a number. She knew it by heart, Belle noticed.

"Patrick, she's here. Yes, all safe and sound." Norah paused, smiling out the window and winking at Belle. "Tell me, how long have you been watching the house?"

Belle burst out laughing. She didn't need to get back at Patrick for keeping her in the dark. Her new landlady had neatly handled that for her.

Norah nodded into the cell phone. "Well, these things take time. Let yourself in. The back door's open. We'll be upstairs, spending that exorbitant salary you've promised Belle. If her taste is anything like yours, every piece of furniture she owns is on its last legs." Her laugh unfolded like the opening measures of an Italian art song. "Patrick, I suggest you hurry before Belle tells me a secret or two about *you*."

Belle watched in utter astonishment as Norah slid the phone back into her pocket, cool as fresh mint in May. Never had she seen a woman so thoroughly put Patrick Reese in his place.

Norah trained her dark, carefully lined eyes on her new tenant. "I can see the wheels turning, Belle. You're wondering what sort of relationship I have with your boss, yes?"

Who, me? Her cheeks warmed again. "How'd you guess?"

"Come next April, I will have lived fifty years on this grand orb, and therefore fancy myself a good judge of both character and motivation. When you figure out those two, the rest is easy." Norah folded her arms and leaned back, as if sizing her up. "You thought we were an item, didn't you?" She shook her head, setting her thick hair and dangling earrings in motion. "Not in the least." Her eyes narrowed ever so slightly. "Patrick Reese is in love with you, my dear. Has been for a long time."

Belle's tongue felt glued to the roof of her mouth. "No . . . I . . ."

"Nonsense. It's in his voice every time he speaks of you. Now that I've met you, it's easy to see why." Norah laid a gentle hand on her arm. "Not to worry. He and I have never discussed it. He's so dense about such things, he imagines it's his little secret."

Downstairs, the back door tinkled open and shut. Norah added in a stage whisper, "Let's let him think we're equally dense on that score, shall we?"

At that, they heard a dull thud and muffled curse drifting up from the kitchen. "The frying pan again," Norah whispered, sending them both off in a fit of giggles.

They were still trying to pull themselves together when Patrick rounded the landing and stared up at them, a sheepish look on his face.

"Have I missed something?"

"Not at all, Patrick. In fact, I think you hit it right on the noggin." Norah winked at Belle then extended her hand, silently

43

inviting Patrick to join them.

His eyes, however, were locked on Belle.

He's older, Belle realized immediately. Of course, he would be. Eight years didn't pass by without taking a toll, but he'd aged more than she'd expected. His handsome head of hair was still thick and full, waving stylishly close to his collar, but his full beard was a new addition and mostly gray at that. So was the hair at his temples.

Then he smiled and became the Patrick she remembered, with a sparkling set of white teeth framed by a permanent tan he'd probably picked up in San Diego. It was a smile that never failed to put her heart into cardiac arrest.

"Patrick." It was all she trusted herself to say.

Trust had always been a problem for David Cahill. Trust meant believing what someone told you, depending on someone to help you. He couldn't think of one person he'd ever trusted in all his twenty-seven years who hadn't disappointed him, hadn't let him down, utterly and completely.

Until now.

"David, is that seat next to you taken?"

He looked up to find a pretty brunette standing there, eyeing the empty seat next

44

to him. Her name was Jennifer Somebody-or-Other, one of the single adults in the church. Her crisp, striped dress brushed by the knees of his jeans as she sat down, rustling in the morning stillness, falling in stiff folds on either side of her.

It was hard not to catch a whiff of her perfume. Flowery sweet, innocent smelling. *Figures.*

"Nice to see you again, David." She displayed a line of perfect teeth, no doubt the product of an adolescence spent in braces. Everything about her pointed to a nice childhood with parents who loved her and cared for her, who sent her to expensive orthodontists and dressed her like a princess. Parents who taught her how to trust God with her whole heart.

It was a lesson he was only now beginning to grasp.

The first time he'd dropped into one of the fold-down seats at Virginia Highlands Christian Fellowship five months ago, he'd been prepared for one of three things to happen: the roof to cave in, the building to be struck by lightning, or the congregation to laugh him out the door.

Or *throw* him out.

None of those things happened. He'd sat there that June day, slumped down in his seat, angry at nothing in particular but angry all the same, while the guy up front in the chinos and the madras shirt talked about grace.

He thought grace was something families mumbled before they choked down their supper.

But Pastor Curt said grace meant forgiveness, and forgiveness was a gift.

A gift? Nobody had ever given David Cahill so much as a sack of free groceries, let alone a gift. Whatever he owned in life had been earned the hard way, through blood and sweat.

And yeah, tears. Not many, mind you, but they'd been there.

Pastor Curt said tears were healing, no matter the reason. "Those who sow in tears will reap with songs of joy." Curt was always quoting the Bible like that, by heart, as if he knew the whole thing cover to cover.

David knew zip. Which was why he spent every Tuesday night at Curt's, studying with a couple of other guys who knew as little as he did. Next week they were starting a series Curt called "The Fruit of the Spirit," the first of which wasn't a fruit at all. It was love.

Love.

David knew all about love. About the giving, not the receiving.

And about the wanting. Definitely about the wanting.

Three

If love is the answer, could you please rephrase the question?

Lily Tomlin

Belle couldn't fathom that Norah's words were true. *Could Patrick honestly care for me? Not love me, of course. That's crazy. But . . . care?*

Belle watched Patrick climb the last two steps to her new apartment. Uncertainty danced around them like dust motes. *Would a hug be too forward?* She tried to read his expression. Surely Norah was wrong about his feelings . . . wasn't she?

Oh my, oh my.

He stood before her now, almost a foot taller than she, still the muscular teddy bear he'd always been — broad-chested and solid. His smile crinkled his whole face, including his hazel-colored eyes.

"You look wonderful, Belle." He slipped his arms lightly around her waist and bent over for a quick, chaste embrace, then stepped back.

Whew. She wondered if the odd mix of relief and disappointment showed in her face.

Norah politely cleared her throat. "Suppose I set the table for lunch while Patrick gives you the grand tour? He's seen these rooms before." She tossed a knowing smile Belle's way then floated down the steps like a graceful bird.

Belle spoke first, stating the obvious. "Norah's amazing."

"Yes, she is." Patrick looked as if he might say something else, then touched her elbow instead. "Let's take a quick look around and head down for lunch. I'd hate for our soup to get cold."

Food was one detail Patrick never missed.

"I'm also anxious to hear more about Chicago." He grinned. "Or we can skip that, if it'll ruin your appetite."

She made a horrid face, looking, she was sure, as if she'd bit into a persimmon. "I've been dining on crow salad for three weeks."

"No problem. This place'll cheer you up." Patrick shifted into the role of salesman the instant they walked into the first room. "Okay —" he rubbed his hands together — "You have two identical front rooms, one on each side of the stairwell. This big one would make a great living and dining room combo." He shot her a sidelong glance. "When you get a dining room set, of course."

He remembered.

Patrick angled his head toward an oak mantel. "Don't you love the fireplace?"

She did love it. And the warm, light gray walls and the immaculate white woodwork and the wide oak boards at her feet. "Patrick, it's perfect. How can I possibly thank you for finding this for me?"

Wait. Don't answer that.

Apparently oblivious to her sudden discomfort, he ambled off to another room. "Back here is your kitchen. Big pantry for storage."

Belle followed him through to a galley-style kitchen that ran across the back of the third floor, with windows on one side and a wall filled with gleaming white appliances on the other. She groaned theatrically. "There goes my excuse for not cooking."

He raised one bushy eyebrow. "Seems to me in Kingsport you made lasagna for our whole staff once."

"So I did. Once. Is that a hint?"

"I'll buy the groceries."

"Did I hear you say you'd be willing to *pay* for something?" She did her best to look shocked. "Where's a tape recorder when I need one? Not a soul will believe me."

"I've changed, Belle." He looked slightly injured.

"Oh, really?" She chuckled. "Explain to

49

me then why you're still driving the Blue Boat."

"Because it runs." Clearly he felt that was explanation enough. "Now it's my turn to ask a question."

She leaned against the sink and swallowed the knot in her throat that was threatening to cut off her air supply. "Okay, shoot."

All at once, Patrick looked as if his tie were too tight. "It's . . . ah, personal."

Uh-oh. "No problem."

"Why did you come to Abingdon?"

Nothing like getting right to the point. She shifted her gaze to the floor, tapping the toe of one boot on the pristine tile, willing her cheeks not to burn. *Keep it light, girl. Don't give yourself away.* "Because I . . ." She looked up at him and gulped down her grin whole. "Because I've never seen you in a beard. Seemed worth the drive."

His suntan brightened considerably as he stroked his whiskers. "I thought it made me look distinguished. More like the owner of Abingdon's hottest new radio station."

"Abingdon's *only* radio station."

"It does have its competitive advantages." His eyes were full of mischief.

Belle pushed away from the sink, nervous energy singing through her veins. In

50

the space of ten minutes, she'd shifted from worrying about how she felt about Patrick to worrying about how Patrick felt about *her.* Her emotions were on edge with questions that didn't have answers. Yet.

"I'm ready to see the rest of the apartment if you are." She used the most carefree, blasé tone she could conjure up.

His steady gaze told her he'd seen right through her la-dee-da act but was smart enough to keep it to himself. They crossed the landing again and ventured into another square room that also looked out onto Main Street through a trio of shuttered windows. "Nice," she murmured, folding back the white wooden shutters.

"This might make a decent study. Another fireplace, lots of natural light —"

"Patrick, when did you start paying attention to home decor?"

He colored again. "Since I'm the one who made the initial arrangements, I hoped . . . well, I'm glad you're pleased."

And so they went, stumbling through inane conversations about floor plans and ceiling heights, talking about everything except what was on their minds. At least, what was on *her* mind. Belle restrained a groan. How had they gotten off to such a prickly start?

When they stepped into the next room,

with its adjacent tile bath, Patrick muttered something about its being the obvious choice for her bedroom then immediately suggested they see how lunch was progressing downstairs.

She nodded quickly. "Yes, let's do." *Before I jump out of my skin.*

Norah greeted them in the dining room with fragrant bowls of black bean soup, rich and dark, served with a dollop of sour cream and crusty Irish soda bread. Belle was grateful for something to focus her attention on other than memories and feelings, and sensed that Patrick felt the same way. "Mmm," was all that was heard around the table until they put their spoons aside at last. From the looks on Norah's and Patrick's faces, Belle was sure they were as thoroughly sated as she.

She was feeling more at home by the minute, thanks to Norah's amiable ways. The woman was wise and confident, at peace with life and comfortable in her skin, which Belle found enormously appealing. In Norah she saw the inklings of more than a business relationship, landlady to tenant. She saw a woman who might provide something sorely lacking in her life: a good and true friend.

Belle chuckled to herself. Calling Norah at four in the morning would be easy. All she'd have to do was bang on the floor.

★ ★ ★

The cell phone in Patrick's pocket rang while Norah and Belle gathered up table linens. "If you two'll excuse me . . ." He punched buttons on the phone. "Patrick here. Yes, David. The transmitter *what?* Oh, bother."

He noticed Belle watching him intently, her eyes like twin lamps, warm and glowing. He could barely concentrate on what David was saying about reflected power and plate current, so taken was he with seeing her again.

"Uh-huh." The stream of engineering jargon flowed on.

She's older. Of course, she would be. Wasn't he? And yet the eight years had been good to her, he decided. Most things hadn't changed — her tiny frame, her long braid, her penchant for jeans and boots, her contagious laugh. Other things were new, like the maturity and confidence he hadn't counted on. She was truly a woman now, not a fresh-out-of-college ingenue. *And to think I called her "kid."* The picture in *Radio & Records* didn't begin to do her justice.

Some women had rosebud lips. Belle insisted hers were more like asparagus — two straight, thick lines drawn across her face. *Yeah, right. Asparagus, my foot.* Her full lips were the stuff of dreams, not casseroles.

53

"Uh, yes, I'm listening, David." *Now.* "Sounds like we might be looking at a new loading capacitor. Want me to come take a look? Not a problem, we just finished lunch. And what a killer meal it was." He winked at Norah, eyeing him across the kitchen. "See you in fifteen minutes."

He disconnected and shoved the phone back in his pocket. "It seems we have a serious glitch at the transmitter site, according to my engineer. Norah, you've met him, haven't you?"

"You forget I've lived in Abingdon all my life." Her animated features grew still for a moment. "David Cahill grew up here. I knew his father, John Cahill, too, though I haven't seen either of them since David joined the air force. A determined young man. Trustworthy. Good with his hands, too."

"Right. Anyway, he's out at the stick now, trying to figure things out."

Norah raised her hand like a confused student. "The stick?"

"The radio tower. Where the antenna and transmitter are located, out on Old Jonesboro Road. David lives there, you know."

Belle looked at him as if he'd swallowed a live frog. "He lives in the *transmitter shack?*"

"Almost. When I bought the land, it included an old farmhouse that was in such bad shape I planned to tear it down. David talked me out of it. A win-win, I'd say. Saved me the money and hassle of having it removed, and gave him something to do in his spare time."

Spare time was not in Patrick's vocabulary and they knew it. It amazed him to discover that his employees had so much of it. "You'll be meeting David and the rest of the gang at our first staff gathering tomorrow morning at ten." He searched Belle's face, looking for a clue to what she might be thinking. Or feeling. "See you then, Belle?"

"I'll look forward to it."

He lowered his voice, hoping to sound as sincere as he felt. "Forgive me for leaving so soon?"

Both women nodded in his direction, then smiled at one another. *What's that about?* He didn't have time to analyze the situation but instead pulled on his coat and offered his farewell from the doorway. No way could he handle another brief embrace from Belle, not when he wanted to pull her into his arms and never let go.

Admit it, man. David's distress call was a godsend.

He needed air and he needed out — quick. Trotting down the steep sidewalk toward the Blue Boat, which was still parked next to the church, he sifted through the hour he'd spent with Belle and decided that although his feelings for her hadn't changed, there was obviously zero interest on her part.

She seemed happy to see him, but not overjoyed. A little skittish, even.

At least I know where I stand. Nowhere.

He threw the car into drive and took off for the outskirts of town where a sharp young engineer and a dying old capacitor were waiting for him.

Transmitters were a piece of cake.

Women were impossible.

"Impossible. The man is truly impossible." Belle draped herself across an overstuffed chair placed at an ideal angle for toasting her chilled feet by the cozy fire. She and her new landlady had spent the afternoon on the third floor measuring windows and room dimensions, then had settled down to share a pot of tea in Norah's elegantly offbeat living room. The old house was charming as could be but, as Belle quickly discovered, difficult to heat.

"I've never seen so many mixed messages." Belle, unlike the house, was plenty hot, certain that steam must be pouring out her ears. "One minute he seems thrilled to have me here, the next minute he's hugging me like I'm his sister. His *little* sister." She shivered — and not only from the cold. "I don't know what to make of it."

Norah's slender feet, wrapped in snug lambskin slippers, stretched toward the grate as the logs popped and spit, sending sparks shooting up the flue. "Belle, it's really not Patrick's fault that he's confused. Look at the scenario. He's a dozen years older, yes?"

"Mmm." She couldn't deny that.

"You two haven't seen each other in ages, correct?"

She sipped her lemon-scented tea, letting it warm her from the inside out. "We talked on the phone a few times each year, but you're right, we've not laid eyes on one another since Kingsport."

"Plus . . . he's your boss."

Her shoulders sank further. "Ay, there's the rub."

"Hamlet," Norah murmured. "Act 3, scene 1."

She sat up straight, nearly spilling her tea. "Norah!"

The older woman, curled up in a massive matching chair, gave her a sideways glance. "One needn't major in theater to know the bard."

"Enough about my life. You're holding out on me, Mrs. Silver-Smyth." A teasing hint of reproof lingered in her voice.

Norah shook a manicured finger in her direction. "None of that 'Mrs. S' business with us, please. You might as well know the truth. I adore the stage, serve as a life-long contributor to the Barter Theatre, and in fact did a turn on those boards myself a long time ago."

Belle's late-afternoon lethargy disappeared without a trace. "The Barter? Oh, Norah, tell, tell. I want to know everything."

Norah gave her a brief history, describing Robert Porterfield, an out-of-work actor who started the theater during the Depression, allowing patrons to barter food for first-rate entertainment.

"Ham for Hamlet? Is that still how it works?"

Norah released a throaty laugh. "No, now they take your VISA card like everybody else. But it's a lovely legacy, don't you think?"

She nodded and listened as Norah spun tales of meeting Ernest Borgnine backstage and being in the audience for the debut of a Tennessee Williams play as a young girl. "All I ever wanted to do was act." Norah's slim shoulders lifted in a poignant shrug.

"I'm with you there. What happened?"

"A man. Men, really."

Belle tried to mask her surprise. "Men, meaning plural?"

"Good heavens, it's not like it sounds!" Norah stirred the fire with a black iron poker. "It was two men, and I married both of them."

Her regally raised brows halted the comment teetering on Belle's lips. She settled back as Norah went on.

"Harry Silver was my first love." She propped the poker against the bricks and added in a hushed tone, "My only love. We were married for eleven months before he was killed in a single-engine plane crash."

"Norah, how awful!"

"Tragic. I was not to be comforted. And because we'd met on the stage at the Barter, I couldn't bear to set foot in the place. For several seasons."

Belle slipped the quilted cozy off the teapot and poured them both a fresh cup of the fragrant liquid. "Of course you couldn't. And your second husband was . . . ?"

"The pilot of the plane."

Belle gasped again, and Norah held up her hand, warding off an imaginary blow. "In very poor taste, I know. My mother certainly thought so. But you see, Randolph Smyth — of Smyth County, mind you — was the only survivor and felt terribly responsible. He kept coming around to offer his condolences, and he had all this lovely money with no one to spend it on, and all this crushing guilt that needed mending, and —"

In spite of the sad tale, Belle laughed. "Say no more. The first time you married for love. The second time —"

"I married for money. Exactly. What a fool I was." Norah stared out the lace-draped window for a moment, then turned back to her tea. "The money lasted longer than the relationship. He left me fifteen years ago for a woman half my age."

"With half your wisdom, I'm sure."

"Naturally, dear, but most men don't fall in love with your wisdom. Take Patrick."

Belle grinned. "I wish you would."

"Do what?"

"Take Patrick. No, I mean it! You two would make a perfect couple."

"Out of the question." Norah's impeccably groomed eyebrows disappeared under silvery bangs. "We have almost nothing in common."

"Like I said, you two together would be perfectly . . . *dreadful!*"

Their laughter rang around the room like the church bells next door, clanging merrily.

Belle shook her head. "The tightwad and the spendthrift, eh?"

"Or the good, the bad, and the ugly." Norah waved her fingers affectionately at a monstrous ginger and white cat, padding into the living room on tufted paws the size of silver dollars. "And here comes ugly now."

The rotund feline examined her through golden slits, as if calculating the effort required to jump up and join her. The appeal of his mistress and her cushy chair proved too much for the animal to resist. He leaped with surprising grace and landed squarely in Norah's lap.

"Sit, Harry."

The cat obeyed, though Belle suspected he intended to sit anyway. Meanwhile, Belle's curiosity was killing her. "You named your cat after your first husband?"

"Why not?" After a few strokes from Norah's bejeweled hand, the cat began purring with such a roar that Belle could hear him from several feet away. "I've always loved the name Harry. You could say I was wild about it." Norah giggled at her own pun. "And he *is* hairy, this Harry." She dropped her head back on the chair and sighed wistfully. "Tell the truth, Belle. How do you feel about Patrick?"

Patrick. Now that *was* a hairy subject.

"The truth? I had a crush on him for two years. I was certain he never knew. Never noticed me."

"Ha."

"Obviously, I missed something."

"Obviously. Now what?"

"I don't know." Belle stood up, suddenly restless. She circled the room, lightly touching an antique spinning wheel here, a handwoven basket there, then stopped to stare at her reflection in the beveled mirror over the mantel.

Was Patrick her friend, her employer, or her future beau?

All of the above? Two out of three?

"I know what I *should* do." She took a deep breath as if to give the idea room to expand. "For the sake of WPER, and our friendship, the best thing I could do right now is locate some good-looking guy for me to focus on and let Patrick find the right woman for him."

Except he is good-looking. And that "right" woman might be me.

Norah, meanwhile, was studying her carefully. "How wise of you." Her low tone reminded Belle of the contented Harry. "Shall we find you a handsome buck in Abingdon?"

She tossed up her hands. "Norah, I've been here exactly six hours!"

"Wise women don't waste a minute." Norah deposited Harry on the floor and rose to her feet. "But I suppose tomorrow is soon enough. On another note entirely, what are your lodging plans this evening?"

"Since my furniture won't arrive from

Chicago until tomorrow afternoon, I brought a sleeping bag with me —"

"A what? You mean penny-pinching Patrick didn't put you up at the Martha?"

"Martha who?"

"The Martha Washington Inn. It's only a block up the street. Stunning place, built in 1832." She shook her head in disbelief. "Not even one night in a fine hotel? Belle, that's criminal. There's no way I'll let you sleep on that hardwood floor up there. The very idea! Bring in your suitcase and I'll get you settled in my guest room down on the first floor."

Clearly the woman would brook no argument, so Belle did as she was told, carrying her tapestry luggage through the downstairs back door. A small but gaily decorated bed and bath were tucked into one corner of the ground floor that housed Norah's business, the Silver Spoon, a gourmet bakery and gift shop.

Belle couldn't resist a quick survey of her surroundings. Small round tables draped in blue-and-white checked linens were scattered among two front rooms, the walls of which were lined with shelves brimming with exotic coffees, teas, and imported foods. Gleaming glass display cases held silver trays with neatly printed signs boasting of the baked goods that would soon fill those trays: scones, brioches, shortbread, croissants, and muffins in every flavor — pumpkin walnut, spice pecan, apple currant, banana peanut, lemon poppy seed.

Belle decided she'd died and gone to bakery heaven.

A whole spice cabinet full of scents wafted toward her — both faint and pungent, tart and cinnamon sweet. She sniffed the air appreciatively. "Is *this* room for rent?"

"Not unless you want to get dressed with half of Abingdon's finest watching you while they nibble on cranberry nut muffins." Norah's voice floated across the shadowy room. "Keep your door closed tight after seven in the morning and you'll be fine." The woman consulted her watch. "Speaking of food, why don't we head down to the Hardware Company for dinner and call it an early night?"

" 'Hardware Company'? What do they serve, *clamp* chowder? Salted nuts and *bolts?*"

Norah groaned. "It's a restaurant, silly."

"Let me guess. Right up the street, past the Martha?"

"You're a quick study, Belle." Norah wrapped two fluttering sleeves around her and hugged her affectionately.

Warm tears stung Belle's eyes. It had been quite a day.

Norah pulled back and regarded her with eyes that held their own faint sheen. "Welcome to Abingdon, my friend. Welcome home."

Four

People have one thing in common:
they are all different.

Robert Zend

Here we go.

At two minutes to ten on Monday morning, Belle stood in front of the double glass doors of WPER, summoning her courage to swing them open and walk into her future.

She'd worn the usual — slim jeans and black boots — but added her favorite blouse and Italian sweater, hoping to project some hard-earned, major-market confidence. Norah, her slender hands immersed in bread dough, had nodded in approval when she'd swept past her that morning, which boosted her spirits immeasurably.

Now that she'd arrived, Belle feared her heart might jump right through her fine linen blouse. Would the staff like her? Would the listeners? *Relax. You've seen this movie.*

And there was Patrick on the other side of the glass, waiting to welcome her, pushing the door open. "Hail, hail, the gang's all here." His broad grin, height-

66

ened color, and twinkling eyes told her he was running on pure adrenaline, less than twenty-four hours before his station was scheduled to go on the air.

"You look happy, Mr. Reese."

"I am," he assured her, guiding her toward the far end of the large, sun-filled room where a half dozen people were gathered around a rectangular table, all eyes on her. "Folks, this is Belle O'Brien, most recently of WTIE Chicago, our midday star."

The assembly greeted her with nods and hellos, each face registering its own unique emotion. Curiosity. Surprise. Detachment. Doubt. She arranged her own face to reflect her gratitude at being there and slipped into the one remaining seat, leaving Patrick to plant himself at the head of the table, feet apart.

It was a stance she knew well. The one that shouted "Patrick Edward Reese, General Manager."

His pale blue striped shirt was ironed to perfection, his bright, patterned tie and navy suspenders carefully chosen, she knew, to make him appear both approachable and in charge. Decisive, a problem-solver, with exceptional reasoning skills . . . the man was a born leader.

And *persuasive* didn't begin to describe Patrick. Hadn't he convinced her to say yes, twice?

Patrick clapped his hands, then rubbed them together, his energy radiating in waves. "Officially, then, welcome to WPER. Each one of you was chosen for your specific gifts, for what you bring to this table."

Seated inches from his elbow, Belle could feel him gearing up, drawing every eye toward him. She'd forgotten what a captivating speaker he was. It wasn't an act, either. The man simply had more charisma than he knew what to do with.

Watch yourself, Belle. Friends, remember?

"Yes, we're an oldies station," Patrick continued, "but the music isn't the whole story. Personality is what we're offering. Genuinely talented individuals with something to say and an engaging way of doing it. That's why our letterhead, our bumper stickers, our T-shirts, will all say this . . ." He paused, clearly wanting their undivided attention as he pulled a handful of vivid red stickers out of a box in front of him. " 'Oldies 95 — WPER — We're the P-E-R in Personality Radio!' "

Nods of approval circled around the table. Belle smiled. *So far, so good.*

T-shirts were tossed on the table next and a scramble ensued while the staff grabbed at the various sizes. She stuffed one marked Small into her black satchel

68

and leaned back, trying not to let her gaze settle on Patrick again — no matter how hard that was to resist.

She'd never seen him look so handsome, so masculine, so utterly in command. *Whoa, girl. Remember what we decided last night?* She frowned. What was that . . . ? Oh yes, to "let Patrick find the right woman." *How disappointed will Norah be when she finds out I didn't mean it?*

Patrick was looking directly at her now, white teeth flashing. "Belle, I know what you're thinking."

She nearly slid out of her chair. "You *do?*"

"You're wondering who's who around this table."

Not exactly.

"Frank." Patrick looked down the length of the table. "You'll be the one to spank the life into this baby tomorrow morning at six. Give us a two-minute introduction. Everybody, this is Frank Gallagher, our morning pro."

Frank was seated at the opposite end of the table from Patrick, obviously staking a little ground of his own. He was definitely the senior member of the staff, Belle decided. Looked about fifty-five, though his toupee made his age harder to nail down. Frank stood up, not as a challenge, but rather, she imagined, to garner their attention.

He soon had it.

"I've been on the air at one station or another in the South or Midwest since 1964." He cleared the gravel out of his throat, then shot a pointed look at the young blond woman to his left. "Longer than some of you have been alive. I've done every format out there, from country to gospel to news-talk. Worked at one station owned by a chicken farmer who lined the studio walls with cardboard egg cartons for acoustics. Did play-by-play for a high school football game by climbing up a telephone pole that overlooked the field and tapping the phone line.

"And yes —" he gazed steadily at Patrick — "I was better known as Frank the Crank back in '67 when I was spinning Top 40 tunes on WHBQ in Memphis. My last gig was mornings in Roanoke. When the numbers went south . . ." He shrugged his shoulders. "Anyway, I'm glad to be here."

"And we're glad to have you, Frank." Patrick led the small group in scattered applause. "Frank was replaced by a couple of young jocks who call themselves the Dual Air Bags." He snorted in mock disgust. "Roanoke's loss is definitely our gain."

Turning to Belle, Patrick softened his voice. "Midday woman, you're up."

Belle debated briefly the merits of staying in her chair, but found herself on her feet an instant later, gently guided by Patrick's hand cupped under her elbow. She plunged in. "I did college radio at ASU." She looked toward the far end of the table. "Not in '64, Frank, but it feels like that long ago." The staff's good-natured laughter gave her a moment to shake off her stray bit of nervousness. "My first real job was in Kingsport, Tennessee." She ran through a thumbnail résumé, watching their expressions alter slightly. Detachment gave way to interest. Admiration. And a question mark.

"Some of you probably know why I'm not in Chicago anymore." A few heads nodded; others gave her a blank look.

She took a deep breath. *One more time.* Five minutes later, the sordid story was behind her. "The hardest part was seeing my friends out of work, right at the start of the ratings period."

The blonde spoke up first. "No offense, but how come *you* were spared?"

Belle studied her for a moment, taking in the woman's abundant blond hair spilling to her shoulders, her barely visible makeup, peachy smooth skin, and blue-eyed innocence.

She can't be a day over twenty-two.

Belle sighed. "They kept me simply because I'm female. The station had run afoul of the EEOC over not having a sufficient number of women on staff, so they created a new position for me."

"Your own sports talk show?" the young woman cooed.

"Not quite." Belle tried not to groan at the woman's naïveté. "I have zero interest in sports, as they well knew. So they stuck me in a sound booth and expected me to record all their promotional spots, their top-of-the-hour identifiers, their liner cards, their sports scores —"

"Great!" The blonde was still enthusiastic.

"— using the name Belle of the Ball."

The men shook their heads, groaning. The blonde looked confused.

"They also insisted I record them in a breathy, high-pitched, Betty Boop style."

The table was silent. The blonde clearly couldn't help herself. "Who's Betty Boop?"

Frank leaned over. "She was a cartoon character from the '30s. Big eyes, short skirts. Squeaky, little-girl voice."

"Ooh!" the blonde squeaked, rolling her eyes.

Frank winced. "Boop-oop-a-doop."

Belle shook her head. "Finally I did what I should have done in the first place. I erased every one of the tapes I'd recorded, emptied my locker onto the new program director's desk, and quit."

The WPER staff broke into spirited applause as Belle eased back into her chair, flipping her braid behind her, feeling her cheeks stinging from the heat that had quickly found its way there.

She had no intention of sharing that story again, ever.

When the group settled down, Patrick nodded at the announcer seated next to Belle. "Think you can top that, Burt?"

The man rose slowly, his protruding belly catching on the edge of the table as he stood. "Naw, Mr. Reese, that's got me beat. Only thing I've heard worse than that was a station that changed to a format of all classified ads. K-ADS. Pitiful."

Patrick laughed. "Almost as bad as the all-Christmas-music station I escaped from. Give us your story, Burt."

"I've spent my whole radio career in Indiana." He reached under his round stomach and displayed a brass belt buckle shaped like the Hoosier state. "See?"

What Belle could see was his stomach covering the northern half of his buckle, from Gary, Indiana, south to Muncie.

"They call me Burt 'Indiana' Jones. Been at WGLD as music director for the last ten years, doing afternoons. I'd still be there except Mr. Reese convinced me it was time to move up to program director." His face split into a wide grin, showing off a size-able gap between his two front teeth.

Patrick chuckled. "Burt thinks 'He's So Fine' by the Chiffons was the last decent tune ever recorded. We're honored to have a man with such discriminating taste running the show."

When Burt dropped down into his chair, the collective attention of the group turned toward the young blond woman who'd managed to still her tongue for a full five minutes.

Patrick nodded her direction, and she spoke suddenly, as if stuck with a pin. "Hi! I'm Heather Young."

Belle pressed her lips firmly shut and forced herself to keep a straight face. *Heather Young? Talk about typecasting . . .*

Heather took another gulp of air. "I graduated from Clinch Valley College last May and majored in English with a special concentration in communication."

"Ever do any radio?" Frank barked.

"Well . . . sort of. I did a commercial once for WNVA-FM in Wise, Virginia. It ran on the air twice." She beamed proudly at her coworkers. "Here at WPER, I'll be doing an all-request show from seven until midnight. This is . . . uh, my first radio . . . *gig?* Is that what you called it?"

Belle felt Patrick's eyes on her and

glanced up. His look was unmistakable. *Be nice.*

Hers was equally transparent. *Who, me?*

"Welcome, Heather," Patrick said, his eyes still locked with Belle's. "Don't let these veterans intimidate you. They all had a first gig once, right, folks? We have one more greenhorn on the air staff." He gestured at a wiry young man with an earnest expression and straight black hair. "Rick Anderson, you're on."

"Hello."

Two syllables and Belle knew they were in trouble. Rick's voice was tuned to a pitch somewhere between blackboard chalk and a rusty bicycle wheel. Surely Patrick didn't intend to use him on the air?

"I'm nineteen —" the young man's eager glance danced from one of them to the other — "grew up on my parents' farm outside Glade Spring, and graduated with honors from Holston High two years ago." His enthusiasm was disarming. Despite the squeaky voice, Belle liked him already. "I'll be running the overnight show, basically keeping the music going. And don't worry . . ." His smile stretched another inch. "I'm not allowed to use the microphone. Ever. Burt will prerecord all the breaks for me. My job is to push the right buttons. And stay awake."

A ripple of laughter traveled around the

table as Rick took his seat and the new staff nodded at one another. *So it begins.*

Patrick straightened and assumed his managerial stance once more. "That does it for our meeting. You'll see three more part-timers in and out this week. Make 'em feel welcome, if you will. I've invited our behind-the-scenes employees to join us for lunch down at the Grill at noon." He indicated the cubicles behind him. "That's Cliff, Jeanette, and Anne back there, busy building a client base for us. David, our engineer, is installing a new loading capacitor at the transmitter site and should be back after lunch."

He nodded at his new program director. "Do whatever it takes to get 'em ready for tomorrow, Burt. I expect the newspapers to stop by, maybe some TV types from Bristol." Patrick grinned like a proud papa. "Dress sharp and come in smiling, folks."

He disappeared into his corner office while Belle and the rest of the staff moved into the main studio. Unlike every other station she'd worked at, all of which had been jammed with flotsam and jetsam and covered with a thick layer of dust, the freshly carpeted, neat-as-a-pin studio was a pleasant discovery. David, the mystery engineer, had done an exceptional job.

Belle listened and nodded as Burt pointed out the "hot clock" — a hand-drawn clock face showing where commercial breaks occurred each hour and what records should be played when.

"At the top of the hour, I want an upbeat '60s tune coming out of the news. Sweep the other quarter hours with something farther down the charts, a nostalgia piece." Burt nodded her direction. "Frank, Belle, you know the drill. Keep the mix interesting. Heather, we'll create a special music clock for you to fit in the requests, and Rick, I'll give you a complete playlist each night. Just push the buttons —"

"And stay awake. I know, I know."

Burt showed them the handful of liner cards posted on a clear plastic clipboard mounted on top of the console — single lines like "Abingdon's Own Oldies 95" — to be read between the songs.

Belle recalled the days when reciting liner cards was all she felt safe doing when the mike was on. *Would Heather have much more to offer?* An odd sensation crept up her spine. Heather was so . . . so *young*. What could Patrick have been thinking?

The green-tinged emotion was easy to recognize: jealousy. Belle sighed. Hadn't she been exactly Heather's age when Patrick hired her the first time?

She dragged her attention away from the animated blonde, whose questions about everything in sight had her coworkers smiling indulgently. The rest of the staff seemed likable enough and more than competent. But, as usual, none of the guys were likely prospects for getting her mind off Patrick.

Radio men were either happily married or loners, drifting from station to station. The only coworker she'd ever dated was in Philadelphia. They'd had too much in common for real sparks to fly, though she did cherish the set of videotapes he'd given her — every episode of *WKRP in Cincinnati*, with all the commercials painstakingly edited out, bless his techno-geek heart.

Listeners made even less likely prospects. They either held her in awe, treating her like a one-dimensional celebrity of sorts, or dated her strictly to earn bragging rights with their friends.

Most depressing.

Belle wandered into the hallway, awash in a sudden, inexplicable wave of loneliness. New job, new town, same old longing to love and be loved. She leaned against the freshly painted wall, head tipped back, blinking hard to keep any renegade tears from slipping down her cheeks. She was certain of one thing: Mr. Right wouldn't be walking through this door anytime soon.

Sherry Robison knew for a fact that finding Mr. Right wasn't difficult — it was impossible. Hanging on to him was harder still.

The late-afternoon sun slanted through the blinds, revealing horizontal glimpses of a seedy Sacramento parking lot, throwing pale yellow bars of light across her paper-thin linoleum floor. The carpet in the living room was worse, an industrial-strength variety with the flimsiest padding money could buy.

She glanced at the plastic kitchen clock. He'd be home soon, swinging open their front door and heading straight for the fridge. He always arrived home hungry. Insisted he was going through a growth spurt. Maybe she'd beat him to the punch and start dinner early. It'd be sloppy joes. Again. With corn and green beans, his favorites. No ice cream, though. She'd polished off the remnants of the fudge ripple last night before she cried herself to sleep watching *The Way We Were.*

Snapping on the gas burner, Sherry pulled down the skillet, seeing her face reflected there for a half-second before the hamburger hit the shiny metal surface. She chopped at the sizzling meat, covering any traces of the woman who'd stared back at her. The twenty-something woman with the familiar short brown curls, brown eyes, and small bow of a mouth. The expression was familiar, too. She'd seen it more and more lately. It was the one that looked suspiciously like defeat.

She'd headed west nine summers ago, a high school diploma in her back pocket and vinegar in her veins. A small-town girl, determined to make her own way in sunny California. A rebel with no cause whatsoever.

Her agenda had been simple: get an apartment, get a job, get a man, get happy. *Piece of cake.*

More like crumbs, she soon realized.

Money didn't go far in Sacramento, so the apartment wasn't much to talk about. Employers turned a deaf ear on an eighteen-year-old girl who'd never held a job — any job — and whose résumé featured four years in pep club as the high point. As for finding a man . . . well, they were there. But the California guys she met seemed too slow in some ways, too fast in others, the kind of trouble that'd sent her packing in the first place.

Nobody cared that she was Sherry Robison, a banker's daughter from one of Abingdon's nicest families. In the Sacramento Valley, she was merely another disillusioned easterner, too proud to go back

80

home and admit she'd made a mistake. A big one.

A few pieces of mail scattered by the phone caught her eye. Had she already read those? She stirred the meat while pouring in the sauce, both hands working on autopilot, and squinted at the stack, trying to remember. The Sears bill was on top, then two more past-due notices from the furniture place. A simple white envelope with a Virginia postmark was on the bottom.

That last one had her thinking hard these days. About doing the right thing. Whatever that was. Nothing made sense anymore. Pinching pennies, juggling aggressive creditors, trying to squeeze in time for night classes so she wouldn't be working ten 'til two at the Florin Mall for the rest of her natural life.

Not a soul back home knew how far she'd lowered her sights these days, how little it took to send her emotions spinning toward the basement. *Face it, Sherry. The joy is leaking out of your life.* She felt it somewhere deep inside her, dripping like the faucet in their garish, green-tiled bathroom. In both cases, she couldn't figure out how to stop the leak from slowly driving her mad.

As if on cue, the front door flew open and a familiar voice hollered a noisy greeting. Despite her melancholy mood, Sherry forced a smile to her face. He deserved that, didn't he?

"I'm in the kitchen, honey." Even as she called out, she knew he was already headed in her direction.

Five

*A blunder at the right moment is better
than cleverness at the wrong time.*

Carolyn Wells

After lunch, the rest of the on-air staff
scattered to gather material for their debut
shows while Belle made a beeline for the
production room, bent on creating a memorable opening, something playful to pique
the listeners' interest.

She settled into the chair, sliding her
hands along the carefully restored console,
breathing in the mingled scents of cut pine,
fresh paint, new carpet. Alone in the pristine studio, she was in her element, surrounded by equipment that gave her the
power to be anything she wanted. With a
push of an effects button and a dash of
dramatics, she could be a sweet shy thing
or a wretched old hag, a British nanny or a
Spanish siren.

Theater without makeup.

She threaded a fresh reel of tape onto
the deck and was pulling the microphone
down toward her chin when the mike
slipped off its mounting and crashed to the
countertop. *Bang!*

At that instant, the studio door *whooshed* open and a startled male voice demanded, "What do you think you're doing?"

She whirled around to find a grim-faced stranger storming toward her, screwdriver in one hand, needle-nose pliers in the other, brandishing both like medieval weaponry. A shock of straight, wheat-colored hair fell over his eyes, shrouding them. In his worn jeans and buffalo plaid shirt, he had the look of an engineer.

An angry one.

David Cahill, no doubt. But hadn't Patrick said he was the quiet type?

"I . . . it slipped." She tried vainly to re-attach the wayward microphone, her heart lodged in her throat. Engineers could get so testy about their equipment.

"Here, let me do it," he muttered, leaning over her shoulder, running his hands over his electronic patient — no doubt feeling for broken bones. Not so much as a slight bruise, she was relieved to notice as he mounted the mike back in place.

"I'm very sorry." She felt terrible and hoped it showed. "Obviously it's brand new, and the last thing you want to do with a microphone is drop it." She waved her hand in a gesture of embarrassment and promptly knocked the microphone off

84

the metal stand — *again* — this time launching it over the console and onto the floor, where it landed with a sickening *thud.*

"Oh, *no!*"

"Good grief."

They both dove under the counter to rescue it. In the dark, cramped space, depth perception became an issue. Their elbows were soon entangled. Two grunts and a gasp followed.

"Ouch! I've got it."

"Excuse me, but that's the chair leg. *This* is a microphone."

"Fine. I'll handle things from here, if you don't mind." At which point their heads banged together with a resounding *crack.*

"Ohh," they grumbled in stereo.

Dizzy from bending over and stunned with a searing pain, Belle rested on her knees for a moment, letting her head clear. She didn't know whether to laugh or cry.

Both had merit.

David stood up first, one hand gripping the microphone, the other rubbing his temple where a visible knot was forming. "You are one hardheaded woman, Miss O'Brien."

At least he knew who she was. *The blockhead.*

"You're quite solid yourself." She nursed

her own injury, a nasty lump growing on the crown of her head. She had to look up the long expanse of his Levi's-clad legs before she made eye contact. "You need to do something about that microphone." Her tone was sharper than she intended, but she was in pain and more than a little embarrassed. "It shouldn't release that easily."

"It was fine until *you* stepped in the studio."

She eyed him through narrow slits. "I've been in this business a decade longer than you have, *Mister* Cahill. I've worked with all kinds of microphones and never — I mean *never* — have I seen them fall off their mountings like this one has today. Twice. What does that tell you?"

She stood up an inch at a time, grabbing the back of the chair for balance until she was eye to eye with him.

Or rather, eye to chin.

Like it or not, she had to admit it was an impressive chin, strong and chiseled along classic lines.

"David." The word was gritted out through clenched teeth.

"Wh-what?"

"Call me David. And what your experience with microphones tells me is that your major-market engineers let you get away with murder."

She could still feel the heat coming off

his chest as he brushed past her to re-mount the microphone. The tension in his voice was palpable. "Do you have any idea how long I had to beg Patrick to let me order new microphones, let alone this Electro-Voice?" Although no longer furious, he was clearly still frustrated with her.

"Knowing Patrick's tightwad ways, I can only guess." She reclaimed her seat and rolled up to the console, determined not to let her own temper get out of hand. In the smoothest voice she could muster, she said, "Let's make sure it survived, shall we?"

He dutifully angled the mike toward her mouth as she slid the fader up. "Test, test. 1-2-3, 1-2-3." She felt him hovering over her and looked up to catch his eye. "Sorry," she mumbled.

She slipped off her headphones and pulled the fader back down. "Sounds fine, thank goodness. And I really am sorry, David." Pushing back her chair to put a bit more distance between them, she gazed up into dark blue-gray eyes, the color of storm clouds at sea, snapping at her behind the latest style in wire-framed glasses.

She took a deep breath. "Suppose we start over. I'm Belle O'Brien. Middays." She extended her hand and watched him turn five different shades of red before he reluctantly shook it. A firm handshake, nonetheless. Strong hands, rough from wrestling with new lumber and old transmitters.

And careless air talent.

He had a swimmer's build, lean and muscular, no bones, no padding. The glasses gave him an air of intelligence, though she wasn't fully convinced. He seemed to be struggling to express himself, brushing his thick, straight-as-straw hair away from his eyes as he spoke. "Sorry to be . . . so . . ."

"Rude?"

"Yes, rude." His head snapped back in her direction. "No, *not* rude. Responsible." He tossed his hands in the air with a noisy sigh. "Look, I'm in charge of this equipment, Belle. I'd like to keep things working at least until we get the station on the air tomorrow."

"Understandable." She pinched off her grin, not wanting to upset the greenhorn further. And he was young, wasn't he? Fresh out of college, Patrick said. Early twenties, then, though he looked older. "I promise to only *speak* into the mike but not touch it, okay?"

He smiled then, full lips spreading across his freshly shaven face. "It's a deal. Now do I get to hear about Chicago?"

She leaned back, dismayed. "Weren't you at the staff meeting?" She knew, of course, that he hadn't been, but felt compelled to act as disinterested in this upstart as possible. "I promised myself I'd never tell that story again. Ask Patrick."

"I did." His smile took a wry turn. "He said I'd have to hear it from you."

She shook her head, feeling off balance all of a sudden. *It must be from that bump on the head.* But she knew better. "What difference does it make?" She waited for his response, watching, fascinated, as his storm-filled eyes steered toward calmer waters. For a fleeting moment, she thought she saw empathy reflected in their blue-gray depths.

His voice gentled, too. "Patrick has talked about you nonstop since I signed on. 'Belle this' and 'Belle that.' I've been waiting for six weeks to hear the rest of the story. From the source."

"I see." With a sigh, she shared her disastrous tale once more. Unlike the other newcomers, David didn't look the least bit shocked. He listened carefully. Nodded. No doubt about it, understanding was etched across his face. That, and something else she didn't have the energy to explore at the moment.

"Betty Boop, huh?" His expression was unreadable. "Why would anyone mess with a voice like — uh . . . like yours?"

"Good question." *What does he mean,*

89

a voice like mine? Is it that bad? She turned back toward the control board, hoping he'd take the hint and leave. He was a nice enough guy, but she had serious work to do, a show to prepare for, and an ego that suddenly needed mending. *'A voice like mine'? Well, thank you very much.*

When she heard him slip out the door behind her, Belle reached for her purse and the aspirin she hoped was waiting for her. *Where does Patrick find these people, anyway? On his front porch?*

"They parked it on the front porch, Belle." Norah tried hard not to sound disgruntled, but she was, truth be told, highly put out. "The moving company — though I hesitate to honor this crew by calling them that — apparently arrived when I was running errands in Bristol. According to Linda next door, it was two beefy guys in a decrepit truck."

"And they left my furniture where?"

Norah could hear the strain in the younger woman's voice over the phone lines. "They unloaded your couch, four-poster bed, and everything else, and deposited them on the porch, right at my front door." Of all the things Norah loathed, incompetence was at the top of her list. "Let me guess. Patrick hired these two."

"For a discounted rate, I'm sure." Belle moaned. "What would you suggest?"

"I'd suggest we get Mr. Reese down here and make *him* haul it up to the third floor." Second on her list of pet peeves were people who cut corners to save two cents. "Your boss probably found the phone number for these so-called movers written on the wall of a public restroom."

"Now, Norah, the man's building a radio station on a slim budget. Suppose I put you on the phone with him while I hustle home? They're forecasting rain for this evening, so the sooner we get my things inside, the happier I'll be. See you in a few minutes."

Norah waited on hold, twisting her silver spoon ring around her finger while she put her thoughts together. Belle was right when she'd said Patrick was impossible. Slap-dash, make-do, bargain-basement impossible.

She heard a *click* on the line, then "Patrick Reese here." His resonant baritone sang across the phone wires.

That was the third item on her list of things to be avoided at all costs: dangerous men with delicious voices.

"Norah Silver-Smyth here." Her tone was a cool retort. "My friend, we have a problem. Correction, *you* have a problem. Where did you find this . . . ah, moving company to bring Belle's furniture from Chicago?"

"Her stuff made it then. Great!"

Norah released a sigh of pure exasperation. "Was there ever a reason for doubt?"

"Well, they gave me such a good price, that . . ." She could sense him weighing his words. "I wasn't certain *when* her things would arrive, is all."

"Oh, it's here. And it's all over my front porch. Did you pay them to actually move it inside, Patrick, or was this a door-to-door arrangement?"

Silence. "Her furniture is on your porch?"

"Covers almost every inch of it. You'll recall it's a rather large porch. Wraps around the entire east side of the house."

"Uh-huh. I'll take care of it. Sorry, Norah. These things happen, eh?" With that, he hung up.

They don't happen to me, sir. She slipped the phone in her sweater pocket, her hands shaking. What was it about that man that made her blood boil? She had to admit he was handsome. Very handsome, in fact. And he did have a velvet-lined voice. But he'd clearly used his charm and good looks to weasel his way through life. Hadn't he talked her into reducing the rent for Belle, giving her an extra-long lease to make sure she'd stay for a while, throwing in free utilities?

The man *was* impossible. Impossible to say no to, among other things.

Prrrrmeow.

Harry the cat made his presence known, rubbing against her legs demanding attention and, more to the point, food. "Oh, you!" She scooped him up and headed for the kitchen to wait for Belle. "Harry, you've kept me company for a decade. Why isn't your feline affection enough anymore?"

She stared out at the gray November skies. Belle was right, rain was in the making. First day on a new job and already her tenant had a hassle on her hands. Norah had to remind herself not to call Belle a "girl," though she seemed young, younger than her thirty-two years. Perhaps it was the nomadic lifestyle she led, or that incredible bundle of long hair, or simply the youthful energy that swirled around the world of broadcasting.

Whatever the case, Belle clearly had more than sweaters and jeans packed in her baggage sitting upstairs in the empty third floor. She'd brought a lengthy list of hurts and disappointments along for the ride. Norah was certain of it.

Hadn't she amassed a sizable collection of her own by that age? One husband in the grave, another whose love had died on the altar of infidelity, leaving her only his name and his money.

Never his heart.

Norah sighed, trying with little success to will away her unforeseen melancholy. She'd been single so long she'd almost forgotten how nice it might be to have a man in her life again. After years of pouring herself into her hometown, her church, her business, serving on every committee and board of directors Abingdon had to offer, she'd found a comfortable rhythm for her solo life.

Hadn't she?

She balanced Harry on her lap, stroking his thick fur, keeping one eye on the cherry clock above the door. *Almost four.* It was only a ten-minute walk from the station. Belle would be there any moment. Would Patrick come over himself and move the furniture up that narrow staircase to the third floor? He didn't seem the type to do heavy lifting.

He managed to knock you off your feet, didn't he?

The realization came out of nowhere, unexpected and unwelcome.

She could categorically deny it. Insist it was hormonal. Call it a midlife crisis in the making. Write it off to a passing fancy. Argue that though they'd spent a great deal of time together since he moved to town, it didn't mean anything. He simply needed someone to show him the ropes, a welcoming committee of one, and she'd fit the bill.

Only one problem. They were lies, every one of them.

She was falling in love with Patrick Reese as surely as he was in love with Belle O'Brien.

The naked truth of it left her breathless, clutching at her chest as if her heart had taken a physical blow. After so many seasons of singular contentment, why now? And why him, of all people? "Foolish woman." She sniffed, unable to keep two stubborn tears from rolling down her cheeks. She hugged Harry tight, but his soft fur and rumbling chest couldn't ease the pain.

Foolish was an understatement. Patrick was five years younger, never married, and treated her like his sister. "His *older* sister," she mumbled into Harry's ample fur. "Besides, every woman in town will have designs on him by Christmas."

Not to mention the fact that he didn't share her enthusiasm for spiritual things. They'd be "unequally yoked," as the Bible called it, unless he had a wake-up call from God.

And then there was Belle. Adorable Belle, who wasn't sure *what* she wanted. So bright, so personable. The woman didn't know how beautiful she was.

Norah dabbed her tears dry, taking deep breaths to settle herself down. "Why, Lord?" She aimed her comments at the pots and pans swinging over her head, knowing her words traveled much farther. "And why Patrick? It's all wrong. You know it and I know it." She didn't expect an audible answer but took comfort in knowing God was, as always, listening, even as she agonized about an overgrown teddy bear who'd accidentally walked away with her heart in his paws.

A tap at the door woke her out of her reverie. Slipping Harry onto the terra-cotta tiles at her feet, she patted her cheeks to make sure they were dry and tugged open the door, setting the tinkling bells in motion.

"Just me."

"No need to knock, Belle." She stepped back, waving her inside. "This is your home now. If and when we can find our way to the front door again, you can use that entrance to take you straight up to the third floor."

"Sorry about your porch." Belle slumped into a chair, a sheepish look on her face. "I realize it's not my fault, but I still feel terrible."

"Pish-posh! We'll let Patrick worry over it." She could feel her old, confident self returning, and was grateful to have her pity party behind her. "Let's cook up something scrumptious for dinner. Whoever ends up hauling that load up the stairs will be ravenous when they're done."

Belle agreed, offering to join her in the kitchen as soon as she carried the smaller items and fragile pieces upstairs. "I'll need to change first. Get ready for my grubby look." Having issued fair warning, Belle disappeared.

Norah began pulling down pans, emptying cupboards, and exploring the fridge while Beethoven blasted away on her kitchen CD player. Had she ever been "grubby," as Belle called it? She looked down at her expensive burgundy slacks, French silk blouse, batik swing jacket, and laughed. *Not in this lifetime.*

Sounds of the front door, repeatedly banging open and shut, meant her tenant was putting a dent in the pile on the porch, but it would take some strong-shouldered men to handle the heavy pieces. Soon the front door closed for good and Belle appeared in the kitchen. Even grubby, she was an enchanting sight in gray sweatpants and an oversized emerald green T-shirt tied at the waist.

Green was definitely her color.

"I love this music!" Belle cranked up the volume on the CD player another notch until the dishes fairly danced on the countertop. "Let me help you toss the salad." She giggled and swirled in a circle as she pitched a tomato in the air and deftly caught it.

It was the happiest she'd seen Belle since her arrival. As they worked together on dinner, Belle had a million questions for her: Where did she find such a fine cutting board, and were the knives really from Sheffield, England, and had she ever seen a more divine color than eggplant?

She paused to watch Belle, a look of childlike joy on her face, slicing potatoes. *No wonder Patrick adores her. No wonder he hasn't even noticed me.* Norah knew that letting her thoughts — or her heart — drift in his direction again would be sheer stupidity. There was obviously zero interest on his part. The sooner she accepted that, the sooner her emotions would be back in line.

It was only then, during a meaningful pause in Beethoven's Fifth, that she heard someone pounding on the front door. Shouting, too, as if they'd been at it a while.

"Good heavens, what's that all about?" Norah hurried through the dining room and peeked through the front windows to see who'd managed to climb over the pile of boxes and furniture to find her doorbell.

"What is *he* doing here?" Not a thing to be done but invite him in. She swung the door open and tossed her arms out in welcome, adding a genuine smile to let him know she meant it. "Come in, you dear man. You're just in time for our movable feast."

Six

Time wounds all heels.

Jane Ace

Standing there in the kitchen, Belle's curiosity got the better of her. Who was Norah welcoming with such abandon? It definitely wasn't Patrick's voice at the door. She dried her hands on a dish towel and made her way to the front of the house, only to meet Norah and the newcomer heading her direction.

"Belle, I want you to meet someone."

With one glance, she wanted to meet someone, too. Thirtyish, tall, with a boyish grin and an abundance of wavy brown hair trimmed close to his ears, the man Norah had in tow was straight out of a men's clothing catalog.

"Matthew Howard." He flashed a toothy grin and thrust out his hand. "You must be Norah's new tenant. I've heard all about you, Miss O'Brien."

Heard all what? She shook his hand briefly, noting it was smooth as a scholar's. She fought the urge to match his grin, tooth for tooth. His enthusiasm was difficult to resist.

100

"Matthew is our associate pastor." Norah waved in the direction of the church across the street. "Earned his doctorate in ministry last May. You've been in town how long, Matthew?"

"Four months." His eyes were still on Belle.

A pastor, then? Ah, well.

"Belle has been here all of one day," Norah was explaining. "That's her stuff you stumbled over on the porch."

"Which is exactly why I'm here, ma'am. Weatherman on Channel Five says it'll be raining by dinnertime. I wanted to see if I could help you get that furniture inside."

"How thoughtful of you." *Very ministerial.* "If you really mean it, there's a delicious dinner in the bargain."

"The Lord knew I needed one decent home-cooked meal this week." His dark brown eyes twinkled. "Meanwhile, let's get started. Are you sure you can handle the other end of the couch, though?"

A male voice floated in from the porch. "I'll carry the other end."

Startled, Norah turned toward the silhouette of a tall, lanky man, framed in her doorway. "Well, isn't this an afternoon for surprises?" Norah's heels clicked across the hardwood floor, then Belle heard a sharp intake of breath. "My stars! You . . . you

101

must be David Cahill, yes? I haven't seen you in ages."

Belle watched a host of emotions move across Norah's face before the woman's features settled into a broad smile. "As the old saw goes, David, 'my, how you've grown!' " The woman's musical chuckle quickly relieved the awkwardness of the moment. "Now, step inside and let me introduce you to my friends. Have you met Belle O'Brien yet?"

Belle watched, dumbfounded, as WPER's engineer moved toward her, a strained expression on his face.

"Belle and I . . . ah, bumped into each other earlier today." He turned to Matthew. "And you're from Abingdon UMC, am I right? I met you at a prayer breakfast a few weeks back."

"That's me. Matthew the Methodist." Both men laughed, exchanging handshakes. "You've got quite a memory, fella."

A prayer breakfast? Belle was incredulous. *The same guy who rants and raves about a tiny microphone mishap goes to prayer breakfasts?*

David was looking directly at her with a steady gaze, as if reading her mind. "Belle probably finds it difficult to believe I've spent much time around ministers."

"No, I . . ."

He was grinning now. In fact, he and

Matthew looked like a pair of goofy book-ends.

Maybe he *had* read her mind. "Okay, I'll admit it, I didn't expect you to be the religious type."

"I didn't expect it either," he agreed, further baffling her. "Anyway, I'm here because Patrick sent me on a mission of mercy."

Norah let loose an elegant snort. "The audacity of that man! Making someone else do his dirty work."

David shook his head. "Actually, I was grateful for the excuse to . . . uh, run into Belle again." She smiled at his intentional pun as he inclined his head toward the porch. "Could I see you alone for a minute, Belle? My ego can only handle this one on one."

Her cheeks grew unexplainably warm. *Does he really need to see me alone?* She followed him out the door and onto the crowded porch. The wind had picked up since her walk home and the skies had darkened with approaching nightfall and a foreboding mass of steel gray clouds.

She rubbed her bare arms, wishing she'd grabbed her coat. "You wanted to tell me something?"

His hands were stuffed in his pockets, yet she had the strangest feeling he wanted to touch her, as if whatever they had to say

103

to one another would be made easier if there were physical contact, instead of two pairs of eyes locked in silence.

Despite the darkening sky, Belle managed to get a better look at him than she had in the studio. It was hard not to stare at those shoulders. Muscular. Solid. Apparently David had tossed around a few two-by-fours in his time. His shirt was tucked in, showing off his narrow waist, and his long legs were wrapped in jeans more weathered than her own.

He spoke at last, seeming to struggle with each word. "Belle, I behaved like a fool in the production studio today." He sighed deeply, then his tongue seemed to come unstuck. "What happened was an accident at best, or my own inept installation at worst. I had no right whatsoever to make you feel . . . well, to suggest that —"

"Relax." She cut him off with a wave of her hand. "I was less than cordial myself. Let's pretend it never happened, okay?" She was shooting for breezy and easygoing, but her heart kept skipping a beat. *You work around men all the time. Why is this guy giving you palpitations?* Nice face, nice build, nice smile. Nice lots of stuff, but she'd been around plenty of nice-looking men before. That wasn't what got her attention. Not really. Besides, David Cahill definitely was not her style.

"I'm sure you're dealing with a lot." She spoke in her most sympathetic voice. "Taking care of all the last-minute technical stuff for tomorrow must be giving you fits."

"Honestly, it had nothing to do with the station." His eyes were an ocean wave, rising toward the shoreline, threatening to drown her. "I found something in the mail this morning that I wasn't ready for, that's all. Guess I was still dealing with it when I came in the studio. Anyway, I hope you'll forgive me for acting like a heel about the mike." Sincerity was written all over his face, from his broad, smooth forehead to his strong chin — not to mention every handsome feature in between.

Handsome? She felt her eyes widen in surprise. *Girl, get a serious grip.*

She did her best to wipe any telltale emotion from her face and gave a slight shrug. "There's nothing to forgive, David, but if it'll make you feel better, you're forgiven."

"Forgiveness is a gift, Belle. Thank you." His gaze was intent, sincere . . . and something else. Something disturbing.

She turned on her heel, feeling lightheaded and off balance. What right did David Cahill have to look at her that way, as if he could see through her, as if he un-

105

derstood, as if he'd known her for years. She'd figure it out soon enough, but right now there were more pressing matters to attend to. A porch filled with furniture, a storm about to split the sky, and a meal to fix for two hungry men . . .

Coward.

She clenched her teeth. *No, just smart. Too smart to fall for good looks and sincerity, no matter how charming the twinkle in his eye might be.*

"Smells like heaven in here," Patrick called out, letting himself in the kitchen door. Norah's cooking was second to none. He'd found himself scratching at her door more nights than not lately, a hound dog begging for a meal. She seemed happy enough to feed him.

He followed his nose into the dining room, only to find four familiar faces gathered around a candlelit table covered with fragrant serving dishes.

"Greetings, gang." He rubbed his hands together in gustatory anticipation. "I hope you saved some grub for your hungry boss."

Belle shot him a look that could toast marshmallows.

David appeared a tad surly himself.

And wasn't that the minister he'd met across the street?

106

Norah spoke first. Her words popped out like ice cubes from a freezer tray. "I'm not your employee, Patrick."

If the floor beneath his feet would open a crack, he'd happily have dropped out of sight without tasting one bite of dinner.

"Of course you aren't, Norah." *Time for the two-step shuffle.* "You're a dear woman who's fed me on too many occasions, and that's a fact. I'm glad someone else is joining you at your table tonight." He nodded in their direction. "Belle. David. And Pastor Howard, isn't it?"

"Matthew." He sank his teeth into a flaky biscuit.

Oh, man. Biscuits with honey butter. Patrick's mouth started watering as he stared at the heaping basketful. "Did you guys manage to get Belle's furniture up the steps?" It was a lame question. The porch was empty so clearly the job was done. But he had to say something besides "Please, may I have a biscuit?"

"Yes, Patrick, they did a wonderful job." Belle's voice was every bit as chilly as Norah's. "Too bad you didn't get here a little sooner to help them."

No use pretending. "You're absolutely right. I'm a heel for letting you handle something my half-brain movers should have taken care of in the first place. Will you forgive me?"

The guys nodded. The women were stone-faced.

Joining them for dinner was looking less likely by the minute. "Please, ladies?" *Wait a minute. Belle hated the word* ladies, *didn't she?* One glance at her face confirmed it. *Yup.*

Wonderful, generous, kindhearted Norah gave in first. "Have a seat, Patrick, your dinner is getting cold." Her voice, he noted with relief, was a bit less frigid.

He pulled up a chair at the end of the table, then realized he had no place setting. They hadn't exactly been expecting him. After a brief scavenger hunt in the kitchen, he came up with the necessary plates and silverware and joined the others, who were laughing now — he could only hope not at him — as they shared platters of thin-sliced Virginia sugar-cured ham, scalloped potatoes, fried eggplant, corn pudding, and green beans the way he liked them — cooked to oblivion with ham hock and brown sugar.

"Norah, girl," he sighed, piling his plate. "They don't cook like this in San Diego. Gentlemen, I'm in your debt for literally picking up where my movers left off, but you have to admit, you've been well paid here."

David and Matthew, their mouths full, could only nod their agreement.

Norah blushed prettily. Fine-looking woman, especially for her age. Turning fifty next year, he remembered. She looked five years younger than that. Maybe ten.

While he relished every tasty morsel before him, Belle regaled the table with a memorable moment from her stint in Kingsport, their first station together.

"I'd been working at WTFM for all of two days but knew most of the music backwards and forwards from listening to it as a teenager," Belle explained. "Then I cued up 'Good Lovin' by the Young Rascals. It has this long, dramatic pause right near the end."

Patrick almost choked on his potatoes. Why hadn't he heard this story before?

"I was on the far side of the studio, pulling some music, and suddenly realized I had dead air. A major no-no in radio. Patrick told me to never, ever, under any circumstances, let a record run out and not be ready with another song, a commercial, *something.* Right, boss?"

She batted her eyes at him playfully, waving her braid. He nodded, cheeks stuffed with eggplant.

"I made a flying leap at the tall stool sitting in front of the microphone, flipping the mike on in midflight. Unfortunately, I had too much momentum going, and the stool and I both kept traveling until we hit the floor with all the accompanying sound effects."

Belle accurately mimicked the *crash, bang, kersplat* of her journey through space, ending with an anguished, "Aaiieeeee!" Her audience of four was hanging on every word.

"Meanwhile, the Young Rascals dove into the chorus again. Imagine my poor listeners, who heard music, then silence, then crashing and screaming, then more music. Here I was, worried about *dead* air, when in fact the audience heard more *live* action than usual."

The dining room erupted with laughter and Patrick put down his fork to join them. He loved watching Belle entertain like this, her amber eyes filled with light, her cheeks tinged with a rosy glow. While he was busy crisscrossing the country, she'd grown into a vibrant, beautiful woman. What could possibly interest her in a turning-gray guy like him? *Nothing.*

Belle caught him looking at her and winked, then she plunged on with her woeful tale. "My listeners heard me moaning and groaning all through the refrain, followed by shouts of people running into the studio trying to find out what had happened. Of course, the only thing that got bruised was my ego. We were soon in hysterics, oblivious to the fact that our

110

little melodrama was being broadcast over five counties."

"And what useful lesson did you glean from this humbling experience, woman?" Patrick put on a stern face, patting his mouth with his napkin in mock disdain.

"Easy." She flashed him a wicked smile. "Don't play anything by the Young Rascals."

David was bone-weary of making do. He adjusted the carburetor of his '75 Ford truck with another snap of his wrench, then slammed the dented hood down in disgust, slicking back his rain-soaked hair. How many times had he messed with the same doggone engine trouble in the last week?

Too many times. Twice, the truck had left him stranded with no choice but to thumb his way into town and catch a ride home later with Patrick. He already owed the man three thousand dollars for the land and the pile of boards that masqueraded as a house. He didn't want to be beholden to him for truck repair money, too.

Money. In the Cahill family, it always seemed to come down to money. Or rather, the lack of it.

He looked first one way down the road, then the other. There wasn't a soul around, and he was a good two miles from

111

home, so his rusted-out excuse for wheels needed to run and stay running, not only tonight but until he'd saved enough money to buy a new engine.

Correction: new *used* engine. He couldn't remember the last time he'd bought anything brand new.

David slid into the cab, ignoring the wet jeans now plastered to his legs, and cranked the ignition. It wheezed, it sputtered, but thank the Lord it started. He tossed up a grateful prayer, shifted into first, and rolled back onto Old Jonesboro Road, a winding two-lane stretch of asphalt that skirted the southwest side of town.

Visibility was less than a hundred yards, so he eased off the gas pedal. With 197,000 miles on the odometer, the truck wasn't worth much, but wrapping it around a tree wouldn't help any. The November sky was utterly dark, not a star in sight, the full moon hidden by thick black storm clouds that had stalled over southwestern Virginia a few hours back and were still dumping an inch an hour. David sighed. His house was in worse shape than his truck, covered with a leaky roof that threatened to collapse any minute. He hoped he didn't arrive home to discover it'd done just that.

Hard to believe that half an hour ago he'd been sitting in Norah Silver-Smyth's knockout of a house, dry as a bone, his stomach full of the best food he'd eaten in weeks. Months. Nice company, too. Patrick was one funny guy when you got him started, Norah was total class, and Matthew had a genuine faith in God that draped around his shoulders as naturally as a well-tailored coat.

Belle was another story. What was her problem, anyway? One minute she was laughing and telling tales, then she was eyeing the pastor, then she was whispering with Norah over some private joke, then she was winking at Patrick, of all things. Wasn't the man well into his forties?

She'd barely given *him* the time of day, except on the porch when they'd been alone. What had that lasted, all of three minutes? Not that he cared. After twenty-seven years, the scattered pieces of his life were finally starting to fit together. The last thing he needed was some radio celebrity knocking him off track. Even if she was a beauty. And she was. A small bundle of fiery, feminine energy, always in motion . . .

Yeah, a guy could get blown way off course by a woman like that. But David Cahill was not about to let another freckle-nosed, curly-haired woman steer him away from the straight and narrow path he'd chosen for his life.

Not this time. Not for all the honey-colored eyes in the world.

Pulling up to the stop sign at Spring Creek Road, he peered through the driving rain toward WPER's antenna, a three-hundred-foot steel tower stationed on the hill behind his house. The red light on top was emitting a slow, steady blink. So far, so good. At the base, the cinder block transmitter building could handle any kind of weather, but radio towers and storms were always a bad combination.

Turning down Spring Creek, he could barely make out his driveway ahead. The relentless rain had turned the narrow dirt circle into a mud slide. If he drove through it tonight, his tires would carve out two permanent gullies he'd have a hard time filling later.

No way around it. He'd have to park along the gravel shoulder of the road and make a dash for the door. Slamming the truck door shut without bothering to lock it — every night he prayed someone would steal the heap and put him out of his misery — he slipped and slid his way across the mud and grass, digging in his pockets for the keys as he ran.

He locked the house every day, but only because the few valuables he owned were inside: his tools, books, and computer. The structure itself wasn't worth one thin dime.

Patrick had planned to tear it down until David talked him out of it. Told him he'd buy the house and two acres, remodel it, make it into a place he'd be proud to call home.

Except David had no intention of living in this town any longer than it took to get the house ready for market. He hoped Patrick would forgive him when the time came to move on, wouldn't think he was an unappreciative heel. The station would be nailed down by then, every kink worked out, all equipment installed. A part-time engineer was all WPER would need. Save them money, too. Patrick would love that part, he thought with a chuckle.

That's why he'd mailed his résumé to WBT in Charlotte that morning. The big one. A fifty-thousand-watt, clear-channel blowtorch, every engineer's dream. He knew it'd take months, maybe years, to get hired there. Still, sending them his résumé was a beginning.

He'd spent his first nineteen years in Abingdon. Long enough for any man. Too long for a Cahill. Coming back after eight years, he felt as if he'd never left.

It wasn't a good feeling.

He didn't know why he'd ended up back here. Habit, maybe. A solid job offer, sure. The need to prove to this town that he could amount to something. Yeah, that was closer to the truth.

But look at this house. Exactly like all the rental properties he'd lived in as a kid. Hammered-together shacks on all the wrong streets in Abingdon. Falling-down houses rented by his falling-down-drunk father. They'd kept moving but their creditors always found them. It was a sorry way to live.

Four years of seeing the world through a serviceman's eyes, four years in college, and a lifetime of devouring every book he got his hands on had shown him it wasn't the only way to live. Not by a long shot.

His front door creaked open and he reached for a light switch, bathing the dilapidated entranceway and staircase with the faint yellow light of a sixty-watt bulb swinging overhead. This place was depressing, especially after being in a house like Norah's. Instead of the fragrance of home-cooked food and cinnamon, his home smelled like mildew and sawdust and worse. The first thing he'd rebuilt was the heating system so at least the temperature was bearable now, and he'd installed a new hot water heater.

Six long weeks of work, evenings and weekends, and most of it in the basement, where it didn't show. It'd be next summer before he'd let anybody from church or the radio station anywhere near this place.

116

If he still lived here then.

He shook off his sopping wet jacket and threw it over the dish drainer, then peeled off his soaked jeans and added them to the pile. *All this so I can get wet all over again.* He laughed to himself, sprinting up the steps and into the remodeled shower. If it took emptying the entire contents of his new hot water heater on his head, he intended to feel clean and warm.

Later, he'd take another look at the letter in his shirt pocket. The one with the photo he'd begged to see, the one that turned his day upside down even before he'd had a head-on collision with Miss Belle O'Brien.

Seven

*Things are always at their best
in their beginning.*

Blaise Pascal

Cinnamon. Definitely cinnamon.

If every morning began with such lus-
cious smells wafting up her staircase, Belle
didn't care if she never left Abingdon.

For that matter, she didn't care if she
never left the snug comfort of her down-
quilted bedcovers.

Mmm.

In the murky darkness, she squinted at
the clock radio inches from her face and
her head shot off the pillow. Twenty minutes before six. Twenty minutes before
Frank Gallagher would hit the remote start
button on the transmitter, firing up 25,000
watts of oldies power. WPER would be on
the air, live with Frank.

The Crank.

She couldn't help it. The name fit him
like a glove. Patrick had tried to talk him
into using his old handle. Told Frank it
suited the format perfectly. "I'm a morning
personality," Frank had grumbled. "Not a
jive-talking disc jockey with stacks of wax

118

for Jills and Jacks. No way. I'm too old to crank the hits. Got it?"

Patrick had backed off for the moment. But Belle was willing to bet Frank didn't know how persuasive his new boss could be.

Sliding to her feet, Belle stretched her tired muscles, sore from too many trips up and down the steps with boxes of valuable cargo. It had seemed valuable when she packed it, anyway. Now it was nothing but a collection of brown boxes stacked everywhere she turned.

Every other box was marked *Stuff.*

Good thinking, Belinda girl. Very helpful.

She tiptoed barefoot through the maze of cartons en route to her antique bathroom and climbed into the clawfoot tub. The shower curtain dangled high above her from a silver oval as the hot water struggled to find its way to the third floor. Low water pressure was a small price to pay for an apartment that would be stunning when and if she got it all together.

The large pieces of furniture were already in place, thanks to David and Matthew, the broad-shouldered duo who'd hauled it all upstairs last night. Matthew the Methodist certainly was a looker, she thought, massaging a generous glob of peach-scented shampoo into her hair. He

119

was kind, helpful, obviously committed to his ministry.

Good for him.

Not so good for her.

Why was that? She was genuinely perplexed. How could she, a woman who'd spent so many years of her life in a church, now find the idea of dating a minister . . . She couldn't put her finger on the right word. *Predictable? Tame, maybe?*

Belle let out a measured sigh, stepping out of the tub and reaching for a textured bath towel. She loved God, of course. Had plans to find a church home, pronto. Especially after all those dry months in Chicago, when her six-day work week meant Sundays were her only day to sleep in.

Sleeping in had become a habit. One she knew needed breaking, and soon. She missed having a church family, a place to call home.

But still. Dating a man like Matthew Howard — okay, he hadn't so much as hinted that he might call, though he did seem rather attentive — dating a minister brought with it certain expectations that she wasn't sure she could deliver. Like wearing dresses instead of jeans, or taming her wild and woolly hairstyle. And if it got more serious than that? Well, she couldn't play the piano, cook the Wednesday night supper, or carry a tune in a bucket.

Why not come up with a few more stereotypes while you're at it, Belle! She shook her head at her reflection in the mirror and continued brushing her damp hair. What minister in his right mind would want a disc jockey for a wife anyway? A woman liable to slip free promotional CDs in the offering plate and station T-shirts in the clothing-drive bin.

"Run for your life, Matthew!" she called out in the direction of the windows overlooking the church, then chuckled. *You're in some mood this morning, girl.*

Almost six o'clock now. She reached over and flipped the radio on, already tuned to 95 FM. A faint hiss, distant static was all that greeted her. Nothing more. Soon that would change forever. The anticipation hummed through her nervous system. She'd never been part of putting a brand-new station on the air before. Hadn't realized until this instant how exciting it could be.

Belle hurried through her morning routine, digging deep in her suitcase to find all the essentials. She'd at least get her bathroom together tonight, and enough clothes pressed and ready for the week. Every station had its own unspoken dress code. This one seemed fairly casual, but she figured on playing it safe this week by wearing some of her favorite sweaters.

Maybe Patrick would notice.

She grimaced. With her luck, that blond, brooding engineer would be the one to notice. Honestly, what was his problem? He was friendly, in a detached sort of way, but she'd swear he was hiding something. The way he looked at her when she pretended to look the other way, then hooded his eyes when she glanced in his direction. Weird. Moody. And too young.

"Though not as young as *Heather* Young," she sang out into the cool darkness of her bedroom, laughing. Come to think of it, those two deserved each other. Maybe she'd have to work on that over the holidays. A little matchmaking to take her mind off the puzzle that was Patrick.

She was in the middle of tugging a new russet-colored cotton sweater over her still-damp hair when the radio suddenly came alive with a drum roll and Patrick's baritone pipes announcing with a dramatic flourish, "Ladies and gentlemen of southwestern Virginia, welcome to WPER-FM Abingdon — Oldies 95!"

The drum roll built into a frenzied crescendo as a classic bass line came pumping in and a voice full of attitude growled, "It's Frank the Crank, baby, here to jump-start your morning with a solid gold memory from the summer of 1969, Oliver singing 'Goooood Morning Starshine.' "

122

Go, Frank, go! Belle gave her sweater a spirited yank, wiping away a tear of sheer joy in the process. Frank the Crank was alive on FM 95, and she was thrilled to her toes. This was real radio, not some computer-generated jukebox. "Hoooeeee!" she hollered into the morning stillness, pulling on her boots with unaccustomed gusto. For the first time in a long time, she couldn't wait to get to work.

Quickly braiding her hair and slapping on her makeup, she practically skipped down the steps to the first floor, where spicy cinnamon mingled with the heavenly aroma of fresh coffee.

"We're on the air, Norah!" She hurried through the darkened gift shop toward the bright lights in the back room. She found Norah slicing bread with the kitchen equivalent of a claymore. "Remind me not to tweak your nose when you're wielding that thing." Belle backed off with mock concern.

Even busy with her baking, her landlady was impeccably dressed. Belle noticed Norah had WPER tuned in as well. Frank the Crank had switched gears and was playing a sentimental single, "To Know Him, Is to Love Him."

"What do you think, Norah?" Belle tipped her head toward the small radio perched on a shelf among a dozen battered cookbooks.

"This is my music, remember?" Norah grinned. "1958. The Teddy Bears have never sounded better."

Belle regarded her playfully. "One teddy bear in particular sounded especially fine at the top of the hour, don't you agree?"

Norah laughed, nudging a wisp of hair off her face with her shoulder. "If you mean Patrick, yes. He has a wonderful voice."

"In the business, we call them *pipes,* like the pipes of an organ." Belle grinned and poured herself a cup of fresh-brewed coffee. "Our man Reese has them in abundance." She found a plate and wandered out to the glass case where the morning's fare was on display. "I'm serving myself a muffin, Norah. What do I owe you?"

" 'Owe me'? Humph. You're my new tenant and my new friend. You don't owe me a dime."

Belle returned to the kitchen, shaking her head, an orange-nut muffin firmly lodged between her teeth. "Huh-uh," she said as soon as she could swallow. "That's not how it's gonna work, or I'll feel guilty every time I come down here. Suppose we keep a running tab for one muffin and one coffee a day, and I'll write a check at the end of the month when I pay the rent."

Norah shook her head, clearly defeated. "Are you always so hardheaded?"

Belle laughed. "Ask David." She gulped down the last of her coffee and shrugged into her coat. "I'm off to make my own debut on WPER. Think warm thoughts around ten o'clock, will you?"

Norah's dark eyes settled on her. "I'll do better than that. I'll be praying for you. Okay?"

"Thanks." She hurried out the back door into the chilly morning, calling over her shoulder as she went, "I'll take all the prayers I can get."

Belle shoved her hands into her pockets and stepped carefully along the steep brick sidewalk covered with a layer of leaves still wet from the night's hard rain. The skies bore no trace of the storm and were instead a clear dark blue, washed clean by the downpour. In the east was a hint of the sunrise to come, in the west, a faint trace of stars twinkling in the heavens. She took a lungful of the fresh-scented air and breathed it out with giddy abandon.

Abingdon was quietly stealing her vagabond heart. Along both sides of the street were houses constructed a century and a half earlier. Solid brick, most of them, with tin roofs on top. Others were sturdy clapboard that had been painted white, over and over, decade after decade. Some had names, like *Marcella,* while others proudly displayed the year they were built on small plaques — 1836, 1819, a few even in the eighteenth century. Belle peered over a white picket fence at a charming garden with a pair of benches facing one another and attached by a wooden canopy overhead. It was easy to imagine wisteria climbing there, with two summer sweethearts sitting knee to knee, gazing at one another with love in their eyes.

Oh, brother! You are *in a rare mood this morning, Belle O'Brien!*

Within minutes she was unlocking the door at Court and Main and mounting the endless staircase. She barely noticed the climb, so excited was she to get there. The station doors sprang open at her touch and she went directly to the on-air studio, making sure the warning light over the entrance had blinked off before she pushed the door open.

"Frank, you're amazing!" She whispered the compliment, not wanting to frighten him.

He whirled around in his chair. "Is that so? A fine judge of talent you are." He barked when he said it, but a crooked grin gave him away. "See that you're in here at ten. Old Frank will be lucky to make it that long with these blankety-blank short records."

"Don't pretend you don't love this." She gave him a cheeky grin and slipped back out. Three hours to show time and already her nerves were humming. What was the big deal? This was small-town radio, nothing to get anxious about.

Right. And kangaroos hop on three feet.

She wandered back into the common central area, curious if she was the first to arrive, other than Frank the Crank. The cubicles stood vacant and their jock lounge — the rectangular table where they'd met — was equally empty. The small fridge, coffeepot, and microwave oven in the corner waited silently for the workday to begin.

The only other sign of life was the sliver of light under Patrick's corner-office door. Had he stayed there all night, unable to sleep? She tapped on the door, heard him holler out an invitation, and stepped inside, eager to see if his unusual taste in decorating had improved.

Oh no. Belle stared at the wall in shock. "Not the deer antlers? I can't believe you've lugged them all over the country. And that fish —"

"Marlin," he corrected with a comical smirk, then waved at the chair across from his desk. "Enough about my decor. Sit, sit."

She slid into the leather chair — a used one, naturally — and regarded him with amusement. He was dressed to the nines in

127

a dark gray, double-breasted suit, white shirt, and a tie that was surprisingly conservative for Patrick. "My, we're spiffy today. You look very handsome and quite managerial."

Here came his hundred-watt smile. "I like the handsome part. And you're looking radiant yourself this morning. Almost like a woman in love. Have you been keeping secrets from me, Belle?"

"Certainly not!"

It was impossible to stop a blush in progress, she realized, feeling the heat climb past the neckline of her sweater and up into her cheeks. She hastened to respond, hoping to deflect his attention from her feverish face. "I can't wait to get on the air, that's all. Funny how being away from your own show for three weeks makes you long for a stint in the air studio again."

"Woman, you're a born broadcaster." He walked around to the front of his desk and rested on the edge of it, closing the gap between them to a mere foot. "If I haven't mentioned it lately, it's wonderful to be working with you again."

"As if you haven't guessed, I feel the same way." She stared up at his tanned and smiling face. Though he had no single feature that stood out — spectacular eyes or a masculine jaw — when taken as a whole, his features added up to one fine-looking man, full of warmth, intelligence, and an irresistible impishness that made him seem more youthful than his forty-four years. *Which is hardly old.* Barely middle-aged. Besides, what's a dozen years between friends?

Friends . . . *Is that what we are?*

It was time to resolve the dilemma, once and for all.

Belle took a deep breath, then reached out to lightly touch the back of his hand. "Patrick, we need to talk."

He slowly turned his hand over until her fingers rested in his, then gave her a reassuring squeeze. She waited, holding her breath, while he searched her face, perhaps for some clue to how he should proceed. When he spoke, his voice was tender, hardly above a whisper. "I think we do, too, Belle." He leaned forward, putting them within batting distance of a kiss.

They were caught just so, in this charming tableau, when the door flew open and Frank marched in towing a stranger dripping with photography gear. "Found this guy snooping around my studio, Mr. Reese. Says he's with the *Abingdon Virginian.* What gives?"

Patrick shot to his feet like a circus performer launched out of a cannon. "Mr. Kildaire, welcome!" He guided the man into his office, nodding a silent message to

129

Belle and Frank. Clearly they were no longer needed. Frank stomped off to the studio, muttering under his breath about newspapers not being worth the paper they were printed on, while Belle gave Patrick a hesitant smile and retreated to the jock lounge.

Going through the motions of brewing a fresh pot of coffee, she forced her breathlessly beating heart to ease back down to normal tempo. She didn't know whether to be disappointed or relieved at the interruption, and that was precisely the problem. Ambivalence wasn't her style in the least, and it certainly wasn't Patrick's. Maybe after his newspaper interview they'd have a chance to chat.

Sunlight streamed through the third-floor windows, infusing the airy room with a luminous glow. She basked in it, making notes, sipping coffee, and watching the station come to life. One by one they appeared in the doorway — Cliff, the sales manager, a beanpole of a guy with an infectious laugh; Jeanette, the promotion director, a sturdy woman wearing chic rhinestone eyeglasses; and Anne St. Helen, who managed the traffic department, which had nothing to do with cars on the highway and everything to do with getting commercial spots on the daily station log. To a person, Belle found them to be small-town friendly and eager to put WPER on the map.

In less than two hours, it would be her turn.

Belle made good use of the time, reading various newspapers scattered about the table — *Washington County News*, *Mountain View Times*, and *Abingdon Virginian* — clipping out articles worth mentioning on the air. She intended to play plenty of music, tossing out a topic of local interest each hour to involve her listeners in her show via the phone lines.

"Belle." Patrick was motioning at her from his office door. "Mr. Kildaire would like to do a brief interview with you, then take a few shots in the production room. You game?"

They exchanged a longer-than-necessary look — one that said, "Let's talk later" — then she directed the newspaper man to the production room for a photo shoot. He asked the usual questions, from "How did you begin your broadcasting career?" to "What brings you to Abingdon?"

Tact was called for here. Answering with "An eight-year-long crush on Patrick Reese brought me to town" would not serve the station or her career well.

Though the thought of it made her smile broadly for the camera.

"Could you roll up to that microphone

131

for me, Miss O'Brien?"

Roll up to it? *Yes*. Touch it? *No way*. Not after yesterday.

She posed as naturally as possible, hoping that the headphones didn't force her curly wisps into a strange new hair-style. "Headphone hair" was worse than "hat hair" for depleting a woman's self-confidence.

She reached up to check for damage and discovered an entire section of curls poking out on top, poodle-fashion, when the door whooshed open and David walked in, tool box in hand. The reporter took that as his cue to exit, quickly gathered his gear, and was gone. David, meanwhile, pulled out various test meters and diodes, prepared to do battle for the worthy cause of clean-sounding audio.

"You didn't touch my microphone, did you?" His voice sounded stern but his wry grin suggested otherwise.

"No, David, I barely breathed on your mike." Belle pointed her nose to the ceiling, pretending to be greatly offended, and yanked off her headphones with a sweeping gesture, smoothing her hair.

"My, aren't we the little actress." He busied himself with the stack of audio pro-cessors in the corner. Belle found her eyes drawn to his broad shoulders, slim waist, long legs. She was used to working with older engineers complete with middle-age spread, thick glasses, and a pocketful of drafting pens. The only thing in David's shirt pocket was David. It was difficult to ignore the pleasant scenery his muscular chest provided.

Good thing he's too young, too green, and too hardheaded. In more ways than one.

"What's wrong with acting?" She deliberately formed her red lips into a petulant pout, on the off chance he'd look her direction.

"Not a thing wrong with acting." He kept his back to her, not missing a beat in what he was doing. "I'm merely waiting to see who the leading man will be." He finally glanced over his shoulder at her from beneath a blond sweep of bangs, his eyes a deep gray. No storm clouds today.

"I never share the stage with anyone if I can help it." Belle gave an exaggerated sniff. She stretched back in the rolling chair, tempted to prop her boots on the counter, then thought better of it. Engineers didn't approve of anything propped on their countertops except elbows. "I prefer doing a one-woman show."

His back was toward her again. "Doesn't surprise me."

David's tone was so neutral it threw her off kilter. *Is he kidding or serious?* She

133

had to know. "Why? Why doesn't it surprise you?"

He stopped tweaking the meters and swung around to give her his full attention. "Because you're a star, Belle, and you love being the center of attention."

Ouch.

She jerked her chin at him. "Patrick sees that as an asset."

"I guess it is, in your business."

"Radio's *your* business, too." She didn't mean to sound so perturbed. But stuff it, she *was* perturbed!

He shrugged. "I'm a behind-the-scenes kinda guy. My ego doesn't need to be stroked five hours a day."

"W-what?" She bolted to her feet. *The nerve of this guy!*

"Belle, I'm only teasing." His generous mouth twitched into the slightest of smiles. "Honest."

"Humph." She tossed her braid in frustration and jammed her hands in her pockets. "Teasing, huh? *Tormenting* might be a better word for it. Anyway, bedeviling people seems to be your favorite pastime."

"Not all people." He shook his head. "Just you."

Her mouth dropped open. "Huh?"

"You heard me." He turned and crouched down to reach one of the bottom meters.

She suspected he was smiling broadly now and trying to hide it. *The turkey.*

"Most women get their feelings hurt easily, Belle, but you actually *enjoy* a fight. Creating a scene is your style. It's that actress thing in you." He turned to look at her again, his smile still in place, not a hint of animosity in his calm expression. "It's not a negative, Belle, it's who you are."

"Oh?" She snapped out the response, feeling her fists clench in her pockets. "And how'd you manage to figure that out in two days?"

"Easy. You talked a lot." His smile broadened slightly. "And I listened."

Heat shot into her cheeks. "Humph." Nothing was more aggravating than a perceptive man.

"Don't get your pretty nose out of joint, Belle." His gaze was steady, his tone warmer. "I like feisty women. Besides, WPER needs a few stars."

Did he say pretty?

She willed her face to cool down, forced herself to look back at him with equal aplomb. "Speaking of which, this little star needs to twinkle herself over to the air studio." Moving toward the door, she tossed the back of her hand over her forehead, dramatically rolling her eyes. "My audience awaits me."

It was definitely time to get out from

under this engineer's too-accurate scrutiny. It was also time to get back into theater, or her coworkers would carry her away in a straitjacket. Seconds before the sound lock cut him off, she heard David's gentle laughter.

At least he was in on the joke. Nothing was worse than waging a battle of wits with an unarmed man.

Frank was waiting for her in the main studio, stacking up the few commercial carts she'd need for her first hour. Carts reminded Belle of the eight-track tape cartridges from the '60s, except these were clear plastic on top and held thirty- or sixty-second commercial spots, cued up and ready to go. Ancient technology and typically Patrick.

"I've also got a CD loaded for your first song, Belle." Frank turned down the monitors so they wouldn't need to shout over the music. "Patrick picked this one. 'Good Lovin' by the Young Rascals." Frank's bushy eyebrows shot up significantly. "Said you'd understand why."

Belle stifled a laugh. *Patrick, you sly fox!*

Meanwhile, Frank's curiosity hung in the air like Snap Davis's lingering cigar smoke.

"It's not what you think, Frank. Trust me."

He shrugged. "Did I ask? I did not. You're up in two minutes. Break a leg,

136

girly." With that, Frank gathered his headphones, two coffee mugs, and a morning paper with the stuffing knocked out of it, and disappeared into the hallway.

She doubted she'd see him again until Wednesday. *He probably sleeps underground during the day,* she decided, giggling. "G'night, Frank," she called after him, plugging in her own headphones, adjusting the mike — *very* carefully — and wheeling the chair up to the console. Ninety seconds and she'd be on the air in Abingdon.

At ten o'clock straight up, she started the cart that broadcast Patrick's top-of-the-hour identification, and flicked on the microphone to add her own carefully planned welcome. When the first note of "Good Lovin' " came blasting out, so did her full-throttle laugh, almost drowning out the music.

She turned off the mike and shook her head. *Belle, really.* At least her new listeners would know she liked to have fun.

"So your theory is 'enter laughing,' is that it?"

She whirled around in her chair to find David standing behind her, hands on his hips.

"Why not?" She shrugged. Might as well pretend it was intentional at this point.

He waved a pair of pliers at her. "Look,

I need to tune a few things up in here and align the tape heads, but I'll be unobtrusive, I promise. Ignore me, okay?"

"No problem." She said it like she meant it. Now she intended to prove it.

Leaving her headphones on, she sang along with the music. Loudly. Brazenly off-key, the only way she knew how to sing. After the Young Rascals, it was Diana Ross, the Dave Clark Five, then Johnny Mathis. She knew every lyric to every hit song from 1954 on. Hadn't she been playing oldies for ten years?

David was practically kneeling at her feet, twisting together two wires underneath the console, when she looked down and caught his eye. "Bet you wish I knew the notes, huh?"

He grimaced and kept twisting.

Some people were just plain fun to spar with.

Belle turned on the mike and introduced the next tune, one of her favorites from Dion and the Belmonts, then busied herself with the program log, keeping one eye on the man at her feet. David had almost disappeared in his effort to reach the processor controls hidden in the farthest corner beneath the counter where nimble-fingered disc jockeys couldn't change the perfectly adjusted knobs.

She smiled in spite of herself. He was

right. She *did* like a good verbal contest now and again. It wasn't flirting. Certainly not. It was merely spirited conversation. *Yeah, that's it.* Patrick was much more her type when it came to romance. David was simply someone she could torment.

Belle scanned her playlist for the perfect song, then cued it up on the CD player. Seconds before she flipped open the microphone, she growled, "Oh, David, this one's for you," then in her best broadcast voice did a rocking intro over horns and bass, hitting the post as Aretha Franklin warmed up for a spelling lesson.

"R-E-S-P-E-C-T . . ."

Eight

There are two tragedies in life.
One is to lose your heart's desire.
The other is to gain it.

George Bernard Shaw

Sherry Robison hurried along the carpeted mall, checking her watch every ten steps, feeling her anxiety creep up another notch. She'd already been late for work twice this week. Not her fault, not really. Josh had been more obstinate than usual the last few mornings, getting in her way while she dressed and made breakfast, grumbling about one thing or another, requiring her undivided attention.

Life with Joshua had its highs and lows. Lately the lows were winning. She'd never leave him, couldn't imagine life without him. But it still hurt to see him struggle, to know what he needed to feel whole and realize it was the one thing she couldn't give him.

The morning sun streaming through the skylights above served as a warning light, blinking at her as she passed under each one: *Late. Late. Late.* A few stores to go and she'd finally be there. Her steps

140

slowed when she realized the wide metal gate was already up. *Uh-oh.* Her boss had arrived before she. *Not good, not good.*

Sherry walked across the threshold, scanning the aisles jammed with circular racks of neon-colored sports clothes. "Jana?" She felt the tension in her voice, the lump growing in her throat. "Jana, are you here?"

The owner of California Casualwear appeared at the back office doorway, her eyes trained on Sherry, her expression hard. "Yes, I'm here." Jana's strident voice carried across the empty store. "The question is, why weren't you here twenty minutes ago?"

Sherry locked her knees to stop them from shaking. "I'm so . . . sorry. It was . . . well, Josh needed —"

"Josh again." Jana moved toward her, a wiry woman with inch-long black hair and angular features. *Like a porcupine.* Sherry steeled herself against the impending onslaught. Jana stopped only inches away, planting her hands on her hips and pursing her lips in obvious distaste. "This is the third time this week you've been late, Sherry."

She hung her head. "I know."

"Even when you are here, you don't give this job your full attention." Jana eyed her critically. "How often has Josh called you

141

at work this week?"

"A few times." She spoke in a cowering whisper, hating herself for it.

"More than a few." Jana's words were aimed like poisoned darts. "Seven times, at least."

"I didn't know you were counting." Sherry felt a hard knot of anger forming inside her. So what if Josh called her occasionally? He needed her, needed to hear her voice. The calls were short. She still got her work done. What was the problem?

"What do you have to say for yourself, Miss Robison? Do you want this job or not?"

Fear stabbed Sherry's heart, chasing away the anger, replacing it with a cold sort of dread. "You know I do. I like selling clothes and helping customers and . . . and I really need the work."

"And I need an employee who cares enough to show up on time and give me their full share of hours." The woman's dark eyes sharpened to pinpoints. "I'm sorry, Sherry, but this is your last day. I'll have your check ready at two when you normally clock out. You're dismissed."

"You don't mean this! Can't you give me another chance?" Her pleas landed on Jana's retreating back. Sherry swallowed the rest of them along with her tears. *Not again.* Not another job to find, not another bill collector to hold at bay, not another long talk with Josh.

It wasn't his fault. It wasn't her fault. If she was honest with herself, she'd have to admit it wasn't David Cahill's fault either, much as she'd tried to pin all her misery on him. No, it was simply life, and life had ceased being simple — or fair — a long time ago.

A leggy teenager strolled into the store on a straight course toward the sale rack as Sherry slung her purse over her shoulder and wandered back out into the mall, disoriented. She was supposed to be at work. Instead she had four long hours to kill. Hardly enough time to figure out what she could afford from the grocery store, let alone what to do with the rest of her life.

Belle O'Brien's first four hours on the air flew by. Listeners called in, welcoming her to town, offering tips about the best places to eat, and chatting with her about all the latest Abingdon news — what groups would be riding in the Kiwanis Christmas Parade and when Washington Countians could expect to see their newly designed flag flying at the courthouse. David stuck his head in now and then, never making a nuisance of himself, but managing to tweak her nose a time or two.

No matter. She always got him back.

143

Her on-a-roll day came to a screeching halt at two o'clock when Patrick showed up long enough to shove Heather in the studio door. "Sounding great, Belle. Show Heather the ropes your last hour, will ya?"

"Do what?" But he was gone and Heather was there in all her youthful glory, waiting expectantly for Belle to suggest somewhere for her to land, it seemed. Her blond tresses fell to her shoulders in perfect waves, her lipstick was a delicate shade of pink, her blue eyes were wide open, shimmering with innocence.

Good grief, I'm working with a Breck Girl.

"Patrick said I'd need my own headphones." Heather's voice was all air and no substance.

Boop-oop-a-doop.

Heather pointed at the console. "Could I borrow your headphones? It'd only be for tonight."

Sure. Why don't you borrow my cashmere and pearls while you're at it? Belle sighed in resignation. "No problem. My cans are your cans."

Blank stare. "Cans?"

"Headphones." Belle mustered as much patience as she could. "Most jocks call them cans."

"Oh." Heather watched her for a few minutes, nodding her head as if trying to

144

take it all in. "What are all those square buttons you keep sliding up and down?"

"They're called *pots*. Nothing to do with flowers. That's short for potentiometer. They're like the volume knob on a radio. Up is louder, down is off. Back when I started in the business, we had rotary pots. Round ones."

"Rotary pots?" Heather's eyebrows disappeared under her blond sweep of hair. "Those sound *really* old. Gosh, did you use rotary telephones, too?"

It promised to be a long hour ahead.

"Sit tight, Heather. I've gotta do a spot break."

"A what?" she heard as she slipped on her headphones. Belle chatted with a listener on the air about the current show at the Barter, *The Taming of the Shrew*, shared the weather forecast for greater Abingdon, then hit the start button on a commercial for one of the few accounts Cliff had already sold, Mike's Quality Dry Cleaners.

"So, by *spot break* you mean these commercials?" Heather asked when the microphone was safely turned off.

"Right. If they don't get played on the air when they're supposed to, or the tape machine eats the cartridge, you'll need a make-good."

"Make a good what?"

"No, a *make-good* is when you re-schedule a commercial."

"Oh." Heather was starting to wilt.

Ease up on her, Belle. It's not a sin to be young. "Don't worry, you'll get the hang of all this jargon soon enough." Belle did her best to sound encouraging. Hadn't Patrick been tolerant about her own lack of experience in the early days? For his sake, she'd be extra patient with Heather Young.

But the more patience she had with Heather, the less she had with Patrick. *That bearded fool! Did he look at the woman's résumé or just her big blue eyes?* Heather's total radio experience had been voicing one commercial at a 6,000-watt station, reading the copy while someone else pushed all the buttons. Heather was in over her head and they both knew it. The thought of leaving her alone to handle a five-hour request show that night made Belle's blood boil.

What could Patrick have been thinking?

Surely he didn't hire Heather for her looks. *Tell me it isn't so, Lord!* By the end of the hour, Heather was in tears, more confused than ever, and Belle was hot. Very hot.

"Heather, don't panic." She patted her arm, uncertain how to console the sniffling blonde. "We're gonna work this out somehow, but you are *not* doing a solo show tonight. It isn't fair to you." *Or to our brand-new station.* "I'll talk to Patrick the minute I'm off the air." Boy, would she talk to him!

At three o'clock when Burt showed up, his arms loaded with music trivia books, Belle ordered Heather to stay put and take notes, then stamped off to the corner office to do battle with Mr. Reese.

By the time she reached his door, she was foot-stomping, rip-roaring, no-kidding mad. She didn't bother to knock, but simply kicked open his door with such force that it swung all the way back and smacked the wall. The marlin jumped, the deer looked shocked, and Patrick sat there, mouth agape, as if he expected to be the third mounted trophy in his office.

"Don't shoot!" He tossed aside the latest issue of *Radio Report.* "At least not until you tell me what I did wrong." His expression softened. "Or is it time for the . . . uh, discussion that was so rudely interrupted this morning?"

"It certainly is not!" Belle slammed the door shut, rattling the transom window above it. "How *could* you?" She choked out the words, near tears she was so angry. "How could you hire a DJ with no radio experience and expect her to go on the air tonight all by herself?"

He looked perplexed. "Is Heather having

147

a little trouble catching on?"

"A *little* trouble? The poor girl is sobbing in the studio, trying to figure out why *cans* don't have green beans in them." Belle advanced toward him, assuming the most intimidating stance she carried in her bag of theatrical tricks. "Patrick, you haven't answered my question. Why did you hire her? Let me guess. You knew she could do radio the minute you laid eyes on her. Is that it? Did you hire her for her pretty face?"

"Her what?" He stood up, looking genuinely confused. "Belle, you gotta be joking. I hired her because she was a good student who was willing to work hard to understand our business. Period. If she needs more time to learn things, I'll come in tonight and work with her myself until she's more confident."

"Humph." Was it her imagination or was steam coming out her ears? "That's probably the way you planned it all along, huh? Working with her every evening, showing her the ropes. One on one."

An amused look crossed his face. "You should hear yourself." His grin grew wider and slightly wicked. "You sound like a jealous wife."

"A . . . a *w-what?*"

But she *was* jealous, and she knew it.

So did he.

Patrick's voice lowered to a gentle murmur. "Belle, don't you know there isn't a woman alive whose face is more beautiful to me than yours?"

"Patrick!" It came out on a croak. "What are you saying?"

"I think you know exactly what I'm saying."

He narrowed the gap between them with three long strides, then slid one hand into hers and tugged her closer still. The temperature in the room shot up several degrees. "I'm saying, my dear Belinda Oberholtzer, that I've been attracted to you from the first time we met at your tacky little college radio station."

"WASU was not tacky," she protested faintly, "and don't you dare tell a soul my real name." *Did he say beautiful?* The word flashed across her mental landscape like a brightly lit movie marquee. He was kidding, of course, using salesman hyperbole to win her over.

Didn't he realize he'd already won, long ago?

"Patrick, I . . ."

With a light touch of his finger on her lips, he stilled her words. "Shhh. Let me finish, Belle."

He was toe to toe with her now. She gazed up into his eyes, wondering if he understood, as she finally did, that he was the main reason — maybe the only reason — she'd come to Abingdon.

"Belle, you're in Abingdon because you're the best person for the job. That's the honest truth of it."

Had he read her mind?

"But the rest of the honest truth is I'm grateful to have you in my life again." He squeezed her hand, obviously struggling for the right words.

"Me, too." *Atta girl, Belle. Very bold.*

"I'd . . . like to know if there could be something more between us."

"More?" She was still croaking.

"A relationship. You know, a . . ." He shrugged, his pearly white grin surrounded by a neatly trimmed beard. "Look, are you busy Friday night?"

"Ah . . . no." She giggled suddenly, feeling like a teenager and sounding pubescent. "No, I'm not busy."

He looked immensely relieved. "Good. I'll pick you up at six for dinner and a show at the Barter."

"It's a date." *A date?* She hadn't been on a date since the Bush administration. Would she remember what to do? What to say? What to wear? Would Norah expect her home by eleven? The whole thing was too weird.

Weird and wonderful.

Patrick sat back on the edge of his desk,

still gently holding her hands, and let loose a hearty laugh. "Finally. After sitting on simmer for ten years, we get to turn the burner up a tad."

"Only a tad." She was doing her best to keep her boots firmly planted when they desperately wanted to do a joyful little jig. "You're still my boss. It could get awkward around here."

"Ahh." He gazed at her, silent for several moments. "Technically, Burt is your immediate supervisor. But since he works for me, of course, you do as well. This calls for the utmost in propriety."

"Utmost." She nodded emphatically.

"We'll take it slowly and talk over things every step of the way."

"Slow is good."

"Suppose we don't mention this to anyone initially. At least until . . . well, until we know if . . ."

Belle nodded, her eyes locked with his. "Until we know if there's something worth pursuing here, or if we're only good friends after all."

"Right."

Except he wasn't looking at her like a friend. She felt more like an icy lemonade on a steamy hot day.

"Well . . . um . . . good. Right." She scrambled for a toehold on her emotions. "We should know where we stand by

Monday morning, don't you think?"

"Monday morning?" He was back on his feet, no longer looking thirsty. "I've waited eight years, and you're giving me five days?"

"Five days is enough." *I'll be lucky to keep it quiet five hours.* "By the end of the weekend, we'll know. Until then, mum's the word, okay?"

"No problem, woman." His eyes darkened slightly and his voice dropped another two notes. "I can win your heart in *three* days, if I have to."

The man had an ego the size of Montana. It was one of the things she liked best about him.

"Now —" He drew her closer. "You can stop fretting over Heather the Young, okay?" He tipped his head down until their lips were a scant breath apart. "Why would I ever want a woman with golden hair when I can kiss one with golden eyes and a golden voice to match?"

As Patrick brushed his lips against hers, Belle waited for an electrical spark, something to send her tingling from her thick braid to her skinny toes.

Nothing yet.

She pressed her lips more firmly against his, convinced the two of them had simply made a bad connection, like a faulty phone line.

Still nothing.

Odd. His lips were moist, his kiss was insistent, his arms around her were snug and warm, but . . .

Nothing. No jolt, no spark, and not even a trace of a tingle.

Not to worry. They could practice Friday night, couldn't they? At the moment, only one thought refused to be silenced: *Norah is not going to like this.*

Norah shook her head emphatically. "I don't like it, Belle, not one bit."

"Why not?" Belle made the question sound innocent enough, though she'd seen it coming. They'd been unpacking boxes and rearranging furniture for three days. Norah had oohed and aahed over her few nice pieces of Carolina-crafted mission oak, collected with care over the last decade. They'd found a spot for almost every one of her meager furnishings, steering away from the one thing that was certain to tie Norah's pantyhose in a knot.

That topic could no longer be avoided.

"This is all wrong for you." Norah pointed in near disgust. "These spartan oak pieces are handsome in their simplicity, but then there's this . . . this overcarved, underwhelming . . . er, what is it, anyway?"

No getting around it. "A hope chest."

"Oh." Norah pinched her lips together,

153

but couldn't keep the laugh from slipping out.

Belle sighed. "I know. It's awful. My parents gave it to me when I graduated from high school." She shrugged. "They were all the rage that year. Cedar-lined hope chests."

Norah chuckled. "What were you . . . ah, *hoping* to put in it?"

Belle stuck out her tongue. "Orange-flowered pillow cases, of course. Green vinyl tablecloths, plastic fish napkin rings, that kind of thing."

Humor came in handy when she had something to hide, and Belle had plenty worth hiding. She was proud of herself for keeping her budding relationship with Patrick an absolute secret, not once letting something slip with Norah or anyone else. Her landlady hadn't asked and she hadn't offered, but it was getting trickier. He was coming to pick her up for their big date in two hours, so she'd have to tell Norah something.

Just not everything.

Not the fact that she'd laughed more in the last three days than she had in the last three years. Nor that holding his hand, feeling his warmth, strength, and affection, had fed her soul more this week than food and water had fed her body in a month.

She'd stick to the safe side of truth:

154

they were good friends.

Norah knelt by the battered chest that bore the scars of too many moves. "And here I'd pegged you as the pottery and baskets type." She undid the latch, then looked up expectantly. "May I?"

At Belle's nod, Norah lifted first the lid, then her eyebrows. "Oh my." She touched a stack of antique linens with great care, smoothing her hands across them, barely brushing the intricate needlework. "These are exquisite." Norah sighed. "You fibbed. Not a scrap of vinyl or plastic in sight."

"My grandmother Oberholtzer's wedding linens from Germany." Belle leaned down to brush gentle fingers across the fabric. "Grandma insists I'll marry a fine man someday and give her lots of great-grandchildren." She shook her head. "Not doing too well on that score, am I?"

"It's never too late." Norah winked. "Don't rule out marriage and children yet."

Belle lifted her shoulders slightly to end the discussion, but it continued to skip through her heart. Could she imagine walking down the aisle on her father's arm, gazing at Patrick waiting at the altar?

No, she could not. Too much, too soon, and too scary.

Norah gingerly tucked the linens back in place. "Want to catch a movie in Bristol tonight?"

"Ahh . . . I'd love to, but I have plans." Belle felt a wave of apprehension move through her. She couldn't explain it, but she definitely was hesitant to tell Norah about what was happening with Patrick.

Did she expect disapproval? A lecture about the obvious conflicts involved?

She stood, smoothing the wrinkles in her jeans as she planned her best approach. "Norah, I need you to keep a secret. Could you do that?"

Norah held up her hand, sending a wristful of slim silver bracelets jingling down her arm. "Discretion is my middle name."

"I never doubted that for a minute." And she didn't. She'd known Norah less than a week and would trust the woman with anything near and dear to her heart. Including Patrick. Even so, the words wouldn't come.

Belle bit her lip. "If you don't mind, I could use some hot tea. Keep me company while I brew a pot, will you?"

Norah followed her into the long, narrow kitchen as Belle opened her new cabinets, enjoying the look of the tidy shelves displaying her familiar dishes and mugs. It wouldn't stay neat for long, but it filled her with a welcome sense of order and purpose. There was the blue-and-white teapot, exactly where she'd put it last night. She gathered the strainer, a tea ball, and the fresh bag of loose sassafras tea she'd uncovered in Norah's shop, and set water on to boil.

"So?" Norah regarded her, a hint of curiosity and something less definable playing on her features. "Do I get to hear your secret?"

"It involves a man, of course."

"Of course. Someone new you've met or a voice from the past?"

Belle looked directly at her, not wanting to miss a nuance of her reaction. "The past. And the present." She cleared her throat, fighting off a sense of dread. *Why is this so difficult?* "Norah, it's Patrick."

The woman's black eyes widened and her customary smile vanished, but only for an instant before her features resumed their usual open expression. "I see."

Did she imagine it or was Norah's voice cooler than it had been a moment ago?

"A lot has happened since last Sunday night when you and I talked about this."

"You mean when you decided . . . how was it you put it, 'to let Patrick find the right woman for him'?" Norah folded her arms over her chest. "Clearly a great deal has taken place since then."

Definitely cooler. Not quite angry, but not happy either.

"You're upset, Norah."

157

"Not in the least."

The older woman's words were calm, but Belle watched her fidgeting with the silver spoon ring on her left hand. Clearly there was something going on under the surface.

"I'm merely confused by your sudden change of heart."

Belle couldn't keep the smile off her face. "Patrick was the one who changed my heart."

"Ah. I see."

She sees something, all right. I just don't know what.

I should have seen this coming.

Norah watched Belle pour the steaming hot tea, the fragrant aroma filling the little kitchen even as despair seemed to be filling her own heart. Tea and sympathy were what she needed, but Belle was in no position to offer the latter. Rather like a cat serving tea to a mouse before swallowing it whole.

Clearly her subterfuge had worked, perhaps too well. Belle was totally in the dark about her feelings for Patrick. No wonder. Those feelings were so ridiculously one-sided. Patrick had never once hinted at there being anything more than a solid friendship between them. He'd flirted with her, of course — didn't most gregarious, good-looking men? — but never with intent and never inappropriately.

Where had she gotten the absurd idea that he might care for her, anyway? Had he so much as brushed her hand in passing, looked at her with anything beyond mild interest, called her any time other than when he needed something?

Norah turned abruptly, focusing her gaze on the view outside Belle's third-floor window, rather than facing the truth that was tearing her heart in two. She could feel it separating, like fabric rending, not along a seam or a well-patched split, but a whole new tear, ripping top to bottom.

She closed her eyes and gritted her teeth, willing away the awful aching in her chest — an aching so real that she imagined a surgeon's scalpel had penetrated her most vital organ.

She'd spent fifteen years avoiding this kind of pain. How could she have opened herself up to it all over again? After all the seasons of hard-earned contentment, of learning to live alone and like it . . . after growing her business and her faith, her twin pillars of support. How could this bearded teddy bear have completely captured her heart without any effort on his part?

Frailty, thy name is woman!

Even Shakespeare offered no comfort this day.

Belle was carrying their tea into the living room, a room Norah had helped decorate. She wasn't sorry, would never regret helping Belle. She was so needy, this girl-woman. Belle needed a friend, she needed to get her spiritual life on track — and she needed to settle down, internally at least, and gain a sense of worth based on something other than her ability to perform for others.

Frankly, Patrick — *her* Patrick — was the last thing Belle needed.

Which is not your job to point out.

Playing the part of the older, wiser woman had suddenly lost its appeal. She got the funniest lines, the most outrageous costumes, but she never got the man.

As she perched on one of Belle's mission oak chairs, teacup in hand, Norah found herself wishing, just this once, she could read the part of the young ingenue, speaking the exact words Belle was saying now with breathless enthusiasm and looking for all the world as though she'd just bitten into a warm fudge brownie.

"Oh, Norah! Patrick is so . . . so mature. The kind of man you can really trust. Isn't it something that we've known each other all this time, but nothing ever came of it until now?"

"Yes, that's something." Norah sipped

her tea then nodded, her face unreadable.

Belle found herself bubbling on and on about Patrick. And so it went . . . Norah nodded; she bubbled. The teapot, hiding under its plaid cozy, grew lukewarm, then cold, and still she bubbled, unable to keep her joy to herself, needing an outlet, someone to listen.

Wasn't it gracious of Norah to show so much interest when none of this could possibly matter to her one whit?

Belle glanced down at her watch and abruptly jumped to her feet, knocking the table with her knee, setting the teacups dancing in their china saucers. "Patrick will be here in an hour. You're the clothes horse, Norah. Come take a look in my closet and help me pick something."

Norah dutifully followed her into the bedroom, where a long wall closet stood open, jammed with clothes in every style and color. "What about this?" Norah pulled out a long-sleeved, brown wool dress with a high neck and a long hemline.

"Good grief, that's a look-but-don't touch outfit if I ever saw one."

Norah simply smiled, then chose another: a pantsuit with a masculine cut.

Ugh. "Worse. Strictly interview apparel. We're talking dinner and a play here, remember?" She pulled out a slim turquoise dress in a form-fitting knit. "This might work. What do you think?"

Norah sleeked one manicured hand over the fabric. "It'll work, all right." She sighed. "In fact, I have a handmade turquoise and sterling silver necklace from Santa Fe that will knock his socks off."

Belle hugged her and laughed. "His socks can stay right where they are, thank you, but I'd love to borrow your jewelry if you're sure that's okay. I'll jump in the shower, then stop by your place on my way out." She caught the woman's eye and held it for a beat longer than necessary. "I can't thank you enough, Norah. For putting your touch on this apartment, for listening while I went on and on about Patrick, for offering to accessorize me in something so priceless. Is there anything I can do for *you?*"

"Yes, there is." Norah's face was tight and drawn, which sent a ripple of discomfort skipping down Belle's spine. Yet another odd sensation in an afternoon that had been full of them.

Norah's voice was so soft Belle had to strain to hear her. "Be good to him, Belle. Underneath all that bravado is the heart of a little boy who needs to know he's loved."

"I will." *If only Norah knew how much the girl inside me needs to know the same thing.*

Nine

When you see a couple coming down the street, the one who is two or three steps ahead is the one that's mad.

Helen Rowland

Patrick was late, of course.

When the Blue Boat came roaring up to the curb at 6:15, Belle was standing in Norah's living room, too tense to sit. She peered out the window, safely hidden by a generous swag of European lace draped in measured folds around the long, narrow opening.

Patrick was wearing his dark gray suit again, the one he'd worn on Tuesday. The one she'd complimented him on, she thought with a shiver of pleasure.

He glanced at his watch, then took the steep wooden steps two at a time. She backed away from the window, nervously smoothing her dress — as if a knit knew how to wrinkle — and did a final once-over in Norah's hall mirror, a gilded monstrosity that stretched from the floor to the twelve-foot ceiling.

She'd chosen the right dress. Norah's exquisite necklace looked custom-made for it, falling below her collar bones in a graceful circle that helped her pointy chin appear a bit less lethal. Turquoise earrings, also mined from Norah's extensive collection, dangled from each lobe. She'd wrapped her braid up in a French knot — also Norah's idea — and confessed that yes, it did give her a more sophisticated look.

When the doorbell for her apartment rang directly above her, Belle practically jumped out of her jewelry. "I'll answer that," Norah murmured from behind her, swinging open the door and apparently catching Patrick off guard.

"Norah!" Belle heard him say. "I was . . . I mean . . . expecting Belle."

"And she's right here, where she's been waiting for the last fifteen minutes." Norah did not sound pleased. "See that you're more prompt next time, sir. The women of this household deserve better."

With that, Norah swung the door open more fully and Patrick stepped inside, looking for all the world like a chastised Little Leaguer.

Do not laugh, Belle. Resist the urge.

When his eyes met hers, she watched his demeanor shift from awkward suitor to savvy executive in mere seconds. As his gaze swept over her from head to toe, yet another expression moved across his face, one that had nothing to do with WPER

164

and everything to do with the evening ahead.

He whistled, loudly.

She blushed, thoroughly.

Since when was Patrick the whistling type?

"Have fun, you two." Norah practically purred as she stood there, stroking a contented Harry draped over her shoulder. The woman seemed to enjoy her self-appointed role of housemother. Belle didn't mind one bit. Having Norah there calmed her jangling nerves and buoyed her confidence for the hours ahead.

Not much had happened in the first three of their five-day experimental relationship. They'd shared one innocent kiss — a fairly forgettable one, actually — several furtive hand-holdings in the hall when no one was looking, and mutual anticipation about their Friday night date.

So much for waiting. The date had officially begun. If he kissed her again, she hoped it would be more like fireworks and less like a damp pack of matches.

Patrick made a big show of offering her his arm, jutting his elbow out for her to slip her hand through. It felt good there, pressed against his muscular chest. With her free hand, she waved good-bye to Norah and they stepped out into the chilly November air. She could see her breath

165

coming out in steamy huffs as they walked in tandem down the steps.

Patrick didn't say a word, merely patted her hand. She felt more like a daughter on her father's arm, en route to her debutante ball, than a grown woman being escorted to dinner and the theater by a new beau. Nonetheless, she had a sense of security and being cared for, two emotions that hadn't visited her anytime recently.

When they reached the curb, she did a double take. "Patrick, you've given the Blue Boat a bath!"

"True confession: I did spend some time at the Buggy Bath Car Wash today. Didn't want you to brush against the Caddy and ruin your dress with dirt from two decades ago."

"Very considerate." She slid onto the up-holstered seats, which had suffered years of abuse at Patrick's careless hand. These, too, had been cleaned, she noticed. In fact, the whole interior was neat as a pin — no roadkill radios in the backseat, no fast food bags balled up on the floor. *Hmm.* He'd gone to a lot of trouble to impress her.

It had worked.

Once Patrick was behind the wheel and navigating the Cadillac east on Main, Belle asked the obvious. "Where are we having dinner?"

He took his eyes off the road long

enough to wink at her. "You trust me, don't you? Abingdon's oldest building happens to have one of its best restaurants."

She prepared herself for a spate of tour guide patter.

"Since 1779, the Tavern has been everything from a stagecoach inn to a field hospital during the Civil War to Abingdon's first post office. The original mail slot is still there."

Belle elbowed his ribs. "Yes, but . . . how's the *food?*"

"Tell me what you think when dessert is served."

Half a block past the radio station, he pulled up to the curb, filling almost two parking spaces, and directed her to an unassuming gray stucco building with an American flag flying out front. One foot inside the door, Belle was immersed in its historic past. Low, dark-beamed ceilings, brick floors, whitewashed walls, and painted blue wood trim, all spoke of centuries gone by. So did candles, resting in the deep windowsills and mounted in tin sconces along the walls. Cherry Windsor chairs gathered around harvest tables, and crackling fires burned in the grates.

"I like it already." Whispering seemed appropriate as she followed him up a narrow, enclosed staircase to the second floor where they were directed to a cozy corner table set for two.

"My pleasure to serve you, Mr. Reese." Their waitress's accent marked her as a Virginia Highlands native. Her uniform was in keeping with the decor, from the white, lace-edged mob cap to her long, full gingham skirt. She took their orders quickly and soon reappeared with their appetizers, portobello mushrooms with feta cheese.

They grinned at one another, took a bite, and grinned some more. Their conversation, stilted at first, hit stride when they landed on safe topics: work-related ones. Community feedback about WPER carried them through the spinach salad. French bread was served with an update on Cliff's success on the sales front. An in-depth review of Heather's progress accompanied the broiled seafood entrées. Dessert, a scrumptious apple tart with cinnamon ice cream, was dished up with a discussion about their upcoming "Happy Together" promotion.

Patrick regarded her over the rim of his coffee cup, his expression suddenly rueful. "Forgive me, Belle." He signaled for the check, then reached across the small table and captured both her hands. "I've been going on and on about the station, when tonight was finally our chance to talk about . . ."

"You and me." *Finally, he noticed.*

"Right." Patrick massaged her palms with the pads of his thumbs. His face reflected a tenderness she'd never seen before, and it both thrilled her to her fingertips and scared her silly.

"You look wonderful tonight." His voice was a soothing rumble.

"Thank you." She didn't know how else to respond, so amazed was she to be sharing dinner with a man she'd admired — no, more than that — a man she'd been enamored with for a third of her life. "To think, after all these years, Patrick . . ." She looked into a pair of hazel eyes surrounded by laugh lines and filled with intelligence.

"Incredible." His smile broadened. "Of course, we could have been having dinner like this eight years ago if you hadn't run away from me to work at WRVQ."

Heat flew up her neck and face. "Run away? Don't tell me you knew."

"Knew what?" He looked confused.

"Knew that I had a bona fide, post-teenage, downright serious crush on you."

"Belle, I had no idea!" His startled expression confirmed it. "Are you sure? I mean . . . why didn't you tell me?"

"*Tell* you? You must be joking." It felt good to laugh and chase away her chagrin at having to admit such a goofy thing. "I would've been mortified if you'd found out. Too embarrassing. One of the inevitabilities of the business, I guess, is falling for your first boss, the one who gave you your big break." She laughed again. "I'm surprised you didn't figure that one out for yourself."

The waitress appeared with the check, which Patrick signed with a flourish and handed back to her. If his mottled blush was any sort of barometer, he was grateful for the momentary distraction.

Belle watched the girl hurry away and shook her head in amusement. "Let me guess. This is another WPER trade account."

"You got it." Every tooth he owned appeared to be on display. He slipped five dollars under his dessert plate. "That's the only money I'll need to spend tonight. We can leave the car at Norah's and save money on parking, too, since the Barter Theatre's right up the street."

She groaned. "I suppose you traded the tickets to the Barter as well." Belle didn't know whether to applaud his frugal efforts or stick his five-dollar bill in the candle flame and watch a grown man cry.

"Better than a trade, Belle." He was obviously pleased with himself. "They gave me complimentary tickets when I told them we might like to sponsor a show this winter. How 'bout that?"

"That's my man. Patrick Scrooge."

He looked crestfallen. "Am I really a miser?"

"Yes." She softened the confirmation with a grin. "It's one of the many things that make you what you are."

"Cheap?"

"Lovable."

With one word, everything around them changed. The clatter of dishes and animated conversations became a distant din as their eyes and ears strained toward one another.

"Belle, if I'd only known you felt that way in Kingsport . . ." His eyes searched hers. What he was looking for she could only imagine. "If I'd known, I'd have never let you go."

She pulled back, perplexed. "Because I had a crush on you?"

"No. Because I was in love with *you*."

Her heart went in two directions at once, plunging toward her stomach and catching in her throat. "In love with me? Patrick, you never gave me the slightest clue —"

"Of course I didn't." He released her hands, tossing his own up in a gesture of distress. "You were my employee, Belle —"

She cut him off with a small cry of distress. "Isn't that what I am now?"

"But this is different. We're more mature and we know what we're getting into this time."

"Maybe *you* know." She stared at the ceiling, her hand over her mouth as she tried to nail down her scattered thoughts and emotions. She was so amazed she couldn't breathe, so shocked she couldn't think, so sorry they'd wasted eight years that she didn't know what to say next.

He solved that dilemma for her. "Belle, I spent two years in Kingsport convincing myself that I was all wrong for you. Too old, too happy being single, too wrapped up in radio."

Tears tickled her eyes and throat. Her voice was pinched. "Couldn't you have given me a chance to vote on whether or not you were right for me?"

"No." He shook his head for emphasis. "You were young, incredibly talented, and had a bright future ahead of you. I needed . . . well, I had to get out of the way so you could keep your career on track."

"How convenient for you that WRVQ came along and made me such a good offer then, eh?" She managed a faint smile, holding the tears at bay a little longer.

His eyes bore into hers for a full minute. *What is he looking for? Is there something I'm supposed to say? feel? do?*

"Belle, it wasn't a coincidence that

172

WRVQ contacted you."

Her stomach dipped again, this time for a very different reason. Her lips seemed to take forever to move. "What do you mean?"

"I mean that I sent them a demo tape of your show and a copy of your résumé."

"You did *what?*" He couldn't have. Not Patrick. "Please tell me you're kidding."

His pained expression told her the awful truth. "I sent it anonymously, knowing they'd hear your talent and hire you and —"

"Patrick!" She stood up, oblivious to her surroundings until the chatter around them ceased and she realized every eye in the small dining room was on her. She sank back in her seat and dropped her head in her hands, unable to keep the tears from flowing full force.

It was all she could do to form the words. "Patrick, how could you?"

"I had to." He reached for her hands, but she snatched them back, plastering them to her head, her face parallel with the table. He pressed on, his tone insistent. "For your sake, I had to let you go. If you'd stayed another month, I'd have begged you to marry me, bringing your career to a grinding halt."

A spark of anger fired in her chest and she lifted her head, glowering at him through tear-drenched eyes. "Wasn't that my decision to make? It was, as you pointed out, *my* career that was at stake."

And my heart. "By not telling me how you felt, by not letting me decide where I'd work next, or if I wanted to leave Kingsport . . ."

She was sputtering now. "I hope you enjoyed playing God, Patrick. Deciding my future for me. Purposely cutting yourself out of it when that would have been . . . would have been the best news . . ."

She slumped in a heap on the table. Her breathing came in anguished gulps as tears streamed down her face. *How dare he!* It was all she could think of, not trusting herself to say it out loud, knowing if she did it would be at the top of her lungs.

"Belle, you have to believe me. I did this for you." The sincerity in his voice merely fueled her outrage.

Grabbing her coat and purse she stood, not risking so much as a glance in his direction, and bolted for the stairwell. She heard his chair scrape behind her, heard him call her name. She hung onto the railing for dear life, fearing in her rush to get away she'd tumble headfirst down the steep, well-worn steps.

"Belle, wait!"

His heavier footsteps behind her spurred her forward, through the reception area and out the door into the dark, misty

174

night. She paused only long enough to shove her arms into her green coat, but by then Patrick was behind her, reaching for her.

His grip on her arm was less than gentle as he swung her around. His words were tinged with anger. "Belle, give me a chance!"

She was gasping for air as she struggled to speak. "A chance to do what? Lie to me again?" The traffic on Main Street gave her all the permission she needed to shout. "How *dare* you, Patrick! How dare you? I trusted you. In my own naive way, I loved you."

"And I loved you, Belle. I still do. Don't you see, I wanted you to have . . . to have . . ."

A possibility dawned on her all at once, like the first streak of sunlight penetrating a gray morning sky. "Of course. You wanted me to have something that you knew you'd never have. A shot at my own show in a major market. Is that it? A vicarious thrill for you, another feather in your manager's cap?"

"No, Belle, that's not true!"

Don't lie to me.

It was worse than she'd imagined. He'd loved her but never told her. He'd sent her away but never told her why. He'd hired her again, knowing all that but revealing nothing. He'd manipulated her career, her heart, her life, all for his own satisfaction.

She shook off his grip on her arm and buttoned her coat with exaggerated motions, her rage and frustration making her hands shake. She could feel her once-tidy hair spilling down her back, scattering pins everywhere. How different things had been when she'd tucked them into place only two hours earlier. Now her eyes were trained on his, ignoring the pleading she saw there. "You are singularly the most selfish person I have ever known, Patrick Reese. You brought me to this station under false pretenses —"

"No!" He didn't seem angry so much as desperate. "I brought you here because you were the best person for the job and —"

"If you say that one more time I'm going to throw up!"

"Belle, it's the truth. I swear to you."

"The truth?" She snorted. "What would you know about the truth?" She managed the last button on her coat and stepped back to take in a deep breath. "I think we can safely say our relationship is over. It was a charming three days while it lasted. Too bad I didn't know it was built on a foundation of lies."

Patrick loomed over her, a thundercloud of a man, his eyes piercing hers, his face wearing so many conflicting emotions she couldn't begin to sort them through.

Nor did she intend to, now or ever.

She took another ragged breath. "Effective Monday, I will no longer be working for WPER." She practically spat out the call letters. "Find yourself another midday woman, Patrick. This one is history."

"You can't do this, Belle." His voice sounded like a wounded bear.

"I can and I will!"

"No, I mean you *can't* do this."

He paused.

She waited.

When he continued, his voice was low, his words spoken with great care. "Belle, you have a personal contract with WPER. You signed it Monday, remember?"

I remember. You don't . . . you can't . . .

"You agreed, in writing, to remain in my employ for six months. In order to get the station established, if you recall. An unusual contract, but you agreed to it completely. After the six months are up, of course, you're free to pursue your career wherever it may take you, but until the second of May . . . you're mine."

"No!"

She turned on her heel and practically ran up the street, her high heels catching on the uneven brick sidewalk. Patrick was right behind her, grasping at her sleeve. "Belle, I'm sorry. I'll help you find something else, something better, come May."

She turned back abruptly, knocking him off balance. "Don't you dare mention helping me. You've done quite enough."

Belle continued her staggering path up the steep bricks, determined not to let him see her stumble.

"Wait!" He was mere feet behind her. "I can . . . I can let you out of your contract, Belle. If you'd rather not —"

"Forget it!" She stopped again, whirling around to confront him. Her face, covered with wayward curls and hot tears, was feverish with anger and embarrassment at being so foolish. "Get this straight, Patrick Reese. I'm going to work every day of that six-month contract for the sheer joy of making you miserable. And unless I give you cause, unless I'm found drunk in the local pub or naked on the Town Square, you can't fire me. Isn't that right?"

His expression was one of pure agony. "That's right. Unless tonight could be considered insubordination —"

The last straw snapped.

"Don't even think it!" It was close to a shriek. "You can't fire someone for . . . for hating you!"

Leaving him slack-jawed, standing there on the sidewalk, Belle stormed off toward home, five blocks away. She let the tears flow unabated, not caring what her makeup looked like anymore, no longer concerned with impressing her date. *Ha!* She scoffed at the thought of how much she'd yearned for a memorable evening.

It had been memorable. Yes, indeed. An evening she'd never forget as long as she lived.

She crossed the street, heading past the Greenway-Trigg building, when she heard the rumble of a Cadillac motor coming around the corner. The car slowed to a crawl beside her and she heard the driver roll down the window.

"Belle, at least let me drive you home." Patrick's voice, muffled by the wind, was pleading.

"I am perfectly capable of walking, thank you. I've done it every day this week and I'll do it every single day until May." She shot him a withering glance as he steered the car along the sidewalk, his window down, his eyes imploring.

"Please, Belle. Please let me explain. You can quit if you want to, you can do whatever makes you happy, but please let me try and make you understand."

"I understand that I've been made a fool of, sixteen ways to Sunday!" She marched over to the car, spotted the theater tickets sticking out of his shirt pocket, and snatched one. "If you don't mind, I'm going to salvage what I can of this evening and take myself to the Barter. Alone."

He didn't try to stop her as she crossed the street and kept walking, and for that she was grateful. She wasn't ready to face Norah with the unhappy news, nor could she imagine sitting alone in her apartment, rehashing this dreadful night in her head, over and over.

No. *The Taming of the Shrew* was the perfect diversion. She'd let the wit of Petruchio and Katherina keep her company. At least *their* love story had a happy ending.

Ten

Being a woman is a terribly difficult trade,
since it consists principally
of dealing with men.

Joseph Conrad

Patrick watched Belle march across the street and out of his life, disappearing into the mist like a forgotten dream.

Except this one had turned into a nightmare.

For a guy who enjoyed being in charge of things, he found his sense of frustration almost debilitating. Why couldn't Belle see what was so blooming obvious to him? That he'd sent her tape to WRVQ for *her* sake, not his. That he'd done it out of love, not selfishness.

That he loved her still.

He was shaking so badly he didn't trust himself behind the wheel, so he pointed the Cadillac toward the nearest open curb space. The engine rattled to a wheezing halt as he slumped over the steering wheel.

You blew it, Reese. Big time. She'd continue working for him, she said. Even though she hated him, she said.

Hate was a strong emotion, he reminded

181

himself. One born of passion, not apathy. *At least she cares about me enough to hate me.* For some odd reason, the thought comforted him. When she'd first arrived in town, he wasn't sure she had any feelings for him at all. Now she had all kinds of feelings. Not the right ones, but it was a start.

He sat there for several minutes replaying their conversation — *Argument, Reese, it was an argument* — looking for holes in his reasoning or in hers, searching for clues to figure out where exactly he'd gone wrong.

I shouldn't have told her about sending the demo tape. She wouldn't have known if he hadn't told her. Never would have found out, either.

I shouldn't have sent the demo tape without asking her. That was closer to the truth, though he had done it for the right reasons. He could fret over his mistakes all night long, but it didn't change the fact that Belle felt manipulated and misled. The bedrock of any relationship, including boss to employee, was trust. Well, he'd simply have to earn hers back.

Shaking his head as if to clear the gloomy fog that had settled over him, he pulled onto Main and continued west, not sure where he was heading. What he needed more than anything was a friend.

He'd been so busy his first few weeks in town, working every minute to get the station on the air, he'd had zero time for developing much in the way of friendships.

That oversight would be corrected, effective immediately.

He considered swinging out to the transmitter site to check things over . . . see if David was home. *Nah.* The guy was probably busy working on his house. He didn't need somebody getting in the way, talking his ear off, slowing him down.

Heather was on the air right now, her first night alone on the board. Maybe he'd drop in and see how she was doing, keep her company. *Dumb idea.* He was the owner of the station, for Pete's sake. He'd make her a nervous wreck. Which didn't take much, with Heather.

He remembered the theater ticket that remained in his pocket. The one for the seat right next to Belle's. *That's it.* He'd find her at the Barter, beg her forgiveness, do whatever it took to make her happy and keep her in Abingdon.

No. The timing was wrong, the place was worse. He didn't want another scene like they'd had at the restaurant. If anyone figured out who they were, it would be bad for the station's image.

Not to mention your ego.

Yeah, that too.

The Methodist church was coming up on his right, the Silver Spoon was on his left. Norah's place. Belle's place. The top two floors were dark, but he could see lamps glowing in the gift shop downstairs. Security lights, maybe. Or Norah baking muffins, getting ready for a busy Saturday morning.

Wait! Norah could use the ticket. Join Belle at the theatre, offer her some female companionship, maybe say a kind word about him. The image of Norah's stern expression last time he'd seen her flashed through his mind. *Okay, maybe not.* Anyway, it was worth a try.

The spaces along the curb were filled, so he parked the Cadillac in the church lot and crossed the street in a handful of brisk strides, heading for the first-floor entrance with the classy, hand-carved sign swinging out front. He rang the bell, an old-fashioned contraption in the middle of the door. A flick of his wrist on the silver handle sent bells ringing inside, same as the set Norah had jingling on her back door upstairs.

If it isn't one "belle," it's another. He grinned in spite of himself. Some night this was turning out to be.

Norah's face appeared in the window, looking confused, then concerned. He felt foolish standing there alone, knowing what

184

must be running through her mind. He shrugged and pointed to the door, which swung open seconds later with another loud jangle.

"Patrick, what's happened to Belle? Were you in an accident? Is she hurt?" Norah's words came in a breathless rush while her dark eyes searched the brick porch, as if he were hiding Belle behind a wooden post.

"Belle is fine," he protested, holding up his hands. "Well, no, she isn't fine at all, she's . . ." He sighed. "May I come in for a minute?"

Norah's eyes, tinged with suspicion, scrutinized him. "I have a feeling this will take more than a minute, Patrick." A mild reprimand lingered behind her words. "I'll work on my muffins while you explain to me exactly what's going on here."

He followed her through the dimly lit shop to the kitchen, where bright lights, warm ovens, and the aroma of apples and cinnamon greeted him. Taking in a deep whiff, he tried to lighten the mood. "Mmm . . . delicious. Can I move in here?"

"That's what everyone says, and no, you certainly cannot." She was stirring batter with a wooden spoon that was getting a serious workout, *whomp! whomp!* against the side of the bowl.

"Norah, you know I'm kidding." He sank down into a kitchen chair, tossing his

185

keys on the table, dreading the direction this conversation would need to take. The sooner he got to it, the better. "Belle and I had an argument."

Norah's spoon paused in mid-whomp. "And . . . ?"

"And she stomped out of the restaurant and walked to the Barter Theatre by herself."

"She *walked* to the Barter? What kind of man would let a woman walk the streets at night? And alone, of all things?" She shoved her spoon into the batter and slammed her hands on her hips. "Patrick Reese, I'm ashamed of you!"

"I'm ashamed of me, too, but she wouldn't get in the car. Believe me, I tried. Followed her for a block." He ran his hands through his hair and exhaled in noisy frustration. "It's no good, Norah. The woman will never forgive me."

Norah's eyes narrowed. "Forgive you for what?"

"Have you got an hour or so?" He studied her expressive face, looking for a clue as to how she might react. *Compassion or judgment?* It was hard to tell for sure. "Look, I really stopped by to see if you wanted to use this other ticket for the play tonight. Sit with Belle, keep her company?"

Norah shook her head. "If she wanted

186

company, she'd have come here first. My guess is, Belle's the kind of woman who requires time alone to work things out. Fear not, I'll be right here when she needs me." She finished emptying the batter into the wells of the muffin tin and slid it into the oven with the smooth precision earned from decades of baking. He enjoyed watching her work, admiring her obvious skills. Hadn't he tasted the fruit of her labors more than once?

Norah set the timer, then turned to him with a hesitant smile. "Now, suppose you tell me your side of things."

Maybe he did have a friend. Norah had been there for him since he'd arrived in Abingdon, showing him around town, offering him advice, feeding him one great meal after another. Like the sister he'd never had. He really oughtta find someone for her, a nice guy, somebody her age or older.

Maybe Frank.

Forget it. She's too classy for Frank. It'd take one sharp guy to keep up with Norah Silver-Smyth, and right now he couldn't think of a single man he knew who was up to the task.

He smiled at her, grateful for her willingness to give him an unbiased opinion on the debacle that was his first date with Belle. Loosening his tie, he leaned back in

187

the kitchen chair, stretched his legs out and crossed them at the ankles, then locked his hands together behind his head. Conversations like this required a comfortable chair, which this wasn't, but it would do.

Norah, meanwhile, was deftly chopping apples, her eyes still trained on him, waiting.

He began at the beginning, the night he'd first heard Belle on WASU and offered her a job in Kingsport. Explained how he'd fallen in love with Belle's voice and the rest of her soon after. How he'd orchestrated her offer from WRVQ. How he'd tucked her in a corner of his heart for eight years, staying in touch, hoping the time would come when they'd work together again, when they'd share something more than their mutual passion for radio.

Despite the sordid, sorry mess he'd made of things, he was proud of himself in one respect: he resisted the temptation to hide any details from Norah, including those that might make him look like a heel.

Never mind "look like"; you are *a heel, Reese.*

Heel or not, he couldn't help noticing that Norah listened without interruption. Really listened, with her eyes, her whole countenance, nodding but not condemning — at least not openly so. She poured him cup after cup of decaf hazelnut coffee. He couldn't stand the taste of hazelnut but drank it anyway while he poured out his pitiful tale.

It was ten o'clock by the time he finished. Exhausted, he rose to his feet, stretching out the kinks in his shoulders and back. "Norah, I can't thank you enough for letting me bend your ear tonight."

She pulled off an oversized oven mitt and waved her hands as if brushing off his compliment. "That's what friends are for, isn't it?"

"Guess so." He gave her a tired smile. "Hope I can return the favor someday when an undeserving guy steps into your life and turns it upside down."

Her own smile was enigmatic. "I'll be sure and let you know when that happens."

"What do I do now?" He yawned expansively. "Any words of wisdom?"

Norah gazed at the man in her kitchen. Even with wrinkles in his gray suit, a tie hanging around his neck in a loose noose, and his hair sticking up Pomeranian style, Patrick Reese was the best-looking male she'd had under her roof in eons. More handsome than Harry, and much easier on the eyes than Randolph, bless his bulging wallet and tightwad heart.

Not that looks were the major consideration here. If that's all she had to resist, she could've managed quite easily.

But Patrick was also charming, funny, bright, and successful. In other words, trouble with a capital *T*. The fact that he was in love with Belle was a serious problem. *Not a problem, a disaster.* The fact that his relationship with Belle was falling apart was worse — a tsunami, an earthquake, a five-alarm fire.

What am I supposed to do, Lord? Give Patrick the prize-winning recipe to woo her back? Stuff Belle with muffins until she agrees to forgive him? Bundle my heart in plastic wrap and store it in the depths of my freezer until further notice?

None of those options were the least bit appetizing.

Norah concentrated on steering her last pan of banana-nut muffins into the oven. She would not succumb to the downward pull of self-pity. Hadn't she wasted enough years saying, "Why me, Lord?" and "Why not me, Lord?" The question now wasn't *why,* but *what.* What wisdom might she offer Patrick to steer him in the right direction?

He was peering at his reflection in a window, knotting his tie, when Norah finally broke the elongated silence.

"So, it's wisdom you want?"

He turned toward her and winked,

sending a few butterflies flitting about inside her. The man was all too aware of his formidable appeal, which, oddly enough, only enhanced it.

"Got any to spare, Norah?"

"I might." She made sure he was paying attention before she continued. "A wise man named Solomon once said —"

"Solomon? You mean Jake Solomon from the *Mountain View Times*?"

If he hadn't been grinning from ear to ear when he said it, she'd have fired a raisin scone right at his prominently displayed nose.

"I know, I know." He held up his hand to deflect her grimace. "Solomon from the Bible, yes?"

She nodded, watching for his reaction. "He said a man of integrity walks securely, but the man who takes the crooked path will be found out."

"Oops." His shoulders slumped. "I've definitely been found out."

"Solomon also said with humility comes wisdom. Your willingness to admit your mistakes should go a long way toward softening Belle's heart. Meanwhile, you need to figure out what sort of relationship you want with her — friend to friend, employer to employee, or man to woman."

His look was pure exasperation. "Can't I have all three?"

"Silly man, of course not." She forced a smile to her lips in a feeble attempt at keeping things light and her feelings hidden. "It isn't fair to either of you or to your staff. You'll need to choose, big guy."

He sat down again, stroking his beard, obviously weighing her words. "My choice is a moot point, Norah. Belle told me she hates me. That rules out friend, employee, or anything else."

If only it were that easy.

She sat in the chair across from him, knees to knees, then realized it was the closest they'd been to one another all evening. She caught the faint scent of his tangy aftershave, sensed the warmth of him radiating like coals in a grate, noted the sheer size of his tall frame dwarfing her kitchen chair.

His proximity unnerved her, yet moving her chair back might send the wrong signal. *How did things get so complicated?* "Hate is a strong emotion," she murmured.

Patrick's face broke into a wide smile. "My conclusion exactly. If she hates me, can love be far behind?" His expression softened. "Great minds think alike, huh, Norah?" He rested his hand lightly on hers, his teddy bear paw easily covering both her hands with room to spare.

More butterflies.

Without warning, his face brightened. "Norah, do you ever pray?"

Pray? Her butterflies turned into bald eagles, banging around in her chest, trying to fight their way out. "Y-yes, of course." *Pray?* She certainly hadn't seen this one coming.

He patted her hands, then leaned back, withdrawing his warm touch. "Well, you mentioned the Bible and I knew you went to church. I thought maybe you'd pray for Belle and me. That things would work out, that she'd trust me again."

"Do I understand you to say you believe in prayer, Patrick?"

A ruddy tint appeared above his beard. "I figure it couldn't hurt."

She chose her words carefully and kept her voice steady. "For prayer to be effective, it helps to know who's listening."

He looked at her askance. "I'd figured on God. Did you have someone else in mind?"

Despite her best intentions, a laugh spilled out, setting her earrings in motion. "God is precisely who I'll be talking to." Her silver jewelry continued dancing, but her features grew still. "You surprise me, Patrick. We've never discussed your relationship with God."

"Hey, I'm not the one with the relationship, *you* are." His tone was abrupt, perhaps sharper than he intended. His gaze refused to meet hers. "Look, it was only an idea. Forget I mentioned it." He looked at her then, and though his words had been gruff, his eyes begged for understanding.

Of course she understood. After Harry's death and Randolph's unfaithfulness, hadn't she worn the same look whenever God was mentioned? Patrick's face was a mirror of her own in those dark days . . . hoping there might be someone she could put her faith in, yet doubting that such a miracle existed. It had taken years for her heart to open up again to the truth of God's love.

She'd honor Patrick's wishes and back off for the moment. But forget he mentioned it? Not for a New York second.

"You're right, I do know the Lord." She knew her easy admission took the pressure off him. "Would you like me to pray for you and Belle right now?"

His cheeks deepened to magenta. "N-now? Oh, no! I was hoping you'd do it later. Alone. Don't you . . . uh, pray when you go to . . . uh, at night?" His discomfort had clearly come roaring back.

"You mean, 'Now I lay me down to sleep'?" *Bless his heart, look at that blush.* She offered him a gentle smile, hoping it might ease his embarrassment. "I'd be honored to pray for you, Patrick." Her smile broadened. "Later."

He looked relieved as he stood up and brushed a dusting of flour off his pants. "You're quite a woman, Norah. Thanks for tonight." He reached down and pulled her to her feet with an effortless tug, then surprised her by continuing to hold her hands in his, barely connecting yet still very much there.

She suddenly felt light-headed — did she stand up too quickly? — then discovered she wasn't breathing. *Foolish woman!* She exhaled with a giggle that sounded as inane as it felt, but at least she was getting oxygen again.

Patrick looked confused. "Did I say something funny?"

"Not at all." *If I'm not careful, I'll be blushing.* "My ears are yours, anytime." *What's* that *supposed to mean?* "Of course, Belle is my friend, too, so she may come knocking on my door as well. I'll be as supportive to both of you as I can." *And keep my own heart out of the fray. Somehow.*

His eyes bore down on her now with an intensity she hadn't seen before. His hands still held hers, with an ever-so-slight increase in pressure. "And when she does come knocking, she'll find a good soul who listens without judging, and talks to God in her spare time. Pretty remarkable, I'd say."

They stood there, smiling at one another, wrapped in a warm cocoon of silence, while she concentrated on remembering to breathe.

Belle made her way along the brick sidewalk toward home, grateful her warm coat held off the misty cold that stung her cheeks. Her solo visit to the Barter Theatre had been awful.

And wonderful.

Awful to be sitting alone, constantly aware of the empty seat next to her, rehashing their conversation, wishing it weren't true that Patrick had deceived her, no matter how noble his reasons.

Wonderful to be soaking up a first-class performance of one of Shakespeare's most entertaining comedies, surrounded by the meticulously restored theater. From the fresh white paint and claret-colored carpet in the lobby, to the elegant light fixtures and spacious stage area, it was every actor's dream come true.

She'd fallen in love with the place immediately.

As she crossed the street, her dark apartment looming above her, she considered seeing if Norah might still be awake and about. She longed to share the highs and lows of this strange Friday night with someone who understood the situation.

Plus, she couldn't wait to tell her about the audition notice posted near the box office for the Barter's late February production of *Much Ado about Nothing.* Seasoned actors were handling the major roles, but they were casting Ursula and some of the walk-on players locally, as well as offering positions for set builders and the like.

Spending the balance of her evening alone at the Barter had been the therapy she needed. Things were definitely looking up.

Though Norah's apartment was dark, Belle could see lights on the first floor so she circled around to the shop's back entrance. Her high heels made navigating the bricks, damp with the night mist, a treacherous task. Slowly she worked her way toward the door, peering through the darkness, grasping for the bell.

Her hands connected with the old-fashioned handle and she prepared to give it a spin when her eyes caught a slight movement behind the lace curtains. Leaning closer to the glass, Belle felt her stomach drop to her toes yet again that night.

Not five feet away from her, in the warm glow of the Silver Spoon kitchen, Patrick and Norah were standing face to face, hand in hand, gazing into one another's eyes.

Eleven

Experience is a hard teacher.
She gives the tests first.

Patsy Cline

David squinted up at the Monday morning sun, yawning its way over the roof of the Virginia Gas Company across Main Street. He hadn't slept worth a flip. After laboring over the letter in his hand last night, he'd floundered around on his lumpy mattress till near dawn.

No use delaying the inevitable. He jerked the mailbox open and tossed in the envelope. As always, a smidgen of his heart was sealed inside, a tiny piece of himself that would never be retrieved.

Along with a personal check. He'd never see that again either.

David knew to the penny how much money he'd sent Sherry Robison so far. Two hundred bucks a month for eight years. Nearly twenty thousand dollars.

The thing he wasn't certain of anymore was *why.*

It wasn't guilt money. Not really. It sure wasn't blackmail. She'd never asked him for a penny. He used to tell himself it was the price he paid for being a Cahill. Nobody expected him to be responsible, so he had to go out of his way to prove them wrong.

Eight years ago he considered it a matter of honor.

Now, listening to Pastor Curt every Sunday, he wondered if it wasn't something else altogether: pride.

Not the good kind of pride, the sort that came from working his muscles or his mind and knowing it pleased God. No, the kind of pride that made him feel superior to other guys, thinking himself a hero when he was a long way from Lancelot.

What was he trying to buy with all that money, anyway?

The answer bubbled up from a deep well inside him: *respect.*

The new, improved David had a little. Not much, but a little. The old, impulsive David had had none and was paying through the nose for it.

He sighed and climbed the steps toward WPER, checking his watch as he went. The staff meeting started at eight, so he was right on time. Sure enough, Patrick was waiting at the head of the table, his suit jacket draped over the chair, his bright red suspenders and pearly whites on full display.

Heather sat by Patrick's side. Dewy-eyed. *Oh, brother.*

Burt was hiding behind the latest issue of *Billboard*, the newspaper-size magazine extending from his Hoosier belt buckle to the eight remaining hairs on his head.

Rick, eyes bleary from a long night on the air, slumped in the chair at the opposite end from Patrick, clutching a can of Jolt.

Frank the Crank was on the air for another two hours.

Only one person was missing.

David poured himself a cup of black coffee and settled into a seat opposite the doorway as Patrick stood to call the small group to order. He noted Patrick's gaze shifting back and forth between the staff and the glass doors.

He's watching for her. David smiled into his coffee cup. Something was going on with those two. They obviously had history together, but this was new. Judging by Patrick's wary look, it wasn't going too well.

The doors sprang open and here she came, her green coat open and flapping, her short, powerful strides the equal of any prowling jungle cat's, her gold eyes snapping.

"Welcome, Belle." Patrick wasn't looking her direction.

"Morning, everyone." She returned the favor, glancing only at her peers as she yanked out a folding chair and dropped into it in a small, graceful heap. "Sorry I'm late."

For reasons he didn't want to explore, David couldn't take his eyes off her. How had he missed those lashes, a thick fringe of dark brown framing her feline eyes? Her generous lips, painted the color of ripe pomegranates, were pouting at the moment. Pressed jeans were smartly tucked into freshly polished leather boots. The little lady was dressed to kill, and the boss man was clearly her mark.

Should be an interesting meeting.

The assembly held their collective breath as each eye — except Belle's — turned expectantly toward Patrick, who exhaled on everyone's behalf. "Let's begin with a heads-up from the sales department." He knocked on the partition and Cliff appeared, computer printout in hand, a crooked smile across his bony features.

"Have I got good news!" Cliff's enthusiasm broke the tension that hovered over the table like wood smoke on a chilly morning. He spouted off the new clients he'd brought in their first week on the air, commended them for their voice work on the commercials, then jumped up to answer his phone. "That's the sound of money, folks. Thanks for making it happen."

"Now —" Patrick's confidence apparently was returning — "Let me share a few faxes and phone messages from our listeners." He pulled several sheets of paper out of his pocket with a flourish and read them aloud, using his rich voice to full effect, probably in part for Belle's benefit.

Yeah, he's got pipes, but he knows it. It didn't diminish Patrick in his eyes; it simply meant the man was human, with his own pride issues to deal with.

On cue, a verse David had recently memorized came crashing through his thoughts. Something about getting the log out of his own eye so he could help someone else with the splinter in theirs. *Okay, Lord. I'm listening.*

"So," Patrick was saying, "all indications are we've got a hit on our hands, thanks to your collective efforts. We'll crank up the Happy Together contest this afternoon on Burt's show." He rolled out the details, how listeners were invited to stop by the Court Street Grill and drop their names in four fishbowls featuring the station's personality photos on the front. "We'll do that until the first of January, then draw a name from one bowl every two weeks, read it on the air, and give 'em nine minutes and five seconds to call in and claim their prize — a date with their favorite WPER personality."

"A date?" Four voices groaned in unison.

Patrick held up his hands. "Relax, not a real date. Just a chance to be . . . uh, 'happy together' with our listeners. Frank will take his winner to lunch at the Hardware Company. Belle, you and your contestant will take off on a hot air balloon ride —"

"Balloon ride?" Belle stared at Patrick, clearly stunned. "But I —"

"Heather's listener will enjoy a matinee performance with her at the Barter, and Burt will have front row seats and backstage passes for the Turtles concert next March. Stop by Leonard's place downstairs and you'll see your fishbowls in place, ready for action."

David watched them grouse about the contest, glad he wasn't part of the deal. Especially that hot air balloon. *No way.* Very little threw him, but heights came close. Ever since he'd watched a classmate at Virginia Tech come tumbling off a radio tower and injure his spinal cord, David had a healthy respect for the dangers involved with tower maintenance. He'd talked Patrick into hiring a service company to handle all the necessary climbing, inspections, bulb changes, and so forth. *Climb straight up three hundred feet above the ground? Not this guy.*

Patrick continued his description of the contest, never once looking at Belle. David, who knew all about wires and volts, would have sworn the atmosphere in the room had become electrically charged. The thickening air was unstable, a perfect environment for sparks to discharge without warning.

"Now —" Patrick's voice was lower, his pace slower — "I'd like to hear your impressions on how our first week went." He folded his arms over his chest, his eyes darkening as he trained them on the auburn-haired woman across the table. "Belle, we'll start with you."

Belle lifted her chin and glared back at him. There he stood, his feet apart in a stance she knew well.

It was the one that shouted, "Patrick Edward Reese, Complete Idiot."

His pale yellow shirt clashed with the silver in his beard, his red suspenders were beyond loud, and his tie would ruin the appetite of most people with taste. Manipulative, a troublemaker, with zero people skills . . . the man was a born loser.

And *clueless* didn't begin to describe Patrick. It wasn't an act, either. The man simply had more blind spots than he knew how to overcome.

She shifted her gaze to the rest of the staff. *What are they so bug-eyed about?* Surely they couldn't read her mind or his, couldn't know what had transpired Friday night.

It was bad enough that he'd abused her trust. Mangled her career. Broken her heart. But then, to abandon her in the street and run to Norah, looking for sympathy. It was pathetic. Disgusting.

And that hurts more than everything else put together.

Which is why she'd gotten up early Saturday morning, thrown her tapestry suitcase into the Pontiac, and driven two hours south, home to Moravian Falls, North Carolina. Her parents were surprised but pleased, and she was grateful to be anywhere but Abingdon, far from Patrick and Norah and more heartache than she knew what to do with.

The cause of that pain was staring at her now, waiting for her to speak. She suspected the other perpetrator was busy baking brioches and thinking of new, more cunning ways to break her boarder's heart in two. Patrick and Norah hadn't seen *her* on Friday night, but my, had she seen them.

And to think I signed a two-year lease to live in that woman's house! She'd confront Norah later. Meanwhile, the tension around the table required immediate attention.

Belle cleared her throat. "Thanks to

Burt's hard work —" she nodded in his direction — "and David's engineering expertise, the week went off without a hitch. Lots of positive calls from people in our target demographics. One listener said we were *almost* good enough to work in Bristol."

Rick hooted. Burt shook his head. But Patrick, unblinking eyes trained on hers, didn't move a muscle. His voice was low when he spoke. "Six months from now, Bristol listeners will be coming to *us*. And we'll be right here where we belong, ready to entertain them." He paused for one beat. "Won't we, Belle?"

She smiled sweetly. "More like five months and three weeks, isn't it, Mr. Reese?" She turned to the wide-eyed blonde by his side. "So, Heather, how was *your* Friday night alone? On the air, that is?"

Norah paced the Silver Spoon, needlessly smoothing tablecloths and straightening tea canisters, keeping an eye on the door and both ears alert to the sound of bells.

And Belle.

Something was wrong. Very wrong. Aside from Belle's falling out with Patrick, Norah sensed some friction in their own relationship. She hadn't seen her, hadn't spoken to her, but she felt the schism in her house and in her spirit. Something definitely was not right between them.

Belle had slipped out before dawn on Saturday morning without saying a word to her about where she was going. *Why should she, Norah? You're not her mother.* Still, no note, no phone call, nothing. *Since when do your tenants need to sign in and out?*

When she'd heard Belle on the air that morning, she knew she was safely back in town, but here it was after four and she still hadn't heard from her. *Maybe if you put a bell around her neck . . .*

It was no good. The guilt, deserved or not, was nibbling at the fringes of her conscience. No matter how Norah tried to justify things, the fact was she'd blithely stood in her shop kitchen, mixing muffins and listening to Patrick's side of the story, while poor Belle sat by herself at the Barter, probably crying her eyes out.

Norah had spent the last three days replaying Friday night over and over, trying to convince herself she'd done nothing unseemly, that her behavior with Patrick had been in keeping with her faith, if not her feelings.

Yes, their hands had touched for a brief moment, but it was meaningless, really, and over before it started. She and Patrick were good friends, nothing more. If the man was attracted to anything about her, it was God's love shining through her.

Oh? And what godly attraction does he stir in you?

It was a question she couldn't answer without blushing. In fact, didn't want to answer at all. It was mortifying enough that she felt such things. Desire. Loneliness. A longing to love and be loved. Intimate memories from her brief but passionate marriage to Harry were no help at all.

She sank into a chair at an empty table, battling the tears that pooled in her eyes, preparing to spill over. After so many years content and at peace as a solo act, she felt anything *but* peaceful.

Concentrating on any task for longer than a few minutes was impossible. Books were scattered through the house, propped open, half read. Invitations to one social event or another remained stacked on the corner of her antique cherry secretary, unopened. The holidays were right around the corner and she had yet to give her menus a second thought, let alone cook up any decorating plans, upstairs or down.

Her mind and her heart were full of a yearning that refused to go away. She wouldn't let herself call it what it really was — a hunger to be held, to be embraced by someone who loved her, a physical neediness that wasn't about lust or intimacy, but was definitely about more than holding hands.

She'd held her desires at bay for so long, she was sure they'd died a natural death, snuffed out by time and a deliberate focus on spiritual growth. "I think I just shrank," she mumbled to herself with a sniff. At her age, it was beyond humiliating to realize she could be so easily swayed by a charming man.

Yet no matter how strongly she was attracted to Patrick, and no matter how great her need, her desires had to be squelched for two very valid reasons: *He's in love with Belle, not me.* The second mattered more. *I love God and it seems Patrick doesn't.*

Simple as that.

Not simple at all.

She stifled a sob, her chest so tight she could barely catch her breath. Her head slumped down onto her forearm, now stretched across the small table, as her misery filled the empty rooms of the Silver Spoon. "Oh, Father, help me keep my mind off Patrick and my eyes on you."

"I could help you with that."

The voice from the kitchen stopped her heart in midbeat. Norah sat up, nearly tumbling over in her haste, and turned toward the kitchen door. Her chest tightened another notch as she felt a wave of heat flow up into her cheeks.

It couldn't be.

But it could.

In the doorway stood her wayward tenant, arms folded over her green wool coat, a look of accusation and pain clearly etched on her face.

"Hello, Norah."

You should be ashamed of yourself! And Belle *was* ashamed of eavesdropping on Norah's anguished prayer. Ashamed, but not sorry. No, the few words she'd overheard had been most enlightening. *I need some discernment here, Lord.*

"The back door was unlocked, so I let myself in." Belle slipped her coat off and draped it over a nearby table, mentally rehearsing the best way to proceed and determining to do so with caution. "Norah, I didn't mean to interrupt your . . . uh, prayer."

Norah rose slowly, her reddened eyes fixed on the floor. "I wasn't praying, Belle. I was begging."

The woman's stark honesty was unsettling. "Begging?" Belle repeated, vying for more time to sort out her feelings.

"Yes." Norah's voice was strained to the breaking point. Her usual elegant posture had given way to slumped shoulders and a chin that tipped toward her chest. Faint trails of mascara followed the contours of her cheeks, and her earrings hung motionless, their dancing days behind them.

Try as she might, Belle couldn't keep her anger toward Norah alive, not with the woman in such a sorry state.

Belle had done her best to stay mad at both Norah and Patrick all day, and instead managed to ruin her appetite and blow off her radio show. She couldn't remember when she'd had a worse day on the air. Fumbling her words, forgetting song titles, pushing the wrong buttons, cutting callers off in midsentence by mistake.

It was amateurish and awful, not to mention immature. Spinning a well-chosen favorite, "These Boots Are Made for Walkin'," only made her feel better for two short minutes.

By three that afternoon, Belle had concluded that Patrick's explanation about Kingsport made sense. She didn't like it, but she understood it. Maybe was grateful for it, now that she'd had some time to hash it over and realize he'd done it out of love.

That was another thing she'd realized: whatever Patrick's feelings for her might be, she didn't love him.

The truth had come to her while tending her bruised ego in Moravian Falls all quiet weekend long. She'd confused a girlish crush with mature love, when in fact the two had nothing in common.

Attracted to him? *Sure.* She apparently wasn't alone in that. But a man she could love till the end of her days? *No way.* She wasn't sure why, but no. Seeing him at this morning's staff meeting had confirmed it. After she'd spent the day sifting through her emotions and the conversations she and Patrick had shared over the years, she was more convinced than ever.

If nothing else, that pitiful excuse for a kiss last week should have tipped her off. Patrick was a friend — a good friend. But nothing more.

And here was Norah — spiritually solid, sophisticated Norah — so obviously in love with him that Belle marveled at her own blind foolishness. Last Friday over tea, she'd sensed Norah's coolness and her own reticence. *No wonder!* Now all those unspoken emotions made sense.

And needed airing.

She put down her purse, softly, as if she feared a sudden noise or movement might put Norah over the edge. Stepping toward the older woman, who still hadn't looked up to meet her gaze, Belle took a deep breath. *No point beating around the bush here.* "How long have you cared for Patrick?"

Norah's head snapped up, her eyes suddenly in focus again. "What do you mean?"

"Nothing, Norah. Honest." She smiled, hoping to ease the anxiety between them, and tried a different tack. "Do you always pray out loud like that?"

She took the slight upward turn of Norah's lips as a good sign.

"No." Norah's face softened. "I generally limit my prayers to a silent conversation." Her slim shoulders gave a slight shrug. "As I said, this was more of an entreaty."

"I've been doing a little entreating myself these past three days." Belle swallowed a lump that appeared to jump into her throat out of nowhere. *Here we go, Lord.* "You know, I used to be pretty plugged into my church." She released a noisy sigh. "Okay, very plugged in. Loved God with all my heart and loved being in his house. I'm not sure how all that got away from me in Chicago, but it did." Her eyes lowered, along with her voice. "Funny how you can convince yourself you don't need to go to church every week, as if worship were an optional thing."

Norah's expression reflected nothing but compassion. "It happens, Belle."

"These last few days, without Patrick to distract me, I've realized I need to put the Lord first in my life. If it's okay with you, I'd . . . I'd like to join you across the street next Sunday."

Norah's eyes filled with tears as she

pulled Belle into an awkward embrace and squeezed her tight. "That's wonderful."

"It's way overdue. I'm . . . I'm glad you understand." Belle was chagrined to feel her own eyes moistening. "Thanks for not pressuring me, Norah, or making me feel guilty."

Norah waved her hand dismissively. "I leave all that to the Lord. His voice is much more persuasive than mine."

Swallowing her tears, Belle chuckled. "Got that right. Now, speaking of persuasive voices, talk to me about Patrick."

Norah turned and walked toward the curtained windows that looked out on the already-darkening sky. Belle waited, content to gaze at the woman's back for as long as it took to get things out in the open.

When Norah spoke, her voice was quiet but stronger. "I've cared for him since we met earlier this fall. Was attracted to him straight off, which was ridiculous."

Belle lifted her eyebrows in surprise. "Why ridiculous?"

"Because he's younger, and —"

She snorted. "Five years, Norah. What's five years?"

Norah's face tightened again. "What I was about to say was, and he's in love with you."

Belle shook her head. "I'm not sure

that's true. Not anymore, if ever. Patrick cared for me, yes. Enough to make sure my career had a chance to grow, enough to keep an eye out for me all these years, but not a forever, the-two-shall-become-one kind of love."

"Have you known a love like that?"

Belle felt her cheeks warm. "No. But I've been around long enough to judge when a man is only a friend. And that's all Patrick is to me, Norah. Trust me, I've thought about this all weekend. Patrick and I are friends. Period."

Hope dawned in her friend's eyes. "Are you sure?"

"Absolutely. If you want him, Norah, he's all yours." Simply saying the words lifted a pressure off Belle's chest she hadn't even been aware she was carrying. The freedom made her almost giddy. "Though why you'd want such a heathen, I'm not sure."

Norah's features relaxed into the hint of a grin. "The Lord knows there's plenty to be done in that department, but Patrick's coming around. The funny thing is, he's really not my type. Too confident, too accustomed to having his own way, and too frugal with a dollar. The man is —"

"Tight, Norah. The word is *tight!*" Without intending to, Belle laughed. Not a loud, honking sound, but decidedly more than a giggle.

At that, a look of relief filled Norah's face, as if some burden of her own was starting to lift. Norah's throaty chuckle echoed hers. "Tight is right."

Belle's laughter became more pronounced. "If he takes you to the Barter Theatre, be prepared to carry a ham." Another guffaw slipped out. "Of course, he'll get the ham on trade from the Court Street Grill."

Having let her laughter loose, now Belle couldn't rein it in. The sheer release of letting go of Patrick, and of all the hurt from Chicago, had gone to her head and come out her funny bone.

Her fit of frivolity continued gathering steam.

"He's so tight, he . . . heeee!"

Norah watched her, wide-eyed. Belle simply couldn't stop. She'd pull herself together for a few seconds, then another spell would come over her and send her off howling again.

"He's . . . he's . . . hoooo!"

Without warning, Norah joined her with a most unladylike snort. Then another. Soon they ran together, a staccato string of short snorts that only made it worse for Belle, doing her best to get herself back on solid ground.

It was a duet of laughter — off-key, off-beat, but right on time to restore their friendship, Belle thought, during a single, lucid moment before she lost it yet another time.

"He's . . . he's . . . hawww!"

Finally, Norah clutched the back of a chair and gasped, "So, what you're saying is, the man is *thrifty*."

Bad move.

Another round of whooping ensued, worse than the last. They leaned on the chairs, they sat on the chairs, they bent toward the floor, seriously considering sitting there instead.

It was in this state that an unannounced visitor found them wheezing, red-faced, and so relaxed their limbs were like gooseberry jelly.

"Obviously I've missed something," their guest noted with a tone of mild disapproval. "Do either of you have sufficient command of your wits to fill me in?"

The women turned toward the doorway in tandem and sang out the newcomer's name on a fresh burst of laughter. "P-paaaatrick!"

Twelve

Nothing spoils a romance so much as a sense of humor in a woman.

Oscar Wilde

"What is so all-fired funny?" Patrick slid into the booth next to Belle. He'd found himself saying that a lot lately, ever since he'd discovered Belle and Norah reduced to a jellylike state two weeks ago. They'd never told him what it was that struck them as being so blinking hilarious. If he'd correctly read their conspiratorial glances, they never would.

Silly women.

Whatever their laughing jag was about, it had made a 180-degree turnabout in Belle's attitude toward him. The romance angle was shot to pieces, that was obvious, but their friendship seemed stronger than ever. *Weird.* The good part was, she'd apparently forgiven him. The bad part was, he was having a hard time downshifting his feelings for her into a friends-only gear.

Except when she acted so dad-blamed goofy. Like now, when everyone at the lunch table was laughing except him.

"Patrick, surely you'd encourage your

disc jockeys to indulge in a little jocularity in their spare time." Belle handed him a Court Street Grill menu and aimed a broad wink at David and Frank, seated across the booth from them. "Or would that be *jock*-ularity?"

"Very punny," Patrick grumbled, while Frank and David sat there like a couple of harvest pumpkins, grinning from ear to ear.

Belle was right about one thing. He did like his staff to have fun off the air. It invariably improved their shows. Frank the Crank was in rare form lately, dragging out all his props from the '60s including his trademark air horn, designed to punctuate his morning patter. Some jocks used a rim shot after delivering their punch lines, but not Frank. Aahh-ooo-gah was more his style.

Every spot break in Frank's show was sold out. Patrick didn't need ratings to tell him the man was a hit. Burt was doing a solid job in afternoons. Heather hadn't started three songs simultaneously in almost a week. Even Rick had successfully stayed awake and pushed the right buttons every night since the first.

Then there was Belle. Warm and witty Belle had won the hearts of the whole town in one month, just as he knew she would. Too bad he hadn't won her heart as well.

Not a complete surprise, this. Before

their disastrous date, before their single kiss — which was, truth be told, kind of a dud — he'd known, deep down, that Belle wasn't the woman for him after all.

A beautiful woman, yes. A good woman, sure. A young woman, definitely. *Too* young. But his woman? *Nah.* He wasn't sure why not, but there it was.

He concentrated on the menu in his hands, then snapped it shut and signaled Brenda, the waitress who usually handled the corner booth that had become Studio G for the WPER crew.

"Let me guess." Belle nudged his ribs. "Grilled cheese, a bowl of chili with jalapeños on the side, and a diet soda."

He hated when she was right. "Wrong. I'm having tuna salad on toast with a cup of veggie soup." Okay, so he'd order his favorite lunch next time. It was better than letting the woman win yet again. *Still . . . tuna?* He hated tuna. His pride would cost him half a bottle of antacids before the day was out.

"Just be glad you don't have a fishbowl sitting next to the register up there, sporting your miserly mug." Belle rolled her eyes in mock disgust.

He hoped she was kidding. The Happy Together contest had been his idea. His and Leonard's, the guy who ran the Grill.

"What are *you* worried about?" Frank

220

barked from across the booth. "You've already got lots of little fishies swimming around in your bowl."

"Whatcha got in *your* fishbowl, Frank?" She gave Patrick a sidelong wink, her eyes sparkling with mischief.

"Humph." Frank was stalling.

"If you don't tell me, I'll look for myself," Belle taunted.

Frank growled in defeat. "Two paper clips, a rubber band, and three official entries."

Belle stifled a laugh. "From the same woman, I'll bet."

Frank snorted.

So did Belle. "I'm right! They're all from Millie, aren't they?"

Millie was Frank's phone groupie, a woman with too much time on her hands and a hankering for Frank the Crank. She called him every morning, sometimes twice, and sent him homemade brownies on a regular basis, which Frank was only too happy to toss out on the staff lounge table for mass consumption.

Patrick felt sorry for him. A middle-aged guy with a middle-aged fan club of one. The man had lots of listeners, but only one Millie.

"Yeah, it's her." Frank scratched at his chin. "She must want lunch at the Hardware Company pretty bad."

"C'mon, Frank, it's *you* she wants."

Belle was merciless, but Frank could handle it, Patrick decided. *Better than you could, buster.* Who knows, maybe Millie was a looker.

His tuna sandwich had no sooner arrived when Belle turned her golden eyes and bantering tongue in his direction. "So, will you be joining us for the Advent Sunday service, Patrick? You said you might."

That one came out of left field.

The Methodist church celebrated the start of the Christmas season in a big way. "The Hanging of the Greens," they called it. It wasn't the first time Norah and Belle had asked him to join them for church, but it might be the hardest to weasel out of. He'd tag along on Christmas Eve, of course. That was tradition, no problem. But this was different. Not a real holiday to his way of thinking, though they kept insisting it was.

Belle's eyes remained trained on his. "Norah's planning a knockout menu for dinner that afternoon. Sure you don't wanna come?"

Dozens of things were easy to refuse in life, but Norah's cooking wasn't one of them. He sighed in resignation. "Sure, I'll be there. What time?"

"Five sharp for dinner. The service is at seven." Belle turned to her coworkers across the booth. "How about you two?"

Frank looked as if he needed his air horn, and fast. "Uh, no, I'll be . . . uh, recording 'Talk of the Town' at noon, then prepping my show for Monday. Sorry."

Patrick had never seen Frank so flustered. The man was beet red and stammering. Maybe he wasn't the only guy at the table who chose to darken the door of a church as little as possible.

He watched Belle shift her gaze to the left. "David, will you join us?"

"Ahh . . . sure. Be glad to." His face said otherwise, Patrick was certain of it.

Belle checked her watch. "You'll need to let me out, boss. Network news is almost over and I'm back on the air in ten minutes." She shot him a sideways smirk. "It takes nine minutes just to climb all those rent-saving steps." The other guys laughed while Patrick slid out of the booth, grumbling under his breath as Belle hurried past him.

Okay, so I'm frugal. What's so all-fired funny about being tight?

Abingdon United Methodist Church was the last place David wanted to be. He should have begged off, told Belle he needed to work on the house, found a valid reason to celebrate Advent somewhere else.

Anywhere but here.

223

Nine years ago, before she'd left town, this had been Sherry's church. He'd never come with her, of course. *Get serious. A Cahill, in this place?* Not then, not in a million years.

Yet here he was now, in the softly lit sanctuary, for no good reason he could think of except maybe the sheer entertainment of watching Patrick squirm. The guy was so uncomfortable it was funny. David stole a glance down the pew, past Belle, then Norah, until he got a good look at Patrick seated next to her, dressed in his blue CEO suit. The man's tie was knotted tight enough to choke a mule. One knee bounced up and down while his hands clutched a hymnal, eyes fixed straight ahead toward the poinsettia-covered altar.

David smiled to himself. *Relax, buddy. God doesn't bite.* Convict? Sure, when needed. Condemn? Only as a last resort, and then not with pleasure.

I oughtta know.

The burden of his many sins — and one in particular — had pressed down on his shoulders for so long the weight had come to feel natural. A penance for his stupidity. Sitting there, surrounded by memories, he felt his past mistakes hovering nearby in the pine-scented air, threatening to crush him again.

I need you, Lord. Right here, right now.

The lights in the sanctuary dimmed as the bell choir filed in, their white-gloved hands reaching for the brass instruments stretched across the draped table in front. Fidgety children hushed without a word as a swiftly rising silence swelled to the rafters, followed by the clear tones of the bells.

O come, all ye faithful . . .

The candles shimmered, their light diffused by the sudden tears that stung David's eyes. He'd been down this road before and knew what to do to keep from making a fool of himself.

Swallow. Blink. Cough.

The solemn bells rang on as his heart sang the familiar carol. He longed to be counted among the faithful. Pastor Curt insisted he was. Every Bible verse he'd stumbled on assured him as well.

But here in this place, where recollections were stirred like cold ashes, his spirit yearned for assurance from the one he'd wronged the most.

The choir finished and glided toward their seats while Reverend Howard moved into the pulpit, his earnest face etched with holiday joy, his words filled with greetings. David liked Matthew, a man who managed to be enthusiastic about his faith without being phony. Maybe if Matthew had been at this church back then, things would have been different for Sherry, spiritually.

Not that it was Sherry's fault. *Not hardly.*

What David had felt for Sherry Robison all those years ago was more about fleshly desires than spiritual ones, and he knew it. They'd both been eighteen, fresh out of high school. A summertime love for him, a walk on the wild side for her.

She'd sworn him to secrecy; heaven forbid if her friends on the right side of the tracks had discovered them some moonlit night, sneaking through the woods and gravel roads that surrounded Abingdon. He was a Cahill, one who lurked along the fringes of nice society. His teachers had always insisted he was bright, exceptionally so. Though his standardized tests demonstrated it, his grades did not.

The classic underachiever. No cash, no connections, no classy clothes, no car, no college plans.

Sherry, the apple of her banker father's eye, had all that and more. A petite pep squad veteran with curly brown hair and a hundred-watt smile, she had the respect of her hometown and David's own adolescent admiration.

Come August, when she'd informed him she was pregnant, he'd been secretly elated. Given a choice, she never would have married him; now she'd have to. But that wasn't how Sherry saw it. She'd laughed, loud and long, uncontrollably, near hysteria. "Marry a Cahill?" There had been a look of genuine disgust on her freckled features. "You must be joking. The last thing I'd ever want to do is marry *you!*"

They hadn't spoken again after that night. When he'd heard she'd left town for points west, he'd screwed up his courage and rang her father's doorbell, asking for her address, determined to send her money to support their child whether she asked for it or not.

Mr. Robison hadn't seen his effort as courageous or generous. He'd thrown David out on his ear with a small check jammed in his jeans pocket and veiled threats about what might happen if he didn't get out of Abingdon fast and keep the sorry news of Sherry's unwanted pregnancy and disappearance to himself.

David didn't tell a soul.

Her friends were informed she'd left for college early.

He'd ripped up her father's check and left town, tracking down Sherry's California address through a mutual acquaintance. When Joshua was born the following April, David started sending her money and a letter for his son every month. The money wasn't enough to live on, he knew

227

that, but it was enough to put food in his son's mouth.

And it was all he had to give. David lived on peanut butter until he couldn't bear the smell of it, drank water instead of expensive canned sodas, kept his truck on the road with baling wire and duct tape. No matter how bad things got financially, through his tour of duty in the air force, then in college, his monthly check to Sherry was always the first one he wrote.

His feelings for her were long gone, but his love for the son he'd never met had grown over the years — exponentially since he'd found forgiveness in Christ. The photo of Josh that Sherry had finally sent last month was sitting on his home computer, a daily reminder to pray for the pale boy with straight blond hair and ocean-colored eyes — a double for his father, David Cahill, two thousand miles away. And his grandfather, John Cahill, the Lord only knew where.

David's longing to see Josh was constant, but it was especially strong at Christmas. How had his son looked that first December as a baby nestled in his mother's arms? As a toddler gazing at the lights on the tree? As a preschooler drawing candy canes? As a first-grader writing wish lists for Santa? Every year he carefully chose one present for Josh, hoping it was something he didn't already own, something he'd enjoy. Something that would let him know he had a father who loved him.

His melancholy thoughts were cut short by the sight of a dozen children — real, not imagined — shuffling up the center aisle dressed in their holiday best. In their small hands they carried chrismons for the enormous tree draped in twinkling lights, waiting for each oversized white-and-gold ornament to find a nesting place among its feathery branches.

Belle nudged David with her elbow and leaned over to whisper, "Look at that little guy with the red suspenders. Who does he remind you of?" She rolled her eyes toward Patrick, her shoulders shaking in a quiet giggle.

David gazed down at her and felt an odd tightening in his chest. She looked prettier than ever tonight, her eyes aglow in the candlelight, a soft white sweater framing her heart-shaped face, her full lips the color of holly berries. No jeans, either. Belle wore a black velvet skirt that fluttered around her knees in a graceful swirl, showing off the legs that were usually wrapped in denim.

Face it, she's all woman, from head to toe. But not your woman, Cahill. Keep your eyes on the tree and your hands to yourself.

It didn't make sense, this thing with Patrick and her. The two were still friends — good friends — but absolutely nothing else. He was sure there'd been more at some point, but apparently Reese had blown it.

Bad for Patrick, but worse for him. He had enough challenges on his hands right now, trying to build an engineering career and rebuild a house, not to mention his Tuesday night studies with Curt. Belle was a distraction, pure and simple. Okay, a nice distraction. Very nice. She clearly wasn't aware of how appealing she was, of the effect she had on him when his guard was down.

Like it was every time he got near her.

Like now.

Help me stay on track here, Lord.

She elbowed him again. Her perfectly tuned cello of a voice thrummed near his ear. "Matthew's doing a nice job with those young children, don't you think?"

Matthew. There's an idea. Maybe he'd drop a hint, get Matthew to ask Belle for a date, take her out of circulation.

Oblivious to his discomfort, Belle pointed to a wide-eyed girl with curly blond locks. "And there's Heather's look-alike." She leaned closer still. "Aren't these children adorable?"

He hadn't realized she was so fond of children. *That's good.* The thought was

230

automatic; then he shook his head. *No, not good at all.* He exhaled in noisy frustration. *Just forget her, man.*

As the congregation rose to sing "O Come, O Come, Immanuel," David made a subtle shift to the right, enough to buy a little breathing space between him and the long-haired beauty who was pressing her elbow in his ribs for the fourth time that evening. *Lord, what am I gonna do about Belle?*

"Norah, what are we gonna do about Patrick?"

Belle stretched her sleep-cramped legs, pointing her bare toes, relishing the freedom of enjoying breakfast in her favorite attire — scruffy clothes and no shoes. She stood and padded toward the window of the Silver Spoon, coffee mug in hand, pleased to be Norah's first customer of the day, arriving downstairs well before the doors opened at seven.

Morning after morning, in the cozy confines of the shop, their friendship had begun quilting itself together with tiny, intricate stitches. While Norah pulled muffins out of the oven, Belle spread fresh linens on the tables. And talked. And listened. Their relationship fell somewhere between sisters and friends, with a dash of mother-daughter dynamics thrown in for good measure. Belle hadn't been this comfortable around another woman since her dorm days. When she thought of Norah, a prayer of thanksgiving wasn't far behind.

Brushing the lace curtain aside, Belle stared out at the dark, shivery-cold morning. If Norah didn't want to talk about Patrick, she wouldn't push it. "Looks like snow." She peered at the thick clouds, bunched up and heavy, filling every inch of the predawn sky. "Do you usually have a white Christmas in Abingdon?"

"Some years." Norah's voice floated in from the kitchen. "Are you going home for the holidays?"

"No." She let the curtain drop back with a sigh. "I'd love to, but somebody's gotta work Christmas Day. That's the thing about radio. It's a twenty-four-seven situation. Patrick has hired three part-timers for the weekends, but everybody's pulling their regular shift on Christmas."

"What a shame." Norah joined her, brandishing a fresh pot of coffee. "Could your parents come up here for dinner Christmas night? I have a spare bedroom, and you know I love any excuse to cook a big meal."

"Norah, would you really do that?" Belle threw her arms around her, nearly sloshing coffee on the woman's silk jacket. "Bless you for offering. Yes, yes! I'll call them later today and put it in motion. They'll be tickled silly. I've missed every Christmas at home since college."

Norah smiled, smoothing Belle's braid with a gentle pat. Almost as an afterthought, she murmured, "Is . . . ah, Patrick going home for Christmas?"

So she does want to talk about Patrick. Belle pressed her lips together, not wanting to let a grin grow there and embarrass Norah. She'd been waiting for this ever since Advent Sunday. Norah and Patrick had laughed together at dinner, sat together at church, lingered together at the door later that evening while she and David had a playfully heated discussion about the best new movie for the holidays.

Patrick never mentioned Norah at work.

Norah never mentioned Patrick at home.

It couldn't be anything but love.

And it couldn't be any more perfect. Why hadn't Belle seen that from the start? She wouldn't push, she wouldn't pull, but Belle intended to cheer from the sidelines at every skirmish, every victory.

Norah and Patrick were, after all, complete opposites. It was a match made in heaven, and the Lord was hot on Patrick's heels. The sooner he discovered that, the better. Norah was clearly more aware of the way the wind was blowing than Patrick was, but she seemed reluctant to bring their budding romance out in the open.

Belle had tried, in as many ways as possible, to throw them together. Maybe another not-so-subtle hint needed to be dropped right now. "You know, Norah, I don't ever remember Patrick going home to St. Louis for the holidays. His parents are gone, his older brother lives in Oregon, so I'm almost certain he'll be staying here in Abingdon. What say we include him in our Christmas dinner?"

"There's a thought." Norah flipped the sign in the window to Open. "Let's set a place for David, too, shall we?"

"David?" Belle scrunched up her face, genuinely perplexed. On Christmas, with her parents here? Wouldn't they make assumptions? "Ah . . . maybe not. Hate to give somebody the wrong impression."

"Oh? Like who?" Norah folded her arms over her chest, the sleeves of her red and green silk jacket gathered in generous folds around her narrow wrists. Her earrings, a cluster of tiny jingle bells, tinkled ever so slightly though she wasn't moving an inch. *The cheeky woman is chuckling!*

"David would get the wrong impression, of course." Belle heard the insistence in her voice and wondered if it sounded more like denial. "Or my parents would." Irritated, she tossed her hands in the air. "Well, *somebody* would! Anyway, you

234

know my new rule: I will *never* date a man I work with again. *Never.* Period, end of discussion."

"Really?"

She hated when Norah said *really.* It meant she didn't believe her for a minute.

"Never is a long time, Belle."

Belle plunked her coffee cup in the kitchen sink, brushing her hands as if to dismiss not only a few muffin crumbs, but the entire conversation as well. "When never ends, give me a call and I'll invite David over for Christmas dinner. Until then, let's stick with convincing Patrick to make an appearance. A promise of food should do it."

A jingle of bells heralded Norah's first legitimate customer of the morning. In good shopkeeper fashion, she headed toward the front, wiping her hands on a linen towel. Belle yawned and scratched her head, shaking her long, loose hair around her like a curtain, as she moved toward the back staircase. "Time for me to head up to my place and shower. See ya later."

"Undoubtedly."

The male voice behind her stopped her in midstretch.

Not him. Not here. Not now.

Thirteen

It's never too late — in fiction or in life — to revise.

Nancy Thayer

There stood David, filling the kitchen doorway, bulky navy parka buttoned to the chin, ever-present toolbox in hand. His eyes regarded her with undisguised amusement.

"Norah asked me to stop by on the way to work and see if I could fix her dishwasher." A smile worked its way across his features. "Said it's been giving her fits."

There stood Belle, one foot on the bottom step, her skin warm with embarrassment from her disheveled head to her brazen bare toes. She was dressed — barely — in an ancient T-shirt and gray sweatpants. Every trace of makeup had been tissued off the night before. "If — if I'd known you were coming —" she felt her traitorous face color further — "I'd have made an effort to be dressed by now."

His eyes twinkled merrily as his smile broadened. "What, and have me miss seeing you in . . . what's the French word? *Dishabille?*"

"I . . . I wouldn't know." She moved up

236

another step, surprised to find her legs shaking. "I took Latin."

"Ah. *Tempus fugit,* especially in the morning." He stepped toward her, stretching out his hand to lightly touch the ends of her hair.

She couldn't blame him. It was sticking out in all directions, including his. But she wasn't prepared for the reaction. The second his fingers connected, something resembling an electrical impulse traveled up to her roots and singed her scalp.

His voice softened, thickened. "You should wear your hair down more often, Belle."

She gulped. "And risk getting it all wrapped around your precious, scratch-and-dent equipment?" She aimed for a breezy, bantering tone, hoping he'd ignore her obvious embarrassment. He was close enough for her to catch a whiff of soap and some muted, aromatic aftershave. Close enough to sense his warmth, pouring right through his parka.

David's gaze moved to her bare toes curled around the edge of the step.

Oh, please. Bad enough he'd found her wild-haired and makeup-free, but *no shoes?* She'd always been a boots-or-nothing kind of woman. Which had never mattered . . .

Until now.

She folded one foot over the other, as if five bright red toes were less offensive than ten. "Sorry to be so casual, David."

He shrugged, his eyes meeting hers. "You're home. Why shouldn't you be relaxed? Besides, I like a woman barefoot."

She tossed her hair with a sassy shake. "And pregnant, too, I suppose?"

The color drained from his face.

"Ah . . . sorry, David. I didn't mean . . . well, that was . . . tacky." She exhaled noisily, as much to dislodge her foot from her mouth as to bring her emotions under control. Not to mention her tongue. *Where do I come up with this stuff, anyway?* She'd merely been bedeviling him as usual, hadn't meant a thing by it, yet his expression suggested she'd hit a nerve. Or offended his sensibilities. *Something.*

She inched up two more steps. "Well, I'm headed off to get ready for work. See you there, I guess." Turning, she ran up the narrow back staircase to Norah's apartment, then darted through her own open door and up to the third floor. Her heart was pounding, and not from exertion or her foolish comment.

David Cahill unnerved her, plain and simple.

She'd almost convinced herself that he was merely a coworker, a friend, someone whose company she found enjoyable. But a coworker couldn't send her heart spinning. A friend wouldn't make her blush and blunder her way through a conversation. And David's company was more than enjoyable. It was . . . it was . . .

Impossible. She grabbed her bath towel and headed for the claw-foot tub, determined to wash away any notion of something developing with David. She'd already made a fool of herself with one near-romance at WPER. It would be a rainy day in paradise before she let it happen again.

Belle can't possibly know.

David kept telling himself that as he fretted over the pieces of Norah's dishwasher spread across her kitchen floor. *No way she could know about Sherry.* He hadn't so much as hinted at his past to Belle, hadn't shared his sordid story with a soul, not even Pastor Curt. *Relax. Belle was only being her normal wisecracking self.* The thought comforted him in some ways, disturbed him in others.

He'd never seen a woman more appealing than Belle as she'd stood there in her wrinkled, comfy clothes, ten perfect toes marching along the edge of the steps like little soldiers sporting red hats, her long hair a mass of tangled curls spilling to her waist, her eyes still clouded with dreams, her freckled face scrubbed clean, her generous mouth free of lipstick for once, begging to be kissed.

No, not begging. He'd be the one doing that.

Belle was so sure of herself, so complete without a man in her life, it seemed. She'd probably been kissed a thousand times by men with more money, more class, more to offer her than a twenty-seven-year degree from the University of Hard Knocks.

The years were another stumbling block. He saw nothing wrong with the five-year gap between them, but Belle might not agree. Patrick, the last man she'd been interested in, was older. Much older. Maybe she preferred a man with a dozen more years under his belt, a father figure.

David tossed his wrench aside in disgust. *So what?* This woman — any woman, but especially this one — was off limits right now. The timing was all wrong. He had career goals, financial goals, spiritual goals, and no intention of staying in Abingdon two seconds longer than necessary.

And that little pep talk is starting to wear thin, Cahill.

The truth was, Belle O'Brien had stolen his heart. He didn't know when it had happened or how. It just had. From the minute they'd bumped heads in the production room, he should have seen it coming. It wasn't just her saucy smile or amber gold eyes or how she filled out a pair of Levi's. It was her love for life, her witty way with words, her growing enthusiasm for her faith.

And that velvety voice.

He'd held his interest at bay while she and Patrick fumbled through the sorriest attempt at a relationship he'd ever seen. What *was* that, anyway? He shook his head, remembering the two of them giving each other the cold shoulder for days at a time.

By Thanksgiving, something had shifted. Patrick became a friend to Belle, period. He, David, became something . . . more. For one thing, she teased him less. He trusted her more. They talked, really talked, in the studio, in the Grill, at her church that candlelit Advent night.

He shoved the dish rack into place and closed his eyes, fighting the image of her standing there on the steps this morning, clutching his heart in her hands. *She doesn't even know.* Know how much she mattered to him. Know how scared he was of putting his feelings on the line. Again.

He sighed, exasperated. The only thing that mattered at the moment was getting Norah's infernal dishwasher back in business. Putting all the parts back where they belonged, he finally resorted to an age-old engineering trick — banging the blasted thing with a hammer. It shuddered to life, spraying him with water faster than he could close the door. He slammed it shut and grabbed a dish towel to mop himself off, willing his temper to stay put.

"So that's how you fixed Frank's old tape deck last week when I wasn't looking."

David jerked around, towel still in hand, and found Belle watching him with a smirk on her face, her hair tamed into a snug braid down her back, lipstick in place, toes out of sight. "You look nice," he said automatically, thinking instead that he'd liked her better dishabille.

She shrugged. "Anything would be an improvement. I see you've worked your magic on Norah's beastie." Her wry expression softened. "She'll appreciate that, David. Thanks."

He also liked her better when she teased and taunted him. A grateful Belle? More dangerous than ever.

"Time to face the music." With a sigh she pulled on her coat and tucked a blue-and-green wool scarf around her neck. "See you up the street."

Here was his chance to put Curt's last Bible lesson into action, the one about being kind, serving one another. *Sure, buddy. It's also the perfect excuse to have some time alone with Belle.* He grabbed his jacket. "I'm finished here. Can I give you a lift?"

She shook her head with a laugh. "You crazy thing, it's four short blocks. By the time you get that sorry truck of yours started, I'll be pouring coffee in the jock lounge."

That's the Belle I'm used to.

"You haven't felt that frigid air out there. Frank's weather forecast is full of snow advisories." He tipped his head in a question. "Sure you don't want a ride?"

"You win." She groaned dramatically, grabbing her purse. "But only because I look terrible with a bright red nose."

He couldn't resist. "What about bright red *toes?*"

She swatted him with her scarf. "Don't you dare tell a soul you caught me looking so frumpy. Got that, mister?" Her tone was stern, her eyes twinkling.

"Got it." He nodded toward the door. "Truck's out front. Lead the way."

Driving up Main Street, he counted his blessings. For one, he'd cleaned out the truck cab earlier that week. He only had a dozen copies of *Broadcast Engineering* behind his seat, instead of four years' worth. And two, the engine turned over on the first try.

Then he caught Belle's eyes focused on

243

the small bundle of letters on the dash, wrapped in a thick rubber band, and realized his luck had run out. Why hadn't he put those somewhere else? *Simple.* He'd never expected to have Belle O'Brien in his passenger seat.

Here she was and there were those letters from Sherry, an eight-year collection of short, meaningless messages. Valuable only because they, along with the picture at home, were his one connection to Josh. If he'd ever had the slightest doubt that Josh was his, the photo put that concern to rest forever.

He couldn't deny fathering him. Couldn't claim to be parenting him, either. Two hundred dollars a month did not a parent make.

He kept his eyes on Main Street and his other senses tuned to the woman next to him who was humming along with the radio while Nat King Cole roasted chestnuts on an open fire. Another blessing worth counting — Belle didn't mention the letters. She had one booted foot up on the dash, inches away from the handful of envelopes, utterly unaware of the incriminating truth inside them.

She didn't need to know. No one did.

It was between him and God. God had forgiven him, and that was more than enough.

* ★ ★

Patrick was sipping a cup of bracing hot coffee when the glass doors to the station swung open, letting in a chilly blast of air along with his engineer and his midday talent, in that order.

David and Belle . . . together?

Nah, they're not together. He's three feet away from her. Patrick took another sip, hardly aware of burning his tongue on the hot liquid. *Her cheeks are kinda pink. Is she blushing? Nah. Cold morning, that's all. Look, they're going their separate ways without so much as a howdy-do. They're not together.*

But the mental gymnastics didn't work. The image of the two of them walking in like that bothered him all day. He couldn't say anything — what kind of a fool would he look like if he did? The thing between him and Belle was over. He knew it was over; she knew it was over. It was over. Heck, it'd never really started.

They were friends. Wasn't it nice to have a friend? He had two friends in Abingdon now — Belle and Norah. How lucky could a guy get? One made him laugh at her funny jokes, the other one made him eat her fabulous cooking. Neither friendship cost him a dime.

Such a deal.

Patrick watched the late afternoon sun,

245

pale and cloud-covered, dipping toward the western horizon. The snow hadn't arrived yet, but Burt was reading the forecast on the air, and the possibility of one to two inches was still there.

Ten days until Christmas. Patrick hoped it would be a white one.

Wonder what Belle's doing for the holidays? He hadn't asked. Didn't want to seem nosy. Or pushy.

Things had settled down between them. With any luck, Belle might renew her contract instead of stomping out the door on the first of May like she'd threatened to. *You almost blew it, fool.* His stomach knotted up so tight thinking about it he reached for a Tums on his desk.

She really *had* become the Belle of Abingdon. A solid gold hit, that woman. The *Washington County News* had called, wanting to do a big feature article on her the first of the year.

He'd said yes on her behalf.

Maybe it would be a good idea to notify her as well.

Patrick got up from his desk, vaguely aware of tightening his tie, brushing the wrinkles in his trousers, wondering if he'd taken an orange-colored Tums instead of the kind that turned his tongue green.

He found Belle standing outside the production studio, talking to Anne St. Helen, recently dubbed the "Traffic Volcano." Excessive make-goods or shoddily produced commercials made Anne blow her top. Wisely, the staff had learned to abide by her wishes and air every commercial exactly when and where Anne wanted them played.

Or prepare to duck.

"Belle —" Patrick watched her carefully — "When you get a second . . ."

She nodded, though her eyes were still focused on Anne. "I'll record that spot before I leave, okay?" Anne took off for her cubicle, shuffling an armload of program logs, while Belle moved in his direction, her familiar perfume arriving first.

"What is it, Patrick?"

He forced himself to sound casual. "Got ten minutes? Or does Anne need that spot immediately?"

She eyed him, clearly curious. "No, it can wait ten minutes. Here or in your office?"

"My office might be best."

She looked concerned, but he ignored it and turned to lead the way. He knew Belle wasn't overly fond of publicity stuff. A newspaper article filled with photos and an in-depth interview, delving into both her professional and personal lives, might send her into orbit.

Better if that happened behind closed doors.

"Have a seat, Belle." He pointed to the chair farthest away from his. *Safety measure.* "I've got some interesting news."

"Oh?" Her gold eyes lit up like candles as she dropped into the chair, braid swinging, and stretched out her slim legs to rest the heel of one boot on the toe of the other. He'd seen that before — her *I'm not the least bit anxious* pose.

Sure.

He grinned, longing to spar with her again, if only for a minute. "Sorry, Belle, it's *not* an offer from New York."

She made a terrible face. "Why would I want to live in New York?"

"It's the number-one radio market, kid."

Belle rolled her eyes toward the ceiling. "Pish-posh!"

He knew where she'd picked *that* up. "No interest in returning to the majors, then?"

"Not really."

Her answer threw him for a curve. She looked surprised herself.

"Patrick, I'm having fun on the air." She shrugged, as if it pained her slightly to admit it. "It's nice to look forward to coming to work again."

He cleared his throat, feeling it tighten. *Go ahead and ask her, man.* "So you'll probably still be here come May, then?"

Her gaze was steady, her features calm.

"Yes, I'll be here. I'm sorry if you've been worried about that."

"Not worried, exactly." *Liar.* "We hadn't settled it, that's all." *And it's taken you six weeks to bring it up, Reese.* Finally, he admitted the truth to her — and to himself. "I'm glad, Belle."

Her smile was utterly genuine. "Me, too."

It'd been so easy, this conversation. What a fool he'd been to put it off. Grabbing a newspaper, he tossed it in her lap. "These good people will be happy to know you're here to stay, since they want to do a big feature article on you, like this one."

She scanned the article with the two-inch headline, half a dozen large photos, an entire page of column type. "Ohh." Belle's eyes widened. "Lots of pictures."

"Think you can handle it?" He knew she'd hate the process but love the finished product. "Might as well let the print media crown you queen and get it over with." He sobered, wanting her to know he appreciated the effort. "It'll be a boon for the station, Belle. Especially our Happy Together contest." Wiggling his eyebrows playfully, he added, "What a lot of fishies *this* will put in your bowl at the Grill, eh?"

"You would bring that up." She shook her head, eyes still glued to the paper, no doubt imagining her own face splashed all over its pages. "When will they do the interview?"

"The week between Christmas and New Year's, if it suits you. Article runs in early January."

Belle nodded. "Why not? That's a quiet week. Speaking of which, what are you doing Christmas Day?"

An odd sensation skipped along his spine. "Uh, same as every year. Watch old movies on TV. Call my brother. Eat a frozen dinner. In other words, nothing."

"Good. You're coming to Norah's for Christmas dinner."

He leaned back in his chair and propped his feet on the cluttered surface of his desk, assuming his own low-anxiety look. "I am?"

"You are. Three o'clock Christmas Day. Promise me you'll come? My parents will be there, too."

"Your parents?" *Wait a minute. What am I missing here?*

"Yeah, the whole thing was Norah's idea." Belle was swinging her foot like a metronome. *Tick tock.*

He recognized it as her *I'm nervous but trying to hide it* look and so assumed his Mount Rushmore face to keep from laughing.

"Norah knew I hated not being able to

go home for the holidays, so she got the brilliant idea of inviting my parents up for dinner, right after I get off the air at three." Her foot stopped ticking. "She wondered if *you* might want to come."

"So this was Norah's idea?" He sensed something important in the air, some message he was supposed to get. *I hate when women do this.* Dropped subtle hints. Expected men to read their minds. Even now, with their relationship — or whatever it was — over, he found Belle's womanly way of looking at things a confounded mystery. Why didn't she just come out with it? Was she saying Norah had designs on him? Was she saying she approved?

Oh, bother.

Belle was nodding. "Yup, strictly Norah's idea." She paused meaningfully, leaning forward in her chair. "She's expecting you."

Does she want me to say yes?

"It would mean a lot to Norah."

It would? "Fine." He tried his best to appear nonchalant. "Anyone else coming?"

Belle's face took on a pensive look. "Funny you should ask. Norah thought we oughtta invite David."

Uh-oh. Another hidden message. Say something safe. "Really?"

"Yeah, I guess she wanted to set an even number of places around the table. But I

251

was afraid my parents . . ." More foot ticking. "Well, I've been single so long, I thought they might jump to conclusions. Make a wrong assumption." Under her freckles bloomed a distinct layer of pink. "Well, you know."

I know what? He blurted out something safe again. "Parents are like that."

She nodded. "I knew you'd understand."

Understand what? Patrick had a sudden flash of insight. "What would *David* think if you invited him?" *There.* Throw the ball in somebody else's court, that's the ticket.

She shook her head. "The guy's a mystery to me. I haven't got a clue what he'd make of it."

Patrick hid his surprise. *So it works both ways, then.*

"David needs a woman in his life, don't you think?" Belle's question seemed loaded, baffling him further.

He lifted his shoulders in a noncommittal way, then had his second bright idea of the afternoon. "Say, how about Heather? She'd be a good match with David, don't you agree?"

"Heather?" Belle was on her feet in an instant. "Heather the Young?" She shook her head vehemently, the most animated she'd been during their entire conversation. "David would never be interested in Heather. She's not experienced enough."

Patrick baited the hook. "In radio?"

"No, silly, in life. She's too naive, too . . . too . . ."

"Young," he finished for her, swallowing a smile. Belle was getting easier to decipher. The woman had feelings for David Cahill and didn't know it yet. *Look at her. Conflicted, confused, fighting it all the way.*

He had no intention of making it easy on her. It was too much fun watching her wriggle on the end of his line. "Heather is only five years younger than David. Twenty-two to his twenty-seven."

"But those five years make a huge difference in maturity." Belle had started to pace. "I mean, when David started junior high school, Heather was only in second grade."

"And you were a senior."

Belle paused midstep and turned to look at him. "There, you see? Age does matter." Her face went through a fascinating series of expressions as she processed their conversation. Obviously she had second thoughts about that last comment. "Age matters until you get older," she corrected, flustered. "Then it hardly matters at all. I mean, when you're . . . uh, older . . . what's five years one way or the other?"

Patrick made sure his expression gave

away nothing. "When does five years *not* matter, Belle?"

She faced him full on, her hands parked determinedly on her hips. "When two people are right for each other, age doesn't matter one whit. Got that, Patrick?"

"Yeah, I've got it." *Do you?* he wanted to ask, but thought better of it. "Tell Norah I'm only too happy to say yes." He finally gave in to a grin so wide it hurt his face. "After all, we're both older. What's five years, one way or the other, right?"

His phone rang, putting an abrupt end to their discussion. As he settled into his chair for a long chat with his banker, he watched Belle gather her things and head for the door, looking thoroughly befuddled.

So. David, then. He was amazed that a twinge of jealousy didn't surface at the thought of the two of them together. Sure, he'd gotten a little green around the collar when he'd seen them walk in together that morning, but the more he thought about it, the more it made sense. Okay, so the guy was five years younger than she was. *So what?* David was mature beyond his years. And Belle was, truth be told, a little young for her age. David was quiet, she was noisy. David was serious, she was fun-loving. Complete opposites.

A perfect match.

Even he knew that was how love worked.

The minute Patrick hung up the phone, David walked into his office looking for some paperwork on the new loading capacitor that was already giving him trouble.

Perfect timing. "Say, David . . ." Patrick focused on digging through a file drawer. "Are you seeing anyone these days?"

"Am I *what?*"

Patrick turned, clutching the necessary forms. "You know, dating somebody special. It just struck me that, if you're not, Heather might benefit from a little male attention. You know, give her confidence a boost. She's doing much better on the air, don't you think?"

David looked as if he'd swallowed a Christmas turkey.

Whole.

With feathers.

"Uh, yeah, I guess so. She's not . . . uh, my type exactly."

"Oh? What type is that?" Patrick grinned wickedly. Another victim squirming under his scrutiny. It was downright entertaining.

"No — um, well, no type. Not — not really." David looked toward the door longingly. "Heather's just a little young for me."

"Not experienced enough?" Patrick was still grinning.

David looked relieved. "That's it. She *is* five years younger than me."

"Yes, but what's five years one way or the other?" Patrick repeated it like a mantra. *Maybe you need to hear it again, too, Reese.* Something Belle had mentioned nudged his memory bank. "By the way, what are you doing Christmas Day?"

David's face became a mask behind his hair. His eyes went flat. "Same as any other day. Work on the house. Slap together a couple of sandwiches. Watch TV."

"Not this year, buddy. Norah is serving a home-cooked feast and you're invited."

The young man's gray eyes opened wide. "I am? Are you sure?"

Patrick nodded. "That's the way I heard it. You were definitely on Norah's list."

His eyebrows lifted. "Do I need to check with her on that?"

David looked so elated, Patrick's heart warmed at the thought of including him in the day's festivities. That's what Belle had said, right? That David was on the guest list? He'd spare Belle the painful embarrassment of extending the invitation personally and handle the whole thing himself.

After all, what were friends for?

"Nah, no need to bother Norah. You're expected at three sharp. Logs on the fire, carols on the stereo, food on the groaning board. Do me a favor, David, and don't tell anyone else at the station, since I'm not sure who else Norah's inviting, okay?"

256

Patrick patted his stomach, visions of biscuits dancing in his head. "I don't know about you, but this bachelor is looking forward to his first decent Christmas dinner in a long time. Elvis can have his 'Blue Christmas.' I want mine swimming in gravy."

"Got that right." David smiled and Patrick saw a new side of his young engineer. Hopeful. Excited, even. Maybe the guy's past holidays weren't memorable. Well, this year would be different.

This would be one Christmas David Cahill would never forget.

Fourteen

*Christmas won't be Christmas
without any presents.*

Louisa May Alcott

On the first official day of winter — December 21 — old man winter celebrated by swallowing the sun earlier than usual. By 5:30, the sky outside David's kitchen window had darkened to an inky black as he reached for another handful of finish nails. He'd been putting in extra hours on the house all week, pushing himself, hammering past midnight. The kitchen cabinets were installed, the tile floor was laid, the counters sanded and ready for their seamless top. The sooner the house was finished and sold, the sooner he'd be gone, pocketing some serious money for a change.

A big change.

A new life, maybe in Charlotte at WBT. He'd sent résumés to radio stations in Nashville and Louisville, too. Why not? Any move up was the right move. The Bible encouraged him to ask, seek, and knock, so he intended to knock on every door he could think of. As long as he'd have the satisfaction of slamming one shut on Abingdon, Virginia, he'd be happy.

Meanwhile, he was determined to get WPER in the best shape he could. Tuned up, cleaned up, ready to hand over to a dependable part-time engineer who knew his way around an RCA transmitter. David already had a good prospect picked out: a fella from Bristol who handled several smaller stations and wouldn't balk at the flea-bitten equipment. It would feel good to walk away having done right by Patrick, having no regrets, no unfinished business, all debts paid in full.

A first for a Cahill.

He tapped a final nail in place on the door frame, running his hand along the wood to check the finish of the surface. The grain was warm where he'd worked it over, smooth under his callused hands. Without warning or invitation, Belle O'Brien invaded his thoughts.

Again.

He remembered touching her hair, feeling its silky texture under his rough fingers. Her throaty laugh played through his head like a musical refrain he couldn't shake. Traces of her perfume had lingered in his truck for days.

He'd barely seen her since that morning he'd offered her a ride to the station. The morning he'd caught her in her bare feet. This afternoon, bustling past him down the

259

steps, she'd waved and kept going, saying something about a choir rehearsal for the Christmas Eve program at her church.

Choir? The woman couldn't sing worth a lick.

She'd found a home in Matthew's church, though, and that was good. He'd bumped into Matthew at the post office and mentioned Belle, trying to stir up a little interest there. David told himself it was the right thing to do, but his effort lacked enthusiasm. So did Matthew's response, which bothered David no end. *What's his problem? Doesn't he know a great woman when he sees one?*

David didn't know whether to be angry or relieved.

He settled for confused. Nothing new there.

An hour ago, he'd turned to watch Belle skip down the steps, braid bouncing, boots tapping, a tuneless melody on her lips. Yeah, he'd miss Belle when he left town, no doubt. *Will she miss me?* Maybe so, maybe no. Two things he'd heard through the grapevine recently gave him a pretty good idea what the answer would be. She'd insisted she'd never date a man she worked with again — he had Patrick to thank for that decision — and she wanted to settle down in Abingdon for good.

Guess that's a big no, Cahill.

He grabbed a dustpan and broom to clean up yet another pile of wood shavings while his thoughts drifted toward the holidays ahead. He'd mailed his package to Joshua in California two weeks ago, in plenty of time to arrive by the 25th. According to Sherry, Josh loved anything to do with science, so David had splurged on a junior chemistry kit. Sherry more than likely would hate the mess, but he knew Josh would have a ball doing all the experiments. Growing crystals, turning potatoes lime green, making the most of bread mold. Yeah, Josh would love it.

Lord, let this be Josh's best Christmas yet.

Without a doubt, David knew it would go down as *his* happiest holiday on record. He'd be in his own church for the Christmas Eve service — who'd have believed that a year ago? — then a bunch from the singles department planned a caroling expedition up and down Main Street. He couldn't sing worth a lick either, but the hot cider and cookies sounded good.

Christmas Day, it was dinner at Norah's. *Man, what a spread that'll be!* He still couldn't believe she'd included him and wondered who else was on the guest list. Norah knew half the town, so it could be a big turnout. Or, maybe just Patrick and him. *Whatever.* Food was food, and

Norah's was the best.

Belle hadn't so much as mentioned it, so he figured she planned to head south for home the minute she got off the air — didn't her parents live only a couple of hours down the road? Yeah, she'd be halfway to Moravian Falls before the gathering around Norah's table said grace.

Maybe Norah'd ask him to pray. The Lord knew he had a lot to be thankful for this year. Much as he'd miss Belle on Christmas, it was better this way. She'd be in Moravian Falls with her parents, he'd be in Abingdon with . . .

The reality hit him like a two-by-four. *Patrick and Norah.* In a strange kind of way, they were *his* parents. Patrick, always building him up, giving him opportunities, teaching him things. Norah, always feeding him, making him feel at home, encouraging him in his faith. His real mother was gone, his real father was drowning in alcohol somewhere, so the Lord had provided a couple of substitute parents. *Well, why not?*

David tossed the dustpanful of sawdust in the trash and brushed off his hands, grinning for no reason other than he felt like it. Four shopping days left. Maybe he'd pick up some new clothes for himself while he was at it. And something for Belle, have it waiting for her when she got back from North Carolina. Small but . . . well, not too small.

Yeah, this was turning out to be one promising Christmas.

Currier and Ives couldn't have painted a more perfect twenty-fifth of December. Outside the historic homes of Abingdon, the frosty morning air was filled with plump snowflakes that fell on the brick sidewalks and turned the town into a winter wonderland. Inside, logs snapped and crackled beneath mantels where stockings bulged with hidden treats and frazier firs stretched toward heaven, an angel or star perched on top to lead the way, a pile of colorful packages stacked around the bottom branches in silent expectation.

No place was more picture perfect than Norah Silver-Smyth's house. Norah made certain of it. She'd turned her fingers into pin cushions threading popcorn garlands for the fragrant tree, so tall it brushed the ceiling. She'd stained her lips red tasting fresh cranberry salad, drawn blood tying holly and ivy sprigs in every possible spot, and nearly tumbled off a chair hanging a huge spray of fresh mistletoe over the entrance to the dining room. And the living room. And the kitchen.

Norah left nothing to chance. Especially mistletoe.

She'd also gone cross-eyed adding each guest's name to a velveteen stocking in counted cross-stitch, each one neatly hung across the massive cherry mantel. *Norah. Patrick. Belle.* And Belle's parents. *Maureen. Robert.*

There was room for one more stocking, she noticed. Too bad Belle hadn't let her invite David. Norah had promised herself she wouldn't push it, wouldn't bring his name up again until Belle did, but it was hard.

Just as she felt Patrick moving in her direction — *and he is, isn't he?* — she wanted Belle to find a man who would simply let her be Belinda Oberholtzer and love her for it.

Maybe David wasn't the one, but Norah felt certain there was something between them. She could feel it when the two of them were in the room together. Static electricity. It made the hairs on the back of her neck stand up to watch them circle one another, wary yet curious.

Norah also knew things Belle would probably never know. Memories of a little boy who grew up on the wrong side of the tracks, whose parents ignored him and his siblings the same careless way they dodged bill collectors and landlords. Norah had seen little David Cahill in his tattered jeans and dirty shirt, hanging out on corners,

264

watching ball games through chain-link fences, collecting bottles out of trash cans to earn a nickel each. She'd known his father, too, from high school. A handsome, articulate man very much like David before alcohol and life's disappointments had dragged him down a hopeless path of self-destruction.

There were other things she knew. More recent discoveries about David. Norah didn't believe in gossip, shunned it like the plague. But people trusted her, often told her things she didn't want to know. She hid them in her heart, telling no one. This business about David and money being sent to support a child, for example, disclosed several months ago by a wagging tongue . . . that story was too private ever to be shared. The young man deserved so much more than an unappreciative banker's daughter and a son he'd never met.

For some reason, Norah wanted better for David. She wanted *Belle* for David. To teach him the value of joy and laughter. To cleanse his wounds with her clever wit and boundless energy. He'd be good for Belle as well. Solid, wise, feet-on-the-ground David would give Belle the roots she longed for without clipping her wings.

Too bad Belle wasn't getting the same message.

Norah had stitched a stocking for David anyway, intending to invite him over for a visit later in the week, then thought better of hanging it on the mantel. *Why upset Belle on Christmas?* Next year, perhaps.

Meanwhile, it was noon and time to tie on her apron and tackle the honey-drenched ham waiting in her refrigerator. In three short hours, the bells dangling from her front door would officially ring in Christmas.

"No, I will *not* play 'Grandma Got Run Over by a Reindeer.'" Belle made sure her voice was gentle but firm. Pint-sized callers on the request line stretched her patience boundaries an extra inch. On Christmas of all days, she was determined to remain cheerful. "I'm afraid *that* single isn't in our studio." Not since she'd conveniently knocked the CD into the trash can last week. "How about 'All I Want for Christmas Is My Two Front Teeth?'"

The child offered a quick response and Belle swallowed a laugh. "Ohh. You already have your two front teeth. Ever heard the tune 'How Much Is That Doggie in the Window?'" She listened and stifled another giggle. "I see. No dogs allowed at your house. Wait a second, I've got the perfect song."

She reached for Burt's stack of

Christmas classics and cued up an old favorite. "Turn up your radio, little guy. The next one's for you." Moments later, Jimmy Boyd's voice crooned over the airwaves, "I Saw Mommy Kissing Santa Claus."

Kisses beat reindeer prints on Grandma's face, hands down.

Belle glanced at the clock. Less than an hour and she'd be smooching the man who'd played Santa for her Brownie troop so many years ago: Bob Oberholtzer. *Dad.* She was anxious for her parents to meet Norah, see her place, meet Patrick. It would be a small but cozy Christmas with the five of them. Nothing romantic, nothing exciting, but special nonetheless.

She had gifts for each one — a gardening book for Mom, a cordless screwdriver for Dad, a hand-painted silk scarf in Norah's favorite jewel tones, and a solid brass, engraved money clip for dollar-pinching Patrick. She couldn't wait to see his face. No — she couldn't wait to see *Norah's* face, she thought, grinning to herself as she flipped on the mike and introduced another set of holiday favorites.

Not one song featured grandma-stomping reindeer.

Parking her headphones on the counter, she stretched back in the chair, feeling her joints creak and pop from too much time in one place. *And too many years in one body, eh, Belinda girl?* She stifled a yawn, looking at her watch again, wishing the hands would pick up speed. It'd been an utterly quiet day, not another soul in sight. Not surprising on Christmas, though she half expected David to drop by and check on his obstinate capacitor or his shaky microphone.

Or her.

Nah, that's silly. Why would David think about her, on Christmas or any other day?

Maybe because she was thinking about him. About how he was spending December 25 all alone. About how it was her fault. Norah had kindly offered to include him in the dinner festivities. *But nooo, Belle O'Brien couldn't go along with that one.* She was too concerned about appearances, about her parents — or Patrick — jumping to conclusions.

Selfish, Belle. Not even a present, a small token of friendship. Nothing.

Her guilty conscience was taking a healthy bite out of her Christmas joy. Should she call him, invite him? "Hi, David, it's Belle. Want to come over for Christmas dinner in thirty minutes?"

Right. Make the guy feel like an afterthought. Besides, Norah had decorated the table Martha Stewart perfect. Setting an extra place would be a nuisance. Wouldn't it?

Belle sighed as she stacked her carts, preparing for the last spot break of her show. There wasn't time to do anything about David now. *Next year, maybe.* Yeah, she'd make sure he had somewhere to land next Christmas. Thanksgiving, too. But for this year, it was just too late.

The last thing David wanted to be was late for Christmas dinner. He checked his watch, smoothed his tie, buttoned his jacket. The image in the mirror amazed even him. His plaid shirt and jeans were stuffed in the closet in favor of a brand-new suit. Blue-gray to match his eyes, the clerk had pointed out. A red silk tie, the most expensive he'd ever owned. Would it be tacky to tuck that forty-dollar invest-ment in his shirt when the gravy went around the table?

He hadn't looked this spit-and-polished since his air force days. With his hair slicked back, it was Airman Cahill all over again. "At ease, boy." He saluted the mirror with a grin. Yeah, it felt good to spiff up. Felt good to have somewhere to go on Christmas. Felt good to have friends like Norah and Patrick.

He eyed their gifts waiting on his newly installed kitchen counter. A coffee-table book about cats for Norah. A radio for Patrick's Cadillac — 1971 vintage, totally refurbished, shiny as new. Next to those, a third package. A small box, the most expensive of all. For Belle.

He shook the tiny present and grinned as it tinkled. *Hardly be a surprise.* He'd found it at the classiest gift shop in town, displayed on red velvet in the window. A 14-karat gold necklace of tiny musical bells, intricately strung together in a delicate strand.

For a moment, he imagined himself slipping it around her neck as she lifted her heavy braid, sending a whiff of perfume his direction. He could see the tendrils of auburn hair clinging to the back of her slender neck. Feel the cool necklace, jingling into place on a bed of faint freckles. Hear her low-pitched voice purring, "Thank you, David. I love it."

But she wouldn't be at Norah's today. She'd be long gone, on the road the minute her show ended. He checked his watch again. Maybe he'd stop by the station before she signed off, give it to her then. Alone. *Yeah, much better without an audience.* If he left immediately, he might catch her.

David ran his hand over his hair once more, grabbed his armload of gifts, and headed out the door, across the wooden porch covered with an inch of fresh snowfall. "Whiter Than Snow." They'd sung it at church last night at the Christmas Eve service. His sins, red as scarlet, were whiter than snow. On a day like this, he almost believed it. He had friends, a place to go, a reason to celebrate. A new memory to blot out twenty-seven Decembers he didn't care to remember.

He yanked the door shut on his pickup and turned the key. The truck coughed and wheezed. "Not today, buddy. Start." The Ford obeyed, launching him across the frozen, muddy driveway and onto Spring Creek Road. His bald tires were no match for the slippery pavement, sending his truck fishtailing up the hill toward Old Jonesboro Road. He eased off the gas, forcing himself to slow down and take his time even as the dashboard clock reminded him that Belle would hit the parking lot in less than ten minutes.

He smiled as he listened to her chatting over the intro to her last record. "Have Yourself a Merry Little Christmas," she sang out as the music swelled and Perry Como took over.

"Think I will, Miss O'Brien," David said into the frigid air, warmed only by the thought of catching up with her before she slipped out the door. The deserted streets invited him to lean on the pedal a little harder, willing Belle to wait, to find something to delay her exit. Minutes later, when he pulled into the empty parking lot on Court Street, David was out of the truck and halfway up the block before the engine stopped shuddering. He took the steep steps up to WPER two at a time. The beribboned jewelry box jingled in his suit pocket.

His chest tightened when he flung open the glass doors, either from sprinting or anticipation, he couldn't tell which. He reached the studio in a half-dozen strides, paused to toss up a hasty prayer, and yanked open the door.

Burt spun around in surprise. "Hey there, David. What brings you here on Christmas?"

Belle was gone. He'd missed her.

Disoriented, David blinked at the balding disc jockey displaying a Ball State sweatshirt and a gap-toothed grin. *Now what?* He felt ridiculous, charging in like a madman in search of a woman they worked with every day. "I . . . uh, just wanted to make sure your turntables weren't . . . er . . . acting up."

"Nope." Burt seemed unaware of David's stretch for an excuse. "They're fine. No wow, no flutter."

David knew that. He'd rebuilt the turntables before he installed them, had replaced the idlers while he was at it. The only thing that went *wow* or *flutter* in that studio was his heart whenever he glimpsed a certain auburn beauty spinning tunes.

"Glad to hear it." David tried to sound upbeat, despite the heaviness settling in his chest. So much for his Santa-style visit. Belle's gift would have to wait until Monday. "Merry Christmas, Burt."

The DJ grunted in response as David swung back out the door. No use letting one small disappointment ruin an otherwise promising day, David decided. He checked his watch again. Ten after three. Dinner was waiting. Good thing Norah's place was only four blocks away.

The engine was still warm as he turned the key and sent the Ford careening up Court Street then sliding down Main, grateful that his was the only moving vehicle on the road. When Norah's three-story brick Victorian came into view, the sight warmed him more than the truck heater ever could. Candles flickered in the windows, evergreen wreaths with a dusting of snow hung on every door and window, and a wispy curl of smoke circled both chimneys, hinting at crackling fires on the hearths inside.

If a better place to spend Christmas existed, David couldn't imagine where that might be.

He spotted Patrick's Blue Boat, parked on Church Street behind a minivan with

North Carolina plates. Turning the corner, he pulled up to the curb and yanked on the emergency brake, angling the wheels toward the sidewalk. Snow and the steep hill made for a dicey combination, especially when the forecast called for another two inches by midnight.

He prayed Belle would take it slow and easy over the mountains between here and home. Did she have a car phone? Norah, prudent woman that she was, probably had tucked her cellular into Belle's purse.

David rounded the corner on foot. Close up, the house appeared even more inviting. An enormous fir tree, wrapped in tiny white lights, strands of popcorn, and multicolored ornaments, sparkled in the bay window. The faint strains of Christmas carols floated down the front steps. He made a mental note to sweep away the snow before he left later that night. Anything to help Norah. She deserved it, not only for including him on her Christmas dinner list, but for all the kind things she'd said and done since he'd returned to Abingdon.

He pressed the packages against his chest long enough to free one hand for the doorbell while he kicked the snow off his shoes. Hearing the sound of muffled laughter, he noticed the enticing aroma of fresh-baked bread and realized he was smiling so hard his cheeks ached. *Man, what a Christmas!*

The door swung open and there stood Norah, wearing a red silk jacket. And a look of utter confusion. "David!" Her voice barely topped a whisper. Her eyes registered dismay.

Uh-oh. He swallowed a lump that suddenly claimed his throat. "Norah?" Something was wrong. She wasn't stepping back, inviting him in. Wasn't flashing her usual smile of welcome.

And was that Belle's voice in the background? Why wasn't Belle on her way to Moravian Falls? What was happening here?

His packages suddenly felt heavier than bricks. His tongue was thick, immovable. A lame "Merry Christmas" was all that came out.

Now Norah was swinging the door open wider, waving him inside, her expression shifting to . . . shock? discomfort? He lifted his feet like lead weights and stepped into the foyer, his eyes riveted on the dining room to his left.

That's strange. Things seemed normal, in place. The holiday table sagged from the Christmas feast that covered every inch — turkey, ham, bowls of fragrant vegetables, with a huge poinsettia as the centerpiece.

Guests sat at each place setting, exactly as he'd imagined: There was Patrick, looking as if he'd been hit broadside by an eighteen-wheeler. A middle-aged man and woman he didn't recognize. And Belle. He'd never dreamed she'd be here. Never imagined she could wear such an agonized expression.

Five place settings. Four taken, one left.

One for Norah.

Not for him.

He wasn't expected. Not included after all.

The pain hit without warning, like a blow from a blunt instrument. The disappointment of two dozen other Christmases pressed down on his chest, squeezing the breath out of him. The memories crushed him — years without trees or decorations, without hugs or presents, telling fibs to friends about what a happy holiday they'd had at the Cahill house. He saw himself as he'd been: a little boy, crying in his bedroom, wishing once, just once, there'd been a plate full of turkey with all the trimmings, or a package with his name on it.

Or a circle of loved ones, seated around a table.

His voice sounded like a stranger's. "I . . . I've made a mistake." He began backing out, feeling light-headed. As if from miles away, he heard Patrick's voice calling his name. Then Belle's voice, more desperate.

It was all a cruel joke. Invite a Cahill for

Christmas dinner? Not in this town. Not anywhere.

Through the wave of painful images that crashed over him, David sensed Norah tugging on his arm. "David, this is wonderful!" Her voice, unnaturally bright, resembled crystal on the verge of shattering. "Come in, come in. We have enough food to feed an army."

He was too disoriented to resist and so allowed her to pull him further into the house. She scooped up his packages and headed for the tree in the living room. His eyes followed her long enough to see the stockings marching along the mantel. *Norah. Patrick. Belle. Maureen. Robert.*

Not *David.* Of course not. He wasn't invited. Why had he thought he was on the guest list?

Patrick. Patrick had said so.

David turned in the man's direction and found his boss moving toward him wearing a face full of apology. "David, there's been a misunderstanding."

Fifteen

Everything is difficult before it is easy.

Saadi

David found his voice, clearing his throat as if the heartache could be as easily dislodged. "It's no one's fault but mine." *For hoping too much. For wanting it too badly.*

"No!" Belle appeared from behind Patrick, pushing past him. Her sweater sparkled with gold sequined stars that matched her eyes, moist and glistening. "It's *my* fault. I was the one who . . . who . . . anyway, my parents are here, David. Come meet them. We're truly glad you came."

He coughed out a response. "Your parents?"

The older couple was standing now. *Of course.* She had her mother's petite stature and her father's auburn hair. How had he missed that?

The situation became more transparent by the minute. Belle and Patrick. Mom and Dad. Norah, the hostess with the mostest. He'd clearly been wrong about Belle and Patrick being finished. *Dead wrong.* Patrick was meeting her parents. Maybe making a big announcement.

278

About tying the knot.

The last thing this party needed was some lonely gate-crasher cluttering up the place.

"I gotta go."

He swung around, yanking open the oversized door and stumbling onto Norah's front porch, nearly knocking off her wreath and all its berry trimmings. The vise in his chest tightened another notch.

"David, please!" Belle was right behind him, snagging the sleeve of his suit. His brand-new suit, the one he'd hoped might impress her. He turned back, reluctant to face her, knowing his anger and embarrassment would be all too apparent.

Belle was inches away from him, her cheeks almost as red as her holiday sweater. "David, I'm so sorry." She looked sincere, but her lame apology changed nothing.

"Forget it." He tried to pull away but her small hands gripped his sleeve tighter still.

"Please hear me out." She craned her neck as if trying to maintain eye contact with him.

It was no use avoiding her pleading gaze. He stood stock still, fixing his eyes on hers. *She wants my attention? So be it.* He stared at her and realized Belle was shivering all over. From the cold, probably.

Her eyes were red-rimmed, swimming with tears. *Must be the cold as well.*

"David, Norah wanted you here for Christmas from the beginning. It was my idea to —"

"Look, you don't have to explain. I get it, okay? I hope you two will be happy."

Before she could say another word, David bolted across the porch and down the steps, nearly falling when his foot hit a slippery patch. He knew she was following him, but he didn't care. Not when she called out his name on a sob, not when the jingling in his pocket reminded him of a precious gift he'd chosen for her alone.

Because he'd let himself care for her.

And he hated himself for that.

Because he'd trusted all three of them.

And paid for it with his heart.

He reached the truck and pulled the door open so hard the hinges groaned in protest. He fumbled for his keys, cursing the cold that made his hands shake until, frustrated, he dropped the key ring in the snow.

Belle was by his side in an instant, snatching them up before he saw where they landed. He watched as her fingers closed around the shiny keys.

She jumped back to her feet with a breathy exclamation. "Ha!" Stepping back, she hid them behind her back, a triumphant gleam in her eyes, a faint smile crossing her tearstained cheeks. "Gotcha!"

He could do nothing but stare down at her. A sprinkling of snowflakes were tucked among the wispy curls that framed her heart-shaped face. Her blast-it-all beautiful face.

Why, Lord? Why this woman? Why now?

Belle fingered the icy keys, debating her best move. Was David ready to go back in the house? *Maybe not.* How could she make him see this was all her doing?

Tell him the truth, beloved.

It was a voice she knew well, and she knew enough to obey without asking questions. She backed up another step to give herself room and took a deep drag of frosty air.

"David, please believe me. When Norah planned this dinner, she expressly wanted you to be invited. I knew that. Patrick knew, too."

"This is supposed to make me feel better?"

"If it's any consolation, I feel worse than you do."

"How do you know how I feel?" he snapped, eyes narrowing.

She lifted her hands in submission, being careful not to lose her grip on his keys. It

281

was clear her hold on them was the only thing keeping him there. Dangling from her index finger, the metal keys chilled her palm the same way his cold stare pierced her heart. *I never meant to hurt him, Lord.* But she had. Deeply. She could see it in those wounded blue-gray eyes.

Another chilly breath. "Norah and Patrick both wanted you here. But I . . . I was the one who said, 'What will my parents think?' " She shrugged, knowing how lame her excuse sounded. "Silly, right?"

David's expression shifted slightly, his brows lifting out of their furrows. One corner of his mouth turned up in a question mark. "What will your parents think about what?"

"About . . ." Belle's mouth slowed to a crawl while her imagination kicked into a high-gear conversation of its own.

Say it!

I can't *say it. David will get the wrong impression.*

He's waiting, Belle.

Let him wait. I refuse to make a fool of myself.

You've already done that. He deserves an apology. And the truth.

Okay, okay, I'm warming up to it.

He was staring at her, still wearing a question mark on his face.

Go on, Belle. Say something. Anything.

"Say!" Her voice squeaked in the key of Betty Boop. "Would you mind terribly if we climbed into your truck? To warm up?" She gulped, ignoring her noisy conscience and waving the keys at him, hoping she looked playful instead of desperate.

He nodded, expressionless, sending her frozen fingers shaking toward the lock. It clicked open and she stepped back, uncertain. *Do I get in on the driver's side or the passenger's?* One look at the snow-covered road solved that problem. *Driver's side.* She used the steering wheel to pull herself up, bemoaning as usual the limitations of her petite stature. Finally settled behind the wheel, she trained her eyes on his and slid back across the seat, headed for the opposite door.

He was inside the truck in two seconds, shutting the door behind him with a rusty bang. Reaching across to grasp her hand, he yanked her none too gently in his direction.

"You're not getting away from me that easily." His tone was neither cold nor hot, but his gaze burned with purpose. "I don't know what's going on here, Belle, but I intend to find out. What does inviting your parents for Christmas have to do with me?"

"N-nothing." *The truth, Belle.* "Okay, something." She groaned in defeat. "Everything. I was worried that my parents might think you and I . . . well, I've been single so long and . . ." She dipped her head, knowing her cheeks had to be crimson. "I was afraid they'd come to the wrong conclusion."

"Do *what?*" The question mark look was back.

"You know. Three couples. Mom and Dad. Norah and Patrick —"

"Since when are Norah and Patrick a couple?"

"Oh, for the love of Mike!" She snatched her hand out of his and folded her arms in dramatic disgust. "Where have you *been* these last few weeks?"

"At work. At home. At church. Same as you." That blasted grin she found so appealing was moving across David's face. "It appears I've missed a budding romance between our boss and your landlady, is that it?"

"It seems you have." She snorted, not caring how unfeminine it sounded.

His only reaction was the slight arch of one eyebrow. "So you were concerned that your parents might mistake *us* as a couple?"

Belle's spine snapped to attention, nearly lifting her off the Ford's bench seat. "You can wipe that wry grin off your face, mister!"

"Wry? Oh, *rye!*" He touched his lips in mock chagrin. "Coulda sworn it was wheat. Or oat. Pumpernickel, maybe?"

"Y-you!" She swatted at him as if he were a pesky fly. "This is exactly the kind of misunderstanding I wanted to avoid. People making assumptions, jumping to conclusions."

His grin faded, one centimeter at a time. His gray eyes softened, darkened. She felt the texture of the air around them changing. Thickening.

David's teasing tone was gone, subdued to a plaintive murmur. "The one who jumped to conclusions today was me, Belle. All along I thought you were headed to Moravian Falls, that I was definitely on Norah's guest list. When I looked in and saw the table already filled and the stockings on the mantel with everyone's name but mine and . . ." His voice trailed off into a lengthy sigh.

She watched him wrestle with some inner struggle, his jaw clenching, working back and forth. Under the red tie, his throat tightened and swallowed. Without question, this handsome, mature, utterly together guy was doing his level best not to cry.

His pain touched her in a corner of her heart she didn't know existed. "David, you're always welcome here," she whispered through the tears in her throat. "You know that, don't you?"

He shook his head, staring out the front windshield in silence. She watched him watching the snow, swirling in circles down the steep street, the sky heavy, a silvery white. The tall pines that climbed the street bent their branches under the weight of the snowfall, mirroring the mood that had settled over the two of them without warning.

When David spoke at last, his pitch was lower than she'd ever remembered. "You're looking at a guy who seldom feels welcome anywhere."

With exceeding care, Belle matched her voice to his. "If you want to talk about it, I'm listening."

"Maybe I'm not talking." He shot a searing glance at her, as if testing her sincerity.

She rested her hand on his elbow, noticing for the first time the fine fabric and cut of his suit. It matched his storm gray eyes perfectly. Fit his muscular form to a T. She forced her eyes to stay focused on his, putting aside the niggling temptations of being this close to a man she found so alarmingly attractive. "David, I thought we were friends. We are friends, aren't we?"

His response was more shrug than nod, but she plunged forward. "The best gift you could give me is your trust. Trust me, David. Tell me why you've often felt left out."

Left out. Pretty good assessment on her part. *Shut out. Pushed out.* Those fit, too. *Can I trust this woman, Lord? You know I need to talk to someone, to share this burden before it utterly crushes me. How much do I tell her?*

The answer was loud and decidedly clear. *All of it.*

He shifted his body to look at her more directly. "Belle, how much do you know about me?"

She seemed surprised at the question, but after a moment she splayed the fingers of her left hand to tick off the facts. "Born and raised in Abingdon. Air force for four years. Virginia Tech for another four. WPER for a first radio gig. Remodeling a house. Single, never married." Her bright eyes lifted in anticipation. "Is there something I missed?"

"Not intentionally." He felt his empty stomach tightening, tying itself in a knot. No one in Abingdon knew except Sherry's parents. No one. They'd kept the secret of Sherry's pregnancy to themselves for nine years. Even Josh might not know the whole story. *Why do I feel compelled to share it now?* Was it sympathy he wanted? Compassion? Understanding?

No.

Forgiveness.

That's what he needed most.

He knew the Lord had forgiven him. Said so right in the Bible. If a man honestly confessed his sins, God faithfully forgave him. Cleansed him, too.

It was other people he worried about. Could *they* forgive him? Not only about his son's conception at the start, but how he'd handled things since then. Should he have followed Sherry to California? Insisted they marry? Dragged her back to Virginia? Sent more money? He'd volunteered to do all of the above and more over the years. Sherry had rejected every offer. Said Josh didn't need a man like him for a daddy. That *she* didn't need him for a husband.

Didn't need his money, either.

She'd kept the money, though. Cashed every check the day it arrived.

He wrote long letters to Josh, month in and month out. Sherry wrote him back maybe three times a year. He'd never heard Josh's voice, never looked in his eyes, never hugged his own son. It was hard not to be bitter. Not to hate Sherry for calling all the shots.

Then again, he knew it had to be hard for her. A single mother, thousands of miles from her support system. Not that her family had ever been supportive. Her friends had left town, off to colleges and careers and husbands of their own while Sherry Robison kept her secret to herself. She'd always been a free thinker. Independent. She'd have fled Abingdon for one reason or another eventually. He'd simply provided her with the best reason of all.

He brought his thoughts back to the present, to the woman curled up in the front seat of his truck, her thick braid draped over her shoulder, eyeing him, expectant. *She doesn't expect* this, *I'll bet.* But she deserved the truth.

Breathing out a silent prayer, he plunged in. "Belle, there's one thing you don't know about me, about my past, that will probably surprise you."

She flashed a set of sparkling white teeth. "I love surprises!"

He winced. "Wrong word. It'll probably shock you."

"Oh."

"You were right, Belle, I never married." His eyes searched hers, anticipating her response. "But I should have."

No reaction. Yet. Merely a question. "Were you in love with her?"

"Love? Who knows. We were eighteen. A couple of rebels. Sherry liked rubbing her daddy's face in it. Me, I liked . . . well, I liked . . . her." No backing out now.

"Oh." Belle's voice was softer. He was relieved that she looked neither curious nor disgusted. Yet.

Hands clammy, his mouth drier than Tucson in August, he licked his lips, stalling. *C'mon, Belle. Let me have it. Tell me I'm a jerk, a skirt-chaser, something.* When her face remained calm, he snapped under the pressure and blurted out, "Do you understand what I'm saying?"

"I think so." She tipped her chin up, as if preparing for a blow. "Were you . . . intimate with her, David?"

Yeah, she understood. He exhaled, relieved to have admitted that much. She didn't look shocked, not really. He'd expected disapproval or disappointment, but didn't see that either. Nor judgment. Yet.

Maybe she'd given in to temptation herself once. Had a wild youth. *Doesn't seem likely, but who knows?* Maybe because it happened long before he turned his life over to God, maybe that gave Belle the ability to accept and forgive him for his . . . indiscretion.

Sin, man. It was sin, nothing else but.

He realized Belle's accepting spirit might vanish when she heard the rest of it, and braced himself for the worst. "There's more to it. We have . . . a son. Joshua. He's eight."

"A son?" Clearly she wasn't ready for

that one. "Where . . . ?" Her mouth opened and closed. So did her wide amber eyes. If she was trying to look blasé about his announcement, it wasn't working.

Surely the last few details would be easier on both of them.

"He lives in Sacramento with his mother. I haven't seen her since . . . well, since." *She doesn't need to know about the money. Or the letters. Enough is enough.*

"You mean you've never laid eyes on your own son?" Now she *did* look shocked. Her eyes snapped in anger. "What kind of woman would do such a thing?"

David shrugged. He wasn't about to defend Sherry's disappearing act, though he knew the crux of it. "She was ashamed, Belle."

"Of what she'd done? Of being pregnant?"

The memory rose up inside him anew and the bitter taste of bile crept along the back of his throat. "She was ashamed to admit I was the father. Because I'm a Cahill."

Belle leaned back, pressing against the passenger door, as if trying to get a better look at the big picture. "Why? What's wrong with being a Cahill?"

"In Abingdon, Virginia, everything." Maybe the rest wouldn't be so easy after all. David ran his hands through his hair, shoving back his wayward bangs in frustration, sensing a prodding he couldn't ignore, much as he desperately wanted to.

Tell her all of it.

He squared his shoulders and forced his voice to sound matter-of-fact, as if the truth didn't still rip his heart in two. "We were poor. The poorest in town. My father was a drunkard, my mother wasn't far behind him. He was the best carpenter for miles around but couldn't keep a job. So, we lived in shacks on the wrong side of the tracks. Moved around. Scraped by on handouts and hand-me-downs."

Belle's face was the picture of dismay. And mercy. "David, I'm truly sorry." She meant it. Empathy rolled off her in waves, filling the air as distinctly as her perfume. It seemed to take her a long time to speak again. When the words came, he heard the tears that lingered just behind them. "What a sad way to grow up. You've done so much when life gave you so little to start with."

She hadn't moved, yet her entire body strained toward him in sympathy. From out of nowhere, he thought of kissing her, just once, just to thank her. A foolish idea he sent back to nowhere and fast.

When his conscience jabbed him again, he released a noisy sigh. "Might as well tell you the rest of it." Which he did. The money he sent, the letters he wrote, the frustration of knowing his son existed yet not knowing him at all.

"How terrible for you." She nodded slowly. "What I really want to know is, what sort of relationship do you and Sherry have now? Not that it's any of my business, of course."

"Our relationship ended nine years ago. Completely."

The look of relief on Belle's face almost took his breath away. Maybe his feelings for her weren't so one-sided after all.

"Sherry and I have nothing in common but Josh. Someday, when he's ready, I hope he'll come find me so we can make up for lost time." He shrugged, fighting the sense of helplessness that always settled in when he thought about his son. "It's hardly an ideal situation, but I manage."

There was one more truth he wanted her to understand. "Christmas is the hardest day of the year for me." The pain of it hit him anew, aching like a partially healed wound split open again by a careless blow. He fought to keep his voice steady. "I think about Josh more than usual, wonder if he's having a better holiday than I did growing up. We never had presents or decorations or turkey on the table." He tipped his head, sizing up her reaction, warmed by the compassion he saw in her eyes. "I

293

guess that's why today was so important to me."

"No wonder." Her words were gentle as a mother's caress. "Will you forgive me for almost ruining Christmas for you?"

Before he could respond, Belle let out a sudden cry of dismay. "We gotta go!" She started fumbling with the door handle, a look of distress flashing across her features. "Norah has been waiting twenty long minutes to find out if she's feeding five or six of us! Not to mention trying to keep the food hot." Belle shoved the door open with her shoulder and gave him an impish wink. "Let's get our story straight. I'm telling Norah you put up a struggle, okay? Fought me every inch of the way."

He stretched out his hand to grasp hers. "It was a struggle, all right. But not about dinner."

Belle squeezed his hand and an electrical impulse shot straight to his heart. "Thank you for trusting me, David. I can't imagine what it took for you to tell me about Sherry. And Josh."

He had to know. "So I'm forgiven?"

"Forgiven? By me?" She squeezed his hand again. "Of course. Your past is just that — passed. God is the only one whose forgiveness is a must-have, and you've already found that, right?"

"Right." He smiled at her, really smiled,

for the first time since that gut-wrenching moment Norah opened her front door. Relief flooded his soul, a dam breaking loose, spilling over, flowing like a river of living water.

Forgiveness. He felt it, he *knew* it.

When Belle slid out of the truck, he followed suit, pushing open his own door and dropping to the icy ground. The snow was falling faster, the flakes thicker, mingling with the gold stars on Belle's holiday sweater as she inched her way across the slippery bricks. Without warning, she lost her footing, waving her arms in vain, grasping at air.

"Daaa-vid!"

He lunged forward, catching her shoulders seconds before she hit the icy walk. How light she felt in his hands. "Easy does it." He was acutely aware of her embarrassment, eager to relieve it. She let out a nervous laugh while he righted her and brushed the snow off her shoulders, secretly grateful for the chance to touch her, if only for an instant.

"Sorry." She was clearly chagrined. "I never was good at ice-skating."

"No problem." He released her quickly, reluctantly. The tinkling of bells in his pocket jogged his memory. "Belle, I have something for you." He fished the small, square box out of his pocket.

Next to the gift she'd just presented to him, this was nothing. Less than nothing, but it was the best he had to offer.

"Here. Open it."

She looked at the gaily wrapped package then at him in obvious astonishment. "David, you shouldn't have! I didn't . . . I . . ."

He shook his head. "No apologies. You've given me more than you'll ever know. Open it. Please."

Like a child, she shook it first, giggling in delight. "Bells! Is that it?"

Watching her tear open the paper, her small hands trembling with excitement, he decided on the spot that Belle's anticipation was worth every penny he'd spent.

She lifted the lid and gasped. "Is it a bracelet? Ah, a *necklace!* David, it's beautiful."

So are you.

He couldn't bring himself to say it. Not now. Not yet. She held up the jewelry, admiring it, the discarded box forgotten in the snow at her feet. Nice as it was, David knew the necklace was a tarnished bit of metal next to its new owner. Her smile far eclipsed the golden gleam of the tiny bells.

"Will you put it on for me?" She blushed slightly, avoiding his eyes. "I never can get these clasps."

David gulped. "Sure." His hands were

steadier than he expected, until he realized the scene before him was unfolding exactly as he'd imagined it earlier that day. An overwhelming feeling of déjà vu drowned him in sensations, as every nerve ending awakened to attention.

There was Belle, turning her back toward him, lifting her heavy braid with both hands, elbows out, creating a graceful dancer's silhouette. Yes, there was the heady whiff of perfume, the wispy tendrils of auburn hair curling along the nape of her neck, the warmth of her body fanning out in steady, invisible waves.

His heart pressed against his chest, pounding out a rhythmic drumbeat, making him feel light-headed, euphoric. Time slowed to a languid pace. The freezing winds swirling around them were forgotten. He toyed for a moment with counting the dozens of freckles on display before him, each one a delicious chocolate dot against the creamy skin below the taut hairs at the base of her braid.

The necklace, man.

He pulled himself together while he drew the ends of the gold strand one to the other and grappled with the tiny clasp, brushing his knuckles against her exposed skin in the process. As if by silent request, Belle dipped her head lower to give him more room, revealing more of herself, vulnerable, trusting.

An idea came to him, unbidden yet welcome.

He couldn't kiss her lips, not yet. But he could kiss the back of her neck.

Surely he could do that.

He gently pushed her braid aside and slid his hands across her narrow shoulders to steady her. To steady himself. A tremor ran through her, so slight he wondered if he'd imagined it. The shoulders beneath her thick sweater felt fragile under his hands. Slowly, reverently, he bent forward. It was an act of worship, an expression of pure gratitude for the undeserved grace she'd shared so freely.

Close, closer. When his lips touched her skin, Belle let out a soft gasp of surprise. He pressed his mouth firmly against her neck, wanting there to be no mistake of his intention. He marveled at the fragrant texture of her skin. He knew he should end it, but lingered a moment longer than absolutely necessary before adding a final, feathery kiss.

One truth remained. She hadn't pulled away. She was, in fact, turning around beneath his hands, perhaps to offer him a sweeter spot for his kisses to land.

Sixteen

Heap on more wood! — the wind is chill;
But let it whistle as it will,
We'll keep our Christmas merry still.

Sir Walter Scott

Belle hadn't meant to slap him.

His kiss had simply surprised her, caught her off guard.

David looked startled himself, standing there, eyes wide, skin flushed, his generous lips parted in shock as if he were about to say something and forgot what it was.

Belle fought for breath and the courage to apologize. "David, I'm sorry."

And she was. *Sort of.* But how dare he take such liberties? Kissing the nape of her neck where she couldn't see him, couldn't have a choice in the matter.

Couldn't kiss him back.

The storm clouds gathering in his eyes prompted her to repeat herself. "Honestly, David, I don't know what came over me. I truly am sorry."

"Not one-tenth as sorry as I am." He ground out the words through jaws that had tightened considerably. Turning sharply toward the truck, he stomped

299

through the snow, his actions exaggerated and stiff, undoubtedly meant to make her feel like a heel for rejecting his innocent overture.

And it was innocent. She knew that the minute she felt his lips press against her skin. A charming show of affection, nothing more. *Wasn't it?* Anxious to make amends, she called out, "Look, I forgive you for . . . for . . ."

"*Forgive* me?" He whirled around, huffing like a steam engine. "Forgive wh . . . whooaa!" Thrown off balance, David frantically scrambled for solid footing on the ice.

Belle watched in frozen fascination as his long legs flew out from under him and his muscular arms shot up into the air. In less time than it took her to speak his name, she was leaning over David, flat on his back. In his brand-new suit. In the cold, wet snow.

"David, are you okay?" She hovered over him, genuinely concerned.

One eye opened. "I don't know yet." The other eye opened. "How come you didn't catch me? I caught you."

She laughed, relieved to hear a hint of teasing in his voice. "Because you're lots bigger, of course." *Lots.* She watched him rise to his feet, brushing off the worst of the snow.

"Serves me right. Shouldn't have gotten mad."

"Shouldn't have kissed me without warning, either."

He met her gaze. "Nope. Not sorry about that one."

He was standing inches from her now, looking down, all seriousness again. A heady boldness sang through her veins as her eyes trailed up the length of his red tie, lingering for the briefest second on his mouth then meeting his eyes again. "I'm not sorry, either."

She watched his Adam's apple dip below his tie, then pop back into view. "Then why'd you slap me, Belle?"

"Instinct, I guess. Maybe I didn't want you to think I was . . . uh . . . that kind of girl."

"What kind of girl?"

"The . . . um . . . kind of girl who lets men . . ."

"Lets men what? Kiss them?"

If David could tell the truth, by ginger, so could she. She sniffed for dramatic effect. "Despite what you may think, I never dated much in high school, hardly at all in college, and less in radio."

"Ohh." The surprised look had returned.

"I'm what my mother called a 'late bloomer.' By the time I . . . uh, *bloomed,* men my age had wandered off to . . . um

. . . a fresher corner of the garden."

David's sudden smile was devastating. "I do believe I see roses blooming in your cheeks right now."

She gulped. "No doubt." Did he understand what she was hinting at? That she'd never known a man? First because they'd shown no interest in her, then because she'd shown no interest in them or in giving herself to anyone but a future husband.

Could David read that in her expression, in her eyes, so she wouldn't have to say the words and risk blushing for the rest of her natural life?

David tugged on her braid, pulling her an inch closer. His voice was a gentle murmur. "What you're telling me is, you're not Sherry."

"Right!" Her sigh of relief could be heard two blocks in each direction. "I'm . . . not."

He closed his eyes for a long moment, then two.

Is he crying, Lord? Praying? She forced herself not to move, not to breathe. Only to wait. When he finally opened his eyes, slowly and without apology, Belle saw a light reflected there that pierced her heart with its honesty.

"To think," he whispered, "that a woman so . . . pure . . ." His voice trailed off. "Grace. You've given me the gift of grace. Again."

She bit her lower lip. "It's not my gift to give. It's God's."

"I know." A single tear slipped down the plane of his handsome face, tracing his chin line, disappearing into the striped collar of his shirt. "You, Belle, are the living, breathing proof of it."

Instinctively, she reached up and pressed her hands against his neck to catch the tear, to spare his shirt. His freshly shaved skin warmed her cold fingers. She felt him swallow, felt his neck tighten as he began to lower his head, saw his eyes sweep closed once more as his lips formed in the unmistakable shape of a kiss.

Her eyes drifted shut. His warm, mint-tinged breath reached her lips a half beat before his mouth did. Despite the chilly air swirling around them, she sensed her skin warming to a toasty glow.

David's hands slipped loosely around her waist, and the tiniest gasp escaped her before she found her lips pressing against his while she held her breath, waiting and wondering and worrying and . . .

Oh, my.

This was . . . this was too good to be imagined. Their lips were a perfect fit, clearly fashioned for one another before time began.

She slipped her hands around the back of his neck, separating their lips for only a moment before they touched again. His kiss was a gentle, caring caress, full of emotion and honesty and respect and every other thing she'd ever prayed for.

Her heart was singing — on *pitch!* fathom that! — as she broke their kiss at last and tipped her head back, vaguely aware of frosty winds brushing across her heated cheeks. "Merry Christmas, David."

His eyes twinkled behind his glasses, which were now covered with a faint layer of steam and ice. "You can say that again." He bent toward her. "In fact, I wish you would."

Norah considered herself an above-average conversationalist. But even a pro runs out of small talk eventually.

Since the minute David Cahill stormed out her front door, trailed by a tearful Belle, Norah had been preparing for their return. Room was made at the festive table for another guest. *Didn't I want six all along?* Symmetry gave her a small frisson of pleasure deep in her bones. The Christmas stocking with David's name carefully stitched across the top was quickly hung by the chimney with care, in hopes that dear David soon would be there.

Soon came and went. *Late* had settled in.

The food waited, no doubt shriveled beyond recognition, warming in her Silver Spoon ovens downstairs. Her three remaining guests, filled to the gills with hors d'oeuvres and eggnog, sat expectantly around her table, strangers to one another, thrown together only moments before the whole messy drama had unfolded in the foyer.

This was not at all the day she'd anticipated, planned for, prayed for, hoped for. Which meant God was up to something, and for that she was exceedingly grateful. After all, what would Christmas be without him?

Patrick was looking at her now, his eyes darker than usual, a hint of a smile playing at the corner of his mouth. *Scoundrel.* She should punish him for his carelessness, for inviting David without informing anyone else. What a lot of unnecessary heartache he'd caused. Still, it was hard to stay mad at a man who meant well and looked so crestfallen when he realized what he'd done.

He'd apologized to her profusely in the kitchen, even after she'd swatted his hand when he reached for a biscuit. He'd grabbed her hand in return, lifted it to brush his lips against her floured palm, begged her forgiveness. When he grinned — his mouth covered with White Lily Flour — she'd laughed until her sides hurt.

How could a woman stay mad at such an impossibly charming man?

Belle's parents were holding up well, considering. A pleasant couple, obviously trying to sort things out, wondering what they'd missed and who the blond stranger was who'd stolen their daughter's heart. Belle could deny it all she wanted, insist her elders were seeing things that weren't there, but it was clear that David had eyes for her alone and vice versa.

Norah smiled to herself. *You don't live fifty years and miss the obvious stuff.* The question was, had the two of them figured it out yet?

As if in answer, the front door swung open, ushering in the snow-covered couple. Belle and David both sported identical red noses and expressions suggesting . . . astonishment? Norah was certain of one thing. David's cheek bore a distinct scarlet handprint, and Belle's neck was a startling shade of pink, showing off a shiny new gold necklace.

My, this is turning out to be a memorable Christmas.

"Finally, you two!" Norah hurried to greet them with a warm hug, steering them to their chairs, waiting side by side at the table. "Forgive us, David, for getting our signals crossed. Naturally we wanted you with us for Christmas. Suppose you sit right here and get acquainted with the Oberholtzers while Belle and I bring in the food."

David shed his soaking wet suit jacket with profuse apologies and dropped into a chair while Norah practically dragged Belle into the kitchen, her curiosity meter on high. She forced herself to keep quiet during the trip down the back steps to the shop kitchen, but the minute they were out of earshot, she pushed Belle into the nearest chair.

"Talk."

"Wh-what about?" Belle's expression was pure as the snow on her front steps.

Norah wasn't having any of it. "Let's start with the necklace."

"David's Christmas gift to me." Belle sighed and held it out for her inspection, smiling wistfully. "Isn't it lovely?"

"Hmm. And I suppose your gift to him was that bright red slap in the face, eh?"

"Not . . . not exactly."

Norah folded her arms with a groan of long-suffering. Young women could be so coy. "What then? Exactly?"

Belle met her gaze without blinking. "He kissed me."

"Aha! Now we're getting somewhere."

"On the neck."

307

Norah's eyebrows shot north. "Belle, he shouldn't have!"

"My sentiments precisely. That's why I slapped him."

"I see." Norah thought about that one for a full minute, then exhaled. "Quite right. Can't have him thinking you're anything less than a gentlewoman."

"Quite right," Belle echoed, clearly relieved to have Norah's support. "But he did apologize, and kissed me again. Properly."

"Ahh." Norah rubbed her hands together, bracelets jingling. "The plot thickens."

"No." Belle stood up. "The *soup* thickens while we stand here letting it cook down to stew." Slipping on oven mitts and lifting the heavy soup kettle, Belle called over her shoulder as she started up the steps. "Who knows? Maybe it's just Christmas. All that holiday cheer and candlelight and mistletoe and presents and so on."

Norah watched from behind as Belle continued up the staircase, forcing her to hurry after her with a basket of fresh bread so she could hear the rest of it.

"Very romantic stuff." Belle had reached the landing. "But it might not be love. It might just be Christmas."

"I wish every day was Christmas." Joshua's gray eyes were round with anticipation. "Don't you, Mom?"

No, she definitely did not. From Sherry's vantage point, Christmas was the hardest day of the year. She collapsed onto the saggy cushions of her secondhand couch and surveyed their apartment. She'd scrubbed it clean, fluffed the pillows, hung as much cheap tinsel around the windows and doors as taste would permit, but it still didn't look like the holidays she remembered from her own childhood.

No way. Not even a little.

She'd brought home a pitiful, free-for-the-taking pine tree on Christmas Eve, to which Josh exclaimed, "That's like the one we saw on the Charlie Brown Christmas special!" Sherry didn't know whether to laugh or cry. She'd been doing a lot of both lately.

Landing another job had been easy enough. Every store in the mall needed help during the holidays — the drugstore that'd hired her was no exception. They'd made it clear, though, that the job ended on New Year's Eve. She'd bought herself time, but not security.

Sherry tipped her head back, willing the tension to drain out of her neck and into the waiting upholstered arms of the plaid couch. When was the last time some nice man had wrapped his arms around her, massaged her neck, rubbed her aching feet,

309

wished her Merry Christmas? Thinking about it bruised her tender heart, already battered from too many *maybes* and *somedays.*

The only mysterious gift under the tree this year was from David Cahill. And it wasn't for her.

"Mom, when do I get to open my presents?" Josh's eyes darted from the big striped box to his mother and back again.

She smiled at him in spite of her melancholy mood. How could she not? His blond hair was sticking up in tufts, his gray eyes with their expressive brows were practically dancing, his smile — minus two teeth — was ear to ear, his pajamas were two sizes too small, showing off lots of skinny, adorable boy. With a son like Josh, it was hard not to smile.

"Do you want to eat breakfast first?" *Dumb question.*

"No! Presents first, Mom."

Of course. She got up and pulled the large package toward him, sharing every ounce of his joy. Vicarious as it might be, it beat no joy at all.

He ran his small hands over the box, pressed his ear against it, sniffed at it like a curious puppy. It was too big to pick up and shake, so he had to satisfy himself with moving it back and forth across the carpet, listening for telltale clues.

"Wanna guess, Josh?"

He assured her that he knew what it wasn't. It wasn't a board game — too big — or a bicycle — too small — or a basketball — too heavy. "Might as well open it, huh?" His hands tore at the paper, turning it into confetti and the floor into a trash heap. "Wow, look! A junior scientist set!"

Gee, David. Thanks a bunch.

But she couldn't be mad at him. Not at David, a man who'd clearly spent many hard-earned dollars on the larger of the two gifts under his son's tree. "That's wonderful." She watched as Josh took out each fascinating piece, turning it over in his hands, wondering aloud what to do with a microscope, and if you could really watch a potato turn green, and did she have one he could " 'speriment" on *right now?*

"Maybe after breakfast." *In the year 2017.*

"Can I send him a thank-you letter?"

Sherry's heart skipped a beat. "N-no, honey. I'll take care of that, okay?"

Josh put everything carefully back in its intended slot, one eye trained on the other smaller gift still waiting for him beneath the scrawny tree. "Is that one for me, too?"

"Silly boy, you know it is. Isn't that your name on the tag, big as life?"

He yanked the package over, taking his time with his second and last present.

311

"Looks like books, Mom."

"Only one way to find out." She watched him pull off the paper, grateful he was such a good reader and wouldn't be disappointed to discover that he'd been right. It was books, a dozen of them from the used bookstore, all his favorite space adventures and action heroes.

"Thanks, Mom! These are cool." He jumped on the couch with his armload of dog-eared paperbacks, looking judiciously at each title, stacking them in the order he wanted to read them. When he had them lined up just so, Josh turned to her with a twinkle in his eye. "Now, where's *your* gift?"

She felt her cheeks grow warm. "Christmas is for kids, Josh. Moms don't need presents."

"Mine does." He slipped to the floor, his pajamas hitched up around his knees, and disappeared into his bedroom, returning seconds later with a small box covered with an entire roll of sealing tape.

Sherry couldn't see the paper beneath all the tape. She smothered a teary giggle, stretching out her hand to receive his gift.

"Merry Christmas, Mom!"

"And to you, handsome boy."

She struggled to open the box while Josh hopped up and down shouting, "It's an ornament! It's an ornament for our tree! I

312

made it at school, all by myself!"

Sure enough, it was. The perfect accompaniment to their tree, a fragile little manger made of Popsicle sticks and cotton balls. "Josh, it's wonderful!" She turned the ornament this way and that, admiring it from all angles. "*You* made this? I'm impressed. Thank you for sharing it with me."

"No problem." He was beaming with pride as she carried it over to the tree and perched it on the most prominent branch. "We didn't make the baby Jesus to put inside, though." He pointed at the empty manger.

"Did you run out of supplies?"

"No. Our teacher wanted us to remember that Jesus doesn't live in a manger anymore or on the cross either. He lives in our hearts."

"I see." Sherry fought a smile. *Christian mumbo jumbo.* His teacher was always filling her son's head with a bunch of Bible nonsense. She might have to address that little problem when Josh went back to school in January.

January. Back to school. Back to no job, no money, no prospects. No use ruining Josh's big day worrying about it. She had another week at the drugstore, didn't she? Plenty of time to worry later.

"Time for breakfast." Three steps and

she was in the kitchen, pulling down the ingredients for pancakes, Josh's favorite. He sat at the kitchen counter to watch her, his blond head cradled in his hands, his wistful expression almost more than she could bear.

She was in the middle of cracking eggs when Josh hit her broadside.

"Mom, how come Dad doesn't send *you* a present?"

Tell him the truth. "Because he doesn't love me."

Josh scrunched up his face in confusion. "Does he love *me?*"

"Yes, he does. In his own way, he certainly does."

"Then why doesn't he ever come to see me?"

She quietly put down her wire whisk, hoping to bring an end to this uncomfortable discussion. "Josh, we've talked about this before. Your father and I never married. So —"

"Couldn't you get married now?"

"Please don't interrupt me, son. And no, we can't get married." She wiped her hands nervously on a dish towel, wishing she had some words of wisdom bottled in her spice rack that she could reach for at a time like this. Something to sprinkle over things. Make them taste better instead of bitter. "We don't love each other. We

314

don't even know each other."

"But he writes you. Every month."

"No, Josh, he writes *you*. Because he loves you and helps provide for you."

"Gee, didn't he *ever* love you, Mom?"

That one landed hard, pressing into her heart until she was forced to feel the pain rather than deny it. "I think he did."

Liar. She knew he did. He'd said so, over and over. *And what did you do with that love, Sherry Robison? You threw it back in his face. Over and over.*

Josh wasn't giving up so easily. "Can't he at least come to see us sometime?"

"Maybe sometime." She knew that was the wrong response, knew where it would lead.

"Sometime? When?" Josh's eyes sparkled. "Sometime soon?"

She slapped the whisk on the counter, gritting her teeth to hold back her anger, to fight back her tears. " 'Maybe' means it *could* happen, but it might not." She picked up the whisk again, gripping it tight. "Anyway, he doesn't know where we live exactly. Only our post office box."

"He could find us, couldn't he?" Josh was just like his father, persistent to a fault.

"He could, but he won't." *Not unless I invite him.* Which she wouldn't dream of doing. *Not David Cahill, king of the write-offs.* The minute she thought it, she real-

315

ized nothing could be further from the truth. A write-off didn't faithfully send letters and money, month in and month out, for a child he'd never met, born to a woman who'd never loved him, who'd laughed in his face, who'd rejected his proposal of marriage and every offer of help he'd ever extended in her direction.

That sort of man could find one lonely woman and one small boy without breaking a sweat. But because she told him to stay away, he did. Because she told him she hated him, he believed her.

Josh broke into her painful reverie with yet another suggestion. "Hey, if he won't come here, can we go there? To Virginia?" Josh had seen the return addresses over the years, knew when his father had moved all over the world for the air force, for college, and now, of all places, Abingdon.

Home. Whatever possessed him to move there? She didn't have a clue. It practically guaranteed that she'd never darken his door.

"No, son, we can't go to Virginia."

Not to Abingdon. Not ever. It would mean facing her father, Mr. George Almighty Robison, who couldn't bear the thought of his little princess being pregnant out of wedlock, who gave her a fistful of cash and a one-way ticket out of town. Told her there was only one way she'd be

316

welcomed back. Alone.

The man didn't even know about his grandson. Or care to find out. At least David wanted a photo of Josh. Had asked for it for years. Her father didn't know Josh existed. Barely knew *she* existed.

Give it up, Sherry. Let it go. She'd tortured herself with this ugly scenario a zillion times over the years. *Enough, already. It's Christmas.*

She forced a bright smile on her face, beaming it in the direction of her only begotten son. "How many pancakes for you, buster?" She winked with pretend enthusiasm. "If you promise to be on your best behavior today, I'll make all your pancakes look like Santa Claus, okay?"

Every mother needed a few acting skills in her pocket. To get through the day. To survive.

Seventeen

*Actresses will happen
even in the best-regulated families.*

Oliver Herford

"My acting is more than a little rusty."
Belle held on to the script for *Much Ado
about Nothing* with both hands, embarrassed to find she was shaking at the
thought of reading Shakespeare again. How
many years had it been since she'd auditioned for a part? More than ten. Even
then, at Appalachian State, auditions were
among friendly rivals who knew each
other's strengths and weaknesses and were
kind enough not to point them out.

This was different. This was the real
thing, professional theater, without a
much-beloved college professor doing the
casting.

Radio could be dramatic, touching,
funny, but nothing came close to the thrill
of performing in front of a live audience
face to face. She'd grumbled more than
once that radio listeners never applauded,
let alone gave standing ovations. Stu
MacGregor, the morning jock in Philly,
once wisecracked, "If a listener claps in the

suburbs and no one's there to hear it, does he make any sound?"

The Barter Theatre was her chance to hear the applause, to see if she had the talent to be more than a voice on the radio — to be a whole person, voice and body, on the stage.

"Norah, if you'll read Antonio's lines, I'll take a stab at Ursula."

"Wrong play, my dear. 'Tis Juliet who takes a stab. Tragically so. Besides, I'd much rather read the part of Beatrice in *Much Ado.* Isn't she the witty one who says, 'I had rather hear my dog bark at a crow than a man swear he loves me'? Hear, hear, sister." Norah held up her mug in a mock toast, winking at Belle, who only laughed.

"Norah, you own a cat, not a dog, and you'd give anything to hear Patrick Reese say he loves you. Don't pull that pose with me."

Curled up in overstuffed chairs pulled close to the fire, Belle and Norah sipped on hot chocolate, frothy with whipped cream and tiny shavings of dark chocolate. Norah never did anything halfway, Belle thought, smiling to herself.

Outside, the late December wind blew hard against the brick house, rattling the windows, beating the wreaths against the wavy glass panes. Inside, the two of them tucked their slippered feet under warm pillows and rattled their scripts in preparation for her big audition at the Barter Theatre next week.

Belle began Ursula's first scene at a masquerade party. "I know you well enough, you are Signior Antonio."

Norah interrupted with a shake of her thick hair. "Belle, you should stand up. After all, you'll need to do so on stage."

Belle sighed in resignation and stood, drawing closer to the fire before she repeated her line. "You are Signior Antonio."

Norah held up her script and read with gusto. "At a word, I am not." Even seated, Norah threw herself into the role, tossing her head back, pretending to wear a reveler's mask.

Belle continued with Ursula's next line. "I know you by the waggling of your head."

Silence. "Sorry, Belle." Norah squinted at the script. "I suppose I should have waggled for you there."

Belle grinned. "Let's take it from the top, then."

Back and forth they went, rehearsing Ursula's four brief scenes, as Belle grew more fretful by the minute. "With less than twenty lines to learn, you'd think I'd have them memorized by now."

Norah smoothed an imaginary wrinkle in her worsted wool jacket. "Surely they don't expect that for an audition?"

"Not expect, no. But I thought it might impress them." Belle read over Ursula's final discourse, a lengthy piece with internal rhyme. "Is it *falsely accus'd* and *mightily abus'd* or the other way around? Honestly, Norah, I hope I don't fall on my face."

"With all your education in theater, I bet you won't." Norah tossed aside the script. "I've always loved this play. Two people, obviously in love but fighting it tooth and nail, until they're tricked into declaring their feelings for one another." She paused, clearly for effect. "Has a familiar sound to it, don't you think, Belle?"

"You mean Beatrice and Benedick, waging their war of wits?" Belle thought of the two characters in the play and their modern counterparts, Norah and Patrick. She sprouted a mischievous grin. "Yes, it does ring a bell. How does the line go? 'Nature never fram'd a woman's heart of prouder stuff than . . .' "

They looked at one another and blurted out in chorus: *"Yours!"*

Norah balked.

Belle bristled.

"Norah, you can't be suggesting —"

"Not suggesting, *telling*." Norah rolled

her eyes dramatically. "You and David are just like those two, throwing verbal darts back and forth, posing like enemies when you're the perfect couple."

Humph. "Well, look who's talking." Belle dropped onto the couch, letting the soft cushions puddle around her. "You and Patrick have created Bea and Ben all over again. Didn't Patrick make some crack during Christmas dinner about your 'rapier wit'?"

"There you go, taking stabs again." Norah's silver hair framed an impish expression. "I suppose we've both met our match."

Belle wasn't certain that David would see her as his Beatrice, or see them as the perfect couple. *The Odd Couple is more like it.* Chatty Cathy and Silent Sam. Well, not always silent. Not when they had time to talk. But here it was, three days past Christmas, and all they'd shared were a few brief visits in the studio during her midday show. Song, chat. Commercial, chat. Nothing more, nothing personal.

Maybe that's a good thing. She didn't need another breath-stealing kiss to tell her what she already knew. David stirred things in her better left unstirred.

"What this rehearsal needs is more hot chocolate." Belle padded into Norah's kitchen, helping herself to cocoa and sugar.

She felt so at home here, in this house, in this town. All she needed was a chance to act on stage again and her life would be fuller than she'd known in years. So what if the part was small. Hadn't she always ended up in supporting roles?

In high school she'd starred as the lead player often enough, but college meant more competition and fewer lines. Her peers all dreamed of New York or L.A. She dreamed of a theater exactly like the Barter. Not a big city — a small town. Not a touring company — a home. Not a star — a stage. A place where she could be someone else for an hour. Theater was the ideal spot for a late bloomer like her.

Norah called from the living room, "Your Hero awaits!"

My hero? David?

Belle grabbed her steaming mug of cocoa and headed for the front of the house, a spark of nervous energy tripping along her spine. *Is he really here? Why didn't I hear him come in?* She paused long enough to catch her reflection in the hall mirror and groaned at her messy braid and smudged makeup. *Hope he's ready for a 'come as you are' party.*

When she rounded the corner and found only Norah sitting there looking smug and waving the script, she stopped in her tracks, her spirits quickly deflated. "But I thought you said . . . ?"

"Act 3, scene 1, Belle. 'Hero,' remember her? The female lead in *Much Ado*? Time to rehearse your scene with Hero."

Belle shot her landlady a scathing glance. "Aren't you the funny one."

"I was merely conducting an experiment. Seeing if young Cahill has indeed taken center stage in your heart."

"A tad premature, Norah." Belle resumed her place by the fire, realizing a chill had settled over her that had nothing to do with the howling winds outside. She *was* anxious to see David, more than she cared to admit to Norah. Or to herself.

"I'm ready if you are. Start where Hero talks about Cupid's crafty arrow. I'm ready with Ursula's first line."

Norah winked at her. "The one about fishing with baited hook?"

"If you promise me you won't wait with bated breath to uncover my feelings for David, we'll get along fine. Deal?"

"Oh, how boring." Norah reached for her own cocoa, long grown cold. "David is off limits, then. For now, the play's the thing."

David clutched the envelope in his hands, afraid to open it, afraid what the contents might do to his equilibrium.

Postal customers milled all around him,

324

riffling through their boxes for mail, dropping envelopes in slots. He was rooted to the spot, staring at the plain white envelope with the achingly familiar Sacramento address. It was the handwriting that was different. Not Sherry's careful printing in ink. These were large letters, some barely recognizable, drawn with a thick pencil. *Abington* was misspelled, but thank goodness the zip was right or the letter might never have found him.

He didn't have to look in the return address corner to know who it was from. *Joshua Robison.* His son.

Waiting until he got home was out of the question, but a crowded post office wasn't the right place to read it either. He slammed the door shut on his postal box, yanked out the key and made tracks for his truck, stuffing the other mail in his jacket pocket.

The bitter winds whipped past him, nearly tearing the sacred letter from his hands. He settled himself behind the wheel, started the engine, flipping the heater on full blast, and took a deep breath. Josh had never written him before. David had always assumed his mother wouldn't let him. Maybe she didn't know about this one, wouldn't have approved if she did.

Lord bless you, Josh.

It was his letter now, his to read and savor. He opened the envelope with exceeding care and unfolded the single sheet of paper, forcing his hands to stop shaking long enough for him to read it.

December 26
Dear Dad —
   Hope it's okay if I call you that. Mom will kill me if she finds out so don't tell her.
   My science kit is great. I turned Mom's tablecloth blue. Not on purpose. Thank you for the Christmas gift.
   I wish we could come to Virginia. Mom says I look just like you but not as tall. Are your eyes gray too?
   I gotta go. Can you write me? If not, that's okay.
   Happy New Year, Dad!
   Your son,
   Josh

The first sob came without warning, a huge racking sound from deep in his chest. No tears, only sound, like a wounded animal. He tossed the letter on the dashboard and crumpled in his seat, giving the pain free rein, a groaning too deep for words.
   Dad.
The weight of it crushed him. A hunger and longing he'd kept at bay for a lifetime

came roaring back, ravenous, insatiable. A hunger to be the father he'd wanted and never had. A father who cared, who showed up, who loved him.

He'd never had that kind of dad.

And neither had Josh.

All those Christmases Josh spent in California, alone with his mother. All those Father's Days, so like his own growing up. No dad in sight. No one to thank, no one to slap him on the back, no one to take him to ball games.

No one to teach him how to be a man.

David groaned again, the tears beginning to flow, stinging his eyes, filling his throat.

The memories split open like tombs that had been sealed shut for decades. His past stretched before him, threatening to pull him under, destroy his hope, and obliterate his joy.

Every unkind word ever tossed his way spun through his mind. *White trash. No-good. Loser. Scum.* Did Josh hear those words at school, on the playground? Did Josh miss having a real father, every day of his life, like he did, even now?

At least Josh's dad was sober, he consoled himself.

At least your dad was around, he realized, defeated again.

It was all his fault. His and Sherry's.

"Sherry." He spat out her name like an

oath into the cab of the empty truck. The word echoed in the stillness, hung there like an unwelcome guest. It would be so easy to blame everything on her. Easy to curse her. Easy to hate her.

But it was too late for all that. God had taken over his heart, at his own invitation. Hate and love could no longer coexist there. He couldn't love his son and hate his son's mother. Not if he wanted to please God.

And he did. By all that was holy, he did.

David pressed his hands hard into his temples, holding back the headache that throbbed beneath his palms. Life had been so much easier when all he had to worry about was keeping the powers that be happy and scraping together two hundred dollars a month.

Those days were nothing but a memory.

Things had gotten downright complicated. His job. His house. Belle. Josh. Ties, obligations, commitments. Everything he'd prayed for felt like a noose around his neck, choking the life out of him.

No.

David lifted his head, dazed, as if someone had spoken.

No!

Those things *were* his life. Blessings from God, every one. So many blessings he didn't know what to do with them all. He sat in the silent cab, looking out at the gray, wintry sky while the truth sank deep into his heart.

From a still deeper place inside him came a rusty chuckle.

Now what, God?

It hurt, this laugh that squeezed itself out of an open wound, yet it carried with it a sensation of lightness, of freedom. He chuckled again, felt it move to his face, forcing his lips upward.

"Lord, I give up." He laughed a third time. "Okay, since these are your blessings, have at 'em."

The sense of freedom grew, filling every inch of his heart and all the space around it.

David threw the gearshift into first, amazed to find himself smiling broadly at the letter on the dashboard. "I don't know what the future holds, Josh, but I know who holds the future. Hang on, buddy. Life ain't over yet. Not by a long shot."

"One more, Miss O'Brien?" The photographer from the *Washington County News* adjusted his wide-angle lens and snapped the last shot on the roll. "Terrific. You've been a good sport about all this."

"Mr. Monroe, ever since WTIE, I've never cared for the phrase 'good sport.'" Belle blinked slowly, trying to bring her

329

eyes back into focus after staring at the bright lights for an hour. Her apartment was a jumbled mess of discarded clothing and displaced furniture, her brain on overload. "We've gone through a ton of film. Hope there's something you can use."

Packing away his cameras and gear, the photographer gave her a broad wink. "Guess I'll have to take these rolls to the darkroom and see what develops."

Belle suspected he used that line daily. Hourly.

Heaven knew they'd spent enough time together. The day had dawned chilly but bright, turning stubborn remnants of snow into a sparkling backdrop for their outdoor shots. There were plenty of those — outside WPER, outside her apartment, outside the Grill, on the hilly field surrounding Virginia Highlands Community College, where she posed with the hot air balloon crew that would send her up, up and away for her Happy Together balloon ride.

She'd almost forgotten about that.

A half-mile-high ride with a complete stranger come March. Nothing separating them from certain death but a colorful fabric envelope filled with hot air.

No wonder she'd put it out of her mind.

She and Mr. Monroe had shot several rolls indoors, too. In her apartment, in the Silver Spoon, in the studio, in the jock lounge with her cohorts — most of whom seemed relieved she was being subjected to this torture instead of them.

Except Frank, who, although he hated newspapers, was dad-gummed disappointed when they didn't feature *him.* Wasn't he the morning guy, the one who *really* put the P-E-R in personality? The nerve of that newspaper, he'd fumed, stomping off to the production room. The very nerve.

Mr. Monroe took the photos while Ms. Bridgewater asked the questions. Belle handled the résumé stuff with ease, tossing call letters at her until the woman's pen approached meltdown. Then the questions got harder.

"Why did you move to Abingdon?" the reporter asked innocently, tapping her tablet.

The truth? Then? Now? What should she tell her? Belle gave her the chamber of commerce answer — great place to work and raise a family — and hoped the Lord would forgive her subterfuge.

That "family" answer sent Ms. Bridgewater down another path Belle wasn't ready to travel.

"Are you engaged, then? Seeing anyone? Or happy being single?"

Shaky ground, this. Belle smiled brightly. "No, not really!" She prayed that her dull answer would be left out of the article completely.

Wait. This is better.

"I'll tell you why I really came to Abingdon." She'd conjured up the consummate detour to steer them away from the personal track and onto something safe. "I'm auditioning for the Barter Theatre." Ms. Bridgewater's pen heated up again, taking thorough notes as Belle chattered animatedly about majoring in drama in college, her yearning to return to the stage, her lengthy rehearsals for the role of Ursula.

Norah was in the room when she hit that part and shot her a curious glance. *Lengthy?*

Belle blushed and kept right on talking. An hour was lengthy, wasn't it?

"We'll be interviewing the on-air staff at WPER as well," Ms. Bridgewater informed her. "See what they have to say about their midday personality."

Belle's stomach did a queasy once-over. "I'm sure they'll have plenty to say. Be sure and take a new pen." *And steer clear of Frank.* Patrick might be a loose cannon, too. Print media was always iffy. Unlike broadcast media, where the reporter only had a recorded voice or image to work with, the print folks could have a field day, easily piecing comments together any which way, making their victim out to be a blinking idiot.

On the other hand, kindhearted print sources could make the interview sound *better* than the videotaped version. Take out all the "uhs" and "duhs" and polish the words till they shone like stars.

Belle flashed her most dazzling smile at the two journalists as they made their way down her apartment steps, arms loaded with cameras and notepads. She prayed they'd be merciful. Show restraint. Run only the flattering photos.

Come next Wednesday morning, she and the rest of Abingdon would find out if her prayers had been answered.

Eighteen

*Learn the lines
and don't bump into the furniture.*

Noel Coward

The Turtles were singing full throttle when Patrick Reese pushed open the door to the on-air studio. WPER's Happy Together contest was kicking into high gear this morning with their first official drawing. He'd collected Frank's fishbowl from the Court Street Grill a few minutes earlier, and handed it to the morning man with a grin he knew was ornery.

No big mystery who was going to win *this* drawing. Millie, Frank's groupie, had stuffed the bowl with dozens of paper fishes with her name neatly printed on each one. Yeah, looked like Frank and Millie would be headed to the Hardware Company for dinner next week. *What I wouldn't give to be a fly on the wallpaper for that meal!*

Still smiling, he closed the door to his office, tossed his coat onto the antlers, and settled into his leather chair, stretching out the last of the kinks in his neck. The place was eight o'clock quiet, his favorite time of

334

day. Spreading open his new desk calendar, a gift from the WPER staff, Patrick turned to the first of January and drew in a deep breath of satisfaction. Pristine squares waiting to be filled with busy, money-making appointments. Nothing like a new year to invigorate the senses.

Unless Norah Silver-Smyth was involved, in which case there was no comparison. The woman invigorated every sense he'd ever thought about and some he didn't know he had.

When did all this happen? He knew the Advent service was the start of it. Sitting next to her, inhaling her perfume — Shalimar, she called it — watching her dark eyes drink in the sights and sounds of Christmas. Yeah, that was the beginning for him. Earlier for her, it seemed. It really didn't matter when, it only mattered that it had indeed happened, for both of them.

Whatever "it" was.

So what if she was five years older? She had more grace and beauty in her silver-ringed fingers than five women half her age. Bright, witty, well-traveled, well-read. Scary, actually. He didn't deserve such a rare jewel and he knew it. What she saw in him, a rough-around-the-edges radio guy, was beyond him. He was just glad she saw it.

Then there was her cooking. He

wouldn't let himself go down that street. Not this morning, not when he'd skipped breakfast, hoping she'd bring him a few muffins later in the morning, like she had all week long, ever since Christmas.

What a day *that* had been. He laughed, shuffling papers around his desk, remembering the whole scene with Belle and David. Those two, with their emotional highs and lows, deserved one another. He didn't need all that youthful angst. Give him a woman who was settled, relaxed, comfortable with herself. Solid. Mature.

A woman of deep faith.

Never thought I'd find that so appealing. But he did. Norah's faith was a real, living thing. It gave her wisdom, strength, compassion for others, and a bunch of other qualities he couldn't put his finger on but very much admired. The final result was the most incredible package of feminine beauty and spiritual depth he'd ever come across in a lifetime.

It scared him to death. No, it scared him to *life.* A new life, with Norah and with the God that she shared so freely with him. *Yeah, so it makes me nervous, so what? My life can use a little shaking up.*

A new year, a new life, a new future. *Such a deal, Reese.* No man deserved it less. Or needed it more.

Patrick snapped back to the present at

the sound of a gentle tapping at his door. He was surprised to find himself choked up and needing to clear his throat before he could call out, "Come in."

The oak door swung open and his two favorite scents wafted in the room — cinnamon muffins and Shalimar — followed by a beautiful woman dressed in a silver gray something that floated around her like a billowing mist.

"Good morning, Patrick." Norah's voice wasn't too many notes above his own, deep and tinged with the sultry drawl of a Southern woman who favored Shakespeare. Country and culture, all wrapped up in one amazing woman. She held out her basket, draped with a checked cloth, and smiled her angel's smile. "Breakfast, beloved."

It was all over.

He had no intention of fighting it for one second.

"The muffins look delicious, Norah. You look better." He took the basket from her hands, setting it aside for later, and moved around his desk to take both her hands.

She seemed only a little surprised at his boldness, not returning his grasp but not pulling away either. Her eyes shimmered, smiling along with the rest of her angelic face.

He drew in a steadying breath. *Say it, man. Now. Go!*

"Norah, I . . . I . . ."

"I know, Patrick. Me, too."

He exhaled in relief. "Really?" *Boy, that was easy.*

"Yes. I hope this isn't moving too fast for you."

"No." He shook his head, stunned, relieved. "How can things move too fast when you're our age?"

She laughed. It sounded like music. "Exactly. Now what?"

He hadn't thought that far. *Just tell her the truth, fool.* "I . . . I only know that you've made me happier than I've ever been. Ever, Norah."

Turning her head to the side, she blushed like a schoolgirl. It was enchanting to watch. Her tone was sweet but firm. "I'm not the only one who's made you happy, Patrick. You know better."

"Yeah, I do." He lifted his head toward the ceiling, feeling a new kind of strength infuse him, a vitality that had nothing to do with youth and everything to do with newness of life. "Norah, will you pray with me?"

He saw tears spring to her eyes. Two more silvery stars in his growing universe, shining up at him. "Yes."

He knew she meant yes to all of it. To his prayer, to their future together, to him.

She said it again, with more conviction. "Yes, I will."

He closed his eyes, pretty sure that's how such things were handled. "Dear God —" he felt awkward yet as certain as he'd ever felt in his life — "Uh . . . happy New Year." *Happy what?* He could tell his palms were sweating.

Norah squeezed his hands and a sense of peace overtook him.

Yeah. Okay. Happy New Year, that's good. "Thanks, God. For loving me before I loved you. And for Norah. For loving me before I loved her. I don't deserve all this, Lord, but I'll take it. I need it."

His chest tightened around his heart even as he felt it expanding, making room for Norah. No, not just for her. For the one who made him, loved him, died for him. *Yes, you, Lord. It's* you *I need.*

In the blink of an eye, the tightness was gone and a sweet, cleansing breath slipped out of him. *Whew. Not so hard.* Almost as easy as telling Norah he loved her. He *had* told her he loved her, right?

He cracked open one eye. *Yeah, I must have. Look at her face.*

She was smiling, wasn't she? Crying, too, bless her beautiful self. What a woman. *My woman.*

Happy New Year wasn't the half of it.

Belle gripped her script and checked out the competition. Shakespeare would have been astounded to find so many potential Ursulas waiting in the wings of the Barter Theatre on a cold Tuesday night in Abingdon. The women, a dozen or more, stood surrounded by painted backdrops from a dozen productions and the colorful litter peculiar to theater.

Alone in the darkened house, the Barter's artistic director was seated center orchestra, waiting to discover his Ursula for the upcoming staging of *Much Ado about Nothing*.

Out of the corner of her eye, Belle sized up the women around her. One was exceptionally tall and slim, like a ballet dancer with a swan's neck. Beside her, a petite woman with a few extra pounds and a lot of mascara. Forty-something. Not the typical attendant for the fair Hero, but as any drama student knew, Shakespearean comedy was open to interpretation.

Next to her, a regal young woman with smooth blond hair tucked into a neat French twist. Her long, simple dress fit the character of a Renaissance gentlewoman. Two or three others also seemed dressed to impress, conveying the message that they'd been waiting their entire lives to step on stage as Ursula.

Belle surveyed her own appearance in a backstage mirror and let loose a heavy sigh. Her slim skirt and boots looked out of place, anachronistic. The sweater was the wrong century completely. *Me, too. All wrong.* Too short, too old, too many freckles, too many curls, not enough practice, and zero theater experience for the last decade.

Lord, what am I doing here?

She knew why she was there, what this audition was about. It was about proving to herself that her college degree wasn't wasted. She'd always considered drama a calling, God's clear design for her life. Had she heard him correctly? *You'll know soon enough, honey.*

Belle's attention to her script was momentarily diverted by the shadow of someone moving behind the sets on the other side of the stage. He — definitely a he — was carrying a load of lumber on his broad shoulders. She couldn't make out a face or his hair color, but the way he moved looked oddly familiar.

"Carpenters," a young brunette whispered in her ear, nodding at the crew dressed in jeans and sawdust. "They brought a new bunch of construction guys in tonight to start hammering together the set. Don't let it throw you."

Like she needed something else to make her nervous.

The women were each to read one scene. Those who impressed the director would be called back to read a second scene with Hero. Silence fell over the backstage gathering as Ursulas were summoned one by one to read with a handsome New York actor already cast as Antonio. His wavy hair and carefully clipped beard were perfect for the part, Belle thought, watching the swan-necked woman glide out for her audition.

She was excellent, much as it pained Belle to admit it. Crystal-clear diction and classic Shakespearean phrasing. *Harrumph.* The petite woman was equally talented, seeming to grow in stature with every line. Belle's spirits sank. The blond princess auditioned next, her acting abilities as close to perfection as Belle could imagine.

"Let's leave now." It was the friendly brunette again, giggling.

"Not a bad plan." But Belle knew it was not an option for her. She had to go through with this, had to know where she stood.

"Belinda Oberholtzer."

Belle almost didn't hear her name being called out. Her given name. *Belinda.* Since all her acting credits, her degree, everything connected to the theater appeared under her real name, she didn't have much choice except to use it. Besides, she was neither Belle nor Belinda tonight.

She was Ursula, attendant to Hero.

Propelled by this last burst of confidence, Belle moved swiftly to center stage. It was hard to glide in leather boots with noisy heels, but she did her best. Planting her feet just so, she lifted her chin. Opened her arms, hoping they appeared graceful, poised. Turned her body ever so slightly toward the audience of one, and flashed Antonio a disarming smile as she held up an imaginary mask and delivered her first line.

"I know you well enough, you are Signior Antonio."

Something was wrong. He was staring down at her, a look of dismay crossing his chiseled features. After a lengthy silence, he blurted out his line, then it was her turn again.

"I know you by the waggling of your head."

But his head didn't waggle, his tongue did, hurrying faster through his lines, as if to end her audition as quickly as possible. She straightened her back, determined to continue, deliberately slowing her words hoping he would follow her lead.

It wasn't helping. The others had sounded so professional, so polished, so right for the part. Any of them would suit. But she did not suit. Her delivery was stilted, unnatural.

Amateurish.

Somewhere, deep inside, a tiny voice whispered the awful truth: *You're not good enough.* Not as good as the others and nowhere near talented enough to win the part of Ursula or any other role.

Her lips moved, the lines were spoken, but her heart heard only the voices of directors past. What had they been trying to tell her, year after year? Why hadn't she listened?

"Belinda, have you ever thought about directing? You have such a good eye."

"With that voice, you could certainly do radio, Belinda."

"Don't be discouraged. The theater isn't for everyone. Do it for pleasure, not for profit."

When she spoke her final line, the truth of Shakespeare's words nearly sent her to her knees: "Graces will appear, and there's an end."

"Thank goodness for that," Antonio murmured in a stage whisper, obviously intending her to hear him. Suddenly he was a good deal less handsome.

From the darkened theater seats beyond the edge of the stage, a voice floated out of the silence. "Thank you, Miss Oberholtzer. Next."

Belle turned, her joints stiff from tension, catching a glimpse of Antonio's smile returning as the next actress swept into the pool of light at center stage. Belle hurried past her, not looking left or right but walking a direct path toward the stage door that would take her into the street, into the night, and far away from the Barter Theatre.

Thank the Lord no one she knew had been there, had seen her make such a fool of herself. No photographer had snapped her picture, no producer had taped her performance — if you could call it that.

She would begin immediately to block out the entire agonizing experience. It never happened. It simply never took place at all.

Who are you kidding? No one except herself. Her decade-old dream of doing professional theater had died, stillborn, with a handful of lines on a bitter cold night. Dead and buried, with nothing left to show for it but a broken heart and an ego left in tatters.

Grabbing her purse, discarded what seemed like hours ago on top of a precarious stack of props, Belle found her way through the shadows to the exit sign above the back door that led to freedom. Freedom from the single most embarrassing ten minutes she'd ever spent in her life.

"Belle!"

She turned with a frightened gasp. *Who*

in the world? The red safety lights back-stage and the swirling dust motes around them made it impossible to see farther than a few feet. She squinted at the form moving toward her, taking shape.

It can't be.

"David?"

He reached her side, his eyes wide with concern. "Belle, I'm —"

"W-what are you doing here?" She recognized the anger in her voice, knew that fear and shame were not far behind it.

"I'm one of the carpenters on the stage crew." His face, what she could see of it, shone with empathy. "I needed the money for new carpet for the house, so I signed on several weeks ago to help with set construction. I had no idea . . ."

"Did you see me —" She couldn't bring herself to say the words. Maybe he didn't see her. Maybe he was back in the set room, hammering away, and missed the whole horrible thing.

But no.

His head was nodding, slowly. "If you mean did I see you audition, yes." His voice gentled to a whisper. "I was standing stage left, in the wings, so I wouldn't distract you and ruin your performance." She could hear him swallow in the darkness. "I prayed for you, Belle."

"Oh, David." Her knees buckled underneath her. She felt his strong hands catch her elbows and pull her back up. Pull her into his arms in a crushing embrace.

She sensed him nuzzling her hair with his chin as she sobbed against his broad chest. Arms pinned to her side, she could do little else but remain tucked against him, a small bird sheltered from the raging storm.

In the long moments that followed, David gave her the kindest gift of all. *Silence.* No words. No questions. What could he say that would make it better?

Her tears slowed, then stopped. Mortified, she pressed against his chest with her head, trying to push herself away. He finally let her go, though he rested his hands on her shoulders. *Smart man.* He knew her well. Knew she would turn and bolt out the door if she could.

She stared at the floor, not trusting herself to look into his eyes, afraid of what she would see there. Afraid she would cry again.

Something had to be said, though. "Thank you, David." It came out on a noisy hiccup.

"No problem." He hiccuped back at her and grinned.

"Aren't you ashamed of me?" She looked up and sniffed, petulant, hiccuping again. "Ashamed of my . . . whatever that was?"

"No way." His grin disappeared. "You weren't ashamed of me." David's eyes looked right through her, offering hope, giving absolution. She basked in the light of it, too grateful to risk turning away from his compassionate gaze, no matter how much it cost her to let him see her so humiliated.

"When it comes to handing out grace, Belle, you do it better than anyone. I'm simply trying to return the favor. Remember what you said to me? 'Your past is just that — passed.' Let it go, babe. You gave it your best shot. No one can ever say otherwise."

She stuck out her lower lip in an exaggerated pout. "Antonio would probably say otherwise." A third hiccup, more pronounced.

David shrugged. "A Shakespearean actor. What does he know?"

He was baiting her and she took it. Her hands moved to her hips, preparing for battle. She was beginning to feel like her old self again. It felt good. "I'd like to see *you* try and read Shakespeare."

He assumed a pose remarkably like Antonio's, though Belle had to confess David was the better-looking one by far. "At a word, I am not," he chirped an octave higher than necessary.

Clever David had paid close attention indeed. Belle rolled her eyes in feigned disgust. "Your British accent is deplorable, sir. Next!" She hiccuped again. Loudly.

From stage right came a chorus of giggles. Belle couldn't keep herself from joining in the laughter. "We've been found out, Antonio. Our ruse is up."

"Or our goose is cooked."

"Something like that." She stifled yet another hiccup. "Look, I've gotta locate a glass of water before I embarrass myself further."

He gallantly offered her his arm. " 'Twould be my privilege, fair maiden, to escort you to yonder Hardware Company for a spot of tea."

" 'Twould it now?" She draped her arm on his with great ceremony. "Carry on, good sir. Will there be a carriage?"

" 'Twill not be, m'lady. The night, though cold, was made for walking. This way, then, shall we?"

They paraded out the exit door, dissolving into laughter before they reached Main Street. Thirty minutes later they were still seated in a cozy restaurant booth, round candles glowing on the table, the freezing darkness held safely at bay while they sipped hot cider and enjoyed breathing the same toasty warm air.

"David, David." She rested her fingers lightly on his, noting how strong his hands were — masculine, with sawdust hidden in the creases, yet the nails were clean and trimmed. An enigma, this man. Did he know, could he comprehend, what having his support meant to her this night? Did he understand what he was doing to her heart, building a home there as surely as he was building a set at the Barter, board by board?

She'd never known a man like David Cahill. Never felt about anyone the way she felt about him. It didn't have a name yet, this feeling, but the fog was starting to lift and the view was getting clearer by the minute.

If you don't stop staring at his hands, he'll think he's grown an extra knuckle. Smiling as she tipped up her head, Belle spoke her heart, straight out. "David, I could never have survived this evening without you."

"I'm glad I was there." His eyes, made darker and more liquid by the candlelight, said infinitely more than his words. "Do you want to talk about it now?"

He wasn't going to make this easy on her. Maybe that was good. She considered his invitation for a moment, bearing the weight of it, then sensing it lift as she spoke the words like a confession. "I learned that I don't always have to be on stage or the star, that it's possible to enjoy something as a spectator without having to be a performer."

"So . . ."

"So maybe I'll buy a season pass to the Barter and let the pros do the acting."

"You *are* a pro, Belle. Just in a different arena." He squeezed her hands, then leaned back in the booth. "Do you know you're the best radio personality I've ever heard?"

Gee, that's original. "C'mon, how many have you really heard?"

He counted on his fingers, one hand then the next. When he got to fifteen, she swatted at him and he backed farther away from her.

"Are you getting ready to slap me again, woman? 'Cause if you are, give me some warning. It took half a day for that last handprint to disappear."

A wave of heat swept out of her sweater and up her neck. "I didn't mean to do that. Honest."

"Huh. I'll bet." He winked at her. "Was there anything else you learned tonight?"

She groaned and slumped farther into the booth. "You're relentless, aren't you?" Pensive, she played with her braid, sorting through not only the evening's emotions, but a decade of dreaming about theater. "I discovered that I'm pretty good at denying the obvious. My professors, not to mention my friends in college, tried to tell me that acting might not be the best use of my . . . uh, talents. If I have any, that is."

"Of course you have talents." He nodded emphatically. "A bunch of them. Knocking off microphones, storing furniture on porches, falling on the ice, slapping men silly —"

She swatted at him again, closer this time. His smile was so disarming she almost missed his next question.

"These professors of yours at ASU. What did they suggest you do with your degree instead of acting?"

The point hit home. "Radio."

"Ah." He nodded in silence. "When God calls, he also equips, Belle. Radio is clearly your calling. Why fight it?"

She sat up, suddenly invigorated. "You're absolutely right. I *have* been fighting it. Thinking it wasn't enough, that unless I was in a major market with a number-one-rated show, it didn't count. That unless I was on stage, my education was wasted." She slapped the table in lieu of leaping on top of it. "You wait until I hit the air tomorrow morning, mister. We'll find out if this late bloomer can't blossom right where she's planted."

His smile stretched from coast to coast below the blue-gray ocean of his eyes. "That's my girl."

His girl?

It wasn't until much later, after David had walked her home, after she'd avoided Norah and her inevitable questions about the audition, after she'd scrubbed off her makeup and climbed into bed, that Belle remembered the significance of the next day.

Wednesday.

The *Washington County News* would hit the newsstands, as it did every Wednesday morning. Except this time, she'd be the featured story.

She scrunched up her pillow, smiling into the darkness of her bedroom. That should make up for tonight. Something to boost her confidence, get her back on her feet again.

Wait.

Hadn't she said something during that interview about auditioning for the Barter? Not much, surely. Just a mention, wasn't it? They'd probably skip it completely. Not to worry.

She'd almost drifted off when another thought poked her awake.

Wait.

What had they asked her about her single life, about dating? Had she said she was or was *not* happy about being unattached? She couldn't remember. Mustn't have said anything too important. Nothing to lose sleep over, that's for sure.

She didn't lose a second of shut-eye. Slept like a log. Right up until Norah knocked on her door well before the crack of dawn and shoved a newspaper under her face, one with a full page of ghastly photos of her and an enormous boldface headline:

"The Belle of Abingdon: Local Radio Personality Seeks Love and Applause in Small Town America."

" 'Love and applause'?" Belle groaned, rubbing the sleep out of her eyes. "Please tell me it's a misprint."

Norah held out a cup of steaming black coffee. "You've already had your first suitor, Belle. The guy who sold me the newspaper wants to know if you're interested in dinner Friday night."

"He *what?*"

"And speaking of applause, how'd you do at the Barter last night?" Norah pointed to the article while Belle stared at it, dumbfounded. "See, there's a whole column about your plans to audition. Everybody will be dying to know what happened. Do tell. Were you the Belle of the Barter, too?"

Nineteen

News is anything that makes
a woman say, "For heaven's sake!"

Edgar Watson Howe

The coffee didn't help.

The steamy hot shower didn't help.

Even Norah's best applesauce muffins didn't improve matters.

Belle's eyes were so puffy from crying she couldn't get close to them with mascara, liner, or eye shadow. Why bother with blush when her cheeks were already stained a permanent pink? No point to lipstick, either, since she was blowing her nose every ten minutes.

Her closet let her down as well. All her favorite clothes were wrinkled, dirty, or both, so she was stuck wearing baggy jeans and a sweater that made her skin look green.

So far this morning, her hair was the only thing not giving her fits.

Brushing it dry with long, slow strokes, Belle kept one eye on the clock. Should she get to work early, hide in the studio, avoid the inevitable commentary from her coworkers? Maybe getting there late was better, minutes before her show, so no one would have time to razz her.

"Oh, fiddle!" Late or early, it didn't make one iota of difference. The most humiliating day of her thirty-two years awaited her. The sooner she faced it, the better. Four blocks and forty-four steps later, facing it *later* seemed like a much better plan.

Three of WPER's finest were already gathered around the table in the jock lounge, the incriminating newspaper spread out before them. Cliff in his houndstooth jacket, Jeanette in her rhinestone glasses, Anne wearing a pencil behind her ear and a smug expression on her face. "Well, if it isn't the woman of the hour."

Cliff, ever the salesman, gave Belle a hearty slap on the back. "Great press for the Barter Theatre. An important client of ours. They'll be thrilled."

"Great."

"While we're on the subject —" Jeanette eyed Belle over her glasses — "I have tickets for you to give away on your show, one pair every hour, starting later this month. For *Much Ado about Nothing*, of course."

"Great."

Anne chimed in. "That reminds me, I'd like you to record a spot for the Barter before you go on the air this morning. Cliff's written it. Kind of a Shakespearean spoof."

"Great."

Patrick's office door opened with a bang. "There you are, Belle!" He waved her toward him, a look of concern on his bearded face. "I need your help on something."

He knows.

He pulled her inside his office, closing the door behind them. He smelled of minty soap and a freshly dry-cleaned suit, making her feel frumpier than ever. "Belle, I've got the Barter on hold on the phone."

I knew it. She managed to croak out a response. "Oh?"

"Since we're a sponsor for *Much Ado* —"

"A sponsor!" *Great.*

"Hadn't I mentioned that? Anyway, from a promotional standpoint, I wanted to make sure you got the part of Elsa."

"Ursula."

"Whatever. Here's the problem. The woman in the office said your name wasn't listed on last night's audition roster. According to the paper, you were supposed to be there."

"Believe me, I was there."

His face brightened. "And?"

She took a deep breath. "Ask them if the name Belinda Oberholtzer is on their list."

Patrick beamed. "Gee, why didn't I think of that?" He grabbed the phone and punched the button. "Miss, I have another possibility for you to check. Got an actress named Oberholtzer on there?"

Belle watched his expression change from expectation, to confusion, to something like desperation. "I see. Uh-huh." His eyes met Belle's when they both heard a peal of laughter coming from the other end of the line.

"No need to make light of it, miss." Patrick's face had turned to the color of wet Georgia clay. "And I'm sorrier than you are. Thanks for the . . . uh, information." He hung up the phone in silence, bravely keeping his eyes locked on hers.

Don't let him hug me, Lord. If he hugs me, I'm a goner.

She almost fainted from relief when he kept his distance.

"Belle, I'm —"

She held up her hands. "Don't say it. It was awful and it's over. I'll survive."

"But all those years —"

"I'll get over it, okay?" Her voice softened when she saw the pity in his eyes turn to compassion. "Not a problem, Patrick. I'm a big girl."

"Actually, you're kinda small." He grinned, obviously relieved. "But you've matured into quite a woman." The creases around his eyes deepened. "David's a lucky guy."

Her stomach turned into a neatly tied square knot. *So much for secrets.* "Th-thanks. I think Norah's pretty lucky, too."

Patrick let out a loud guffaw, chasing away any tension in the room. "Are you kidding? I'm the blessed one in that relationship and you know it."

She watched a softness come over his bearded face, transforming it so completely her mouth dropped open. "You're hiding something from me, old friend. Something exciting, unless I miss my guess. Out with it."

In a few, halting sentences, Patrick described his visit from Norah on New Year's Day. Belle found her own disappointment fading away as her boss shared his life-changing discovery with her.

When Patrick finished, she was the one hugging *him.* "That's wonderful!" She squeezed his teddy bear chest then stepped back, brushing away a tear. "Two kinds of love, eh? One for now and —"

"And one forever." He nodded sheepishly and Belle decided she'd never seen him so genuinely happy.

"When's the wedding?"

The ruddy color was back. "Oh no, you don't. We're a long way from that, Belle."

A voice floated in from outside the office. "A long way from what?"

They both turned to find Norah standing

in the doorway wrapped in a teal-colored wool coat, a muffin basket resting in her gloved hands. "Did I miss something?"

Belle chuckled. "Nothing Patrick can't fill you in on. Gotta go, you two. Spots to record and a show to prep."

"Wait a minute." Patrick thrust a handful of pink phone message slips into her hands. "You'll want these."

"Huh?" Belle thumbed through the stack of unfamiliar names. "What's all this?"

"Admirers." His grin covered half his face. "A dozen or so guys read your article this morning and decided if you weren't happy being single, they might be able to do something about it. Those came in on the business line. Frank took twice that many on the studio phone since six this morning."

Her groan covered half an octave. "Great."

"Better not let David see those." Norah offered Belle a knowing smile as she brushed past her. "You know how jealous these radio men can be."

David, jealous? The notion of it warmed her to her toes, buoying her along in a wave of pleasant euphoria all the way to the production studio. All through the recording of a commercial for the Barter. Right up until she entered the on-air studio where reality struck again in the form of

360

Frank Gallagher. A highly peeved Frank Gallagher.

"Mornin', Frank!" Belle sang out.

"So says you." He tossed her the music log with little ceremony. "Better pull the tunes for your show now, since you'll no doubt spend all five hours on the phone with your fans. These are for you as well." He slapped a second stack of pink phone slips on the countertop. "Though why you'd want to talk to these love-starved fools only you would know."

Poor Frank. Belle understood exactly what prompted his sour mood. She studied his broad back, his carefully positioned toupee, his ancient coffee cup, his newspaper opened to her article.

"Frank, I'm sorry they did a story on me first. Everybody loves your morning show and —"

"You think I'm bothered by this?" He wheeled the chair around so quickly it made her jump. "Not on your life, girlie. Old Frank's been around long enough to see how this works. A pretty girl sells more papers than a middle-aged guy in polyester pants." He sniffed for effect and turned back to the board. "Besides, Jake Solomon at the *Mountain View Times* is talking about doing an article on me. Sometime soon, he says."

"That's terrific, Frank." *Bless his heart.*

Belle knew the perfect thing to boost his ego. "By the way, I didn't get the part at the Barter last night. Made a blooming idiot of myself, as a matter of fact."

He spun around again. "No kidding!"

She almost laughed out loud at the look of relief on his face, especially when he tried hard to appear sympathetic and failed miserably. "Yup." She shrugged her shoulders, playing it to full effect for his benefit. "No weeks of rehearsing for this woman. My evenings are my own." She winked at him. "I seem to remember that last night had some disaster-making potential for you as well. How'd your dinner with Millie, the winning contestant, go?"

His eyebrows gathered like storm clouds brewing over the Appalachians. "I've been talking about it on the air for the last three hours. Don't you ever listen to my show?"

"Every single morning, Frank." *Maybe the man's ego didn't need boosting after all.* "But today I was too busy licking my wounds over the article."

"What's the matter, wasn't it accurate?"

"Oh, it was accurate, every painful word. Not a misquote on the page." She sighed, putting down her things. "I simply forgot the cardinal rule for interviews — never say anything you don't want seven thousand people to read about." She began yanking out music CDs for her show, talking over

362

her shoulder as she went down the wooden wall rack. "So, tell me about last night with Millie."

"It was . . . nice."

Whaddaya know. "Details, Frank, I want details."

"Tall, slim, my age, curly dark hair, good sense of humor." He cleared his throat with exaggerated fanfare. "We're going out again tomorrow night. On my dime this time."

"Frank, you sly thing!"

He'd already slipped on his cans and turned on the mike for a long stop set, chatting about weather and upcoming events. His bass voice boomed, "Be sure to join our own media darling, Belle O'Brien, broadcasting live from Dollar General Store this afternoon from four until five. Take advantage of their January White Sale savings and meet the Belle of Abingdon."

Do what? Her spirits and her jaw dropped in tandem. The minute Frank's mike was off, she grabbed the liner card promoting her appearance and read the awful news for herself. "Not today, please don't tell me this. I'm wearing zero makeup, dowdy clothes . . ." Her diatribe dissolved into a groan. "Whose idea was this?"

"Patrick's." Frank flashed a lethal grin. "Figured he'd capitalize on the newspaper publicity. Let you get out there and meet your adoring public, face to face."

"Great."

She'd have barely enough time to run home between her show and the remote broadcast to change and slap on some makeup. The fistful of phone slips in her hands convinced her she couldn't go "as is," since some of her admirers might show up whether they needed a new set of towels or not.

Minutes later, it was her turn on the microphone. She tossed up a silent prayer for energy and enthusiasm, both of which were sadly lacking at the moment, and dove in. "Belle O'Brien here to keep your day spinning along, starting with a number-one record from January 1970. B.J. Thomas and 'Raindrops Keep Fallin' on My Head.' "

And that's about the only thing that hasn't happened today. Not yet, anyway.

Frank's advice about needing to get her music ready turned out to be prophetic. The studio request line rang nonstop all morning with calls that fell into two categories, same as the messages on the pink slips. Some wanted her to know how disappointed they were, the usual "you don't look like you sound" comments. In ten years of doing radio, the only response she'd come up with to that one was, "Sorry, I'll try harder tomorrow."

Or — and this was by far the majority — the callers were men wanting to know if they could "meet her sometime." Prepubescent teenagers whose voices changed keys three times in one sentence. Salesmen on cell phones, yearning for a little human contact on the road. Men in their sixties who kept calling her "young lady" and saying how much she reminded them of their own daughters. Lonely guys from neighboring towns like Meadowview, Chilhowie, and Damascus, the town she'd driven through back in November. Students from Emory & Henry College and VHCC, back from the Christmas break, assuring her she "didn't look bad for an older woman."

Great.

During the network news feed at noon, she made the unfortunate mistake of choosing the Grill for her take-out lunch. A newspaper rack waited silently inside the door, hitting her between the eyes with that headline one more time. While she stood at the counter, trying to ignore the sidelong glances and elbow nudges her presence had set into motion, Leonard came lumbering out from behind the sizzling grill, wiping his hands on his grimy apron and grinning in greeting.

"Take a look at that fishbowl, Miss O'Brien!" He grabbed it off the display rack and shook it at her. "Betcha got twenty new ones since this morning. Guess that makes you the Belle of the *Bowl,* huh?"

"Very clever, Leonard." She smiled in spite of herself. "How about a turkey on whole wheat, light on the mayo?" He was back with her sandwich in record time, but not soon enough to prevent a few good-natured verbal volleys from the regular diners who knew her. Thanks to the paper's thorough reporting, now they knew even more about her.

Studying the group of photos for the tenth time that day, she decided they might not be as awful as they'd first seemed. Had she ever seen a photo of herself she really liked? The one with the hot air balloon crew, a pose of her climbing into the big rattan basket they called the gondola, was a nagging reminder that her own "date with a winner" would be coming up in a little over a month. The listener part made her nervous, but the ballooning itself was scarier still. Patrick had convinced her she'd be plenty safe, despite David's insistence that he'd get a group from church to pray for her from takeoff to landing.

Where *was* David, anyway? She dashed back up the steps, sandwich in hand. She hadn't caught so much as a glimpse of him all day. He usually stuck his head in the studio while she baby-sat the news feed and nibbled on lunch, but not today. The afternoon dragged on. Though the music was upbeat — Animals to ZZ Top — she found her spirits were sagging, especially each time she promoted her upcoming remote broadcast. *Why today, Lord?* His silence spoke volumes. Clearly she was expected to cram all her misery in one day, get it over with, then jump back into joyful living on Thursday.

When she flew out of the studio at three, Belle reminded herself that in two hours it would all be over and she could crawl in bed and pretend this day never happened. Meanwhile, lots had to happen. In less time than it took her to hurry down Main Street, run up and down the steps and fire up the Pontiac, Belle also squeezed in a hasty iron job on her favorite pants and jacket, smeared some color on her freckled face, and squirted on an extra dose of perfume for good measure.

Bad idea. Her fragrance, like a flower drawing bees, had men swarming around her at Dollar General Store. Microphone in one hand, towels in the other, she was doing on-air chats with Burt back at the studio while listeners stood around and listened to her bubble about white sale bargains. While she hawked the wares, they

gawked and stared. It was beyond embarrassing.

With fifteen minutes left on the air, she'd
run out of interesting things to say about
the sale items. "The sheets are flat, the
towels are thick" summed things up in a
hurry. Interviewing shoppers, though, was
disastrous. As soon as she stuck a mike in
someone's face they said, "Hey, I saw you
in the paper. You don't look the same in
person."

Great.

Forty-five minutes later, she finally unloaded her portable broadcast gear in the
parking lot behind the station on Plumb
Alley, so named because it ran plumb
through town. Avoiding the few remaining
icy patches that lurked in the corners of
the lot and between the bricks in the sidewalk, she made her way up the hill, then
up the steps, clunk-clunking the equipment
behind her, biting her lip to keep from
saying something she'd regret.

And to keep from crying.

It had been one endless, ragged day. Ten
more steps and she'd be at the station
door, where everyone would be long gone
except Burt in the studio. Looking down at
her feet to keep from tripping over the
cords and wires, Belle almost landed in the
lap of a long-legged man seated on the top
step. With something in his hands that, for

a blessed change, was *not* a copy of the *Washington County News.*

Finally, she did cry.

"Is that any way to thank me?"

David watched as Belle sagged onto the steps, equipment sprawled everywhere, tears streaming down cheeks made rosy by the cold.

"Sorry," she croaked, digging through her purse, probably for a tissue. He pulled a white handkerchief out of his back pocket and offered it to her with a shake.

"Here. It's clean, honest."

She took it, eyeing the other item in his hands but saying nothing. He gingerly sat it next to him on the landing and waited for her to pull herself together.

"What are you doing on the steps? Did you lock yourself out?"

He shook his head.

"Were you afraid I wouldn't bring back the remote gear in one piece?"

Another head shake, though he couldn't help smiling at that one.

She, however, was frowning. "You wouldn't dare ask me about my day, would you?"

"Don't have to, Belle." The wear and tear on her was obvious. After the Barter last night, then the article this morning, it was no wonder she was wrung out. "If it helps to hear it, I'm sorry."

She nodded, clearly not wanting to go down that avenue for another visit anytime soon.

Truth be known, he was particularly sorry about the paragraph where she talked about being single and not being happy about it. About not seeing anyone special right now.

What am I, chopped liver?

The answer was obvious. *No.* He also had never taken her on a date. Which might be a good thing, considering his plans to leave town someday were picking up speed.

Belle's eyes were glued to the clay pot by his side. "What are those?"

He handed her the flowers, tall green stems with delicate white blooms clustered at the top. "Paper-whites. Little bulbs coaxed into flowering for a beautiful woman in January so she'll remember to bloom where she's planted."

She looked like she might start crying again.

He shifted down a step. Geared his voice down while he was at it. "It's a good day for bearing gifts, Belle. The sixth of January."

Her glistening eyes widened. "Epiphany."

"The day the Magi appeared." He nodded and offered her a hand, meaning to help her stand up. Instead, she stayed put and hung on for all she was worth. Her warm touch was soft yet insistent. The smallness of her hands made his own seem too large, too rough. Especially since he'd hammered and sawed at the house all day, reinforcing the staircase to the second floor.

"Magi or not, I'm glad *you* appeared today. Finally." Her lower lip edged out in a pretty pout. "Where've you been?"

He had to know. "Missed me?"

The lower lip pushed out further. "Answer my question first."

"Not unless you let me take you to dinner."

The lower lip dropped in a gasp. "Do you mean a date, David, or are we going dutch treat?"

How had he gotten himself into this? Seconds earlier, he'd prided himself on never taking her on a date, and now here he was, doing precisely that. *And loving it, Cahill.*

He squinted at her as if sizing her up. Unnecessary, when she was the perfect size. He'd found that out when he'd embraced her last night. She fit snuggly under his chin. Her arms circled his waist just so. Her lips landed right on top of his heart. Or rather, where his heart used to be before she stole it.

She asked you a question, man. "Ah . . . since you studied Latin and I studied French, Dutch isn't our language, wouldn't you agree? I'm paying, of course."

Belle smiled for the first time since she'd landed on the steps. Maybe the first time that day. Her eyes sparkled with mischief. "Are we talking the Martha Washington Inn for dinner, then?"

He snorted, yanking her to her feet along with him. "We're talking Bubba's Best Barbecue." *And we're not talking about the envelope in my pocket. The one with the solid gold job offer from WBT in Charlotte.*

They dragged the equipment inside the station doors, parking it out of harm's way, and headed down the steps. He could sense her mood lifting and hoped he was part of the reason why. Although it was Epiphany, a night for gifts and revelations, he couldn't bring himself to reveal his latest news, not yet. Not until he saw the station in North Carolina. Not until WBT's management explained the terms of their generous offer. Not until he decided if and how Belinda Oberholtzer fit into his future.

Twenty

Money often costs too much.

Ralph Waldo Emerson

Swerving to pass a guy whose cruise control was set on crawl, David adjusted the mirrors on the rental car. Nice to be able to use an interior button to handle all that instead of rolling down both windows and shoving things around by hand, the way he did on the truck. That piece of junk was sitting at Ratcliff's Auto Clinic and Body Shop getting the engine worked on while he tooled down Highway 16 in a brand-new borrowed Taurus, pointed toward Charlotte.

Not a soul in Abingdon knew where he was headed or why.

He was good at keeping secrets. All through his growing-up years, he'd tried to keep his dad's drinking a secret. All through the service and college, he'd kept his shabby upbringing hidden from his buddies. And hadn't he managed to keep Josh a secret from everyone he'd ever known for eight long years?

Everyone except Belle.

Which was why the WBT offer was

burning a hole in his conscience. His dream station. The money and security he'd longed for waited for him three hours south of Abingdon. He hadn't hinted to Belle about it, even after more than two weeks. Instead he talked to the Lord non-stop and begged for wisdom.

He couldn't risk telling her, not yet. What if she told Patrick? Or told Norah, and *she* told Patrick? *Belle wouldn't tell a soul, and you know it.* Well, what if she got all weepy about him moving? Worse, what if she didn't shed a tear and wished him well, sayonara, good riddance? The whole thing gave him a headache.

Take in the scenery, man. Get a grip.

The late January day was cold but sunny. Now that he'd left behind the snowy mountains of the Blue Ridge, there wasn't a patch of white stuff in sight as he drank in the rolling hills of western North Carolina, heading south toward the Piedmont Plateau. *Beautiful country, this.*

Great weather for working on the house, he realized with a guilty start. He'd worked hard all Saturday at the station to earn this day off, worked all yesterday after church pulling down the crumbling plaster in his living room, feeling bad about laboring on Sunday, convincing himself he could continue to worship while he worked.

His set-building gig at the Barter had

paid for the carpet that waited upstairs for him to install. But with that side job over, his bank account was back to zilch. Again, still.

Money, always money. And time. It would take him another three months to finish the house. Less if he had help. The supplies were covered. What he needed was an extra pair of carpenter's hands. Friends from church had generously offered, but he was down to the problematic stuff he'd never ask a novice builder to tackle. The kind of detail work his father had been a master at. On his sober days.

Thinking about his dad meant thinking about Josh, yet another situation that had sent him to his knees often this month, ever since the boy's letter. He didn't dare call or write him back — Sherry would have a fit. He hadn't told Belle about that one either. *Too complicated.*

He hoped Josh would write again, but he hadn't. Clearly the kid needed a father. Why hadn't Sherry found herself some laid-back California kind of guy by now? She was cute enough. Friendly enough. *Too friendly.* Why didn't she marry somebody and let the man adopt Josh as his own?

Over my dead body.

The thought hit him hard, knocking the breath out of him for a second. He didn't want anyone else to father Josh. His only child, his look-alike son. *Selfish, David.* Yeah, well. It wasn't pretty, it was merely the truth. Taking the job at WBT would at least let him send twice as much money every month. Maybe more.

Not that the job was his yet, not hardly. He had a long day ahead with plenty to prove. To himself and to the chief engineer at Jefferson-Pilot's flagship station with 50,000 clear-channel watts in a top-fifty market in a city surrounded by half a million people. The Queen City it was called, after Queen Charlotte Sophia, the wife of King George III.

The city might have a queen's name, but it didn't have a Belle.

He sighed, determined to concentrate on transmitters and towers and not the auburn-haired temptress back in Abingdon. It didn't help that he'd gone out of his way to drive smack dab through the middle of Moravian Falls. And he ignored the obvious when WBT came booming in on his car radio, playing the Fifth Dimension's "One Less Bell to Answer" as the lead-in for the station's midday talk show.

He'd call Belle tonight when he got home. After he saw what WBT had to offer and what the job entailed. The salary and benefits were no doubt double what Patrick was paying him. Whether he took the job or not, he had to know if he was good enough. Had to know if he had enough talent and drive for the big time.

Stretching his shoulders, grown stiff from sitting behind the wheel since dawn, David consulted the map stretched out on the passenger seat. He'd be there in half an hour. A quick glance in the rearview mirror convinced him that he still looked decent. Clean-shaven. Since his beard grew in blond, he could get away with a few more hours before the shadow showed.

His hair looked better than usual, thanks to a fresh trim from Belle, who'd insisted on cutting it last week. Said she'd always done her younger brother's hair. As Patrick would say, the price was right, plus it didn't look half bad. The best part had been her nimble fingers running through his hair, tickling his scalp, putting all his senses on alert when she leaned over him, the scent of her perfume filling his head.

Enough, Cahill. Think transmitters. Think towers.

The traffic around him had grown more congested, the scenery more urban. *Not long now.* Out of habit, he straightened his glasses, smoothed down his tie, tucked in his shirt, eyed his suit coat hanging in the backseat. *Big day, fella. Don't blow it.*

Belle stretched her fingers, grown stiff

from writing. The stack of mail on her coffee table didn't seem to be shrinking, though she'd already written a dozen letters, hoping her listeners would be pleased with a handwritten response. Even if every one said, in essence, "No, thanks, I'm not interested in dating anyone right now, but I really appreciate your invitation."

Liar. She didn't appreciate them one bit.

That's not true either. She appreciated the trouble they took to listen to her show, to read the article about her, to write her a letter. It was the dating inquiries that undid her.

Two days after her newspaper story, the phone calls eased up in time for cards and letters to start pouring through the station's door with her name spelled every which way. *Bell, Bella,* and *Bailey* for the first name, *Obryan, Ober,* and — her personal favorite — *O'Brainy* for the last.

Like the phone calls, they fell into two categories, discussing either her appearance or her marital status. If they wrote, "I thought you'd be a blonde," she referred them to the lovely and talented Heather. "I thought you'd be younger" prompted her quick reply, "Me, too."

Letters from prison inmates were a staple of disc jockey life, but not this many, not in a couple of weeks. She consoled herself with the fact that her faithful prison fans

wouldn't be hounding her for a date anytime soon, not like the other writers who
offered their bucket seats for her to sit in
the next available Saturday night. Men of
every age and ilk tried to tempt her with
trips to Bristol for a movie, jaunts to
Kingsport for a concert, or mile-high
climbing expeditions up Mount Rogers, the
highest point in Virginia.

It left her dizzy and gasping for air just
to think about it. So did the prospect of
answering all the mail staring back at her.
She shuffled through the remaining stack,
pulling out a few that looked more promising than the others. Typed letters on
classy stationery. Letterhead bearing the
logo of one of the law offices in town.
Might be nice to know a good lawyer. Another from a med student, interning at
Johnston Memorial Hospital, right up
Court Street. *Handy guy to have around
when we launch the Happy Together balloon.*

Should she take the risk? Write back and
agree to meet one of them, if only for a
root beer float at the Grill? The idea was
enticing, but only from one standpoint —
it might get David off high center and
moving forward in her direction if he
thought he had some competition.

Things had been going along swim-
mingly, from Christmas right through

379

Epiphany, at which point their relationship stalled like an old Ford truck. Like *his* truck, in fact. He'd used the rusty clunker as an excuse to get out of a trip they'd planned to White's Mill, an 1840-vintage grist mill three miles outside of Abingdon. This morning she'd noticed his Ford parked at Ratcliff's Auto Repair and decided David had taken the day off to get his truck worked on, maybe pick up some more supplies for his house projects.

Heaven knew he'd spent enough time and money on that place lately. More than he'd spent on her. What was his rush? The roof was solid, the outside was painted, the kitchen was nearly done. That's what he'd told her, anyway. He hadn't invited her to the house yet. Kept saying he wanted to wait until it was totally done. *Silly man.* She wasn't getting any younger and these letters were starting to sound more appealing by the minute.

Not as appealing as David.

Okay, okay. True. She'd never laid eyes on these mystery men, but she'd run her hands through David's silky, wheat-colored hair, snipping away the ends, shaping it up, taming his bangs, doing her best to comb her way into his heart.

She closed her eyes, letting the letters scatter across her lap. The memory, days later, was still strong, tactile. She could feel his fine, straight hair falling through her fingers, like corn silk, completely the opposite of her own thick, curly locks. Could see once more the goose bumps that had skittered up his neck when she'd massaged his scalp. "This improves circulation and stimulates hair growth," she'd explained, grateful he couldn't see her blush.

Rubbing his scalp *did* do those things, but it also made his eyes drift shut, made him release the softest sort of moan, a sound so faint she was certain he wasn't aware of it.

She'd heard it, though. Watched his mouth twitch, his face relax, succumbing to the spell of the mesmerizing comb against his scalp. Didn't she feel the same way at the hairdressers?

Well, not quite the same way.

The real eye-opener that day was seeing what David Cahill looked like without his glasses on. It utterly destroyed her equilibrium, so much so she had to sit down and stare at him.

"David, I had no idea!"

"Idea of what?" His look convinced her he didn't have a clue.

"What amazing eyes you have." She gulped, twisting the scissors in her hand until she realized her carelessness might cost her two fingers. There he sat in Norah's kitchen, wearing a towel around

381

his shoulders and a tentative smile on his face, a look of expectancy, clearly waiting to hear what was so amazing about his eyes.

For starters, it was the brows, she decided. Thick but not bushy like Patrick's. Darker than his hair. The color of nutmeg. Carefully arched in a graceful, masculine curve. Expressive. Commanding. To think those brows had been hiding behind his wire-rimmed glasses all these months. *Years, probably.* If the man ever wore contact lenses, he'd have to fight women off with a two-by-four.

She'd be the first in line. With a chain saw.

His eyes studied her studying him. Blue-gray, she'd known that. But not *that* blue, not *that* gray. The intensity of color was startling. An entire Pacific Ocean captured in two orbs, rimmed with a narrow black circle as if to hold the waters at bay. Surrounded in purest white, then trimmed with thick lashes, the same delicious shade as his brows.

David Cahill might have grown up poor, but when it came to good looks, the man was richer than his fondest dreams. Or hers.

Belle had realized the only way the man would get a straight haircut that day was if she stood by his side, or better still, faced his back. There she had merely to fight the sensations of his hair and skin under her fingertips, and the visual appeal of his broad shoulders. Not his eyes, those captivating, knee-weakening eyes.

Rrrringggg!

The portable phone in her lap sent her scurrying to answer it, strewing letters all around her feet. Her dreamlike trance gone, she did her best to sound normal as her heart marched in time to a kettle drum beat. "Hello?"

"Hi."

The kettle drums wouldn't hush anytime soon. It was David.

"Hi yourself. Where've you been all day? Had dinner yet?" She glanced at the clock on her oak mantel. *Nine-thirty. Dinner? Good one, Belle.*

Long pause. "No, but I'm not hungry. Had a big lunch. Listen, could I come over for a few minutes? I know it's kinda late."

Her alarm would ring at six, but she could tell something was on his mind and she definitely wanted to hear about it. "Sure. I'll meet you at the front door in fifteen."

Enough time to spiff up, whip the apartment into shape, make a pot of decaf coffee. *Snap, crackle, pop.*

She yanked open the door to find him making his way up the steps, wearing his best suit and an enigmatic smile. Now that she'd seen what those eyes had to offer, his glasses dangerously disappeared. She focused on his mouth instead and realized that move didn't improve the situation one smidge.

"Come on in." She stepped aside as he eased past her, offering her cheek in case he wanted to plant a quick kiss there. He did. Too quick. The kettle drums inside her were replaced by snares beating all out of rhythm, making her light-headed as he followed her up the stairs. "My, aren't we dressed up for a Monday evening cup of decaf?"

"I didn't want to take time to change clothes."

She didn't ask for more details. Didn't want them, in fact. "I'll pour us both some coffee. Have a seat in the living room." When she walked back in balancing two mugs and a sugar bowl on a tray, she noticed he was eyeing her mail, gathered once again into a tall, tidy stack.

"Fan letters, Belle?"

She shrugged, putting down the tray. "Yeah, I suppose." Should she mention they were all from men, most wanting dates? Would that push David forward or push him away, for good? A risky business, this.

He looked up, smiling, innocent. "Mind if I read a few?"

"Ah . . . no, I guess not." Now the risk was his. *Serve him right if he gets his nose out of joint when he reads them.* On the other hand, he might pick out a few prospects and tell her to go for it, with his blessing. *What a mess.* Enough to give her a whopper of a headache.

He found the prisoner letters first. The high-schoolers, the senior citizens, the poignantly desperate ones. He seemed to relax, tossing each one aside as if in relief. When he reached the one from the med student, he slowed down. Seemed to study it more carefully.

Belle watched him out of the corner of her eye while she sipped her coffee in silence. *Say something!* He skimmed the next few, slowed down again when he got to the one from the attorney. And the professor from Emory & Henry. And the owner of Abingdon's nicest men's store.

He put them down finally and grabbed his coffee, sloshing some over the side. "Sorry." He stabbed at the spill with a paper napkin. His eyes — stormier than usual, she noted — were aimed directly at hers. "So, how are you going to answer them?"

She didn't like the accusation in his voice any more than she liked the defensiveness she heard in her own. "Most of them are getting a polite, personal, 'thanks but no thanks' letter back from me." She pointed at her stationery, heavy cream-colored paper with a bold *B* embossed at the top.

"And the others?"

You tell me, David. "I . . . don't know, yet."

They stayed like that, coffee mugs in hand, neither one moving, no one speaking, only staring at one another, for a full minute. Longer. She sensed the hairs on the back of her neck rising to attention over the spot where he'd kissed her on Christmas.

Tension swirled around them, chilling the air, forcing her to break the silence before she started visibly shaking.

"David, you came here for a reason tonight, something besides these letters. Talk to me. Above all, we're friends, remember?"

"Friends, is that it?" He let out a frustrated sigh. "You're the best friend I have, Belle. I don't mean to make light of that. I came tonight because I wanted to tell you face to face what's been going on with me."

Finally.

"I went to Charlotte today. For a job interview. With WBT."

"A *job?*" She knew she'd barked it out like a four-letter word and abruptly tried to amend herself. "An engineering job, then?" *How can he look so relieved when I'm so undone?*

"Right. Assistant to the chief. Great salary, great benefits. And of course, the equipment is state-of-the-art."

"Of course." What broadcaster didn't know WBT, *The Voice of Charlotte?* Her heart was collapsing from the pressure. Leaking along the fault lines. She was surprised she was still conscious, still able to form words that made sense. "When . . . when would you start?"

"Belle, I haven't accepted the job yet."

The leaks stopped. "You haven't?"

His oceanic eyes inched closer to hers. "No. I told them I'd need some time to think about it. To . . . finish the house, wind up some . . . details here. I told them I couldn't give them an answer until the first of March."

Five weeks. New leaks threatened to spring out along several stress points, including her eyes. "Am I a 'detail,' David?"

He slowly put his mug down on the tray, then took hers and dispatched of it as well, never losing eye contact with her for an instant. His strong hands slid around hers, wrapping them in a blanket of warmth. "You're a detail, all right, Belle. The most important one. I'm here tonight to see what you think of this offer.

Of me moving to Charlotte."

He's gotta be kidding. Doesn't he know what I think, how I feel?

David rushed to continue. She could see the excitement building in his face, hear it in his voice. "It's the job I've always hoped for. Prayed for, the last few months. A chance to use my God-given talents and the skills I've worked so hard to . . . well, it's . . . perfect."

She nodded, swallowing hard. "I remember the feeling, wanting to work at a major station, to try your wings." She also remembered how, years ago, Patrick had gotten out of her way so she could do exactly that. He'd set her free, though she hadn't known it. Then.

Is that what David needs, Lord? Is that what you're asking me to do? Let him go, give him wings?

"Don't you have anything to say, Belle?" David looked distraught at her lack of response, and no wonder.

It didn't help that she couldn't explain herself, couldn't catch her breath for the weight that pressed on her chest. She gathered up every ounce of courage she'd tucked away for a rainy day and said what needed to be said. "I'm happy for you." *And heartbroken for me.* "It's a great job. You can't turn it down." *But I wish you would. Oh, David, I wish you would!*

388

He said nothing, only brushed the palms of his hands across her cheeks in a gentle caress. His eyes said it before his lips did. "Please tell me what you want me to do."

"Oh, no, you don't." Her voice sounded like a stranger's, hoarse and monotone. "This is for you to decide. I'd never want to stand between you and such a terrific offer. And it is terrific, right?"

He mumbled the salary.

"Make that *very* terrific." She sighed, struggling to regain her voice and the tattered edges of her heart. "Go as God leads, David. We'll both make it a matter of prayer. No matter what you decide, we'll always be friends. Yes?"

Although he nodded, his eyes were saying something else, a cryptic message she couldn't decipher.

"Meanwhile, you've got to finish your house and get it on the market. Can you manage that in five weeks?"

His chin was working, his neck had tensed. "Not alone."

"I'll be glad to help." *Grab a shovel, Belle. Dig your own grave while you're at it.*

"No, thanks. I mean . . . thank you, but I'll need to hire someone. A carpenter or two, someone who knows what they're doing." He sighed. "That means a bank loan. Pray for that if you're going to pray

389

for anything. Otherwise, I'm looking at three months to complete the house, and WBT won't wait that long. They've assured me of that."

"I can pray for a loan, no problem." She could also loan him the considerable funds she'd stashed away since arriving in Abingdon. But that would be interfering with God's direction for David's life. Wouldn't it?

If the Lord provided a bank loan, then Charlotte was meant to be David's new home. And if not, then David was meant to be hers. *Thy will be done, Lord. But you know precisely which way I'm voting.*

David stood up and stretched. "Belle, it's late. Gotta let you get your beauty sleep. Not that you need it." He tugged on her braid, his eyes warm with affection, she was sure of it. "So, what are you gonna do about those Romeos who want to meet you?" He nodded in the direction of the letters.

She sighed with overstated indifference. "Guess I'll pick the most promising one and write him." *It's not nice to be sneaky.* Except sneaky always worked. "After all, with you moving to Charlotte, I'll have to find something to keep me busy."

"The most promising one, eh?" His eyes darkened considerably. "Don't do anything foolish, Belle. You never know what kind of kook might write a letter."

"Fear not. After I've chosen one, I'll let everyone read the man's letter and get their opinion. Plus, I'll meet him in a public place. Not a thing for you to worry about, David." She patted his hand, steering him toward the door. "Get a good night's sleep. Dream happy dreams of WBT and Charlotte and all that lovely money."

He stumbled out the door and down the steps, evidently thrown off by her ploy. She *would* pick one of these letters. Yes, indeed. Write the stranger back, arrange to meet him soon, throw her arms around him if necessary. Whatever it took to make David Cahill jealous, make him understand that the future he'd always hoped for was right here in his hometown.

In her arms.

The salary was awful, but she'd make certain the benefits were positively breathtaking.

Twenty-one

*The ideal love affair
is one conducted by post.*

George Bernard Shaw

By Wednesday morning, Belle had narrowed her choices down to two of her on-paper admirers — the store owner and the college professor. Stable types. Not as likely to move away to, say, North Carolina, like the med student who'd take off the minute he finished his residency.

Not as likely to sue her as the attorney might, once he figured out what she was up to.

She'd already started writing her responses, doing her best to sound interested but not *too* interested, when Burt stuck his head in the studio and tossed her the day's mail.

"Found a boyfriend yet, Belle?" His gap-toothed smile made him look like a pirate.

She couldn't help but smile back. "I'm keeping my options open."

"Couple of 'em here worth looking at." He nodded at the latest stack, then disappeared when she whirled around to introduce the next song.

Belle flipped on the mike. "It's quarter after eleven on a barely-above-freezing Wednesday, but we're keeping things cooking in the studio with this number-one-with-a-bullet hit from October 1967, the Box Tops singing 'My Baby, She Wrote Me a Letter.' "

She talked right up to the post, hitting the last word before the vocalist punched in. It always made her feel sharp, on top of her game. *Who knows who might be listening?* A future beau, for all she knew. A hot L.A. programmer, driving through town. *Nah.* She'd found her home. The perfect town. A wonderful church. Only one heartfelt desire left. *Well, two.* But the husband had to come first, then the kids.

Which brought her to the newest pile of mail. She sifted through the letters quickly, reading a few lines then moving on, intending to give them the interest they deserved later. One envelope caught her eye, though. Made her pause longer than usual. Plain white bond paper, nothing fancy. Neatly typed, probably on a computer. An Abingdon post office box for a return address, but no name. The usual postmark, a dual cancellation stamp for Bristol — Tennessee *and* Virginia — mailed yesterday.

Hmm. She sliced it along the flap, taking care not to cut the letter in half with her razor-sharp opener. The page was covered with type. *A chatty sort, eh?* Single-spaced, business-looking. Until she read the words.

January 26
Miss Belle O'Brien
WPER-FM 95
Abingdon, Virginia 24210
Dear Miss O'Brien,
   Since that first day you hit the air-waves, I've heard nearly every minute of your shows and loved them all. You have a genuine enthusiasm for life, a contagious, caring attitude, and a great laugh. I also appreciate the wise and witty style you use to handle callers, and the gentle way you let your faith shine on the air.

He had her attention. Yes, he most certainly did. The letter was signed "All Ears," so no clue there. She kept reading.

   I'm a single guy, close to thirty, been around Abingdon for a while, and still haven't found the woman of my dreams. Appearance doesn't matter to me, although judging by the photos in the paper, you're an exceptionally beautiful woman. Other things matter much more, though.

Definitely a guy with his head on straight. No question his letter beat the college prof's, hands down. Maybe she'd make this one her second choice. There was more:

I've prayed for a woman who would share my joy in Christ. Share my desire to have a family and create a life together. A woman who'd fill our house with laughter and receive my love with open arms. Who'd offer a full measure of grace for all the things I'm sure to do wrong in a lifetime of loving her. I'm hoping that woman is you, Miss O'Brien.

Belle was surprised to find her hands had grown clammy, her throat dry. This guy didn't mince words. That "receive my love with open arms" part touched her at the core. And what a clear, unapologetic faith! The Lord knew how much she needed that, to keep her strong, keep her on track, to lead by example.

Clearly, this letter was her first choice. Maybe her only one.

In return for her love and affection, that woman would have my whole heart as her dwelling place. My complete attention would be given to her needs and hurts. My utter devotion would be hers, guaranteed for a lifetime. My boundless passion would ever be at her command.

How could she be getting teary over a stranger's letter?

And how dare the Box Tops decide to stop singing so suddenly like that? She jammed another button on the control board and segued directly into the next song, throwing the music format right out the window. Junior Walker and the All-Stars crooned, "What Does It Take to Win Your Love?" while she finished the letter, sniffing all the way.

I'm not a perfect man, Miss O'Brien. Not even close. But my spirit tells me that you are all these things and more, a woman to be reckoned with, a woman to be cherished. I've listened carefully, and I believe I'm a pretty good judge of character. Yours is priceless.

Could we take a chance and find out more about one another? Name the time and place and we'll meet. Somewhere you'll feel safe. If it's the Lord's will, I hope someday you'll discover that the safest place you could ever be is in my arms.

With respect and admiration,
All Ears in Abingdon

She used the letter to fan herself while
her head was spinning. *Who is this guy?*
Surely not a real person. Still, there *was* a
post office box number. It may have been
written on a computer, but not *by* a computer.

Nope, this was a real man. Close to
thirty, he said. Single, local, a committed
Christian. *And what a way he has with
words!* Belle kept fanning her heated
cheeks and punched up another tune, her
third in a row, this one a classic from
1966, the Righteous Brothers' "You're My
Soul and Inspiration."

Without warning, the studio door burst
open. Startled, she slapped the letter
against her chest and spun around.
"David!"

He stood there, hands on hips, looking
like nothing short of a major-market engineer. In other words, unhappy with the on-
air talent. "When I heard three in a row
and no Belle, I thought perhaps you'd
fallen asleep at the switch." One expressive
eyebrow arched above his glasses. "Are you
planning on talking today, or did we
change to a 'less talk, more rock' format
while I was gone Monday?"

The nerve of this man! She refolded the

letter and slipped it into her purse, intentionally delaying her answer while she built up a good head of steam. "Since when do you worry about what I say or don't say on the air, not to mention which music clock I'm working with?"

His shrug was clearly meant to infuriate her further. "Burt asked me to keep an eye on things while he's meeting with a client."

"Humph." She'd turned her back to him, stacking up carts and doing her best to give him the cold shoulder. Two of them, in fact, plus a cold neck. A very cold neck.

He was standing directly behind her now. If she backed up, she could roll over his toes. Twice, if she rolled fast enough.

"Speaking of meeting people, Belle, you looked pretty interested in that letter when I came in. Is he the lucky guy you've chosen to meet?"

She tipped her head back and looked straight up at him. Confound it, the brute even looked handsome upside down. "What's it to you, I'd like to know?"

He spread his hands apart. "Not a thing. Curious is all." His tone lost its teasing edge as he slowly turned her chair around and knelt down so they were eye to eye.

Her bravado slipped away as quickly as it'd appeared.

"Do me a favor, will you, Belle?"

She gulped and nodded. *Anything except throw that letter away.*

"Today is the day I meet with the bank. About a loan for the house, so I can hire a couple of guys to help me finish in time for WBT. Nobody else knows about the offer but you. Nobody. Will you pray for me? In fact, will you pray *with* me, right now?"

She nodded. "Let me get in and out of this next commercial set before Patrick comes in here asking for my head on a platter."

David stayed where he was while she spun around and did a quick back-sell, listing the songs and artists of her three-in-a-row "special music sweep." She read the weather and a liner card, then punched up the first commercial, relieved to let the equipment handle everything else automatically.

"Now." She turned back, her heart skipping a beat when she discovered he'd slipped to both knees, inches away from her. "Well, well, just what I've always dreamed of. A man kneeling at my feet."

"Get used to it, Belle. Every man in town is willing."

Not every man. "Let's pray."

They bowed their heads and David went first, begging the Lord for mercy when he met with the bank at three o'clock, asking

399

that the loan officer be fair and hear him out.

Belle echoed his prayers, adding her own silent entreaties between the lines. *Your will be done, Lord. If he's supposed to go to Charlotte, let everything happen that needs to today at the bank. If it doesn't happen, then give me the courage to ask him to stay, Lord. For me.*

Belle could hear the stop set ending, her cue to be ready to introduce the next song. She cleared her throat and clicked on the mike. "From 1967, one of Dionne Warwick's dozen top-twenty hits. 'I Say a Little Prayer for You' on Oldies 95 W-P-E-R."

She winked at David making his way toward the door, obviously amused by her selection, and turned off the mike. "Hey, it's my show, right? Let me know how it goes at the bank."

Minutes later, she stole a glance at the letter sticking up out of her purse. *Very tempting, that.* Would it hurt to meet him? If David *did* get the loan, if he *did* take the job, wouldn't it be wonderful to have such a man as a friend? *Don't fool yourself, Belle. You are not thinking brotherly thoughts about this guy, whoever he is.*

The truth was, she felt guilty for thinking about him at all. *And I wouldn't be thinking about him if David weren't so cir-*

cumspect about his feelings! If he'd simply say, "I'm leaving town, it's been nice," she'd be fine with it. In a few years.

Or, if he'd announce, "We're getting married and moving to Charlotte," she'd be fine with that, too. And be dressed in thirty seconds.

One thing was certain. Despite her promise to David to let everyone read this letter and give her an opinion, she intended to keep it safely tucked away from prying eyes. Norah would think she was crazy to consider meeting a stranger like that. Patrick would insist she have a police escort. Heather would tell her to throw the letter away, then dig it out of the trash and write the man herself. Especially after Heather's disastrous movie date with her not-so-Happy Together winner. The tub of hot buttered popcorn in her blond hair was apparently only the beginning of Heather's dreadful night at the cinema, poor thing.

And David would undoubtedly be jealous if he saw this listener's letter . . .

Which was why, come to think of it, he'd be the one person she *would* show the letter to, the one person she'd tell about her plans to meet the man. A little jealousy might prompt David to articulate his own feelings for her. Though she doubted he'd be half as eloquent as her mysterious "All Ears."

Hmm. Hope they're not big ears.

Belle reached for the letter again while the Casinos waited in the wings to sing their one big hit, "Then You Can Tell Me Good-bye." She went through the motions of introducing the tune as her eyes scanned the opening words of a letter she suspected she'd be reading off and on all afternoon.

Dear Miss O'Brien,
Since that first day you hit the airwaves, I've heard nearly every minute of your shows and loved them all.

David sat in the outer office of the bank, cooling his jets, waiting his turn. He gazed through the wooden venetian blinds. The afternoon sun was doing its best to shine, eclipsed by heavy cloud cover. More snow in the forecast, Belle had announced. *Welcome to midwinter in the Virginia Highlands.*

The marble floor glowed with the rich patina of age. And money. Abingdon Bank and Trust had been around a long time. David, who kept his checking account at a bank in Bristol, had chosen this location for two reasons. First, because Patrick banked here and assured him his name would help grease the skids. David hadn't told Patrick why he needed to borrow money for the house remodeling, just that he did. Patrick hadn't batted an eye or asked a single question.

The other reason he'd picked this place was simpler: Sherry's father didn't work there. The last David remembered, Robison was at Citizens First Bank. Or whatever their name was now. Banks seemed to put their names up with Velcro lately. He hadn't seen the man since he got back to town in October. Who knows? Robison might not live in Abingdon anymore. In any case, this wasn't his bank and that was all that mattered.

David read over his copy of the loan application again, filled out with care the day before. Although he'd only been employed four months, his college and service records were top-notch. He'd worked hard to make sure of it.

His references were chosen with care: Patrick Reese, because he was his boss, and Norah Silver-Smyth, because she was a class act who knew the whole town. As long as his loan officer was some young guy who didn't know a Cahill from a katydid, he figured he'd be as good a risk as the next guy.

His house would be collateral. The loan money would go for labor. It would take about ten thousand dollars, he'd calculated, every dime of which would be paid back the minute the house was sold. The

403

way houses were moving in Abingdon, it would be gone in sixty days and he'd still come out ahead. Way ahead, if the Lord was merciful.

The door opened and a thirty-something man in a striped tie and yellow shirt stepped out. *Perfect.*

"Welcome, Mr. Cahill. Sorry to keep you waiting. My manager and I will be happy to sit down and discuss your loan application now." The young banker waved him into a corner office, one with thick blue carpet, natural woodwork polished to an elegant sheen, and tasteful, gilt-edged paintings lining the walls.

The decor was meant to intimidate. In David's case, the effort was superfluous. The man sitting behind the huge mahogany desk was intimidating enough. It wasn't his height, though he was taller than average. Or his strong jawline, carved out of the same marble they'd used for the bank lobby floor.

No, it was who he was. And what he stood for.

"Mr. Cahill," the young loan officer was saying, perhaps sensing a change in the atmosphere and wanting to do his best to smooth things over. "Meet our brand-new vice president of the loan division, Mr. George Robison. Sir, this is David Cahill."

The man behind the desk stood, a column of gray granite in his Brooks Brothers suit. His cold eyes shrank to black slits. "No introduction necessary, Chuck. I know Mr. Cahill and his family well. Leave us alone, please. I'll take things from here."

Belle placed the two letters side by side. His exquisite letter to her; her own much-labored-over response to him. The man, whoever he was, had clearly poured his heart out to her. She wished she could do the same. But he had the advantage. He'd heard her on the air, every day, for months. Had read a long article about her, seen her photos. Maybe had stopped by her remote broadcast at Dollar General, not introducing himself, just hanging around to watch.

Ugh. She didn't want to think about that. Gave her the willies.

Her show over, Belle was hiding in the production studio hoping no one would come looking for her until she'd gotten this letter safely signed, sealed, and delivered to the post office.

Quick, before she chickened out.

Quick, before someone read the two letters, his and hers, and declared her certifiably crazy. Her plan was iffy, no doubt. But not dangerous. Meeting him at the

Grill would keep things from ever going over the edge.

Besides, she had to do it. Had to get David's attention, force his hand. *Wouldn't it be easier to simply confess your feelings to him?* The thought had nagged at her all afternoon. Sure, it would be easier. But WBT had complicated things. If he really wanted to move, she had to give him the space to do so. Going with him was out of the question, since their relationship hadn't reached the happily-ever-after stage.

Yet here she sat writing a letter to a stranger who was already talking about marriage! She might not have the talent for acting, but no question she had the artistic temperament for it. *Up, down, up, down . . .*

Taking a breath to steel her nerves, she scanned her letter for the fourth time that hour.

January 27
Dear All Ears,
I must admit, your letter got my attention. Such a wordsmith you are! It's odd to have you know so much about me when I know so little about you.
Thanks for your kind words about my show, in particular for noticing that I'm a Christian. I'm ashamed to admit my faith got put on a back burner for a few years, but God has faithfully

waited for me to come to my senses and make him first in my life. I've found a great church family here in Abingdon and am learning what it means to trust God completely.

Then why wasn't she trusting God to work things out with David? The thought needled her conscience. She ignored the jabbing pain and kept reading.

Your desire to find a godly wife is admirable. And appealing, I must admit. Only the Lord knows if I could be that woman. The qualities you offer in return are generous to say the least. Love, affection, attention, passion, devotion . . . you must know those things would ring any woman's chimes. Especially a woman named Belle!

Was that too much? Too positive, too encouraging? She didn't want him to think she was ready for the altar. Heaven forbid. *And you will forbid it, won't you, Lord? Stop me from doing anything rash and losing David in the process?*

Maybe this wasn't such a great idea. She pressed on, hoping the next section would let him know her heart was already spoken for.

I'm not perfect either, Mr. Ears. I'm

also not as lonely as the article sug-
gested. There's someone special in
my life, a man I've known for three
months. I'm learning to care for him
more deeply every day. Because he
might be moving away this spring,
things are up in the air with us right
now. It seems only fair to warn you,
though, that my heart, my mind, my
soul are filled with thoughts of him
around the clock. Perhaps by the time
we meet, that will be resolved, one
way or the other. For both our sakes, I
sincerely hope so.

Looking forward to hearing back
from you soon and learning more
about what makes you tick. If you're
serious about meeting me, I'll be at
the Court Street Grill having dinner
Friday at five o'clock. Thanks again
for your lovely letter.

With gratitude,
Belle O'Brien

There. She'd been honest, fair, and encouraging, right? The door stood open for
him to walk through, as long as he understood what the situation was.

What is the situation, Belle? Simple. She
wanted this kind stranger to write back immediately. Agree to meet her. Turn out to
be almost everything she ever wanted in a

man. *He couldn't be everything. That was David.* But enough to make David see the writing on the wall. To take one solid step in her direction. *One step, Lord. I'll run the rest of the way.*

David had to make the first move so she'd know it was God's will and according to his plan. She'd gone off on enough tangents without touching base with God first. Not this time. *Your way or no way, Lord.*

Belle laughed out loud, filling the four empty corners of the brightly lit production studio. *Not "My way or the highway"? You really have made some progress.*

She signed the letter with a flourish of her dark green pen and folded the thick, creamy paper with care. Sliding it inside the matching envelope, she sealed it with a lick and a promise and flipped it over to add his address. Only a post office box, no name, as secretive and mysterious as he was.

"Your turn, Mr. Ears." She headed out the door as she consulted her watch. *Minutes away from four.* The post office was a twenty-minute walk. She'd have to hustle to get there in time to buy a stamp and get her letter in the mail. *Good thing the snow hasn't started yet.* She bundled up, calling out a general good-bye to all within earshot, and charged down the steps.

A cold, biting wind greeted her when she

reached the street. Tugging her scarf tighter around her neck, she put her head into the wind blowing hard out of the west and pointed herself toward the post office, ten blocks away. Maybe she'd walk as far as the house and jump in her car. *Nah.* It might take longer to find a parking space. As David had reminded her a hundred years ago or so, *tempus fugit.*

Flying along Main Street as if her boots had wings, she passed Abingdon Bank and Trust, wondering how things had gone with David's loan. An honorable, hard-working guy like him? Surely a no-brainer for the loan officer. Naturally they'd given him the money.

Which meant if she was going to get David's attention before his eyes were permanently fixed on WBT and North Carolina, she'd have to make tracks.

Twenty-two

Truth or tact? You have to choose.
Most times they are not compatible.

Eddie Cantor

David remained standing even after Chuck, the junior loan officer, backed out of the corner office, tail tucked firmly between his legs. Even after George Robison indicated by a perfunctory wave toward a hard wooden chair that David was expected to sit.

David preferred to stand.

This wasn't the time or the place or the circumstance he would have chosen, but this meeting was destined to happen someday. He would not face it sitting down.

The banker did sit, finally, pulling a slim file folder toward him and opening it with some ceremony. David could see it was his loan application, a copy of his bank statement, a letter from Patrick stating his employment terms, and his own sketch and photos of the house and property. Everything in order.

Resting his elbows on the paperwork, George Robison steepled his fingers and trained his metallic gaze on him, not meeting David's eyes but focusing on a point in the middle of his forehead, shutting down any avenue of communication.

The corners of the man's mouth had not budged from the firm, hard line David had seen there when he'd walked into the office. The older man managed to maintain that line when he spoke. "You know, of course, that a loan on this property is out of the question."

David felt his stomach drop to his knees. He gritted his teeth to keep his disappointment from showing. "Why is that?" *He knew why, he just wanted to hear the man say it.*

"When the property was originally sold to Patrick Edward Reese last September, that shack you live in was appraised at one thousand dollars. Not worth the wood and nails it's made out of, in other words. I believe it was of such little value it was slated to be torn down. Am I right?"

"That was the original plan, yes. I offered Mr. Reese three thousand dollars for two acres and the house. You'll see the property sale agreement in that file folder. The one under your elbow." David could not, would not be intimidated by this man. He'd followed the law to the letter in this real estate deal with Patrick. Had already paid him off, owned the house and

412

land, free and clear.

What had Sherry called her father? *Mr. George Almighty Robison?* No way, not for this radio engineer. There was only one Almighty in David's life, the only ultimate authority he answered to.

"A shack is still a shack," Robison insisted. "Hardly worth my risking a ten-thousand-dollar loan on a pile of wood that could come crashing down around your ears while the unpaid debt crashes around mine."

David clenched his fists by his side, struggling for control. In the recesses of his memory, the list he'd been studying at Curt's house unfurled like a banner: love, joy, peace, patience, kindness, goodness, faithfulness, gentleness, self-control. *I need the whole fruit basket today, Lord.*

"Mr. Robison, have you looked over the recent photos of the house? I think you'll see a marked improvement, all according to code, all done with the proper permits and inspections. I had a realtor do a walk-through, and she estimated with the completed work done in time for the big spring real estate season, the house will be worth six or seven times the amount of the loan I'm asking for. She suggested a ninety-day balloon loan. Pay it all off at once, upon sale or three months, whichever came first."

The man looked as if he'd swallowed a live weasel, so pronounced was his disgust. "Which realtor is that, pray tell?" When David shared her name, Robison merely shook his head. "These weekend open-house types are hardly licensed appraisers, let alone mortgage loan specialists."

David cleared his throat, fighting for time and begging for patience. "I'd be happy to pay for an official appraisal."

"Which would be a requirement if we were proceeding with this loan application. Which we are not."

Here we go. "I'm afraid your reasoning is not, by law, sufficient to turn down this application without serious consideration, Mr. Robison." He prayed his nights in the library studying the current laws for borrowing money in the state of Virginia would pay off for him now.

The veins in the older man's neck were throbbing as he rose to his feet. "What did you say to me?"

"I said I need a detailed response, in writing. Proof that credit reports were done, references checked —"

"*References?* Cahill, the last time we saw one another, I handed you a check and an ultimatum. Do you recall what that was?"

Finally, Robison had gotten to the core issue. It had nothing to do with now. It

414

had everything to do with then. The black slits that served for the man's eyes had acquired a glint that stiffened David's spine. He made certain his words were equally straight, like arrows, aimed at the heart.

"Yes, Mr. Robison, I recall it well. The date was August 28. The check was for one hundred dollars, which I ripped in two, if *you* recall. And the message you gave me was to leave town and never tell a soul about Sherry's pregnancy."

"And?"

"And that's exactly what I did, sir." *Except for Belle.*

"You did much more than that, young man!" The banker's jowly face was purplish and shaking. "You drove Sherry away. Drove a wedge between her and the parents who loved her, who gave her life and every luxury she could ever want. And she threw it away for what? For *you.* For a lousy, worthless Cahill!" He leaned over and pounded his desk, punctuating his words. "She never called. She never wrote. We don't know if she's dead or alive. Because of you. You and your no-good drunk of a father —"

"I will *not* have you speak of my father that way!" The words rushed out before David could stop them. "My father was many things he wasn't proud of, but he was never ashamed to have me as his son."

415

The truth of that hit David so hard he bent over slightly, as if he'd been kicked and all the air knocked out of him.

Say the rest of it, David.

"Sherry might have stayed in Abingdon, sir, if she'd thought her father felt the same way about her. But she didn't. Your shame drove her away, not me. And your pride kept her away. I haven't seen her in nine years myself, Mr. Robison. But I do know this. She's definitely alive."

George Robison dropped to his chair, clearly stunned. David was feeling a bit overwhelmed himself. He never thought he'd find himself defending his dad, but he'd done so. Was glad of it, too. Never imagined that Sherry had severed all contact with her parents. Hard to say who was the more stubborn one, Sherry or her father. Both were cut out of the same cloth, that was obvious.

Watching the banker wrestle with the news of his daughter's well-being, David was suddenly struck with another blinding bit of truth. *Joshua.* If Sherry's family didn't know about her whereabouts, it was almost certain they didn't know about Josh.

His son. George's grandson.

It wasn't his place to tell them, either. Sherry had kept the news to herself for a reason. David was undoubtedly looking at that reason right now.

Mr. Robison composed himself. The steel gleam in his eye returned, sharper than ever. "I appreciate knowing that my daughter is alive. Rest assured I'll find her, whether she wants to be found or not. Meanwhile, I suggest you look for your money elsewhere, Cahill. There's some fool out there who will loan it to you, though a few choice words from me ought to dry up your financial prospects in this town in a hurry."

He stood and swaggered toward David, striking a pose meant to menace. "As for this office, I never want to see your face darken my door again." He squinted at David, turning his features to stone. "I believe you've heard me say those words before, boy. Should have listened then. Listen now."

David had no need to see this man again, ever. That's what made it easy to extend his hand as he turned to leave. Easy to drop it when his offer of a handshake was ignored.

He'd listened, he'd learned, he'd obeyed God.

That was all that mattered.

Weary from doing battle, he stumbled out into the lengthening shadows of a late afternoon, bone tired yet oddly elated. Granted, his loan hadn't been approved.

There's an understatement! Not a dime, not a dollar. He laughed to himself and headed on foot in the direction of the post office, needing the exercise, the air in his lungs, the chance for his head to clear.

No wonder he was elated.

He'd faced the darkest part of his past and survived. With his faith still intact, his honor still his own. Never mind the money. There were other ways to get the house finished in time. He'd work around the clock. See if WBT would stretch their offer to March 15. Ask Patrick for a short-term loan, a couple thousand to buy him a much-needed transfusion of skilled labor. *Where there's a will . . .* Yeah, God's will.

Somehow he'd make it happen. George Robison wasn't going to ride him out of town on a rail, not this time.

He crossed the street, dodging cars and wintry winds, practically jogging to keep warm. A quick look at his watch told him the post office would be closing any minute. No matter. He only needed to check his mailbox and drop a stamped letter in the slot, and the lobby was always open for that.

Trotting across Wall Street, he dug in his pocket for his ring of keys, then pushed open the glass door into the post office. The warm air welcomed him like a friend. He swung left into the first row of boxes and collided with a small woman wearing a familiar green coat.

"Belle!"

"David?"

"What are you doing here?"

Their question, in unison, bounced off the metal walls full of mailboxes that surrounded the narrow space.

"You first." Belle tugged her purse closer to her side, her cheeks pink.

"I stopped by to check my mailbox, like I do every afternoon on the way home from work." He fiddled with the keys, searching for the long gold one that would open his mailbox. "And you?"

"I needed to buy a stamp. To mail a letter." Belle looked like the cat that had been caught seconds after swallowing the canary, stray feathers tickling the corners of her mouth in a most charming way. "It's addressed to a man whose mailbox is right along this row."

"No kidding." He looked around as if such a man might leap out of a corner, key at the ready. "Who is he?"

"He signed his letter 'All Ears.' "

David felt his eyebrows slip under his bangs. *Well, well.* " 'All Ears,' huh?"

Belle dug in her purse and pulled out a white folded paper. "Since this was your idea, maybe you'd like to read it."

"*My* idea?"

"Remember? You agreed to review the letters I'm responding to in a more . . . uh, personal fashion. I've decided this is the only guy I'll write back to in any encouraging way. The only one I'll agree to meet."

He unfolded the letter with a snap. "So we're meeting him now?"

Belle sniffed, looking over his hands as if she hadn't already read this letter, probably many times. "Well, *I'm* meeting him. If he's willing."

David thought he'd been through every emotion possible during his loan interview with George Robison. It seemed there were a few more sentiments he'd be exploring this afternoon, starting with the ice running through his veins right now. Belle seemed excited about meeting this man. A stranger to her, and an audacious one, judging by the tone of the letter David was reading.

"Why are you doing this, Belle?" He hadn't meant for his voice to sound so abrupt, his words so demanding.

She blinked. "You know why. Because . . . because you . . ."

He grabbed her shoulders, feeling them tense up through the heavy wool coat. "Because I have a chance to better myself? Because you don't care whether I stay or go?"

"How dare you put words in my mouth!" Belle's eyes snapped as sharply as her words, gold sparks of fire that illuminated the dim corners of the empty post office.

He let go of her shoulders, aware he was squeezing them hard, probably hurting her. "Then *you* put the words there." His tone was more insistent than belligerent. Could she hear the difference? Was there any? "Belle, tell me why you want to meet a man you don't even know."

When I know you. When I care for you.

He was an imbecile to let this foolishness go forward when he could stop it right now. By telling her the truth.

"All right. I *will* tell you why." She looked around, clearly desperate for a chair to fall into. Or a big, dark hole. Why had he pushed her so hard? Whatever she was going to say, he deserved.

"I'm meeting this man because . . ." She was fading again. "Because I'm trying my best to let you move to Charlotte with no strings attached." Her voice caught. "To give you the freedom to follow your heart wherever it leads, without confusing the issue with . . . with . . ."

He kissed her.

For a long time.

It was the only way to make sure she didn't say something they'd both regret. *No strings?* Was the woman crazy? She had more strings tied around his fingers

421

and toes than the Lilliputians used on Gulliver.

Belle started to pull away. The heat in her cheeks told him she was embarrassed. *Too bad.* He pulled her toward him again, mashing his mouth on hers, more worried about staking his claim than impressing her with finesse. She didn't pull back, wasn't fighting him.

When he finally let her go, they were both breathing hard, warming the air around them so thoroughly that his glasses steamed up. He took them off to wipe them dry while Belle stared at him with a faraway look in her eyes. Maybe it just seemed far away because he couldn't see farther than two feet.

He slipped them back on and she offered a crooked little smile. "David, have I ever told you what amazing eyes you have?"

"Yes, ma'am, you have." He pressed his lips against her forehead, wanting closure, a seal of approval. "Still think you wanna meet this Mr. Ears?"

"Too late." She sighed, buttoning her coat and moving toward the door. "I've already mailed the letter. Friday evening at the Grill. Five o'clock. Maybe he won't get the letter in time. Might not show up, either." She backed toward the door, the darkening sky providing a backdrop through the double panes of glass. "See

422

you at work tomorrow."

"Wait for me." He dropped a letter in the outgoing slot, then quickly emptied out his box, keeping one eye on Belle as he flipped through the few pieces of mail. *Nothing from California.* All he needed to know for the moment.

He jammed the letters in his pocket and hurried after her, steering her into the parking lot then tucking her arm snugly inside his own. "How 'bout I walk you home? Never know what kind of crazies might be out this evening."

Belle laughed. Loudly. "None of them could be crazier than the man who just assaulted me in an empty post office."

"Assaulted? The very idea." He jerked his chin up. She wasn't the only one who could be dramatic. "Did you scream? Call for help? Try to get away?"

She dropped her head, shoulders shaking, still laughing. "No. No. And never mind." She shot him a sideways grin. "I'll bet Norah has some soup on tonight. Are you game?"

Norah's soup? Belle's company? He tipped his glasses down to give her a full-court wink. "Such silly questions you ask, woman."

Norah heard them on her porch before she heard the doorbell, their voices ringing

423

in the frosty air. *David and Belle.* Just as it should be. She reached up for another two soup bowls, ladled the aromatic potato cheese chowder into the deep-dish stoneware and carried them into the dining room as they pushed open the front door, right on cue.

"Welcome home!" She loved seeing the looks of astonishment on their faces as they rounded the corner and found their soup waiting. "Thought you might be hungry."

"Norah, you are . . ." David scratched his head, seemingly at a loss for words. " 'Incredible' doesn't capture it, but it's a start. I guess some bread would be too much to hope — oh my. Look at this."

She floated back into the room, a long cloth-covered basket in hand. "Hoska bread, fresh out of the oven. Somebody's favorite, I recall."

"Mine!" her guests chimed, laughing as they tore off their coats and scarves, eagerly preparing to break bread together.

Norah slid into the seat at the head of the table and reached for their hands. "Pray with me." They bowed their heads and she offered a simple, heartfelt entreaty for the Lord's blessing on their lives. More prayers went heavenward than those that were spoken aloud. *Knit them together, Lord. Let them see you in each other's hearts, so they'll know your will and de-*

sign for their future.

The prayer finished, they dove into the soup, spoons first.

"Speaking of the future," Norah said, then realized they wouldn't have a clue what she was talking about. "Ah . . . the future of . . . uh, your house, David. How is that coming? I know you were looking into some options for finishing it more quickly."

"You mean the loan I applied for?" His voice was subdued, pensive. "Thanks for letting me list you as a reference, Norah. Unfortunately, they turned me down."

They couldn't have. "They what?"

"David, why didn't you tell me?" Belle looked suitably crushed for a brief moment, until another expression dawned on her face, like the sun coming up over the Blue Ridge on an absolutely clear morning. "Wait! That means —" Belle clamped down on her lips and refused to say another word, content to beam her rays in David's direction while Norah merely observed the sunrise in the young woman's face.

My, if it isn't Epiphany all over again.

Norah pressed the banking subject a bit further. "It's odd they'd refuse you the loan, David, when they clearly hadn't done their homework. They never called me about that reference, for instance. Nor Pat-

425

rick, to my knowledge."

His face grew still. "I'm not surprised."

Norah felt a slight twitch in her chest, the one she always trusted to warn her when something wasn't right. "Who was the loan officer in charge? If you don't mind my asking."

"George." He swallowed his soup with a noisy gulp. "George Robison."

Norah watched Belle's expression. No reaction. The name meant nothing to her. *Good, good.* It meant everything to Norah. The whole ugly picture was prominently on display.

"I see. Wasn't he at Citizens First for all those years?"

"Uh . . . I believe so." David's eyes reflected a pain Norah comprehended only too well.

I know, I understand, Norah wanted to say. But she couldn't. She wasn't supposed to know about a certain banker's daughter and a son born out of wedlock and an honorable young man raised in a house full of sorrow, determined to do the right thing, financially and every other way. She should have been privy to none of that confidential information, whispered to her by the town busybody.

Yet here she sat, knowing what she knew. Knowing what had to be done to right a very old wrong.

Twenty-three

*You don't know a woman until
you've had a letter from her.*

Ada Leverson

Norah's heels clicked across the marble floor, a muted staccato amid the secretarial buzz that greeted another workday at Abingdon Bank and Trust. Yes, the receptionist assured her, Mr. Robison was in his office this morning. Would Mrs. Silver-Smyth kindly take a seat?

She would. For the moment.

Norah slipped off her kid gloves and slid them into the deep pockets of the ankle-length fox coat. Her look was calculated, intentional, an art form Randolph Smyth had taught her fifteen years earlier. Appearance was everything, he'd insisted. Power. Money. Influence.

What a lot of rubbish.

Today, though, Norah wanted — needed — to appear influential. For one reason. She was determined to make a difference. Though dressed to kill, she prayed a funeral wouldn't be necessary. Smothering George Robison in guilt was not her idea of a good time, but helping him do the right thing? That activity suited her to a perfect T.

The heavy paneled door to the corner office swung open and George marched out, wearing an expensive suit and a smile that went no further than the corners of his mouth. When his black eyes landed on her, they practically danced, taking in her luxurious coat and fashionable attire in one long head-to-toe leer.

"Mrs. Silver-Smyth!" He offered his hand to her, which Norah pretended not to see as she swept past him and into his office, gently shaking her silver head for sheer effect.

"Nice office, George." She gave the room a cursory glance and tossed her slim leather purse onto a wooden chair. *Was David forced to sit there for interrogation yesterday?* "Seems you've moved up in the world. This space is decidedly more impressive than the one you had at Citizens."

He looked suddenly unsure of himself, as if he couldn't decide whether to stand or sit, smile or not smile. He finally sat. And smiled, though she noticed it didn't improve his features in the least. A frown surely waited in the wings. She'd watch it move center stage soon enough.

"What brings you to my office this morning, Norah?"

He'd used her first name deliberately, no

doubt wanting to put them on equal footing.

"Well, George —" She flashed a smile meant to tip things in her favor again — "It seems a grievous error has been made."

His faced paled slightly. "By the bank?"

"No. By you." She let that sink in, watched his brow furrow, imagined him mentally sorting through papers and calendars, looking for some detail that might have slipped past him.

Finally he shrugged. "I'm afraid you'll have to tell me, Norah. What have I done?"

This time? She could point out so many. The years George and Randolph — husband number two — spent quietly shifting assets so that when Mr. Smyth left her for a younger woman he took most of their resources with him. Then there were the dozens of occasions when George had pledged to sponsor one community event or another, only to leave Norah high and dry when it came time to produce the funds.

Still, nothing came close to his most recent misstep. The others had been bad business decisions on his part. It was only money. She'd managed. This one involved a young man who'd paid dearly for one mistake.

And paid. And paid.

She made sure George was staring straight at her, then began. "Yesterday, David Cahill came here looking for a loan. A small, reasonable loan any hardworking homeowner might request. Very little risk involved. But you turned him down. Because nine years ago he loved your daughter Sherry."

"What . . . you . . . !" George was sputtering.

"He wasn't good enough, was he? A Cahill, poorest of Abingdon's poor. So you've decided he isn't good enough now. Is that about the size of it?"

"This is categorically none of your business!"

For an instant, she imagined herself in David's shoes, literally standing in the same spot yesterday, facing the wrath of this man. *Brave soul.* She was in no danger whatsoever. George Robison couldn't touch her. Couldn't hurt her the way he'd undoubtedly hurt David.

"You're exactly right." She tuned her voice to its coolest tone. "It isn't one bit of my business. It is *your* business, however. Loaning money to those who deserve it. Investing in the future." She leaned on his desk, manicured hands fanned out across its mahogany surface. "Your daughter's future, for starters."

"What about my daughter?" His bellow

had a trace of panic behind it; then a dark expression crossed the man's face. "Norah, have you been consorting with her all these years, helping her hide from the family who loves her?"

"Certainly not." *Hide?* "Am I to understand that you haven't seen Sherry since she left town?"

He slumped in his chair, staring out the window. Things were worse than Norah imagined. *Does he even know about his grandson?*

When George spoke, his voice was so low she almost missed the words. "We haven't seen or heard from Sherry in nine years. At first we were furious with her. Didn't try to find her. Figured she'd come crawling back for money eventually." His features stiffened. "She didn't. We didn't know where to start looking. What town, what state."

"At what point did you stop trying to find her?"

He sighed heavily, his expensive suit wrinkling around him, as if it had suddenly grown too big for his drooping shoulders.

"We gave up when it became clear she didn't want to be found. Didn't want to come back."

"And you blame David for this?"

He straightened up, bristling. "Who else? He's the one who . . . who . . ."

431

"George, really." Norah shook her head, letting a faint smile stretch across her lips. "It takes two and you know it. They were impulsive kids."

His eyes narrowed. "You knew? You knew why she left? About the pregnancy?" His voice rose to an anguished pitch. "Who else knows? The whole town?"

"I doubt anyone knew at the time." She gave a dismissive wave and tossed a quick prayer that the woman who'd told her in the strictest confidence had let the tale-telling end with her. "Sherry left town so quickly and then, at your prodding, so did David. I've certainly not heard it bandied about. The key is, the two of them knew what happened and knew it was wrong. Still, in their own ways, David and Sherry have both tried to do the right thing since then."

"What 'right thing' is that?"

"Caring for Joshua."

George clambered to his feet, sending his heavy leather chair careening against the bookcase behind his desk. *"Joshua?* Joshua *who?"*

"Joshua Robison." *Lord, give me strength.* "Your eight-year-old grandson. Sherry's son. David's son." She paused, not wanting to rush his reaction, wanting it to sink in. "I'm sorry Sherry didn't tell you herself, George." *Very sorry.*

She continued to wait, letting the truth do its work on the man's heart. Surely he had one somewhere in there, buried beneath years of denial and pain. And guilt.

"Here's something else that will surprise you. David has been sending her money for eight long years. Even when Sherry didn't want it. Or him." Norah was improvising now, less certain of her facts, but more clear than ever about the desired outcome.

George's voice became a mere shadow of its former snarling self. "Cahill sent her money?"

"I have it from a reliable source that David sent Sherry two hundred dollars a month. For eight years."

Ever the banker, George stretched across his desk for a calculator and punched in the numbers. Sinking back down into his chair, he whistled under his breath. "Nearly twenty thousand dollars."

She nodded at the sum. "A lot of money for an airman to come up with. Or a college student. Or a radio engineer, trying to remodel his first house." Norah patted the man's clammy hand and straightened up, feeling the atmosphere in the room growing lighter. *Glad you're here, Lord. He's coming around, isn't he?*

"A grandson." George kept nodding his head, swallowing hard. His eyes, black as they were, had a watery sheen Norah hadn't noticed before. "No wonder Sherry didn't come back. I told her . . . I told her the only way she could come back is if she . . . if she came . . . alone."

Regret was stamped across his face like a brand.

Norah blinked before her own eyes betrayed her and added a slight smile to her voice, hoping to soften the hard edges of truth. "Good thing she's as stubborn as you are, then. Carrying the child to term, creating a home for him. It takes a good dose of starch to raise a child by yourself." She stole a quick look at her watch and the appointment book open on his desk. "You have a busy day ahead, I see. And a great deal to think about." *Here we go, Lord.* "May I offer an idea worth considering?"

He nodded slowly.

"This isn't something you *have* to do, understand. Merely a suggestion of what an honorable man might do. What a good father might do."

"Oh?" He cleared his throat. "What's that?"

She slipped a silver-edged note card from her purse. On it was a recommendation for him to mull over, one she'd come up with after fretting over it all through the dark hours of the morning. She placed it in front of him without another word and watched him read it. Within seconds, the veins in his neck were bulging, either from his anger or her audacity, Norah wasn't sure which. She pressed on before she lost her nerve.

"David did what you weren't willing to do. He claimed the child as his own. Put his reputation and his money on the line to do it." *Almost there, Norah.* "Now's your chance to step up to the plate. Show your daughter she's forgiven. Show David he's respected for doing the right thing when he didn't have to. Show Joshua he's loved by a family he probably doesn't know exists."

Norah pulled his appointment book toward her and flipped it over to Friday. "You've got an opening tomorrow at four o'clock. I'll see that David is here, waiting in the lobby. Handle it as you see fit, George. Just remember this —" She moved toward the door, then turned for her parting shot of grace — "You didn't know the whole situation. Now you do. For whatever wrongs you've done here, God's forgiveness is big enough to handle them. The choice is yours. I'll be praying."

Norah pulled the door closed behind her and floated across the marbled floors and out onto the sidewalk on a cloud of relief. She was amazed to find the world still spinning on its axis. The midmorning sky still shone with pale gray sunlight. Her pricey high heels still hurt like the dickens.

435

Whatever came of this visit with George Robison, she'd accomplished the two things she'd set out to do. Told him the truth about David and cleared the path for reconciliation. "It's up to you now, George," she said to no one in particular, sliding her car key in the lock, smiling broadly.

It truly was a beautiful day. Perfect for a drive. She turned the ignition and the Lincoln purred to life. *A quick jaunt to Damascus, perhaps?* Fourteen miles southeast of Abingdon. A sleepy town where another father went about his business — sober and solvent, if the rumors were true — unaware of what a fine young man David Cahill had turned out to be.

Time he found out, Norah decided. She giggled like a woman half her age, about to do a deed only a woman her age would dare attempt. *My, but we're feeling feisty today!* She, who never meddled in anyone else's business — ever — was about to meddle again. *But my intentions are pure, Lord.* Of course they were. Children needed their parents, didn't they? And sometimes, parents needed their children even more.

She'd stop by the house and change first. No silks and furs needed for this gentle, humble man, one who knew only too well what he'd done wrong. She couldn't wait

436

to tell him all that he'd done right.

David took a long breath, steeling him-self, then unlocked the post office box.

Yes! It was there, just as he'd hoped. He made short work of the envelope, disposing of it in a nearby trash can, and leaned back on the wall of metal mailboxes for support, physical and otherwise. The wall felt cold against his back, though he barely noticed the temperature or the late Thursday after-noon gloom, so focused was his attention on the letter he was unfolding with care.

Cream-colored paper, thick. A *B* em-bossed on it. *How like Belle.* The tone of her response was friendly, yet tentative. *No wonder.* She didn't know who was reading her letter. Yet.

His eyes drank in the words, smiling at her line about chimes and Belles. He loved when the halls of WPER rang with her laughter. *Definitely more musical than her singing.*

The next paragraph sent his heart skip-ping wildly around his chest as he read each word, letting the truth he found there sink in. *"My heart, my mind, my soul are filled with thoughts of him around the clock . . ."*

His knees buckled, sending him inching down the wall. Belle was talking about *him,* confessing her feelings about him to a virtual stranger. *Lord, I had no idea!* His parka suddenly felt too hot, too tight, keeping him from breathing.

She thought about him, she said. All the time, she said.

He filled her soul. *Filled her soul.*

If that wasn't love, it was striking-distance close. He wanted to confront her on the spot. Track her down at the radio station. *You're wooing her, remember? Not confronting.*

He'd written her for one purpose, to drag her attention away from those other pain-in-the-neck letter writers and get it back on him. Where he wanted it to be, longed for it to be.

"All Ears" had worked. Too well. *If you can put your feelings on paper, Cahill, you can say them face to face.*

He kept reading. She wanted to meet him tomorrow night. *No problem.* He'd be there early, be waiting, be certain she saw him and understood his feelings.

Because those feelings had a name now.

He loved her. It was love and nothing less.

No more holding back, no more playing games, no more waiting for her to make the first move. *Too risky.* He'd almost lost her to some mystery man when she was everything he could hope for, everything he'd prayed for in a woman.

In a wife.

That's what it would take. Commitment. A promise for the future. Belle was old enough to know what she wanted. And if she wanted him, if she'd take him as is, he was hers. All hers.

He tucked the letter in his pocket and made his way toward the truck, already composing the note he'd write back and drop in the mail within the hour.

One more day, Belle. This time tomorrow he'd be driving toward downtown Abingdon, freshly shaved, wearing a new white shirt and a clean pair of jeans. With a threadbare wallet in his pockets. With a ramshackle roof over his head and a beat-up, run-down truck in his driveway. And with a heart so full of love it might not fit through the doors of the Court Street Grill.

Belle slipped on her cans, listening to the Marvelettes winding down, singing along in her customized key, making up her own words to "Please Mr. Postman."

Please let there be a plain white envelope for me . . .

It wasn't merely a song, she decided. It was a prayer.

She turned on the mike and trilled, "That was the first number-one single for Motown Records back in 1961. I'm Belle O'Brien, spinning your favorites on W-P-

E-R Oldies 95. Weather, coming up." She flicked off the mike and shook her head. *Dull, girl.* Her whole first hour had been that way, a distracted, disjointed mess, with one eye trained on the studio door, wondering when Burt would come strolling in with the day's mail.

Her first "All Ears" letter had arrived on Wednesday. He should have received her letter Thursday. Now it was Friday. *Your turn, fella.*

When Burt showed up with a smattering of correspondence, Belle tried to act non-chalant as she waved him back out the door while sliding a letter opener along the seal of a telltale white envelope. The minute the door swooshed shut, she tore out the sheet of paper as her heart leaped into her throat.

Disappointment sent it thudding back into place. *So short!* Not the long, soul-bearing epistle she'd hoped for, just a few brief lines from her mysterious admirer.

January 28
Dear Belle,
   Hope you don't mind my using your first name. After reading your letter a dozen times, I feel as though I'm getting to know you better. The real, true you. The woman, not the radio personality.

Your renewed commitment to the Lord thrills me. To be honest, though, I'm not as thrilled to hear about this man in your life who fills your thoughts day and night. Does he know how blessed he is to have a woman like you care about him?

You also deserve to know much more about me. Will you trust me to do that in person, tonight? I'll be counting the hours until I see you at five o'clock.

Listening with all my heart . . .

P.S. Just so I'll know you're definitely coming, would you play "Cherish" by the Association when you sign off? Pay attention to the lyrics, Belle. Cherish is the word.

Whoever her anonymous correspondent was, he'd chosen a most romantic record for her to play.

Stop it, Belle! Don't get off track. She grabbed the appropriate CD for later in her show. This was about getting David's attention, not winning the heart of Mr. Ears.

Did David know how blessed he was to have her care about him? Not yet, maybe, but soon. One dinner spent with her mystery man ought to push David over the edge the minute he got wind of it. She'd make sure the news blew in his direction.

441

The letter from Belle was one thing. David had expected that. Had watched her mail the thing yesterday afternoon, in fact. Before he kissed her. Before soup. But this note from Norah Silver-Smyth, waiting in his mailbox at work, this was something else again.

David shrugged off his parka and unfolded the letter. No stamp or address. She'd obviously dropped it by the station in person, maybe after her morning muffin round with Patrick. Would Belle bring him breakfast like that every morning? *Nah. Never happen.*

Norah's elegant handwriting covered the pale silver stationery with loops and swirls that took some time to decipher.

David,
So nice of you to join us for chowder Wednesday. Consider this a standing invitation to join us for a bowl on Soup Night whenever you're free.

Consider it done, he thought with a grin. He'd even bring his own spoon.

I know you're under the gun to finish your house. Will you be working on it this Sunday? Suppose Belle and I bring dinner over, something simple

442

you can wolf down between hammer blows. Of course, I haven't asked Belle yet, but I know she'd love to join us. Say, two o'clock?

He loved the idea of food. Visitors were another thing. Getting underfoot, slowing him down, asking questions, seeing his house in such a sorry state of midrepair.

Then again. Belle. Dinner. Not a tough decision.

One last thing. I talked to Abingdon Bank and Trust, and you need to stop by Friday at four o'clock, if that's convenient. Something about a check. A new credit check, perhaps? Hope something good transpires. See you Sunday!

Fondly,
Norah

"Stop by" for another dressing-down from George Robison? *No way.* He flung the note at his desk, understanding more clearly than ever why Sherry had left and never come back. The man never knew when to quit.

One problem. Norah was the one who asked him to be there. That was reason enough for him to stop by the bank, even if it meant facing another round in the carpeted ring with George. Maybe the man had taken his challenge seriously, gathered credit reports and so forth. They'd probably called Norah for a reference and one thing led to another. *Who knows?*

Six hours from now, he'd find out. Whatever happened there, it wouldn't matter nearly as much as his rendezvous later with Belle. He glanced down at his jeans and white shirt — he was dressed for the Grill, not the bank. Too bad for George, he figured. Grabbing a stack of engineering logs to review, he stared up at the speakers that piped WPER into his tiny work cubicle. The knot of tension in his chest began unwinding at the sound of her voice spilling out, warm and vibrant.

My beautiful Belle.

He intended to be all ears, all day, while he worked and waited until she played her last song. No visits to the studio, no risking giving himself away.

He worked diligently for three full minutes, then tossed aside his papers and headed toward the studio, anticipating her intoxicating perfume and luminous gold eyes, less than twenty feet away from him.

Belle was seated at the console, back to the door, her long braid stretched down her back. How he longed to pull out those tidy twists and run his hands through the curly mass of it, spreading it over her

444

shoulders, inhaling the fragrance of her.

"Belle?"

Her head jerked up and around with a guilty start as she stuffed a piece of paper in her purse, never taking her eyes off him. "Hi."

He knew what the answer was, but he had to ask. "Whatcha reading?"

Her eyebrows arched. "Wouldn't you like to know?"

What if I said, "I do know." What if I tell her now?

No. He needed to give her time to figure it out for herself. Let her feel in control of things. For all he knew, she'd already put two and two together and was playing along with his game, strictly to amuse herself. Or embarrass him.

Belle didn't look amused, though. She looked pensive. "It's another letter from Mr. Ears. I'm meeting him for dinner tonight, in case you'd forgotten."

She's testing me. "Oh, right. Totally slipped my mind. What time was that again?"

"Five." Her glance sharpened. "Not planning on joining us, are you?"

"Not this guy. In fact, I have an appointment at the bank around then." *Which had better be finished in time or George is toast.*

"I thought the bank . . . well, I thought that was over."

You think a lot of things, Belle. Bless you, you think about me. He stood there, grinning what he knew to be an idiotic grin. She'd put it there, that grin of his. Because he loved her. *Keep saying it, Cahill. Practice. I love you, Belle. I love you.*

She stared at him, waiting for an answer.

"I'd love . . . uh, to know what . . . the . . . uh, bank is thinking, too." *Get it together, man!* He realized the goofy grin had returned. "Guess I'll find out later this afternoon."

On that note, he backed his way out of the studio, pointing at the speakers. "Your song's over." *And we're just beginning. You'll see, woman. Soon enough.*

Twenty-four

Pandemonium did not reign, it poured.

John Kendrick Bangs

David knew trouble was afoot the minute he stepped inside Abingdon Bank and Trust. Chuck, George's young gopher, stood outside the hallowed corner office, frantically motioning him over.

"In here, Mr. Cahill."

The room was empty, the imposing desk unmanned. David stood and waited, eyeballing the yawning wooden chair. *Not Wednesday. Not today, either.*

George showed up minutes later, striding into his office, shutting the door behind him with a decided bang. "Have a seat, David."

"I'll stand, thanks."

"You'll *sit!*" The man's foul mood was written all over his face like a scrawl of red graffiti.

David sat. At least his body did. "Is there a reason I'm here?"

"Don't be smart with me, young man." The black eyes shone with a deadly glint, worse than last time. "I'll make this short and sweet. Norah Silver-Smyth showed up here yesterday. Gave me a piece of her mind."

I'll bet she did. "No kidding."

"Gave me a piece of information, too. About a boy named Josh."

Norah knew about Josh? *Impossible. Unless . . .* Unless Belle had told her. David could barely get out the words. "What did she tell you? About Josh, I mean?"

George leaned over his desk, a pair of meaty hands pressed on the gleaming surface. His voice was a low growl. "Norah told me the only thing I needed to know. That I have a grandson. You might have mentioned that yourself, Cahill."

David kept his tone even. "Sherry had eight years to tell you, sir."

"And you were busy those eight years, I hear. Sending checks for a kid you never met."

Belle, again. It had to be. She'd told Norah. Who'd told Sherry's father. David swallowed hard. "Supporting Josh seemed the honorable thing to do."

"*Honorable?* Norah used that word, too. Told me what she thought an honorable father ought to do in this situation."

"And?" It was all David trusted himself to say, so ragged were his thoughts. How could Belle do that? How could she have betrayed him? The woman he confided in . . . the woman he loved?

George reached in his pocket for a piece of paper. Small, like a check. He slapped it in front of David, face up. "This was her idea of honor."

David stared. It was a check, but not a small one. Twenty thousand dollars. Made payable to David Cahill. Not drawn on Abingdon Bank and Trust, but on the personal account of George Allen Robison.

"Sir?" It sounded like a croak. It *was* a croak.

"Ten thousand to finish your house. And another ten for . . . good measure. That's the way Norah put it." The man's voice had become surprisingly steady.

David picked up the check, making sure it was real. "I don't know what to say."

" 'Thank you' would be a beginning."

The check was real, all right. The largest check he'd ever laid eyes on. And it had his name on it. His house could be finished in a month. *Less.* He could buy a decent truck. *Or put a down payment on a new one.* Come March, he could load that truck with his worldly possessions and head for Charlotte, North Carolina. A man with a solid future, a distant past, and no regrets.

Make that one regret. With a long braid.

In thirty days, Abingdon, Virginia, would appear in his rearview mirror for the last time. It couldn't happen fast

449

enough to suit him.

George's voice snapped him back to the present. "Do you have a picture of my grandson?"

"A photo? Why? Do you want proof?" David hadn't meant to grind out his words like that. The pain of Belle's betrayal overwhelmed him, seeking an outlet, a target.

George grunted. "Norah's word is good enough for me. I just . . . just wanted to see what the boy looked like, that's all."

David pulled out his billfold, flipping it open to the school photo Sherry had sent him before Thanksgiving, and held it out for George's inspection. "Joshua Robison, age eight."

The man's face became stone gray, utterly still. He did nothing, said nothing, for a full minute as he studied the blond little boy with the winsome smile. He sighed at last. "The kid's yours, no question about that."

No question. "And yours, sir. Your grandson. No question about that, either."

"Which is the only reason you're holding a check for twenty thousand dollars, Cahill. It's not guilt money. I had nothing to do with . . . what happened eight years ago. With that baby being born. Consider this a refund. For money hard earned and well spent."

David folded his wallet and slipped it

450

back in his pocket, his eyes trained on the man across the mahogany desk. *Lord, he's so hard to read.* It wasn't clear if George was happy with this solution or felt forced into it.

A scenario that never would have happened if Belle hadn't told Norah. The check, paper-thin, weighed heavy in his hands. The things he could do with it spun through his mind, over and over. For a guy who grew up poor on the wrong side of town, it was a fortune.

But was it a godsend?

He knew one thing he could do with it. The same thing he did the last time George Robison handed him a check. He could walk out the door and rip it in half. Keep his pride, if nothing else.

Which would leave him no option but to stay in Abingdon for another three months to finish his house and thereby lose the job at WBT. Which would force him to walk through the doors of WPER every day for the foreseeable future and look at a woman who'd given away his secrets and broken his heart.

"Thank you for your generosity, Mr. Robison."

The banker stood, buttoning his suit coat closed over his considerable girth. "I don't expect to see you again, Cahill. Do we understand each other?"

"We do." David rose to his feet, the folded check tucked in his shirt pocket. "I hope . . ." It had to be said. "I hope you'll get to meet that grandson someday."

The gray granite was back. An impenetrable stone wall that David couldn't do more than acknowledge with a slight nod. Minutes later, he stood in the twilight of a January afternoon, the last rays of feeble sunlight fading into the horizon that swallowed the end of west Main Street.

He turned east, toward WPER . . . toward the Grill, where Belle undoubtedly waited for her Romeo. She'd played "Cherish" at the end of her show, exactly as he'd asked her to, while he'd sat smiling in his cubicle at work. His heart had done a slow dance to the music, imagining Belle wrapped in his arms, tucked tightly against him, humming along in a key all her own.

The tightness in his chest shifted up a notch. *A fool for love is still a fool.*

A quick glance at his watch assured him Belle was probably already at the Grill, waiting. He had barely enough time to stop by the station. Make a quick phone call to WBT. Get a short letter ready and drop it in the mailbox outside the station for the five-thirty pickup.

He had to hurry, before he ran out of time. Or conviction.

Belle stared at the yellow-striped walls of the Grill, disappointment seeping through her bones. She was tired of looking at the clock above the WPER fishbowls, tired of seeing the minute hand crawl five minutes past the hour, then ten. Fifteen.

Stood up! She'd never been stood up in her entire life.

Of course, she'd never agreed to meet a man like this before either. A stranger. *A complete stranger!* It was obvious she'd lost her mind. *Too many times around the old turntable for you, girlie.*

She'd caught a glimpse of David dashing past the Grill door on his way up to WPER, looking like a man on a mission. She'd hoped the mission would be saving her from a disastrous evening with Mr. Ears, but no such luck. He'd kept right on going, didn't so much as glance in the direction of the Grill on his way by.

Humph. Some Friday evening this was turning out to be.

She *had* mailed her letter to Mr. Ears, right? Been clear about her intentions to meet him? Played "Cherish," like he'd requested? Leaving nothing to chance, she'd arrived at the Grill fifteen minutes early. Sat by the window. Wore her favorite red knit dress, an eye-catching number that made her burst into a chorus of "W-O-M-

A-N" every time she slipped it on.

She was counting on Mr. Ears to have some eyes, so they'd bug out when he saw her in it.

She could see them now, those blue-gray orbs widening with surprise, then admiration. The color would deepen to the hue of a tempest-tossed ocean. His lids would drop to a dangerously low —

Whoa, girl! This isn't David coming to meet you. No matter how much she wished that were true. It was "All Ears" who would get an eyeful of her bright red, dressed-to-kill ensemble, not David.

Unfortunately.

At the moment, though, only one man was eyeing her and that was Leonard, whose apron was battle-scarred from a busy Friday at the Grill. He poured her a second cup of coffee, asked if she wanted a menu. "Or are you waiting for someone?" he said with a knowing wink.

But he couldn't know. Nerves, that's all.

Those same nerves shot her out of her seat when she spied David bolting out onto the sidewalk but not turning in her direction. She flung open the heavy glass door of the Grill as if it were cardboard. "David, wait!"

He turned, looking confused.

No, not confused. Angry. He looked angry. Breathing hard from the rush of adrenaline, she waited for him to speak, to put her at ease. To offer some encouragement.

"Belle, I'm in a hurry."

That was not encouraging.

"So I see." She gulped, trying to tamp down her emotions. "I thought you might be . . . uh, hungry and thinking about dinner at the Grill and —"

He held up his hand to stem the flow of words. "Look, I've gotta drop something in the corner box before they collect the mail."

She stood there with her mouth hanging open, watching his blue parka turning away from her. *David, rude?* The man was many things, but brash and inconsiderate had never been in his repertoire. At least, not since she'd gotten to really know him. Something was wrong, something bigger than her plans to meet Mr. Ears for dinner. David had had plenty of time to put his foot down about that. *If he'd wanted to. If he cared.*

She intended to put her foot down about *this,* though. "David, wait." Scurrying after him, she wished she'd skipped the silly heels. So what if they matched her red dress? So what if they made her legs look half an inch longer? David hadn't looked at her eyes, let alone her legs.

As if he'd read her thoughts, David

stopped and spun around again, fixing his cold gray gaze on her. In the twilight, his cheeks were two ruddy spots; his generous lips were parted but not smiling. "Don't make this any harder than it already is, Belle."

"Make what harder?" She skidded to a stop, a sense of foreboding washing over her. She wanted to touch his sleeve, connect to him somehow, but his mood made such a thing impossible, far too risky. "Talk to me, David, please. Now. Tell me what's wrong." In an attempt to lighten the mood around them, she leaned toward him and wiggled her eyebrows. "Is there some dark secret you haven't told me yet?"

"Secret?" It exploded out of him. His eyes smoldered, heated by an intensity she didn't understand. He lifted his hands then threw them back down, frustration coming off him in waves. "I've told you too many secrets already, Belle."

She stepped back and closed her eyes for a moment, fighting the threat of tears. "You're not making sense." Her voice was thick, her emotions conflicting, nameless. "There's only one secret you shared with me. About Sherry and Josh. I'm glad you told me, but it doesn't change anything . . . between us. It doesn't change . . . how I feel about you."

"Well, it changes how I feel about you."

It hurt like a physical blow, numbing her insides, leaving her gasping for air. "What have I done? Are you going to tell me? Or make me guess? David, your behavior —"

He cut her off with a hiss. "You want to know what you've done? Made a mess of things, is what. You told Norah about Josh. And Norah told George Robison."

Belle was too stunned to argue, let alone think straight. Instead she blurted out, "Who's George Robison?"

His eyes were storm clouds, his words a low thunder. "Sherry's father. The man who refused my bank loan on Wednesday. Not that you would concern yourself with such mundane issues. You were too busy sharing a juicy bit of gossip —"

"That's not true!" If he could interrupt her so rudely, she could do the same. "I don't know who told Norah, or why she told George, but I do know this. I've not shared the story of your past with a living soul. No one. Don't you know I would never *do* such a thing?"

The clouds in David's eyes parted and a look of pure agony shone through. "You mean . . . you didn't . . . ?"

"Of course not." She shook her head, relief running through her veins. At least now she understood why David was so undone. "You must have thought . . . well, you . . ." Her voice trailed off as he reached out, swept her into his arms, and pulled her toward him. "You must have —"

"I must have been an idiot," he finished for her, bending down, forcing her head to tip back slightly, bringing his face closer to hers. "I'm as sorry as I can be, Belle. Forgive me for jumping to the wrong conclusion? For not trusting you?"

It was hard to miss the tenderness in his eyes when they were so near. His lips were close, too. Right there, inches away. "Of course I forgive you, David." She felt the air around them warming. "You were simply caught off guard. And if Norah told George, you can be sure it was somehow for your benefit. She's crazy about you. It's easy to see why you'd think . . . anyway, it doesn't matter."

"Yes, it does matter." He slid his hands along her shoulders and cradled them behind her neck. "*You* matter."

She caught her breath, wondering . . . hoping . . . *praying* the tone in his voice meant what she thought it did.

Say the words, Cahill.

He looked down at her, at her shining gold eyes and grace-filled face. *You love her. Say it. Now. Go.* He inhaled the evening air, sweet with the scent of her, and formed the words with his mouth. "Belle, I . . ."

458

She kissed him. Kissed *him!* Crazy woman, didn't she know he was about to tell her something important? Oh, but this was fine. This was more than fine. Her full lips were pressed against his, gentle but insistent. What was it Belle compared them to? Asparagus? *Mmm.* They tasted more like berries, the color of her delicious red dress —

Wait. She wore this dress for Mr. Ears, not for me.

Confound it, he wished he hadn't thought of that, not while he could feel her long eyelashes tickling his cheeks. But he had to know, had to be certain.

"Belle." He broke the kiss, still hovering over her mouth, savoring the closeness of her. "Weren't you supposed to meet Mr. Ears at the Grill?"

She looked up, her eyelids at half-mast, her smile delightfully askew. "Oh, that . . . he never showed. I'm . . . glad."

"Are you, now?" He felt his own grin stretch across his face and realized it had been hours since he'd smiled while listening to "Cherish" on the air.

Which she'd played for another man.

"You're sure you're glad he didn't show?" He needed, in some perverse way, to chase away any doubts, to know that he'd claimed her whole heart. "You won't regret not meeting him? The man who

459

longed for you to fill his house with laughter and receive his love with open arms?"

"My, but you have a good memory, David." She was flirting with him now, her voice a decided drawl. "For a man who saw that letter only once, it certainly made an impression on you."

"Not half the impression you made on me the first time I saw *you*." He had to get her attention away from the letter-writing Mr. Ears and on to safer territory. "Could we step inside the stairwell, out of the cold?" He tugged at her arm, unlocking the door and ushering her inside the dimly lit landing, the stairs to WPER stretching up into the darkened space above them. He pulled the door shut and leaned against the wall, shaking off an unexpected shudder.

Better she never know the truth about the letters. It made no difference at this point, did it? She'd chosen him over her mystery man, that's all that counted. "All Ears" was history. David knew for a fact the man would never write her again. The thought made him chuckle.

"Are you saying you laughed when you first saw me, then?" Belle was more alert, eyeing him closely.

"No, not at all." *Watch yourself, buddy.* "If you recall, our relationship started with a bang. A head banger at that."

"So it did." Her eyes had left his and were focused on the envelope sticking out of his pocket. The one he'd meant to mail some ten minutes ago. A long white envelope, with only the return address showing. His return address. A post office box.

"What's that?" Her eyes widened.

Outside on Court Street, a knot of people streamed by, their voices muffled. Inside the stairwell, things had grown quiet indeed.

"A . . . letter." He worked hard to keep his voice steady, his tone light. "Why?"

The look on her face told him why. So did her words. "I've seen those plain white envelopes before. Twice."

"They sell 'em by the dozens at Walgreen's." His light tone now qualified as desperate. Even he could tell that.

"Not with that return address printed on it, just so." Belle reached in her purse and pulled out two more envelopes. Same white, same style of type. And the exact same post office box in the corner. Her hands were shaking. "What's going on, David?"

He forced himself to smile, to look as ingratiating as possible, as if the whole thing were a game, meant to be fun. "You're such a bright woman, I'll bet you already figured it out. So you tell me, Belle. What do *you* think has happened here? Go

461

ahead, you talk. I'll listen. After all —" he forced his smile to broaden — "I'm all ears."

Thwat!

She'd meant to slap him this time.

He was sure of it. Sure he deserved it, too.

Though it wasn't much more than a petulant swipe, it stung like anything. He resisted the urge to place his own hand there and massage away the pain, see if she'd torn off any skin.

Lord, I've messed up here, major league. I need your wisdom. Don't let me blow this.

"Belle, I'm truly sorry." *Again. Still.*

"Well, you should be!"

Here was a side of Belle he'd not seen before. Hoped he'd never have occasion to see again. A hopping mad, face flushed, arms flailing Belle. She was a small woman, but when she got angry, she looked bigger, swelling up like a tropical puffer fish, and about as poisonous.

The truth, man, tell her the truth.

He dove in. "I never meant to mislead you." *Not on purpose, not exactly.* "You said you would choose the most promising letter and write to him, arrange a meeting." He shrugged and begged for sympathy with his eyes. "I wanted to be sure the letter you chose was . . . mine."

"Why?" A hint of hysteria hung behind her words. "So you could make a fool out of me, watch me fawn all over this mystery guy, telling him all about *you*, so he'd . . ."

Her face became the color of her dress. Only redder.

"Ohh, noo." She groaned and slumped against the other wall. "You read the letter I sent to him, didn't you? I mean, to you . . . I mean, *about* you."

He felt his own skin grow warm. "Yes, I did read it. A dozen times. I'm glad you think about me, Belle. I think about you all the time, too."

"Oh, you . . . !" Her fluster suddenly fizzled. "You . . . do?"

"Yes, Belle." He lowered his voice to a soothing murmur, hoping he'd seen the last of her red-tipped fingernails poking at his chest. "Pretty nails, by the way." *Yeah, there you go. Drown her in compliments. That'll help.* His eyes drifted over her, his gaze appearing to calm her further. At least she wasn't stomping her high-heeled foot anymore. "The red matches your dress perfectly, I see." He knew squat about colors and clothing, only that women ranked them right up there with food and shelter. "Am I to assume there's a nice set of matching red toes hiding in those spiffy shoes?"

"Humph!" She'd folded her arms over

her chest, not resembling a puffer anymore, but still packing a dangerous gleam in her eyes. "Not likely you'll ever see those toes again, Mr. Cahill. Or shall I call you Mr. Ears? Your ears aren't particularly big, but they do hear things that aren't said and make promises they can't keep, and —"

"Wait a minute." He dropped down a few inches to get her attention, make eye contact. "What promises did I make in my letters that you think I won't keep?"

She yanked one of the envelopes from her purse and unfolded it with great showmanship. The Barter Theatre folks had it all wrong: Belinda Oberholtzer was a born actress.

"There are four promises, as I see it." Belle began reading aloud in what he recognized as her radio voice, "Promise number one: She'll have 'my whole heart as her dwelling place.' Well." She stared pointedly at his chest. "A decent size home, I suppose, though hardly a royal palace."

"It would be if you lived there. As my queen."

"Oh." She feigned disinterest and continued reading. " 'My complete attention would be given to her needs and hurts.' " She sniffed dramatically. "I've seen no evidence of that this evening."

"Ah, but the evening is young." He wiggled his eyebrows meaningfully.

She pretended not to notice. "Here's a third promise. 'My utter devotion would be hers, guaranteed for a lifetime.' Puh-*lease!* How could a man possibly make good on such a guarantee?"

"With a wedding ring."

"Ah . . . I . . . see." But she didn't see his teasing smile, or her own becoming blush.

He was toying with her now. "Is there a fourth promise, Belle?"

She stared at the letter and gulped, finally mumbling, " 'My boundless passion would ever be at her command.' "

"And . . . ?"

"And that better come *after* the wedding ring!" she snapped, folding the letter along well-worn creases.

He slipped his arms around her in a loose embrace, feeling her pulling as far away as she could, pressing back against his hands, still fighting him. *Lord, she deserves those four promises. More. Help me say what needs to be said tonight. Starting now.*

"Belle." He inched her closer, nuzzling her hair with his chin, feeling her relax the slightest bit. "Will you forgive me? For being so jealous, so afraid you'd find someone else to make those promises to

465

you, that I . . . lied to you." *That's what it was. A lie. Not a game. Forgive me, Lord.* "Do you remember what else I wrote in that letter?"

In a tiny voice she croaked, "Which paragraph?"

"The one that ended, 'I'm hoping that woman is you, Miss O'Brien.' Remember that line?" Under his chin, he felt her curly head nod. *Now. Go.* "Is that woman you, Belle?"

Wrong, Cahill. You're forcing her to say it first. He took a deep breath. Before his words poured out, Belle moved her head again, up and down.

She's nodding. *She's nodding!*

"Belle, I love you." *There. Done.* She was still nodding. *Good, good. Keep talking.* "I meant every word in that letter. I'm sorry it's taken me this long to tell you . . . how I feel." His voice was hoarse, uneven, a thousand emotions squeezed into a few words.

Such important words, though.

He pressed on, needing to voice his feelings, wanting her to know everything. "The only time I ever told a woman I loved her, she . . . laughed. Hard." The catch in his throat surprised him, threatened him.

When he felt her begin to shake under his hands, he fought for equilibrium and feared the worst. "Please, Belle. Look at me. Are you . . . laughing?"

She looked up.

No. She was not laughing.

Tears were streaming down her face. Her sobs, which she seemed determined to hold inside, made her shake so badly she was forced to release them in small, airy gasps.

It was several minutes before she could speak and make sense.

"David —" she sighed, then hiccuped — "David, I can't believe it was you, writing those letters. All along, it was you."

"Are you glad?" In the shadowy stairwell, he caught a glimpse of her eyes, sparkling like twin moons, and her smile, which told him what he needed to know.

She thumped his chest, well-padded by the parka. "Of course I'm glad. I planned that whole letter thing for one reason. To make you jealous."

"Which you managed to do quite well."

She put her hands around his waist only long enough to snag a handkerchief out of his back pocket. "What year was this last washed?" she muttered, then blew her nose in it anyway. Leaning back, she squinted at him. "Are you sure you know what you're doing, confessing love to a woman who is five full years older than you? A woman who has a great face for radio? If we were in a bright light —"

"Which we aren't, but if we were, I'd be

looking at the most beautiful woman in the universe."

"Says you."

"And who else needs to say it, pray tell?"

He had her there.

"But look at these lines around my eyes." She tilted her head sideways to give him a better look. "See those?"

He took her face in his hands, treasuring the feel of her soft cheeks resting in each palm, and gently kissed the corner of one eye. Slowly. Then the other. "Don't see a thing."

She sighed. "This hair, then. Too thick, too unruly, not a smooth mane like Norah's, not . . . uh, David, what are you doing?"

He'd untied the ribbon that held her braid in place and began pulling the plait apart, taking his time, enjoying the feel of her silky, curly locks as they unwound in his hands. He watched her eyes turn to leaded glass as his hands reached the nape of her neck.

"Someone once told me —" He massaged his fingers into her scalp in small, expanding circles — "that this improves circulation and stimulates hair growth."

"Huh-uh. My hair dothn't need to grow. Pleath thtop."

He wondered if Belle realized she was slurring her words.

"Seems to me you also complained about your lips once. Too thick, too straight, you said."

"Athparaguth." She nodded then, clearly not trusting herself to say another word.

"Well, I happen to love fresh asparagus, which means I love your lips exactly the way they are." To prove it, he kissed her thoroughly, molding his lips to hers, fanning her hair across her shoulders and down her back as he did. When the kiss finally ended, he pulled her against him, marveling again at how perfectly she fit there. "You are just the right age for me, Belle. Just the right size. Smarter and more beautiful than I deserve. But most important of all, I believe the Lord has brought us together for a reason."

"What'th that?" she mumbled against his chest with a sigh of contentment.

"Eathy —" His laughter filled the gloomy stairwell with a joyful noise — "We can help each other get to the main post office on time for the last pickup of the night." He gave her a final squeeze, then released her and pushed open the door. A wintry breeze swirled around them. "We'll toss this envelope in the mailbox out front, then have dinner as planned, shall we?"

She looked up, the blurry stars in her eyes seeming to focus again. "Are we talking the Grill?"

"No, woman, we're talking the Martha Washington Inn." He relished her gasp of surprise. "Let's just say I've been blessed with a . . . bonus of sorts today. Thanks to Norah. And George. And you."

"A bonus?" She sounded suspicious, working to keep up with his long strides as she stumbled along in her ridiculous red shoes.

He had to admit, those high heels did nice things for her legs. *Bet she doesn't know that.* Women sometimes missed the obvious.

"David . . . you didn't . . . take the job at WBT after all, did you?"

He stopped. Letting her catch up, letting her see his face when he told her. "I ran upstairs and called them right before you saw me tonight, Belle. Turned the job down. I've got a house to finish. And other details to work out."

"Am I back to being a detail again?" She tapped her red-heeled foot impatiently.

"You are *the* detail, woman. The reason I'm staying. Does that spell it out for you?"

"Ohh." She smiled her dreamy, asparagus smile. "I'm so . . . relieved." Belle climbed into his truck from the driver's side, muttering softly, "Gee, this feels familiar."

"Yeah, sure does." The engine started with a roar. He pulled her closer for one more kiss, simply because he could. And because he was certain she'd kiss him back. Without laughing. "We've come a long way since Christmas, Belle."

With miles yet to go . . .

He pushed the thought away as they drove into the starry night.

Twenty-five

Work is love made visible.

Kahlil Gibran

The list was endless, David decided. He threw himself down on a lumpy second-hand sofa and reviewed the ever-growing inventory of tasks that needed to be tackled before his house was done. *His* house. And to think he'd actually expected to pour all this energy into a place and then sell it. *No way.* This was his home now.

He'd attended the early service that morning to get his Sunday started on the right foot. Nothing was more important than worship. Not even Belle, though she was mighty high on the short list of priorities in his life. Especially after dinner Friday night at the Martha Washington Inn.

The woman was a vision by candlelight. Her pale, freckled skin glowed with its own incandescence. Her amazing red dress earned her an entire restaurant of admirers, none more attentive than he. Her laughter filled the room — and all the corners of his heart.

He'd told her he loved her and he meant

it. She hadn't said it in so many words, but she'd nodded in all the right places. *Works for me.* In the next few weeks, they'd know if their love was meant for a lifetime or a season.

He didn't need a few weeks. He didn't need an hour. He knew. But Belle needed time, it seemed. He could wait. Meanwhile, he had a house demanding his every waking hour.

He'd tackled plumbing and heating when he first moved in. It was hard to function dirty and cold. Though he remembered vividly many childhood winters when he'd done just that. *Never again. Not this Cahill.*

Late at night, stretched out on his bed with the quiet house settling around him, he wondered if that wasn't his whole motivation for remodeling the house. To complete the projects his father had never finished. To prove that a poor boy with nothing could grow up to be a rich man with something.

Not rich as the world defined riches, but rich in the things that mattered. In faith, in friends, in family. Faith and friends were in place and growing; family was a dream waiting to be born.

"Patience, man!" he roared into the stillness.

His voice echoed against the four living

room walls, bare except for the plasterboard he'd nailed up last week. *And
speaking of patience.* Those walls needed
taping, drywall mud, and sanding. Hard
enough for a crew of two or three to
handle, but a real bear for a handyman
trying to go it alone on evenings and weekends.

Some of the single guys from church had
helped him nail the plasterboard up, but he
couldn't impose, couldn't ask for more of
their time. Three rooms, a stairwell, an upstairs hall? *Nah.* He couldn't ask people to
deal with that. It was endless hours of
work he'd have to do himself.

Especially since the twenty thousand dollars was history.

It'd been a kick to look at that check, to
think about spending it, to add up all the
labor and supplies it could buy. But it
couldn't buy honor. Couldn't buy pride.
Definitely couldn't buy peace of mind.
He'd earned those things the hard way and
they weren't for sale.

Heading to the kitchen for a soda, he
smiled as soon as he hit the room. At least
the kitchen was done. From snazzy cabinets to new counters to the ceramic tile
floor. The almost-new refrigerator had two
recognizable items in it — gray lettuce and
green cheese — but by jingo, the room
looked good. Big selling point, the realtor

had assured him. Good reason to keep it, he'd assured himself.

He'd finished the outside stuff. The roof, replacing the boards on the front porch, painting the clapboards white, those things had happened late last fall, before it got too cold to work outdoors. All that was left was inside work. Refinishing the pine floors in the living room, installing the carpet in the two rooms upstairs, the drywall hassle, and all that woodwork and trim. And wall-papering. And painting.

The detail work his father had excelled at during his dry spells. The same skills John Cahill had passed on to his son.

Skills that were serving him well these days. *No time like the present, fella.* He took the steps up to his bedroom two at a time, tossing his good clothes on the back of a chair and finding his grungiest jeans and sweatshirt. Norah and Belle wouldn't arrive with Sunday dinner for another three hours. The floor sander in the corner downstairs was whispering his name.

"Shhh!" Norah gently jabbed a silk-swathed elbow into Patrick's side. "Didn't your mother ever teach you to whisper in church?"

Patrick dutifully dropped his booming baritone to a low-pitched murmur and bent closer. His warm breath on her cheek sent a quiver vibrating through her heart.

"Remember, woman. Church is a new experience for me."

"Ah, so it is." How easily she forgot that Patrick's newfound faith was only weeks old, so quickly was he learning and growing. God was clearly at work in Patrick's heart. *Yours too, Norah girl.*

She tipped her head toward his as they rose for the opening hymn. "Mother wouldn't even let me whisper during the sermon. She made me write notes."

His eyes on hers were full of mischief. "Got any paper?"

Minutes later, seated again, she offered him a small tablet in jest, and was surprised to see him slip out his pen and begin scrawling on it with a bold script while Matthew Howard ran through the weekly announcements. She tried not to stare at the paper — hadn't Mother cautioned her against that rude behavior as well? — and waited for him to finish writing whatever bit of foolishness had momentarily turned his attention away from the morning service.

Finally, he slipped the pad into her hand, his eyes fixed on the altar, his expression blank except for a slight twitch at the corner of his mouth.

She glanced down and read the few sentences. A well-timed, spirited arpeggio from the pipe organ kept her gasp of amazement from filling the sanctuary. "Patrick! Are you . . . do you . . . mean this?" Her fingers gripped the pad of paper while she struggled to get an equally firm grasp on her wildly beating heart.

She read the note again. There was no mistaking his words.

I love you, Norah. There's nowhere else I'd rather be, for the rest of my days, than right here by your side. Will you marry me, love of my life? Just say yes.

"Patrick, I . . ."

"Shh." He pressed a finger to her lips, a playful grin tugging at his mouth as he poked at the tablet with his pen and underlined *Just say yes.*

"But shouldn't we . . . ?"

He pried the tablet from her hands and flipped to a blank sheet. She couldn't bear to look away this time as he wrote.

I've prayed about this for a month. God says yes. Your turn.

It couldn't be that simple, could it? She'd buried two husbands, cried an ocean of tears, mended her ragged heart twice. Could she risk a third gold band on her ring finger, a third vow of commitment for a lifetime?

Could Patrick be the one? Had God indeed saved the best for last?

Her hands trembled as she reached for

the pen and paper and added one word across the bottom in a shaky script that skitted across the page in rhythm with her heart.

Yes!

"Are you going to tell me, or do I have to guess?" Belle watched Norah packing enough food for a dozen hungry men into an enormous wicker basket. Fried chicken, biscuits, cole slaw, baked beans, corn with limas, and brownies by the truckload all disappeared into a square picnic basket lined with Norah's familiar blue-and-white checked napkins. Belle shook her head. "Who's going to eat all that?"

"David will tuck away most of it. In case you haven't noticed, that man of yours has a powerful appetite."

That man of yours. Belle shivered at the delicious sound of it. She'd seen David's appetite in motion at the Martha on Friday night. The man ate all his dinner, most of hers, and made cow eyes at the man's plate next to them until she threatened to kiss him right there in the restaurant, if only to keep his lips occupied.

That ploy did not work.

He stole a kiss when no one was looking and still ordered a second dessert.

That man of hers had looked more handsome than ever in such an elegant setting, wearing his jeans, white shirt, and a tie scrounged out of his glove compartment. The Martha would never be the same.

She watched Norah dance around the kitchen, convinced the woman was up to something. "Granted, David can eat some serious food —"

"And whatever he doesn't eat today will keep nicely in that pitifully empty fridge of his."

"How do you know it's empty?"

Norah twirled in her direction, her flowing jacket following in a graceful swirl. "A guess, nothing more. Honestly, have you ever known a single man to have a decent collection of leftovers?"

"Absolutely not. Most of the guys I dated didn't know what a leftover *was*. Nor did they own a single roll of plastic wrap, let alone storage containers. If you peek in a man's margarine tubs, you're guaranteed to find nails and screws."

Norah nodded, laughing. "Precisely why you're taking a whole box of plastic zip-up bags."

"*I'm* taking? What about you?"

"Oh, I'll join you soon enough. You go ahead." Norah winked. "I have important business to take care of first. Which means you'll have a little time alone with David. But only a little, mind you."

"Fear not." Belle snapped a mock salute.

"We are a trustworthy twosome."

"I don't doubt that for a minute." Norah's tone was softer. "Sharing the same faith and convictions makes all the difference. Still . . ." Her smile spread from earring to earring. "Let's not tempt the flesh and take too long about making certain decisions, eh?"

"If you're talking marriage, please don't. David hasn't."

Well, there *was* that brief mention of a wedding ring Friday evening in the stairwell, but he was merely teasing her. *Right?* She was in no hurry, not after behaving so impulsively with Patrick. Hadn't that turned out for the best, though? Norah's constant smile was proof positive that it had.

"Besides —" Belle added, studying Norah with an appraising eye — "You're a fine one to talk about delaying decisions and avoiding the inevitable trip down the aisle."

Norah's face turned a rosy hue. "I suppose you're talking about Patrick. And me." She sighed, patting her cheeks as if to cool them down. "All in good time, my pretty. All in good time."

"Humph. Now you sound like the Wicked Witch of the West." Belle grabbed the heavy lunch to go. "Which makes me Dorothy, complete with my red braid and basket. Where's Toto when you need him?"

"Harry will have to do." Norah scooped up the inanimate object curled up at her feet. "Though I fear he couldn't care less about Kansas."

"Harry's all yours." Belle headed for the back door, grabbing her coat off the chair, then turned. "See you at David's. At two, promise?"

"Oh, I'll be there on time." Norah's features were filled with expectation, hinting at a well-kept secret. "I wouldn't miss this get-together for all the ham in Virginia."

David had worked up a king-size appetite, steering the circular sander back and forth across his living room floor, hand sanding the corners and the pine mantel. His back and shoulders ached from the effort and his stomach growled in agreement.

A battered windup alarm clock on the windowsill reminded him he had less than half an hour to get cleaned up and ready for Belle and Norah's visit. He looked around the room, shaking his head in resignation. *What a mess.* Sawdust and wood shavings covered every inch of the living room, throwing a fine layer of dust over the foyer and into the kitchen, the only room worth bragging about.

At least he'd get himself clean, he decided, brushing the worst of it off his sleeves as he headed toward the steps. The sound of tires turning onto his gravel driveway jerked his head toward the window. A Pontiac.

Belle.

Dressed in work clothes, by the look of it, and bearing a basket almost as big as she was.

He watched her pause in his drive, gazing up at the house. Why hadn't he brought her here before? *Ego, man.* He'd wanted everything to be finished so he could impress her with his carpentry, his prowess with saw and sander. Instead, she was seeing the *before* picture — and it wasn't pretty.

Belle didn't appear discouraged by what she saw. Was smiling, in fact. Man, did he love her smile. *Name something you* don't *love about her, Cahill.* Right again. She was moving toward the porch, weighed down by a basket that, big as it was, still probably didn't have enough food for the three of them. *A shame.* He'd hate either of the women to go home hungry.

He let her knock first, not wanting her to know he'd been observing her every move, then yanked the front door open with a flourish and a broad smile. "Welcome."

"David, it's wonderful!"

Three words and she'd stolen his heart all over again.

Keeping his eyes locked on hers, he reached out and carefully took the basket from her hands, surprised at how heavy it was. It was soon at his feet, forgotten, as he pulled Belle inside and closed the door behind her, folding her into his arms where she most certainly belonged.

Outside, the last day of January spread its mantle of gray sunshine over the frozen farmlands around David's house. Inside, it was quiet and warm, a cozy oasis with a fire burning in the grate, fed with freshly cut pine that crackled and warmed every corner of the room.

Belle broke the weighty silence with a giggle. "I may be crazy about you, David, but not crazy enough to kiss a man with sawdust all over his face."

He lifted one hand long enough to sweep away his bangs, sending a cloud of sawdust raining down on the top of her head. "Now we match." He slipped off his glasses, also coated with dust, he discovered.

Belle's eyes took on a mischievous twinkle. "Didn't I warn you about those eyes of yours? They're lethal weapons, my friend, sawdust in your eyebrows or not."

"Suppose you brush me off, then, while I shut these peepers you think are so dangerous." He let his eyelids drop and in an instant felt her small hands lightly moving across his forehead and over his hair. Her touch was feathery, like a kitten batting at a ball of yarn. Was it his imagination or could he hear her smiling?

"You've been working hard today, David." Those soft hands of hers had finished with his hair, his forehead, and were carefully smoothing away the dust around his eyes, his nose.

His mouth. She seemed to be taking her time there.

Hmm. He spoke, the words muffled by her fingers hovering over his lips. "Does this mean I have more sawdust there?"

"Just clearing a space."

Ohh.

He opened his eyes in time to watch her stretch up on tiptoe, her own eyes wide, and press her lips where her fingers had been only seconds before. They gazed at one another as they kissed, her hands moving up to his shoulders, his down to her waist.

So right, so right.

He held himself back, not wanting to frighten her.

Does she know what this does to me? What her eyes are telling me, even if she can't say it with words yet?

He broke the kiss. Had to, needed to.

"Belle, I . . . I'm glad you're here."

"Me, too." She tweaked his nose, then

bent to pick up the discarded basket. "Norah promised to be here at two. Hope I didn't throw you off being early."

Throw off? And then some. "No problem. What's for dinner?"

She rattled off the menu, making his mouth water more with each word. "If you like, we can set things out. That is . . . uh . . . if there's somewhere we can eat that isn't . . ." She peeped in the direction of the kitchen.

"Yeah, there's a table in there. I'll put a fresh cloth on it." He grinned. "Then you won't see the sawdust."

They made quick work of it, putting out three place settings, finding dishes and glasses, storing the perishable food in the fridge until later. "Will you show me around while we're waiting?" Belle's eyes shimmered with anticipation.

"Promise you won't notice the mess?"

She wrinkled her nose at him. "Oh, I'll notice, but I promise not to say anything. How's that?"

He pulled lightly on her braid, steering her in the direction of the other rooms. She seemed impressed with what he'd done so far. Especially the new tile in the bathroom and the decorative wood trim on the staircase. She asked intelligent questions, offered suggestions he intended to pursue, and kept saying it was wonderful, which made his chest expand right along with his ego.

I want her to love this place, Lord. To love me, the man who rebuilt it. The man who loves her so much it hurts.

"Who's that?" Belle gazed out his second-floor window, looking toward the intersection where a pickup truck was turning onto Spring Creek Road, headed their direction. "Anybody you know?"

He stood close to her, enjoying her nearness as they stared out the window together. No, he didn't recognize the truck. A Chevy. Fairly new, a nice one. *Don't I wish mine were in that kind of shape.* Three-quarter ton. It would carry a bunch of lumber. Had some wood piled in the bed, he noticed, as it slowed down approaching the house. Sure enough, the truck was swinging onto his gravel drive, right below them.

"Whoever they are, they're here." Belle started to turn, then gasped. "It's . . . it's Norah! In a pickup, no less. Will wonders never cease?" She squinted through the glass. "Who's the guy with her?"

David felt his entire nervous system kick into overdrive, his attention riveted on the man getting out of the truck.

Tall. Lanky, but muscular. Dark blond hair, starting to thin on top. Wearing work clothes and a solemn expression. The man stood there, assessing the property, shading his eyes as he bent his head back.

When the man's eyes — the same blue-gray as his own — connected with his, all movement ceased.

"It's my father."

Belle's soft gasp sounded far away. His heart was beating so loudly it drowned out her words, threatened to leap right out of his chest. *His father.* He hadn't seen the man since he'd left Abingdon eight years ago. Had spoken to him once, when his mother died. Hadn't come to her funeral, which he suddenly regretted more than anything he could think of.

His father. *Here.*

"David, your dad? Really? What . . . why . . ." Belle was scrambling for words, obviously as surprised as he was. "Did you invite him?"

"Not hardly." *Nor would I.* "It must have been Norah's idea." *Again.* The knock at the door sent them both heading toward the staircase, Belle first, then him, moving as if through water with slow, measured steps.

He'd barely reached the landing and turned when the front door swung open and Belle stepped aside to welcome the newcomers. Norah ventured in wearing an expression that suggested hope mingled with apprehension.

His father's face was easier to understand. The man looked grim. Scared to
death. And sober, if his clear eyes were any
indication. David watched him scan the
rooms on either side, then lift his head toward the staircase. Their eyes met again,
closer this time. David could see the man's
eyelids flicker, his mouth tighten.

Tension stretched between them like a
rope. Belle and Norah faded from view. It
was only the two of them. The stillness was
thick, the silence was deafening.

Time came to a standstill.

He could bear it no longer.

"Dad."

His throat was pumping like a rusty well
as he swallowed again and again, fighting
against the flood of tears that threatened to
choke him right where he stood.

His father didn't move, only waited in
the doorway, waited for him to say something else, to invite him in, give him permission.

He's waiting for me to . . . to say . . .

He couldn't make the words come out,
couldn't make his feet move forward, down
the rest of the steps, into the foyer, to the
doorway where a man waited in silence.

No, not silence.

His father's lips were moving. His voice
was barely above a whisper.

"Son."

He didn't know who moved first, didn't care. In the blink of an eye, they were locked in a fierce embrace. Their hoarse sobs echoed in tandem through the empty house.

His father had come home.

God welcomed me home, didn't he? Then I can do the same.

Because of grace.

They stood slapping each other's strong backs. Shaking hands, then embracing again, without a word. Shared memories and emotions and unstated truths swirled around them until the air seemed to change color. Seconds went by unnoticed. Eventually, haltingly, things wound down into a throat-clearing sort of chuckle.

"Well." His father spoke first. His eyes were lowered, his face a study in conflict. "Your prodigal dad has finally come home."

"I'm glad." And he was. Alcohol had taken his father away from him. Sobriety — and humility — had brought him back. "You look good, Dad."

His father's gray eyes regarded him, steady, determined. "I'm a recovering alcoholic, David."

As if he hadn't known that. Still, the confession was obviously painful for his father, tightening the cords of the man's throat.

"I know, Dad. I understand."

"Appreciate that, son." He shifted his weight onto his other foot. "Though the truth is, you oughtta hate me for what I did. Causing you so much heartache growing up."

David watched him swallow hard. "Never mind that now, Dad. It's over. Believe me, I've made plenty of my own mistakes since we parted ways."

His father nodded and they exchanged a glance that covered a multitude of seasons and as many sins. "I've been sober for four years, son. Since your mother died. Moved to Damascus to start my life over. Got full-time work there as a carpenter."

"Of course." David smiled in spite of the emotional tug-of-war going on in his heart. "How'd you find me?"

His father nodded in Norah's direction. "She found me. Drove to Damascus last Thursday. Tracked me down like a regular Sherlock Holmes."

"Pish-posh." Norah shrugged at his praise. "It's not too difficult to find a skilled carpenter with John's reputation in a town of nine hundred."

His father's voice grew warmer. "She told me about you, son. About how you'd made your way in the world. Joined the service. Got a college degree. And a good job. Found a house of your own. And a nice girl." He nodded at Belle, who blushed furiously. "Norah thought it was time I came and saw for myself how you'd turned out."

John paused.

David waited.

"I couldn't be prouder, David. I know I had nothing to do with it. Did more harm than good. But still, I'm proud of you." He cleared his throat again. "I'm also here to help you get this house of yours finished. Evenings, weekends, I'm yours. It's a nice place, son. Together we'll make it look even better. Are you game?"

"Sure, Dad." David's eyes threatened to fill up again. He used his tried-and-true method of swallow, blink, cough, and managed to keep the tears at bay. Barely.

He needn't have bothered. The women were sniffling, big time.

Even his father's voice was gruff. "Guess I owe this little reunion to Norah Adams . . . uh, Silver. No, *Smyth,* is that it?" He tossed up his hands in frustration. "Woman, I never can keep all those old husbands of yours straight."

She laughed through her tears. "It's easy, John. The only thing that remains are their names. They're both gone now. Deceased."

Belle seemed surprised at the news. "Randolph Smyth, too?"

Norah nodded with a pensive sigh. "It was in the Bristol paper last week. Heart attack."

For a moment, no one spoke. It was awkward, David realized. The death of a man who'd walked out of her life so long ago. "I'm sorry," he offered. *You're a regular conversationalist, Cahill.* But it felt appropriate.

"Thanks." Norah sighed, as if a door had closed on a part of her life. Her face brightened a little. "It was a long time ago. Those feelings are buried with him for good now."

His father gave Norah a sideways glance. "You'll pardon me for asking, but might that mean you're available? You always were the prettiest girl in our class, Norah Adams. The dream of every red-blooded adolescent boy in Abingdon."

Everyone laughed, especially Belle. "David, it's patently clear where you learned your flirtatious ways. And Norah *is* spoken for. Isn't that right, Norah . . . Norah . . . hmm. Let's see. How would *Reese* sound?"

Norah turned a shade of red not seen before in nature.

David winked at Belle, sending a spark in her direction that boomeranged back.

His father, clearly confused but obviously happy to be there, merely smiled.

Belle's lighthearted comment had served as a breath of fresh air, blowing away the discomfort of all that came before it. David imagined for a moment the joy of spending the rest of his life with such a woman.

Which whet his appetite. Which reminded him of a refrigerator full of food.

"Folks, if it's all right with you, I say we continue this conversation over fried chicken. The kitchen is right this way."

Belle went ahead of him, quietly adding a place setting. Making room for one more at the table, he realized with a smile.

Just like Christmas.

Twenty-six

There are no secrets better kept than the secrets that everybody guesses.

George Bernard Shaw

"Mom, is this like Christmas?"

"No, Josh." Sherry shook her head, still in shock. "We've never opened a gift like this on Christmas or any other day." She stared at the calendar. *February 4.* David's support checks usually came on the fifteenth of the month, give or take. Not this early.

Besides, no way was it a support check.

It was a miracle.

Josh bounced up and down on the couch next to her, his eyes sparkling with boyish enthusiasm. "C'mon, let me look at it again."

She held out the check, cautioning him not to touch it, just to look. Her hands were shaking. Her insides were shaking.

One piece of paper and her whole world was transformed. It meant everything was okay. The debilitating effects of five weeks without a paycheck would vanish. *Poof!* Just like that. She could pay off the creditors. Get caught up on her rent. Buy some decent clothes for Josh. Fix her car. Better yet, trade it in on something dependable.

Take classes. *Yes!* She could finally look into college courses. Maybe while Josh was in school. She could afford a sitter now, too. Her head was spinning, her heart racing.

"How many zeros is that, Mom?" Josh's eyes were big as zeros, trying to count them all.

"It's twenty thousand dollars, Josh." She whispered it, afraid someone would hear, would come and take it away, say there'd been some mistake.

Josh's voice was awe-filled. "Wow. Did an angel send this?"

"Not an angel." *But close.*

The check was made out to David Cahill. Endorsed by him and made payable to her, in his handwriting. The note in the envelope simply said, "Josh needs this more than I do." Probably true, but it didn't explain why the check was drawn on her father's account.

George Allen Robison. With their home address. The house she grew up in.

Did that mean her father knew about Josh? Finally, after all these years? Had David marched in and demanded this on her behalf? Maybe her dad wanted to send her money but didn't have her Sacramento address.

Nah. He coulda found me long ago.
They both knew that.

She didn't understand where the money came from. She only knew it was the single most incredible thing that had ever happened in her life.

Other than Josh, of course.

"So Mom, what are you gonna buy first? This *is* like money, isn't it?"

Gathering him up in her arms, she pressed the tip of her nose against his. He loved when she did that. Said it tickled. "Young man, we're going straight to the bank and then to the grocery store." She hugged him tight, tears streaming down her face. "The first thing I'm buying is fifty jars of sloppy joe sauce."

Belle O'Brien had discovered a talent she didn't know she possessed: hanging wallpaper. As long as Norah was at the other end of the long roll, Belle was fearless with paper and paste.

This came after three weeks of finding out what she *didn't* do well. No matter how hard she tried, no matter how much she wanted to help David and his father finish the house on Spring Creek Road, she had to face the truth. Taping drywall was not in her skill set. Neither was painting trim without accidentally coating an additional two inches of newly stained floor or windowpane or freshly primed drywall.

But once Norah taught her the mysteries of measuring and hanging wallpaper, she'd hit her stride. After the men did the dirty work, the women arrived with food fit for kings and buckets of wallpaper paste. The men made the rooms solid and secure. The women made them beautiful. *What a team,* Belle thought, as February passed in a blur of activity.

Patrick often came by to watch. He was not permitted to touch a single tool. He *was* allowed to touch Norah, but only on the lips, and only if she was feeling exceedingly generous. Norah was there to work, she insisted, not play spin the bottle with her beau. Her *serious* beau, Belle couldn't help but notice.

As for Belle, she cherished the time with David. Watching him work in his element, muscles in motion, his clever mind coming up with creative solutions to problems, all fueled her appreciation of his talents. Yet it was seeing his relationship with his father begin to heal and grow stronger that most warmed her heart.

God was at work. His grace and mercy were flowing everywhere. True, David and his dad had a few verbal battles, mostly over the best way to measure trim. Even when it ventured into personal territory, though, they resolved things, moved forward.

She liked John Cahill. An older version of David. Handsome, physical, smart, intense. He walked in smelling of Old Spice; wore jeans and a white T-shirt, always. He was proud of his work. Prouder of his son. David told him about his own son, Josh. Showed him his picture. Three generations of Cahill males, she realized. Blond-haired, gray-eyed, strong-chinned Cahills.

When would David finally see Josh? She still couldn't imagine what kind of mother wouldn't want a father for her child, especially a man as fine as David. *Her loss, my gain,* Belle thought, then chastised herself for being selfish.

When it was certain they'd finish by the end of the month, plans for a house-warming party were put in motion for the last Saturday night in February. Norah and Patrick put their heads together for the guest list. It included the entire crew from WPER, David's friends from his church, Belle's friends from hers, and Norah's friends from all over.

"The more the merrier." Norah's eyes twinkled with mischief. "Trust me, we'll have all sorts of things to celebrate by month's end."

Patrick mentioned springing for the food, though Belle was sure she'd misunderstood him. *Patrick? Paying for something?* Impossible.

His San Diego tan was fading. So had his regular references to other markets, other stations. It was obvious that Abingdon had become home for him, just as he'd planned.

She was so busy working at the station all day and on David's house most evenings, that Belle didn't pay attention to an appearance schedule Burt posted in the studio. *Much Ado about Nothing* was opening at the Barter. It was sponsored by Oldies 95, which meant before each performance, one of the radio personalities was expected to stroll out on stage and welcome the audience on behalf of WPER.

Tonight, February 25, was her night.

"Norah, I can't do this." Her bedroom had an after-the-cyclone look. Discarded clothes draped about, jewelry in heaps, shoes in piles. She stood there in her slip, holding up yet another fashion possibility, then groaning and tossing it nowhere in particular. "I give up. I don't know what to *wear,* let alone what to say."

Norah held court on a mission oak chair, offering wise counsel. "Of course you know what to say, lovey. You do this kind of emcee thing all the time. Just be Belle. Make them glad they came. Short and sweet. Funny. And warm, as only you can be."

"But Norah, the *Barter.* The stage."

Can't the woman see what this will cost me? Norah had helped her work through the catastrophe of her audition for days afterward. Surely she understood what the evening ahead meant, what it would take to get her back out on that stage.

"You're not there to act. You're there to be yourself." Norah rose and gave her a much-needed hug. "That's the role you were born to play. Break a leg."

Belle finally settled on the red dress. The David Dress, she'd named it. Knowing he would be there, center orchestra, cheering her on, was good news and bad news. He'd seen her make a fool of herself on that stage once before. She couldn't bear the thought of it happening again in front of so many people.

Especially in front of people who might remember a certain newspaper article about Belle O'Brien and her crazy dream of doing theater.

She arrived half an hour before curtain and paced the floor backstage until she realized she was making the stage director nervous. She wouldn't need a microphone, since the acoustics of the old theater were breathtaking. She wouldn't need notes for a one-minute welcome. What she needed was a calm spirit and she knew where to turn for that.

Lord, help me think about the audience

instead of myself. Let your joy shine through me and give me strength. If you're on stage with me, I know that whatever happens, I'll survive.

At precisely eight o'clock, the stage manager gave her the nod and she entered stage right, the bright stage lights hitting her like an oncoming freight train.

Hadn't she faced lights like that hundreds of times in her career? *Not to worry, girl. Remember what Norah said. "Just be Belle."*

She took a deep breath and plunged in. "Good evening and welcome to the Barter Theatre, one of the oldest continuously operating regional theaters in America. My name is Belle O'Brien and I do the midday show on WPER-FM —"

Without warning, the audience burst into applause, first one section, then the other, until the whole house was clapping with gusto. In particular, a little knot of people front and center. *Norah. Patrick. David.* And not just them. *Heather. Burt. Rick.* Even Frank the Crank, bless his craggy heart.

She shot a look of concern in Patrick's direction. *Who's running the station?*

He shot a look back. *Relax. Break a leg.*

She didn't break a leg, but it did appear she charmed the crowd, if their reaction was to be trusted. She shared a brief story

501

they found amusing. Invited them to listen to the radio station. Described the historic building they were sitting in. Gave them a quick introduction to the play. And welcomed the artistic director to the stage.

It was the same man who'd judged her unimpressive attempt at Ursula.

He sidled up next to her, smiling at the applauding audience as he whispered in her ear. "Why play the part of someone else when you're so talented at playing *you?* Congratulations, Miss . . . uh —" He winked. "Oberholtzer."

She floated off the stage, down the steps, and into the waiting arms of a man who put Antonio, Claudio, and the rest of them to shame. Mere mortals in velvet doublets and hose, men who wouldn't have the faintest idea how to swing a hammer or sand a wood floor.

Let alone hang wallpaper.

Two days later, Belle's wallpaper skills were on display for three dozen of Abingdon's finest, as David threw open the doors of his refurbished farmhouse for a Saturday night of celebration and good-natured inspection.

He'd waited a lifetime for a place to call home, with pride. That time had finally arrived.

"Where's Norah?" He scanned the

roomful of friends, old and new, looking for a familiar head of silver hair. "I haven't seen her since she dropped off the food six hours ago."

"Mmm." Belle finished another one of Norah's delicious orange pecan muffins wrapped around thinly sliced sugar-cured ham. "Hard to tell, with so many folks here, but I don't think I've seen Patrick either."

Candles glowed on the mantel, on the windowsills, and all through the kitchen. Party music filled the downstairs — oldies, of course — which made it hard to talk without shouting. He was content to slip his arm around Belle as they surveyed the living room together.

There was Matthew the Methodist, chatting with Heather Young, of all people. *Interesting.* Frank the Crank had Millie on his arm — those two were a regular item now, yet another reason the WPER staff had started calling the place "The Love Boat." Rick and Burt were hovering around the food table, stuffing their faces with Norah's food.

"Where *is* Norah?" Belle wondered aloud. A commotion at the front door answered her question. Norah was inching across the threshold. Perched in Patrick's arms. Wearing a silvery white lace dress.

And a sheer white veil.

A veil?

Belle's shriek of delight rang through the noisy room. "I can't believe it!"

A spontaneous cheer rang out in the foyer as David steered Belle through the throng. Patrick was making a big show of dropping Norah to her feet, sweeping her into a precipitous dip, and planting a major smacker on her pretty pink face.

The blushing bride, David realized, grinning broadly. *Well, what do you know?*

Belle's cello voice was squeaking like a violin. "Norah! What in the world . . . ? I mean, when . . . ?"

Patrick cleared his throat with a booming broadcaster's *ahem.* "Now that we have your attention, ladies and gents, may I introduce the first and *only* Mrs. Reese, my beautiful bride of one hour."

The room exploded in celebration. Paper napkins were tossed in the air and Rick dug out a CD featuring the Dixie Cups classic, "Chapel of Love." As if on cue, the partygoers made an aisle for Norah and Patrick to walk down, arm in arm, until they reached the fireplace across the room and demonstrated another showstopping kiss.

"The whole story, please," Belle called out.

Patrick cheerfully obliged. "You'll remember, I spent a few years in Tennessee, so I knew all about their marriage laws.

You don't need to be a resident. No appointments needed to get a license. No waiting time, no blood tests, and at our age —" he squeezed Norah affectionately — "no need for our parents to sign the certificate for us."

Norah nodded, her eyes sparkling, her smile dazzling. "My charmingly cheap husband decided that since we were already having this get-together, it would make a dandy wedding reception."

Patrick pretended to be embarrassed and shrugged. "The price was right. A quick trip to the county clerk's in Bristol, thirty-six dollars in cash, and the woman of my dreams is all mine. We hope you'll share in our joy. And look at the bright side." He flashed his infamous white teeth. "You didn't have to spend a dime on a gift."

Another general cheer rang out before the guests started lining up to congratulate the happy couple. Belle ran up first, hugging Norah for the longest time, David noticed. *What is she thinking? Feeling? After all, she had designs on Patrick herself once.* He watched the women together, both their faces radiant, and realized Belle was only happy for Norah, nothing else. *Put it to rest, man. Ancient history.* The only direction he needed to look was forward.

She made her way back to his side, slipping her arm around his waist, looking up at him. He could see the wheels turning. *What, Lord? What's on her mind?* He had a pretty good idea. Lace dresses. Long veils. Marriage licenses. *Now, Lord? Here? Is it too much, too soon?*

He'd do a trial run. *Yeah, that's it.*

"So, Belle, what do you think of this happy news?" He kept his voice steady, his gaze steady, his hands steady. His insides were a joint-jumping mess, but she didn't need to know that.

"I think it's wonderful." She sighed, her golden eyes glowing like stars, her voice a cello once more. "How 'bout you?"

"Wonderful." *Is that the best you can do?* The place was all wrong, he realized that. Too crowded, too noisy, not the least bit romantic. She'd want that, wouldn't she? A quiet, cozy corner at the Martha. Candlelight. Soft music. Him on one knee. Two, if it made her happy.

He looked down at her, his heart bursting. *Oh, Belle. Marry me. Be mine until heaven.* Maybe if he said it with his eyes, she'd know, she'd understand. The words would have to wait until later, but he wanted her to know now, right now, how he felt, what he longed for.

She simply smiled up at him, then turned to see about some food for the newlyweds.

So be it. Later. He watched her as the evening progressed, making people feel welcome in his new home, serving their guests more punch, more food, more hugs. It was eleven o'clock before the crowd began to thin. Maybe by midnight he'd have her to himself. Not for a long time, but for long enough.

Amidst the hubbub, he almost didn't hear the shrill ring of the phone in the kitchen.

Who in the world? Everyone they knew, it seemed, was there. Could be the station. They had a part-timer at the helm, which meant anything might have happened, from a cart that jammed to transmitter failure. At times like that, he was grateful to have the 'mitter shack perched on the hill behind his house.

He made his way through the throng in the kitchen, elbowing past a group from his Sunday school class to get to the phone on the wall, still ringing for all it was worth.

He grabbed it a half second before the answering machine kicked in. "Hello?"

"David?" A woman's voice. "Is this . . . David Cahill?"

Vaguely familiar. Sounded about his age. Definitely a Virginia accent.

"Yes, this is David Cahill." Why were his palms suddenly clammy? "Sorry about

507

the noise. We've got a housewarming going on here."

"Oh." The woman paused for a long time. "David, it's Sherry."

"Sherry?" A cold steel knife of pain slid through his heart. "Sherry . . . Robison?"

"Yes."

Is that all the woman had to say after eight years? "Yes?"

He swallowed a bitter lump in his throat. "Where are you?"

"The Comfort Inn."

Not here. Not in Abingdon.

"You're in town?" He gulped, trying to get his bearings, collect his thoughts, which were spinning out of control. Around him in the kitchen, everyone was smiling, chatting, normal. On the phone was a disaster in the making. "What are you doing in Abingdon?"

He heard her take a deep breath. He also heard a young voice in the background and his throat tightened. *Josh.* "Is Joshua with you?"

She laughed a little, sounding relieved. "Of course he's with me. I could hardly leave him behind in California. Josh, come say hello to your father."

"Your father." His son.

He waited an agonizing thirty seconds before a young boy's jubilant voice came on the line. "Hi, Dad!"

"Josh." David squeezed his eyes and turned his back to the crowd in the kitchen, hoping no one noticed. He thanked the Lord that Belle was somewhere else at this exact moment.

"How are you, son?" A lame thing to say, but a start.

"Great, Dad! I like Virginia. We saw horses. Mountains, too."

"It's a nice place. Shouldn't you be in bed by now, Josh?"

"Nah. I slept in the car. We drove forever. Took us a week to get here, Mom said. We traded in our beat-up car. This one's cool. It's bright yellow."

"That's good, Josh. Let me talk to your mother now, okay?" *Because I intend to get some kind of explanation.*

"I'm back." Sherry paused, then whispered something to Josh that David couldn't decipher. Finally, her voice came on the line. "David, you still there?"

"I'm here." *Not in great shape, but I'm here.* "The question is, why are *you* here, in Abingdon?"

Her voice softened. "David, you once asked me to marry you. I . . . I laughed, remember?"

"I remember." *Like I could forget.*

"Well, I'm not laughing now." Her voice was barely above a whisper. "I'm here to say yes."

Twenty-seven

*I could sooner reconcile all Europe
than two women.*

King Louis XIV

Sherry could tell that David was surprised. Shocked, probably. It might have been better if she'd written first, or called. It just made more sense to go with her heart and come on home to Virginia.

Settling things out west had taken no time at all, not with thousands of dollars to grease the skids. She'd made a few calls to Abingdon before she left California for good. She found out David was definitely single. Remodeling a house out on Spring Creek Road, someone told her. For all she knew, he might be building it for her and Josh. Wouldn't that be wild?

After all, hadn't the man sent her money every month for eight years? More faithfully than a lot of guys who were forced to by the courts.

Hadn't he mailed her a check for twenty thousand dollars three weeks ago? Why would he do that if not so she could get her life in order and come back home? Home to Abingdon, home to him. Surely that's what he'd been trying to tell her, in his own quiet way.

Most men would have disappeared long ago. Not David Cahill. He loved her, plain and simple. What other explanation could there be? He'd obviously carried a torch for her for eight long years.

Well, then.

She was back in town, determined to light that torch for good. The phone line had been silent for several seconds, so she jumped in. "I guess you're kinda surprised to hear from me after all this time."

"Kinda." His voice, a deep, masculine rumble, sent shivers up her spine.

"That's understandable. I'm . . . I'm anxious to see you, David. Josh is, too, as you can tell. Could the three of us have breakfast tomorrow? Or lunch, maybe. You'll want to sleep in after your wild party, huh?"

"It's not what you'd call a wild party, Sherry. Just some friends from work and church."

"Church?" *Don't tell me the man's gone religious on me.* "I didn't know you went to church."

"Yeah, I do. Every Sunday."

"No kidding." Eight years was a long time, she reminded herself. People changed. Did that mean he wouldn't be interested in her physically? *Not a chance.*

511

Not David Cahill, the guy who chased her through the woods on more than one moonlit night. And caught her. Once. Some things about a man might change, but not that.

"Let's meet at noon, then." She forced herself to sound lighthearted, nonchalant despite his seeming lack of enthusiasm. It'd never occurred to her that David might not be thrilled to see her, to have her home. That's what he wanted, right? Maybe he was just shy about it, now that she and Josh were finally back in town. She'd help him adjust to the idea. And fast. "Know any good restaurants?"

"Ah . . . how about we . . . eat here?" He sounded uncomfortable. "Money is kinda tight right now."

"Sure, sure." That was better anyway. His place. More personal, more private. Let Josh see his new home right off the bat. *After our tiny, ugly apartment, Josh will think it's a palace.* "I'm pretty sure I can find it, but if you'll give me directions, that'd be helpful." She jotted down a few notes. David's voice was unusually low. Almost sad. Maybe the party hadn't gone well. Cost him money he couldn't afford.

She knew all about money hassles.

Those days were over. Forever, she hoped.

"So, we'll see you at noon." She could

512

feel her heart picking up speed at the thought of seeing him again. Was he still a skinny guy, blond hair falling in his face, with blue-gray eyes like Josh's? Come to think of it, she'd been eyeballing a pint-size version of David Cahill for eight years. Not a chance she wouldn't recognize him. *Not hardly.*

"Joshua eats anything but fish. Me, I'm not picky in the least. You learn to eat anything when funds get tight." She paused, realizing how that must have sounded to him. "Uh . . . David, I know I said this in a letter once, but I want you to know how much those checks meant to us. The money went right for groceries, every month. We would have starved without you." A little dramatic, but she wanted to make him feel important, appreciated.

"I did what I could, Sherry. I'm sorry it wasn't more."

More? Gee whiz, the guy is a saint! She'd better sew things up with him in a hurry, before another woman in town found out what a gem he really was, Cahill or not. The time hadn't been right before. He was settled now. Had a good job. A house. The timing was perfect.

The timing could not have been worse.

David hung the receiver back in place, numb to his toes. What had he done?

513

Agreed to make lunch for Sherry and Josh Robison, that's what.

He couldn't risk being seen with them in a hotel restaurant, having people making assumptions, spreading rumors. Not to mention if Sherry made a scene . . . No, home court was best.

He looked around at the stacks of dirty paper plates, empty glasses, discarded napkins. At least he wouldn't have to cook, not if they'd willingly eat chicken salad and country ham. Food was the least of his concerns. The auburn beauty walking toward him was what worried him most.

Belle stretched up and kissed the end of his nose. "You're looking awfully serious for a man who hosted the grandest housewarming event of the decade." Her full lips opened wide for a heart-stopping smile. "Come say good-bye to Norah and Patrick with me."

Grateful for the distraction, he followed her into the foyer where the happy couple was making their much-heralded exit. "We're off to the Martha," Patrick announced with a roguish leer. "See you Methodists at the second service tomorrow."

The newlyweds found their car, mysteriously draped with crepe paper and strung with tin cans, a hand-lettered *Just Married* sign poking up in the back window. Good old Frank the Crank, David guessed with a half smile. He waved the two off, noticing most of the others were gathering their coats and heading for the crowded driveway as well.

The hour was late. Not too late, he hoped. He desperately needed to talk to Belle. The sooner the better.

"At last I have you all to myself." Belle curled up at the end of the couch, angled close to the fading embers of the fire in a room that had suddenly grown chilly. She'd been watching David closely, ever since she'd found him standing in the kitchen earlier, looking as if he'd lost his best friend.

It had been an emotionally taxing month, she knew, what with the decision about WBT, facing Sherry's dad at the bank, reuniting with his own father. *No wonder the guy looks worn out.* She crooked a finger in David's direction. "Come and sit with me, handsome. I've got something to tell you."

"Me, too." He poked some life into the fire then joined her on the couch, pulling her into his arms. "You go first."

She gently pulled back from his embrace. *Look him in the eye, woman. Let him know you're serious.* "David, it's taken me a long time to admit something to myself.

515

Now that I have, it's time I told you." She could hear the trembling in her voice, feel the dryness in her mouth.

Wet your lips. Make them move. Go!

"I love you, David. With all my heart, I love you." Despite her best efforts to hold them back, tears sprang to her eyes. "You're the kindest, wisest, most godly man I've ever known. I know you've waited a month to hear this. I'm sorry it's taken me so long. Tonight seemed like . . . well, the perfect time."

There. She'd done it. *Not so horrid after all.*

But he wasn't smiling. *Why isn't he smiling, Lord?* Her heart was behaving like a set of snare drums again, a flurry of beats without rhythm.

It was worse when he finally spoke. "Belle, I'm . . . I'm so . . . grateful."

"Grateful? David Cahill, grateful is what you feel when your mother does your laundry. Not when a woman pours her heart out and says she loves you."

She could feel her chest tightening, a sob building. *No! No dramatics, Belle.*

When his long arms reached to pull her closer, she planted her hands firmly on his chest. "No, you don't. This isn't something you can cuddle and make go away. You had something to tell me, yes? Suppose you get on with it before I make a bigger fool of myself." *As if that's humanly possible.*

"Belle, I love you. You know that."

She sniffed, her chin buried in her chest. "Good of you to mention it again. I'd almost forgotten."

He put one finger under her chin and lifted it up until their eyes met. Sincerity filled his face. Relief, she suspected, filled hers.

"I've said it as many times in as many ways as I possibly can." He dropped his hand and leaned back, obviously needing the distance. "I . . . I got a phone call tonight that . . . surprised me."

"Who from?"

"Sherry Robison."

A gasp escaped her lips before she could catch it. "That . . . *that* Sherry?"

He nodded, looking grim.

"Why? Where is she? What was she calling about? Was Josh with her?" Belle realized she sounded ridiculous, hysterical. "Tell me some good news. Quick, before I faint."

"I don't have any good news."

She didn't faint, but she did slump over convincingly. "Don't tell me she's here in Abingdon." It came out on a moan. When he didn't answer her immediately, it was worse than if he'd said the words. *Yes. She's here.*

With some effort, she lifted her head. "Why did she come back, David?" *I don't really want to know. Tell me anyway.*

"I'm . . . not sure."

Yes, you are. She wants you back. I can see it on your face. All over your handsome face.

"Oh?" It was all she trusted herself to say.

He told her then. About the check from George Robison. How he'd mailed it to Sherry. How she'd apparently used the money to wind up her affairs in California and move back home.

Belle groaned two full octaves. "When are you seeing her?"

His eyes darkened. "How did you know?"

"I'm a woman, David. In case you hadn't noticed."

"I noticed, Belle." He said it through clenched teeth.

"I know how we women think. She's going to use your son to get you back."

David abruptly stood to his feet. The gaze he fixed on her was as hard as his jawline and every bit as stubborn.

"That's outrageous, Belle. The woman hasn't spoken to me for eight years. The last time I heard her voice she was laughing in my face. I'm eager to see Josh, yes. But Sherry? No way. The woman means nothing to me, do you hear me? Nada. Zip."

"I hear you. And I believe you." Any trace of humor in the moment had vanished. She, who always sought out silver linings, saw nothing but black clouds ahead, starting with his brooding gray eyes.

She stood, too. Though her hair barely brushed his chin, she wanted to seem strong, able to handle this bump in the road. *Not a roadblock, Lord. Please don't let it be a roadblock.*

David's voice was firm, matter-of-fact. "I'm having the two of them over here tomorrow for lunch. No big deal, leftovers from the party, a chance to meet my son. A chance to explain to Sherry that, should she entertain any ideas of us getting back together, that's an impossibility." He slid his hands down her arms with a strong enough grasp to get her attention, to force her to look up at him, whether she wanted to or not.

And stuff it all, she wanted to. Sherry or no Sherry, this was her man and she loved him. Intended to keep him. Fight for him, if necessary.

His eyes were clear, his words convincing. "I love you, Belle. You have nothing to worry about here. I'll call you the minute they leave tomorrow. Better yet, why don't you come over at three and meet them both? She'll see how serious our relationship is and that will be the end of it."

Was this a tiny slice of silver lining? "Promise you'll tell her I'm coming, so I won't feel stupid barging in on your cozy threesome."

"I'll tell her. Everything will be fine." He circled his arms around her in an embrace clearly intended to end the conversation. His warm kiss, suitably long and utterly persuasive, chased away the last of her doubts.

When he finally lifted his lips from hers and checked his watch, he angled his thumb toward the door and murmured, "You'd better head for Main Street, sweetheart."

"What? And leave this mess for you to clean up? No way." Belle slipped out of his arms and began gathering up the debris. "I want this place to shine tomorrow. Sherry will take one look at it and *know* you have a woman in your life who loves you. Got me, mister?"

David's laugh rolled across the room, warming her to her toes. "Yeah, I got you, Belle. And like it or not, you've got me."

Sherry got there exactly at noon. David watched her pull up in her car — bright yellow, just as Josh had described it — then sit there.

Why doesn't she get out? David opened the front door, impatient to see his son. Hadn't he waited long enough? He stepped out on the porch as they began climbing out of the small car.

She's older. Of course, she would be. Wasn't he? The eight years hadn't taken much of a toll on her, though. She was still a small thing, with a few more womanly curves. Still had curly brown hair. Wearing it shorter, maybe. Looked good on her. Her face had filled out. Softened. She was smiling. Wearing a lot of makeup, he thought, but she looked nice. *Very nice.*

Then Josh ran around to her side of the car, and David had eyes only for him.

The resemblance was uncanny. The hair, the eyes, the build. He was staring at his own school pictures from third grade come to life. His chest constricted so tightly he couldn't speak. *Welcome home, Josh,* he wanted to say. *I love you, son.*

Then Josh grinned, big enough to show off his missing teeth, and David felt the vise around his chest relax enough for him to breath again.

The waiting was over. His son was here.

"Come in!" David pushed open the door behind him. Sherry hadn't taken her eyes off him for a second. *Is she disappointed? Have I changed so much?* Josh ran ahead of her, stumbling through the door, then turning to be sure his mother was coming close behind. Sherry brushed past David. Closer than necessary, he thought. *Blushing, too.* Her perfume was nice. Like a flower.

Finally, she spoke. "What a great place." Her eyes met his. "Did you do all this?"

He was surprised to hear his voice sound normal. "Good bit of it. My dad helped, too."

"Your dad?"

He understood the incredulous look on her face.

"No offense, but I didn't think your father could hammer a straight nail. At least, not when I left town."

David rushed to his defense, trying not to bristle. "The man's changed. Been sober for four years. Doing well for himself, living in Damascus."

"That's terrific." She smiled brightly, seemed sincere. "Josh, you got anything to say to your dad or are you gonna stand there and be shy?"

David grinned at the boy who was holding his mother's hand like a younger child might. David hunkered down, bringing his eyes in line with Joshua's, now open wider than ever. "I was shy at your age, Josh. No problem." He squeezed the boy's shoulder, longing to hug him for all he was worth.

"I'm not shy. I'm scared."

They both laughed and Sherry tousled Josh's hair. "Scared of what, young man? David is as trustworthy as they come. Aren't you, David?"

He straightened to his feet and she looked at him then, really looked, with a steady, knowing gaze. The gaze of a woman who'd known him better than anyone else — including Belle.

Her voice had softened and she spun the words out like liquid gold. "David Cahill is, above all things, a man to be trusted."

He felt the heat rising from his chest, crawling up his neck. *What is she getting at?* He tried to brush it away with a casual response. "Thanks . . . I think."

"No thanks necessary." She smiled, a half smile this time, full of secrets. "Joshua, your father is the kind of man who always does the right thing."

The boy beamed at him. "Gosh, that's good, isn't it?"

"I try." He didn't like the way this conversation was going.

"You do more than try, you succeed." Sherry patted his arm, sending him a message that he was doing his level best not to receive.

"Let's eat." He said it more forcefully than he meant to, though neither of his guests seemed to notice. "I've got everything spread out in the kitchen."

Sherry fussed over the remodeled room, noticing all the details and nodding her approval. He watched as her eyes took in the new cabinets, almost as if she were loading them up with her own groceries.

Lunch proceeded without a hitch. They ate everything he offered them. Josh especially was stuffing food in as fast as a boy missing two teeth could chew. David knew the signs. *He's gone hungry more than once.* It had been tough for Sherry in California, tougher than she was making it out to be with her breezy description of ocean cliffs and giant redwoods.

When she asked for a tour of the house, he obliged her, hurrying through the upstairs bedrooms, noticing how she lingered there, measuring both rooms with her eyes. He spent more time in the living room, showing off his father's built-in bookcases and the mantel he'd refinished to a fine umber.

As soon as his shyness evaporated, Josh had a million questions about the house, about the radio station, about the truck. *What a great kid!* David kept thinking, over and over. He answered Josh's questions with all the enthusiasm the boy deserved, while Sherry listened, her eyes glowing with an unsettling light.

The clock on the mantel caught his eye.

Nearly three. Thank the Lord, the cavalry would soon be there. "Sherry, I've invited someone to join us this afternoon."

"Oh?" The single word carried the weight of several. *Who?* and *Why?* no doubt.

"Her name is Belle O'Brien." He laughed, feeling awkward for not mentioning this sooner. *And why didn't you, man?* "Actually her name is Belinda Oberholtzer, but her radio name is Belle, so that's how we all think of her."

Sherry looked immensely relieved. "I see. A coworker, then."

"More than that." *What is your problem? Just say it.* "She's my . . . girl-friend."

A host of emotions moved across Sherry's face. Surprise, suspicion, anger, determination. "Your *girlfriend?* David, I'm shocked."

He didn't know whether to laugh or be offended, so he kept both to himself and asked the obvious. "Shocked that someone might be interested in me?"

"No!" She was upset. More than upset. "Shocked that you'd . . . ah . . . Suppose we let Josh watch a little television while you and I take a walk around the property."

Without a word, he flicked on the set in the living room, then grabbed their coats

525

and headed out the door. *Whatever line she's selling, I'm not buying.*

As they moved across the frozen yard, she spoke first, in measured tones. "David, apparently there's been a misunderstanding."

"On your part, maybe." He was hot, could feel his blood pumping under his skin. He willed himself to remain calm, hear her out.

Sherry could be so convincing. Manipulative. She'd been batting her eyes at him for the last three hours. He knew the signs. She wanted something, expected something from him. The sooner they got it out in the open, the better.

"What is it you want, Sherry?"

Her eyes flew open as if she'd been struck. "What do *I* want? I thought *you* wanted something. Specifically . . . me."

"I beg your pardon?"

They stopped and faced one another, their breathing sending puffs of steam into the frosty air. "David, when you mailed me that check, I thought you were telling me to come home. To Abingdon."

"What?"

Her words came out on a sob. "I thought you loved me, David. That's why I'm here."

He was undone. How had this happened?

He clenched his fists and prayed for guidance. "I did love you, Sherry. A long time ago. For months after you left, I hoped you'd come back to me, marry me, let me help raise our child. But you didn't come back, so I stopped asking. Stopped begging." He sighed at the painful memory. "Stopped hoping."

"I did care for you, David." Her voice was strained, her words halting. "In my own way, I did. But I couldn't marry you. Surely you understood that. Not a . . . a Cahill. Not then. But seeing the life you've created now . . . Well, you've redeemed yourself, David."

Ahh. There's my answer. Thank you, Lord.

He lightly touched her elbows through her heavy coat, wanting her to hear him clearly. "You're wrong, Sherry. I didn't redeem anything. The Lord redeemed me. He saved me from myself. From my bitterness. From hating you and mistrusting women in general. The Lord set me free from all that."

"The Lord?" She scrunched up her face in distaste. "You really have bought into this whole church bit, haven't you?"

"Not church." He had to make her see the truth. "Not a building, not people. The Lord Jesus. He's the one who's made all the difference. He's the reason I could send that check to you, no strings attached."

"That's funny —" she all but spat the words at him — "I saw all kinds of strings dangling from that check."

"I'm sorry you did, Sherry." He exhaled, frustrated, looking for a way to make amends. "I'm not sorry you came home, though."

For a moment, a glimmer of hope shone in her eyes. "Really?"

He nodded. "It's time for you to patch things up with your family, don't you think? And I need to get to know Josh. Really know him. He's a terrific kid, Sherry. You've done a fine job of raising him."

She stepped backward. The soft angles of her face had sharpened. "So. This is all about *you,* then. You seeing Josh. You bringing my dad and me together for a boxing match so you can sell tickets."

"No, I —"

"I gave up everything to come home to you, David!" Her voice was shrill, cutting through the icy air. "You owe me a chance. A chance to be part of a whole family. A chance to have a father for Josh and a husband . . . a husband for me. I've been . . . so . . . so . . . lonely."

Sherry's shoulders collapsed. Her anguished sobs tore at his heart. Whatever the truth behind her words, her tears were real.

Should I hold her? Comfort her? He didn't want her to jump to conclusions.

Hang the conclusions. He was not the kind of man who stood by and watched a woman suffer, especially if her pain was due to his own misguided attempt to do the right thing.

He reached out and pulled her into his arms. She came willingly, though it made her cry harder, her sobs echoing in the frozen stillness of the countryside. At a loss, he smoothed her hair, murmured the most encouraging, honest words he could think of. When she seemed too weak to stand on her own, he tightened his grasp, pressing her against his blue parka, praying for wisdom.

But it wasn't wisdom that drove up in a Pontiac.

It was Belle.

Sherry's sobs had distracted him, or drowned out the sound of Belle's engine, until she'd pulled up within a few feet of them. While Sherry clung to him, Belle only stared. Long enough to see his desperate expression. Not long enough for him to explain.

Belle hit the gas, sending her car spinning toward Spring Creek Road, throwing a spray of gravel at his feet.

Twenty-eight

Love to faults is always blind.

William Blake

"Whose fault is it again?"

Norah sighed, shaking her head. Her life-long journey with Patrick was twenty-four hours old and they'd already hit their first speed bump. "It's no one's fault, darling. Not David's and certainly not Belle's. Sherry Robison simply appeared at the other end of his phone line last night after we left the party."

"Humph." Patrick squared his shoulders as if to do battle. "Cahill better take care of our Belle, or he'll answer to me when her heart gets broken."

His fierce expression made her swallow a laugh whole, sending her earrings on a merry dance. "Don't polish your armor just yet, good knight. Belle can manage things." She ventured into the closet and brought out a fistful of hangers. "Wait until she gets back from David's place. We'll no doubt find out everything is under control."

"If you say so." Patrick yanked open the dresser drawer she'd emptied for him and began filling it with socks. Not in pairs, not in stacks, just willy-nilly.

Forever is a long time, she reminded herself, watching him stuff dress and sport socks into the drawer with abandon. Soon those same socks would be hiding in corners, gathering wool under furniture, wrapping their fuzzy threads around unsuspecting dust bunnies.

It was a sure bet she'd be the one rounding them up for a trip through the wash.

New husband, new socks, same old story.

But hadn't he been the handsomest thing yesterday, standing before the county clerk, wearing his freshly pressed suit and a narrow black tie? She'd stumbled over her vows more than once, lost in his dark hazel eyes and devastating smile.

"Mrs. Reese?"

Barely listening, she continued to gaze at him, remembering their first hours together at the Martha . . .

"Mrs. Reese!"

"Oh!" She snapped to attention, feeling the heat sting her cheeks. "Sorry. Not quite accustomed to the sound of that."

"Get used to it, woman." A sly grin stretched across his beard. The remaining socks landed on the floor in a jumbled heap. "Were you daydreaming just now, my dear?" He eased his arms around her, drawing her toward him.

She gave him no resistance. Couldn't if she'd wanted to.

"Thinking of anyone I know?" He slipped off one dangling earring, then another, lightly kissing the sensitive spot behind each ear.

In seconds she felt like the blushing bride she most certainly was, being wooed by her teddy bear of a bridegroom. "I was thinking of you, naturally. Of us. Last night."

"Oh, at David's party?" His kisses eased down her neck.

"No, silly. Uh . . . later."

"On the porch?"

The lips against her skin didn't contain the slightest hint of a smile, though she was certain she felt the corners of his mouth beginning to curl. So, for that matter, were her middle-aged toes.

"Not then. Later."

"In the car, perhaps, Mrs. Reese?"

She groaned. "No . . . later!"

"Hmm." His hands were rubbing her shoulders and back, relaxing her, gentling her. "There wasn't much after that, really. Except the Martha."

A throaty sigh escaped her lips. "Precisely."

"You'll have to forgive me, beloved, but

the daily rent at the Martha is too steep for your old cheapskate hubby. Will home do?"

"Home will do very nicely." She laced her fingers through his hair and tipped his head back until their eyes met. "Have I mentioned how much I love you, Mr. Reese?"

"Not in the last ten minutes." His eyes darkened and the lids dropped to half mast. "Suppose you tell me again."

"Not again! Not again, Lord!" Belle was filled with a cold fury. She managed to keep the car on the road, but her emotions were veering wildly over the map of her heart.

Last November, when she'd discovered Norah and Patrick gazing at one another in the shop kitchen, had been awful. This was worse. Much worse.

She'd only had a crush on Patrick. David Cahill was the love of her earthly life.

Patrick and Norah had merely been holding hands that night.

David and Sherry had been embracing. Fervently, it appeared. She'd seen them the minute she turned off Old Jonesboro Road. Recognized David's blue parka right away. Easily guessed who was wrapped in his arms.

And where was Josh? The boy wasn't

even in sight. Wasn't he the whole point of their cozy Sunday get-together?

She wiped away a burst of hot tears, knowing they were the only ones that would dare interfere with her justifiable thoughts of homicide. It would have to be a humane method, she decided. No knives or guns. Death by chocolate, maybe. Kill them with kindness. "Oh, fiddle," she grumbled, slowing down for a stop sign. "It's Sunday. You can't go bumping people off on the Lord's day. It's not proper."

Besides, she knew there was an explanation. Hadn't David's look of despair told her what she needed to know? That all was not as it appeared, that something had happened? Maybe he'd just told Sherry about a certain Belle O'Brien, the love of *his* life. *There's a calming thought.* Maybe he'd just informed Sherry that he'd be willing to see Josh often, but not her. *Better, much better.*

Or maybe — just maybe — things were exactly as they appeared. David's first love, the mother of his only son, had come home at last to claim what she thought was rightfully hers.

The tears returned for a second round. Belle felt her spirits drooping, past her boots, under the Pontiac, and all over Main Street. Matthew's morning sermon floated through her mind. "Cast all your worries upon the Lord," Pastor Howard had admonished them, "because he cares about you."

Believing that was one thing. Acting on it was another.

She'd leaned on the Lord to get her through the debacle that was Chicago, and he had. When everything fell apart with Patrick, God was there. The embarrassment of the Barter audition faded in the warmth of his steadfast loving-kindness.

Now, her future with David dotted with question marks, she found herself with a fresh armload of worries and only one place to drop them that made sense.

"All yours, Lord." It came out on a croak, but it was a sincere croak, full of determination. "David is yours, Sherry is yours, Josh is yours. Work that whole situation out to your satisfaction, Lord." She sniffed, the last of her tears drying, making her cheeks feel tight and drawn. "One more thing, Lord. Could you wrap your arms around me in the meantime?"

The gray afternoon light, slanting low in the winter sky, beckoned her to follow its meager rays, up and down the streets of Abingdon until, an hour later, she pulled into the single parking space behind the brick house she called home, and yanked on the brake.

Fine. She wouldn't do anything drastic.

Not overreact. Not think the worst. She also wouldn't call him. David was the one who had the explaining to do. *Let him call me.* In the meantime, she'd make a concerted effort to leave her fears in the Lord's capable hands and press on with her life.

A few chocolate chip scones from Norah's bakery case would help matters greatly.

Belle wasn't so easily assuaged come Monday morning. Scones and muffins were not filling the hole in her heart left there by one heartthrob of an engineer who was noticeably absent when she arrived at WPER. The phone message he'd left her Sunday evening was cryptic — "Not to worry, Belle. I'm working things out here. I love you. Trust me, all is well."

"Well, then, where are you?" She yanked CDs out of the rack for her show, slapping them on the counter.

"He needed to spend the day with his son," Patrick informed her when she went looking for David during the noon newsbreak.

"He took the day *off?*"

Patrick looked up from the clutter on his desk. "Yeah. You know, vacation days? Most people make use of them, Belle."

"Will he be here tomorrow?" She

sounded like a lovesick fool. Well, so what? She *was* a lovesick fool.

"He better be here tomorrow. You and your Happy Together winner will be lifting off from the VHCC campus at four o'clock sharp. Since you're broadcasting live from the air, David will have to outfit the gondola with the remote equipment. Yeah, he'll be there." A twinkle sneaked into Patrick's expression. "Not worried, are you, Belle? Not after yesterday's sermon?"

"I *did* cast my worries at the Lord's feet," she insisted with a dramatic ruffling of feathers. "Problem is, I keep going back to find them again."

"Wait until you get to my age." Patrick's toothsome grin was contagious. "You won't remember where you put them."

Good old Patrick. Always there to cheer her up. More so now that he'd set up housekeeping with his new bride in their brick Victorian. He'd been there Sunday afternoon, moving in, when Belle arrived back from David's house, resolute but glum. He'd listened patiently while she spilled out the whole sorry story of an old girlfriend and a young son. As always, he handled the news with aplomb.

Good old Patrick.

"Maybe that's what this is all about." Belle passed a hand over her aching temples. "I'm too old for David, is that it?"

Her sigh was huge, filling Patrick's office, practically breathing life back into the mounted marlin. "After all, Sherry is *his* age, twenty-seven, and I'm so much older."

"Older?" Patrick was clearly put out with her. "David loves you as much as I adore my new landlady. He simply has some issues to work out with his son. Why don't you grow up?"

"That's my whole problem! I *am* grown up. *Too* grown up. Thirty-two and counting fast."

"Your body may be thirty-two, but you're behaving like Heather right now." His heavy brows formed a menacing V. "Do I make myself clear?"

It was clear, all right. His beard was sticking straight out from his face.

"Got it." Her peevish tone disappeared instantly. "When I see David tomorrow, I'm sure he'll explain everything."

"Josh, let me explain why your mother and I won't be getting married." David pulled his kitchen chair closer to the young boy who was sitting across from him with his hamburger parked in front of him, untouched. "Okay, son?"

Josh nodded, his full lips pulled to a narrow line across his small face.

He's not happy about this. David under-

538

stood only too well a child's deepest need to have a solid home with two parents who loved their offspring *and* one another. Josh had been talking about it off and on all morning, not understanding about love or respect or compatibility or trust, only seeing that the thing he wanted most in life — more than Nintendo or Game Boy — wasn't going to happen.

"Josh, there are two basic problems here." *Keep it simple, man.* "For one thing, your mother and I don't love each other."

"Did you *ever* love my mother?" Josh's voice cracked, splitting David's heart in two.

He exhaled, gathering his thoughts. "Yes, I did. Before you were born, when your mother lived here in Virginia, I thought I loved her very much." He had no intention of explaining the difference between love and lust to an eight-year-old. He hadn't understood it himself at eighteen. "But your mother didn't love me. She told me as much, many times. Then she moved away, to California. And after a long time, the feelings I had for her went away, too."

Josh nodded, a faint light of comprehension flickering in his gray eyes.

David dropped his voice to its gentlest pitch. "Did your mother ever say she loved me, Josh?"

The boy stopped nodding. "No."

"There, you see? But there's something more important you need to understand, son. Your mother says she doesn't love God. But I do, very much."

Josh's head drooped. "I know. She thinks that's weird."

No surprise there. "The Bible tells us that those who love the Lord should be yoked to — married to, that is — other people who also love God. Does that make sense?"

"Sure." His little shoulders shrugged in agreement. "That way you have something in common. And somewhere to go when you're in trouble."

Smart boy. "You're absolutely right, Josh. A faith that's shared holds a marriage together, a family together."

"Will we still be a family?"

David swallowed hard. "You'll always be my son. That'll never change. Ever. And we can see each other a bunch, since your mom tells me you're going to stay in Abingdon. Have you met Grandfather Robison yet?"

"Yeah!" Josh's head bobbed up and down. "He gave me the neatest train set." His voice dropped to a conspiratorial whisper. "Know what? At first I thought he looked pretty scary. He's really big and stuff. But he cried when he met me. Cried harder than Mom. Isn't that wild?"

"That's wild, all right." David gulped again, but still found himself choking out his words. "I'd have given anything to be there, Josh." Bringing his emotions under control for Josh's sake, he veered off on a different slant. "You have a second grandfather, you know. My dad. We're having dinner with him tonight. Think you can handle meeting another grandpa?"

"Will he bring me something, too?" Josh's enthusiasm quickly faded when he saw David's lifted eyebrow and exaggerated scowl. "Just kidding, Dad. He doesn't have to give me a gift. Meeting him will be good enough. Does he look just like us? That's what Mom said."

"After you meet him, you tell me. Then tomorrow afternoon, you and I are going to be part of a hot air balloon launch. How 'bout that?"

"Way cool! Will *you* be in the balloon, Dad?"

"Not me, son. I don't . . . uh, handle heights very well. But you'll get to meet Belle. The lady I told you about?"

Josh's eyes grew wide. "You mean *she* is gonna fly? Man, she's really brave!"

"Uh-huh." David tucked a napkin under Josh's chin, determined to get some lunch in the boy. "She's brave, all right." *Brave or crazy, I'm not sure which. Just keep her safe, Lord. For me. Keep her very safe.*

"That's her." David waved toward Belle, who was dressed in all the colors of a clown on Parade Day, surrounded by ballooning gear in the same rainbow hues. "See her, Josh?"

"She's pretty easy to pick out, Dad." The young boy scampered across the grass, a capricious March wind whipping his jacket around him, while David lengthened his stride, determined to be there when his son met Belle for the first time.

She stood, watching them moving toward her, her eyes switching back and forth. Even from a distance, he could read the anxiety etched on her freckled features. "Hello there, beautiful!" he called out, hoping to put her at ease. When she offered a tentative smile, he knew the worst was behind them.

Bounding up to her like an enthusiastic puppy, Josh thrust out his hand. "Hi, I'm Joshua Robison!"

Belle squeezed it, broadening her smile. Her eyes swept over the boy from head to toe. "My, but you *do* look like your father, don't you?"

"Yup. Mom says Cahill men are hams some."

"Are what?" Belle wrinkled her nose. "Oh! Handsome." She winked at him over

Josh's head. "She's right about that one. My name is Belle O'Brien."

Josh nodded. "You're a disc jockey, right?"

"Most days. But this afternoon I'll be a passenger in a hot air balloon. Wanna watch?"

"Nope." Josh shook his head. "I wanna go."

Belle bent over until she was eye to eye with the boy. "I wish you could, Joshua, but the passenger list is full today. Maybe sometime you and your dad could go hot air ballooning."

Josh pushed his lower lip out in a pronounced pout. "Nope. Dad said he doesn't like high places."

"Is that so?" Belle stood again, her eyes searching David's. "I didn't know that."

"Yeah, well now you do." He hated this, hated having Belle see him as anything less than manly or courageous. The heat in his face only added to his shame. "It's a long story, Belle. A good friend of mine was in a tower accident. He fell, and . . . anyway, I've decided that I'm . . . happier on firm ground."

Her face registered understanding. "So you don't climb the stick either?"

He exhaled a noisy sigh. "Right." He looked down at Josh. "Which means, buddy, if you want a balloon ride someday, our brave Belle will have to be your traveling companion, okay?" He ruffled the boy's hair, still amazed to have him there, in Abingdon. A part of his life. *For good, Lord, please?*

Josh looked disappointed but didn't say anything. *Poor kid.* He'd probably heard "we can't afford that" his whole life and decided no really meant "no money." Maybe the check from Sherry's father would help erase some of that.

He watched Belle as she listened to Josh's version of his cross-country adventures on Interstate 40. Each time he described it, the boy made the drive longer, the weather wilder, the cities larger. To hear Josh tell it, Memphis was the size of Montana.

No question, David would have to sit the child down for a father-son chat about honesty and truth-telling. He'd be the one to teach his son about their heavenly Father, too. The very thought of such a scenario filled his chest with a warm sense of pride, of responsibility.

Father and son. Yeah, it felt good, felt right.

The idea of marrying Belle felt right, too, he reminded himself. The sooner he told her that, the better. As of this moment, though, he'd be walking down the aisle with a peacock. The object of his affection was covered in bright colors, head to toe. Bulky yellow sweater, purple scarf looped around her neck, a pair of blue jeans — brand-new, from the stiff look of them — and screaming red sneakers. *Where do women get this stuff?*

He tossed her a playful wink. "Kinda flashy in the wardrobe department today, aren't we?"

"Yeah," Josh chimed in. "You look like a box of crayons!"

She exhaled with noisy frustration. "Patrick's idea. He wanted me to match the colors of the balloon. Said it would look good when the cameras started rolling."

David surveyed the wide expanse of the campus green, deserted except for the balloon crew and a few students between classes. "Uh . . . what cameras?"

"My point exactly. This is hardly a Big Media Event, not even in Abingdon." She leaned toward him and dropped her voice to a husky pitch. "Though I'm thrilled a certain radio engineer paid a visit to the launch site."

He shrugged with exaggerated indifference. "Somebody had to bring you the broadcast gear."

For a split second, she fell for his subterfuge. "Wh-what? You mean — ?"

"What I mean is, I don't ever intend to be apart from you for two days, ever

545

again." He grinned broadly. "Is that under-stood?"

Her cheeks now matched her sneakers. "Ohh. So things are . . ."

"Things are fine." He rested his hands on Josh's shoulders, squeezing them with fatherly affection. He couldn't do it enough. "Josh and I are getting to know one another while Sherry enrolls for classes next semester and finds an apartment." He paused, his eyes trained on hers. "For the two of them."

Belle's relief was written all over her face. "How wonderful! Wonderful that . . . er . . . Josh will be here in Abingdon. With you."

He held her gaze. "And with you. You two are a quite a pair."

"We are?" Belle and Josh looked at each other in amazement.

David reached for Belle's hand, twining her slim fingers through his own. "You're both small, energetic . . . and full of ba-loney."

"Hey!"

Two sets of narrow eyes pointed at him, with frowns to match.

"You forget," he chided them gently, "I love baloney."

Their frowns began to turn the corner.

"And I love the two of you more than life itself. That's the thing you have in

546

common most of all."

Josh ducked his head, obviously not accustomed to such tender words from a man, but liking it just the same.

Belle's eyes were glistening. "I'm not wild about baloney, Josh. But I sure do love your dad."

She said it!

His heart made a path toward the sun. "You do, huh?" He swallowed a threatening lump that appeared out of nowhere. "Suppose we continue this conversation tonight after you touch the ground, Belle. My place, at seven o'clock?" He slid his wire rims down to give her a full-tilt display of raised eyebrows and the gray eyes she seemed to find so irresistible. "If you don't mind, beloved, I have a proposal I'd like to make the minute you land on terra firma."

For a second she stared at him, startled, then Belle threw back her head and laughed. "Are you kidding? After that confession, I may never touch the ground again."

Touching the ground became an important subject over the next thirty minutes, as Belle watched the balloon crew at work, spreading out the colorful envelope with diagonal panels sewn in brightly hued zigzags that flapped and fluttered each time a hint of wind skipped past.

The wicker basket looked rugged enough. At least as sturdy as the kind grocers used to pack fruit, she decided. Heaven knew she'd dressed the part, in berry blue, banana yellow, and cherry red.

David was busy strapping the remote broadcast equipment in the gondola while Josh jumped up and down on the sidelines, full of running commentary. A few curious students hung in the background — none with a camera or reporter's notebook, she noted. Patrick and Norah showed up minutes before four o'clock, binoculars in hand, escorting her contest winner, a teenager who stared at the inflating balloon with genuine terror in his eyes.

Bless his heart, there wasn't a thing to be concerned about.

Still, as the zero hour approached, she realized they'd both benefit from a few words of instruction before they climbed into a mere basket and floated over Abingdon. She made her way toward Tim and Patrick, who appeared to be having an intense discussion about the weather.

She cleared her throat to get their attention. "Say, fellas. What makes the balloon rise?"

"Hot air." Patrick gave her a sly wink. "You should have no problem creating plenty for them, Belle."

" 'Fraid not, sir." Tim, the pilot of the balloon crew, pointed to a huge fan and propane tank. "The fan creates the air when we do our cold inflation of the envelope. The propane tanks in the basket provide the heat. The only thing Miss O'Brien needs to do up there is smile and look pretty."

Belle liked Tim already.

"Almost ready." He scanned the horizon. "It's a bit windier than I'd like, Mr. Reese, but as you pointed out, we've postponed this flight twice already."

"Go, go." Clearly, Patrick was impatient with the process.

Windy? How windy? Wind was necessary for ballooning, wasn't it? "Tim, we're perfectly safe, right?"

His mouth said yes. His eyes suggested something else.

Josh, never far behind her, tugged on her elbow. "Don't fall out of that basket, Belle!"

"Yeah, please don't." David's eyes were full of teasing. "It would ruin my day."

"And mine." She smiled and tightened her scarf, gazing at the March sky, feeling a slight breeze circling around her. Only a slight one, though. *Nothing Tim can't handle.*

Finally, she turned to her contest winner, a loyal listener who'd stuffed twenty entries in her fishbowl. "You ready, Paul?"

The teenager's eyes were saucers. "I'm . . . I'm not sure I . . ." He gulped, watching as the crew fired the dual burners, which quickly lifted the envelope upright, straining against its tethers toward the pale blue skies above.

The crew, perched on the edge of the basket to keep it from lifting off, were waving furiously. "C'mon, you two!" Tim stretched his hand in their direction.

"Miss O'Brien, I . . . I can't!" The pimply young man looked ready to faint, his Adam's apple lodged in his throat.

Poor Paul!

"Not to worry. I'll be taking photos while I'm up there. I'll send you copies." She winked and gave him an impromptu hug. "No one will know you weren't up there with me unless you tell them, okay?" She patted his shoulder, noting the visible relief written all over his face, then dashed toward the basket and the waiting crew.

They dumped her inside with one heave-ho and little ceremony. *Good thing we didn't have cameras rolling for that little exercise in grace.* "Ta-da!" she said lamely, adjusting her clothing.

"Where's Paul?" The pilot had to shout above the burners.

"Not coming." She would never call the boy *chicken.* She would call him *smart.*

"It's you and me against the wind, Tim."

"Wait!" Josh suddenly bolted in their direction, his arms outstretched, his small gray eyes pleading. "Can I go?" He whirled around with a look of desperation. "Dad, please, can I take his place?"

"Josh, I —"

"Fine with me," Tim blurted out. "Toss him in the basket, sign a release form, and we're outta here." He pointed at David. "You're his father, right?"

Belle watched David gulp, clearly caught off guard. "Uh . . . right."

"Does that mean I can go, Dad?" Josh was beside himself with joy, hopping from one foot to the other. "Please? I promise I'll do everything they tell me to do."

The balloon strained at its tethers, forcing a quick decision.

"Yes, I guess . . . I guess you can, son."

One of the crew members shoved a form and a pen in David's hand. Belle watched him sign it, wondering what must be running through his mind. A once-in-a-lifetime opportunity for his son. A longing to make him happy. And a healthy dose of parental concern for Josh's safety.

"Frankly, we need him for the weight," Tim shouted over the roar of the propane burners. "Not a thing to worry about. Climb in, little fella."

Belle pulled their junior passenger into

the basket, her hands brushing David's, her eyes locking with his. "I'll take care of him, David. I promise."

Tim fired the dual burners again. "Weigh off!"

The crew jumped clear off the gondola and Belle scrambled for her camera, expecting the balloon to shoot into the sky like a ball held under water too long, exploding above the surface.

Instead, it danced along the grass for a few feet, lifting gently upward. Another shot of heat from the burners and it picked up lift speed. Between blasts, Belle called down to Patrick and Norah, who were official chase crew mascots for the afternoon, "See you when we land! Don't lose us!"

As if anyone could misplace 105,000 cubic feet of rainbow-colored balloon.

Josh captured the moment in one breathless word: "Wow!"

The sensation was like nothing she'd ever experienced. Her stomach was somewhere around her knees. She felt light as a feather. *And the sound!* So quiet, so absolutely still, except when Tim fired the burners, loud and hot, right above her head. Between blasts, she realized she could no longer feel nor hear the wind. *Eerie.*

She listened to WPER on headphones, monitoring Burt for his on-air cue to go live. In seconds, she was broadcasting. "From the rooftops of Abingdon, I'm Belle O'Brien with my special guest." She winked at Josh, wide-eyed at her side. "We're a thousand feet above Virginia Highlands Community College, headed for a piece of sky near you."

Describing the view below, she lowered her voice to match the hushed sensations around her, then shouted over the burners when Tim shot a few million BTUs of heat into the envelope, lifting them higher. "We're traveling southwest above Lee Highway, with a beautiful view of the Blue Ridge Mountains on our left, the Norfolk Southern Railway rolling through town on our right. The one that blows her whistle every morning at eleven, right in the middle of my show."

She was amazed at how calm she sounded, how calm she felt. Clicking off the mike until her next break, she took a dozen pictures of the awe-inspiring view, still marveling that she couldn't feel any breeze whatsoever.

"Where's the wind, Tim?"

"You're in it. We move with the wind, not against it." He chuckled, shaking his head. "First time up, eh? I'll have a pin for each of you when we land. Nice little cloisonné number, custom painted with our colors and design."

"Cool!" Josh's voice was reduced to a breathy squeak.

"Thanks, Tim." She beamed back at him. *What were you so worried about, girl?* Ballooning's a piece of cake. The launch was gentle enough. They'd sit back down on the grass just as easily, no doubt.

Bristol and the state line between Virginia and Tennessee stretched out in the distance. Below them was the route Patrick and Norah had taken last Saturday when they eloped, she realized with a grin. *You couldn't call it eloping. Not at their age.* The Virginia Highlands Airport appeared on the right, while directly underneath, motorists were honking and waving out their windows. She waved back, careful not to lean too far over. *Gravity still happens.*

Looking over the edge from a safe distance, she realized how small everything appeared from that perspective. People looked tiny, houses looked like pieces on a Monopoly board, highways looked like narrow concrete ribbons. Problems looked smaller too, she thought, glancing at Josh with a guilty nudge to her conscience.

Josh was his father all over again. Which meant he'd be nothing but a blessing to her life, no matter how things worked out.

With the intuition of a child, he seemed to sense her gaze bearing down on him and looked up with a toothless grin. Without a word, he slowly slid his small hand into hers, natural as you please, shooting like an arrow straight to her heart.

Twenty-nine

A hero is no braver than an ordinary man, but he is brave five minutes longer.

Ralph Waldo Emerson

Belle gulped and squeezed Josh's hand, warm and sticky in hers. "You're a brave guy, Josh, jumping on board at the last minute like that."

He shrugged. "Nothing to it."

"Your dad went back to the transmitter to monitor the broadcast, and everybody else is right down there." She pointed over the edge of the gondola. "See them?"

Below them on Highway 11, the chase vehicle rolled along more or less their same route. She could spy Norah's silver hair pressed against the window. Imagined Patrick by her side and the rest of the crew, keeping in touch with Tim on their car phone and his cellular.

She sensed they were shifting more to the south as she finished her second broadcast of the hour. *Whaddaya know?* They were parallel with Old Jonesboro Road now. *Heading toward David.*

Watching the familiar road unfurl below her, she indulged in a dozen pleasant memories of the evenings she'd navigated that country road, headed for another wallpaper project at David's. When an on-air cue from Burt on her headphones caught her attention, she turned on the microphone for her final broadcast aloft.

"Hello again from the skies above southwest Abingdon, where a few clouds have moved in as we begin our descent toward a friendly farmer — we hope — and a flat field. The ride has been picture perfect, with nary a breeze to knock us off course. My pilot Tim and I are —"

She felt it. A wind — *wind?* — hard from the north, pushing the balloon forward instead of letting it drop gently toward the waiting earth.

"Wind shear!" Tim hollered above the blast of the burners, while frantically tugging at the vent line.

"Josh, sit down!" Belle did her best to not sound panicked. "That's it, honey. Hang on to the tanks."

Belle suddenly remembered her microphone was on. "Ah . . . a wind shear is what my pilot tells me we're experiencing. A radical shift in wind speed and direction, if I recall my earth science textbook correctly." She fought to keep her voice steady, calm, in control, while her heart leaped into her throat as she watched their erratic descent.

She took a deep breath, then pressed on with her commentary, clinging to every broadcaster's code: *Never let 'em hear you sweat.* "Since I've not landed in a hot air balloon before, I have no idea if we're traveling at the proper speed or angle, though it does seem a bit steep. And a little fast. Make that more than a little fast."

They were preparing to land, no doubt. But not in a farmer's rolling field. They were headed toward the rocky hill behind David's house. The hill with a radio tower on top.

A glance at Tim confirmed her worst fears. His face was gray, deadly serious. His hands were working the only two controls he had at his command — the burners and the parachute vent. He could control up and down movement of the balloon. Forward movement, though, was up to the winds, which were quickly becoming March-like. Unpredictable.

And frightening.

It wasn't supposed to happen this way, Lord. Gently up and gently down. Like in the movies.

The wind shifted suddenly again, and she dropped the microphone. Afraid to bend over and retrieve it, fearing the movement might make the basket unsteady or disorient Tim, she crouched inside the gondola, wrapping her arms around a shivering Josh, and watched in horror as the rough, hilly ground grew closer.

The strong winds were pushing the deflating envelope forward, pulling the basket behind at a precarious pitch. She could barely make out WPER on her headphones, but thought she heard Burt calling her name.

"Burt!" She screamed it in the direction of the microphone now caught underneath one of the propane tanks. "Burt, we're trying to land. We . . . we're near the transmitter site on Spring Creek Road."

Much too near.

Seven hundred feet below them, David's newly shingled roof came into view. What a nice job he did, she thought absently, her senses on overdrive. Ahead of them she saw treetops. A small hill. A tall tower.

Three hundred feet of steel tower.

With a red beacon on top, blinking for all it was worth.

Warning! Warning!

The shadow of the balloon on the ground was growing bigger. If they could simply steer a little to the left, she thought in a lucid moment, they could miss the tower completely.

But Tim wasn't steering. Couldn't.

He was cutting off the blast valves. Shutting down the fuel tanks. Yanking on the vent line. Shouting on his cell phone.

Gripping the sides of the gondola.

"Hang on, Belle!" She could hear the terror in his voice, see it in his eyes, see her own terror mirrored there. Josh was whimpering now, clinging to her yellow sweater, asking over and over for his mother.

Lord, help us! Please!

Her mind was whirling as she clamped her hands down on either side of the basket, backing down into one corner of it, shielding Josh with her body and trying to put as much distance between them and the target that loomed before them. The guy wires of the radio tower were dangerously close, close enough to see in detail, thick cables extending a hundred feet in three directions from the base of the tower, holding it up by sheer tension.

The concrete-block transmitter shack at the base was growing larger by the second, too. The truth blindsided her: *David is in there.*

"David!" She screamed his name out of pure instinct, though she knew he'd never hear her.

"Daaa-vid!"

Then, a revelation: *He can hear you, Belle. Use the mike.*

Squeezing one hand behind the propane tank, she wiggled her fingers in the tight space, trying desperately to locate her abandoned microphone. *There!* She pulled it loose with two fingers, easing it up and over the top of the tank.

With her headphones lost in the confusion, she didn't know if she was broadcasting live or merely communicating with David, a few hundred feet below her. "David! David, we're headed straight for the tower! Get out of the transmitter shack now. *Now!*"

The door to the concrete building flew open. She could see his face as he watched her, helpless. She wanted to comfort him. To comfort herself. "We still might clear the tower!"

No. They were descending too fast for that.

Seconds before impact, the gondola swerved, barely grazing the top section of the tower. *Yes!* Her heart leaped with immediate relief, until she was thrown to the basket floor with a sickening thud, pinning Josh beneath her.

A strange silence, sudden and complete, filled the gondola.

She didn't dare move an inch. Wasn't sure she could. Her leg was pinned underneath her at an awkward angle, hurting like the dickens. It was obvious even to her untrained eye what had happened. The envelope itself had snagged on the tower, straining the suspension cables of the gondola as it snapped back, sending the basket crashing into the tower from the rear.

"Tim, we're caught on the tower!" She could barely get out the words, barely project her voice above the half-deflated envelope, whipping around the tower like a huge, noisy flag.

Her words were wasted on Tim. He was crumpled on the basket floor at her feet, unconscious.

She felt the boy stir beneath her. "Josh, are you okay? Does anything hurt?"

"I'm . . . I'm scared."

Suddenly, a fresh gust of wind tossed the basket away from the tower, then brought it banging back, then swung it away, then brought it crashing back again.

"Ohh!" Every collision made Belle's leg ache more. Woozy, she struggled to find any good news, a silver lining in the dark and cloudy present. At least they were no longer going up. Or forward.

Down, however, was still a real possibility.

Why was the basket shaking? *No.* It was her. *Shock.* She felt light-headed. Dizzy. And scared out of her wits.

She couldn't go into shock. Couldn't. Josh needed her.

Hugging him close, she smoothed his hair and patted away his tears. "I'm here, honey. Don't be afraid. Your daddy is . . .

not far away and he's helping us right now. You'll see."

Let it be so, Lord.

She didn't know all the intricacies of broadcast engineering, but she knew this much: the antenna on top of the tower radiated 25,000 watts of power. Dangerous if a person got too close. She looked up, disoriented from the swaying basket, and judged the distance to be fifty feet.

David would have dropped the power by now. Called EMS and the fire department. David knew what to do. He was so good. *So good.*

"That man of mine," she mumbled, losing a grip on consciousness, feeling her world starting to spin as her head dropped down on Josh's small shoulder. "Be mine, David. Be mine."

"Belle! Josh!" David had shouted until he was hoarse, realizing that distance and the wind were conspiring against him. *If they're even conscious.* He wouldn't let himself think past that grim possibility.

The gondola was a good fifty feet below the antenna. Far enough to be safe from electrical shock. *Thank you, Lord.*

That also meant they were two hundred and fifty feet above the transmitter. Above the hard ground. Above him.

The basket, badly damaged from the first

563

collision, was not weathering the constant battering well. The winds that had blown the balloon off course had picked up speed, making the tower sway more than usual, sending hundreds of yards of nylon balloon material flapping in the wind like a sail, then wrapping itself around the tower.

To make matters worse, the smell of rain was in the air.

Lord, give me wisdom here!

He'd called Sherry on the cell phone. Couldn't even bear to tell her the details. Prayed she'd forgive him for such a fool-hardy decision.

Only one thought consumed him: the two people he loved most were in that balloon. He had to do something — and fast.

The rescue teams were on their way. The chase crew would be here any minute. So would the media. They'd all heard Belle on the air, shouting for help. Shouting his name.

"David! David!"

He couldn't wait any longer, couldn't stand around and watch the people he loved hang precariously in a basket, wondering any minute if it might fall. If they'd be rescued in time.

"David! David!"

He wiped his sweaty hands on his jeans, then grabbed the thick gloves he kept in the transmitter shack for emergencies. This

564

situation definitely qualified.

He pulled on thick-soled boots, grabbed a long rope and other crucial climbing gear, stuffed his cell phone in his pocket, and jumped onto the narrow ladder that led straight up, three hundred feet.

Hold on, beloved ones. I'm coming.

The first twenty feet were easy. Thirty, forty, fifty. He felt his blood pumping. Felt the wind on his face. He paused, not letting himself look down. Only up, up at Belle and Josh in the basket. *Alive and well, Lord. Please.*

Sixty, seventy, eighty. The muscles in his legs were starting to ache. His arms, too. He'd need all four in good working order to go the distance. Ninety. One hundred feet off the ground. The contrary March winds whistled around his ears, sending the tower swaying a full foot one way, then the other.

Without warning, the basket banged against the tower, almost knocking him off. *Help, Lord!* His foot slipped and his bravado with it. He hugged the ladder, waited until his foot found the rung, until his heart stopped pounding on the walls of his chest.

Almost halfway. He couldn't look down, couldn't look out at the treetops, at the expanding view around him. He kept seeing his college friend, dropping off that radio tower like a stone, hitting the cement base. Alive but paralyzed for life.

No! He wouldn't think about himself. Only Belle. Only Josh.

Keep them safe, Lord. Help me get there in time.

He looked up and kept climbing.

At one hundred fifty feet, the muscles in his legs were screaming, threatening to cramp up on him. He was slowing down, he knew that. But he had to keep going. A fragment of a verse he'd memorized spun through his mind: "For the joy set before him, Christ endured the cross." *This is just a lousy radio tower, Lord. Nothing as awful as the cross. If you can do that, I can surely do this.*

One hundred seventy feet. One ninety. Two hundred. He stopped again, breathing with ragged gasps. In the distance he could hear the wail of the sirens. EMS, the fire trucks, they were all on their way. But he'd been here first. He'd had to do this.

For Belle. For Josh.

For himself.

To prove he could. To prove he loved them more than his own life.

He could hear Josh now. Whimpering, it sounded like.

Thank you, Father. He's alive, he's alive! It spurred him on. Helped him ignore the pain shooting through his arms and legs. He kept his eyes trained on that basket.

Ten more feet.

It took every ounce of energy he had left to call their names. "Belle! Josh! I'm here."

The whimpering stopped. "Daddy?" His son's voice was tiny, faint, almost lost in the wind.

"Josh! Is . . . is Belle okay?"

Silence. His hands gripped the tower tighter still, straining to keep his wits about him. *No, Lord!*

"D-David?"

Belle's voice. He almost lost his footing when the relief hit him like a shock wave. "Belle! I'm almost there. Hang on."

Two more steps. His eyes never veered from the battered basket. He knew she didn't dare stand, though he could see her gingerly working herself around to peer through a palm-sized hole in the side.

"Oh, David."

Their eyes locked. He took in her bruised cheek, the cut on her chin, the fear in her eyes.

"Are you okay?" Her wide eyes were fixed on him. "I mean, how did you climb . . . ?"

"Belle." He struggled to breathe, to hang on to the ladder, to keep his equilibrium. "Never mind me. Are *you* okay?"

"Yes. Well, no. My leg is . . ." She

smiled weakly at him. "Never mind. Josh is scared but he's okay. Aren't you, Josh?"

All he could see was a blond head and wide gray eyes filled with fear.

"I'm . . . sorry, Josh. I should never have . . . I'm sorry." His words fought against the ever-increasing winds and the guilt that tore at his heart. He forced himself to move up higher still, above the basket so he could assess the damage, inside and out. The news was not good.

"Tim is breathing but unconscious," Belle informed him. "No blood, thank goodness. Ohh — !"

Another sudden, stiff breeze knocked the gondola around in a half turn, sending them scrambling for something to hold onto in their wicker prison.

They needed help and pronto. Better yet, they needed a miracle. "Belle, I can see the fire trucks pulling up to the house. They'll be up here soon. Can you hang on?"

"I'll try." The words croaked out. "As long as I can see you, I'm not as scared."

He barely heard Josh add, "Me, too, Daddy."

Their teary smiles galvanized him into action. He moved another foot up the tower, close enough to grab two of the suspension cables that supported the basket. He had to make them stable, keep them from banging around any longer, destroying the basket and all hope for a safe rescue.

Removing the rope from his tool belt, he eased one end around the cables. Doing it with two hands on solid ground was tough enough. Clinging to a swaying radio tower, two hundred fifty feet up, made it nigh impossible. Struggling to steer the rope into a circle, he caught a movement below him out of the corner of his eye and realized Belle had tucked Josh in the safest corner of the basket and was standing to help him tie the knot.

"Pull!" He shouted against the wind, watching her wince as she did as he asked. The Lord only knew what injuries she'd suffered. Below them, he heard the trucks getting in position, hoisting ladders. "They're coming, Josh! Can you hear them? They'll be up here before you know it. I can see your mom's car down there, too. Are you okay, son?"

Josh nodded, his cheeks tearstained but smiling.

So brave. Like his courageous Belle, reaching across the abyss between them to yank on her half of their square knot.

She was gasping for air as she labored over the rope. "David, I can't . . . believe you . . . did this."

He shook his head and gave the rope a

sharp yank, grateful to watch the basket stop swaying at last. "That's love for you."

Her eyes, still golden in the fading afternoon light, filled with fresh tears. "David, I do love you. So much."

Muffled voices far below them offered assurance that help was on the way. "It could take them some time to get up here, Belle."

She wrapped her arms around a shivering Josh. "We can wait. It seems a whole lot safer in here than . . . where you are."

From the other side of the basket, Tim stirred. Groggy and disoriented, he lifted his head and squinted at his passengers. "Wh-what . . . happened? Where did we land?"

"We didn't . . . yet." Belle patted his leg reassuringly. "We're still aloft. Sort of."

Tim looked instantly more alert. "Aloft? What is this . . . heaven?"

David laughed in spite of himself. In spite of his aching arms and cramping leg muscles. "Almost heaven, fella. Stay right where you are. This thing is none too steady, even with the knot we tied."

Tim scratched his head. "You tied the knot?"

This time it was Belle's turn to laugh. "It's not *that* simple."

"Sure it is." David propped his chin on the crossbar, drinking in all her disheveled glory, her arms around his son, her eyes on him. "Norah and Patrick made tying the knot look easy enough."

Her eyes narrowed. "What are you saying?"

From a hundred feet below them came the sounds of firemen, climbing closer by the minute.

"I'm saying let's continue this conversation when we get you three safely out of this fruit basket and on the ground. You 'bout ready to head down the ladder, Josh?"

Many agonizing minutes later, the first crew members reached them, bearing heavy climbing gear, leather safety straps, and, for good measure, a thermos of hot coffee. Josh was eased down first, crying but courageous nonetheless. Tim, once he got his bearings and a shot of caffeine, climbed down the tower without much assistance.

Belle, with her injured leg, posed a greater challenge. It took three men, a complicated pulley arrangement, and — farther down — a trip in the cherry picker to get her on firm footing. David was beside her every step of the way, encouraging, coaxing, making sure she wasn't in more pain than necessary.

"David, stop fussing," she kept saying. He knew better. The woman loved when

571

he fussed over her for any reason. He figured this particular reason would last them about two hundred years.

Sherry stood on the windy hillside, her heart permanently lodged in her throat. *Josh! Why can't I see Josh yet?* Swirling around her were EMS personnel and television camera crews, sparring for positions, bumping against her.

A burly cameraman glared down at her and barked out, "Excuse me, ma'am, but I need to get my tripod set up."

"And I need to get my son down from that radio tower!" It came out on a sob. She turned away, ashamed of the hot tears that sprang to her eyes. Couldn't he see how awful this was for her?

"Wait a minute! Is there a child up there? Are you the mother?" The cameraman changed his tune in a hurry, waving over a reporter. "Phil, over here! This woman's son is in the balloon."

In seconds she was surrounded by camera lenses and eager bodies clutching notebooks. "I really don't know anything." She worked hard to get the words out, to make sense of what was happening. "The . . . the child's father is up there, too. He's . . . he's the one rescuing them, don't you see? He's . . . saving my son."

They fired questions at her: Why was

Josh in that balloon? Had his father flown with him? Was her son hurt?

She had no answers to give them.

"What's the father's name?"

That was one question she could answer. "David Cahill. He's the engineer at WPER. He's Josh's father. He's . . ." Catching sight of some movement above them, she turned away, stumbling closer to the tower base, pressing against the thick yellow tape the police were using to hold back the growing crowd of onlookers.

There! Climbing out of the basket . . .

"Josh!"

He couldn't hear her, she knew that, but she waved and screamed his name anyway. "Josh!" Far above her, she could barely pick out his small blond head, his striped sweater, his blue jeans. Oh, but it was him. *Yes!* It was her son. Safe in his father's arms.

Josh. The center of her universe. Her first love. Her only love. The only person in her life who really mattered —

Just Josh. Not David.

The realization hit her like a gale-force wind. She loved one person, and only one: her son. She didn't love David. That was the truth of it. And he didn't love her. That was the truth, too.

Oh, but he was rescuing her son! She'd be grateful to him forever for that. And she would tell him so, the minute he put their son safely in her arms. She would tell him . . . she would tell him he was . . .

Forgiven.

More than that. She would ask *his* forgiveness. For taking his son away. He deserved that, surely. A sudden wave of heat filled her face. Yes, he deserved that. She'd put the man through eight years of torment. He deserved . . . something. An apology was a beginning.

"Josh!" He could hear her now, she was certain of it. *"Josh!"*

He was strapped to the substantial back of a fireman as the man slowly made his way down the tower ladder, foot by agonizing foot. She knew her boy would never let go of those shoulders for a second, not even to wave at his mother. The waiting seemed endless, but he was getting closer.

The minute the fireman's boot touched grass, she ducked under the yellow barrier and threw herself at the young boy whose arms now stretched toward her.

"Mom! Dad saved me. I'm safe, I'm safe!"

David inhaled deeply. If Patrick wanted media coverage, then he by cracking got it. The Bristol television stations had their crews there, satellite trucks circled around the tower base, and reporters from all three newspapers jockeyed for the best photo ops of the rescue.

As the cherry picker lowered him with Belle, herky-jerky toward the grassy hill, David's eyes sought out Josh. And Sherry. Dread filled him, cold and hard. Could the woman possibly forgive him for carelessly risking their son's life?

There she is. Josh was barely visible, so tightly was Sherry hanging on to him. David saw her glance his way, and their eyes met.

He nodded slowly in acknowledgment as she moved toward him, Josh's hand in hers. He prepared himself to be slapped, cursed at, made into a public disgrace. He deserved it and more. The minute she was within earshot he called out. "Sherry! Please . . . I'm sorry. So sorry. Is Josh okay?"

She came as close as she dared, with all the trucks and equipment around them. He was amazed to see the hint of a smile touch the corner of her mouth. "Thank you for saving his life, David."

It was the last thing he expected. The last thing he deserved.

"Sherry, didn't he tell you? I'm the reason he was in that balloon. It was all my fault. I —"

She shook her head now, almost laughing, it looked like. "Nice try, David, but I've been this child's mother for eight years. I know how persuasive he can be." She shot him a knowing look. "He's nearly as stubborn as his father. Don't beat yourself up about this. You're forgiven, okay?"

The word stuck in his throat. "F-forgiven?"

"Yeah." She began backing away as an EMS vehicle made a circuitous path toward Belle. "Forgiven. For all of it, okay? The whole thing."

Grace. Again, Lord. It had been raining grace every day since Christmas, falling in great, cleansing drops. He never lost his thirst for it, could never get enough.

He forced himself to speak, though only one thought filled his heart. "Thank you." *Is that all?* What else was there to say? "Thank you, Sherry."

Thank you, Jesus.

She turned to go, though Josh lingered behind her, his eyes still trained on David's. "Bye, Dad."

"I love you, Josh. See you soon, okay, buddy?"

Josh waved, then turned as a camera flash caught him reaching up to hug his mother's neck.

David lowered his gaze, overcome with emotion. When he looked up, Sherry had turned back toward him. Her eyes locked with his.

"David, I . . . I'm sorry, too. For . . . for a whole lot more than a shaky balloon ride." Her chin was trembling, but her gaze remained steady. "I was . . . I never should have . . . uh . . . laughed. Let alone left." She dropped her head and shrugged her shoulders.

It seemed to be all she could manage, but it was enough.

After eight years, it was more than enough.

What had Belle said on Christmas? *The past is just that — passed.* So be it. He'd gotten his son back. The rest didn't matter anymore.

Only one woman mattered and she was a mere two feet away from him, being strapped to a stretcher. He turned to give Belle O'Brien his absolute, undivided attention.

"What time is it?" Her voice was hoarse, the dark circles under her eyes a reminder of her ordeal.

He looked at his watch, all the while keeping one eye on her. "Almost seven o'clock. Why?"

She licked her parched lips, then tried to smile. "We were supposed to meet at seven, remember? You had something important you wanted to tell me. Some proposal . . ."

His grin, dry lips or not, was ear to ear. "Oh, that."

"Yes, that!"

The EMS crew tucked a blanket around her and rolled her toward the waiting ambulance as she wriggled her head around to watch him follow her.

"Promise you won't let them take off without you." It was a warning, not a request.

"Don't worry, Belle. I'll never leave your side. Ever." He let them get her stretcher settled in the van, then climbed in after it, perching on a narrow side bench as they slammed the door shut. Inside the van, all was blessedly quiet. He could almost hear her heart beating. Maybe that was *his* heart, making such a racket.

He cleared his throat, ignoring the ministrations of the medical team who were poking thermometers in her mouth and checking her pulse.

"It *is* nearly seven o'clock, so I suppose there's no point delaying things."

"No point whatsoever." Her eyes were gold stars, twinkling in the dim light of the van. If she was in pain, it wasn't showing on her radiant face.

"It's like this. Belinda Oberholtzer, will you marry me?"

"Oh, David." Out of nowhere came a hiccup. "I thought you'd never ask."

Thirty

*The sad part about happy endings
is that there's nothing more
to write about.*

Tammy Wynette

Belle wrapped herself in a luxurious terrycloth robe that stretched from the bottom of her chin to the tops of her ten scarlet toes and emerged from the fragrant, steamy bathroom wearing her most beguiling smile.

Her eyes drank in her surroundings. The corner suite at the Martha Washington Inn had sumptuous burgundy carpeting, expensive antique furnishings, ivory and gold walls, and a chandelier poised above a truly enormous king-size bed.

What it did *not* have was David.

Silly man! Was he playing games with her, tonight of all nights? Her emotions were not to be trifled with, especially at this precise moment when they were spinning in a dozen directions.

She had waited all her life for her wedding night. She did not intend to wait a single moment longer.

After she looked under the bed, where he

wouldn't have fit if he'd tried, she found instead a plain white envelope on her pillow. *Belinda* was handwritten on the front. No return address.

Then again, he'd hardly need to mail it.

She smiled as she picked up the letter and opened the flap, slipping out a single sheet of paper. Dated today, the fifth of June. Written while she showered, judging by the time noted below it.

Ma Belle Amie —

The cur. He already had her laughing, choosing her all-time favorite '70s song. Well really, how could it not be?

Have I told you often enough today how beautiful you looked on your father's arm? A vision in white lace, your tiny hands filled with fragrant blossoms, your face filled with love. Love for your Lord, love for me. Belle, you took my breath away.

As if he didn't steal her own breath! Waiting at the altar, dressed in black formal wear from the tip of his handsome head to the soles of his strong, courageous feet. Feet that had climbed to her rescue. Even when it had scared him beyond all comprehension. *My husband, my hero.*

Standing by your side, I couldn't

tear myself away from your eyes, glowing like costly gold coins polished to a rare sheen. A hint of tears made them glisten all through the ceremony. I loved that, Belle. I love you.

She could barely read the words swimming before her on the page.

And oh, that dress, Belle! A perfect fit for your perfect body. I am your husband now, so I can tell you that I have never found anyone more desirable. You are everything your Creator intended a woman to be. I am humbled at the thought of all that waits for me.

She was using the letter as a fan now, being careful not to brush her cheeks, lest they singe the paper.

Listening to your voice as you spoke your vows was like hearing a finely crafted instrument, played by a master. The beautiful speaking voice that has charmed the hearts of many will be the sound that greets me in the morning and wishes me sweet dreams at night.

If only he knew what the sound of his

voice did to *her*. Sent shivers up her spine.
Made her heart beat faster. Warmed her to
her very soul.

*I have only one thing to ask of you,
Belle. A small favor from one who
loves you more than life itself . . .*

The letter ended abruptly. No signature,
no postscript.

"What?" Belle flipped it over. "What one
thing? What small favor?"

She heard a soft footfall at the door and
looked up to see her beloved David,
closing the door behind him, wearing a
matching robe and a rakish grin.

"There you are, handsome new husband
of mine." She tuned her voice to the key of
purr. "Now, tell me. What one favor would
you ask of me?"

"Don't sing."

"Don't . . . ! Why . . . why you —" She
sailed one of the Martha's fluffiest pillows
in his direction, but to no avail. The man
was laughing. *Laughing, blast it!* And getting closer by the minute.

"I'll sing if I want to, you . . . you —"
She tossed a bedroom slipper at his
shoulder, and nearly took out an antique
lamp instead.

"Okay, wife of mine. You're welcome to
sing, as long as I can choose the tune." He

was almost toe to toe with her now, his eyes filled with merriment and something else that made her heart skip a beat, then two.

She stuck out her lower lip. "What is this? An all-request show?"

The man's grin was wolflike. "You could say that." His arms circled her, as if she could go anywhere with her legs pinned against the edge of the bed. His voice dropped to a wolfish pitch, too. "I'd like to hear something from, say, the Crystals? September 1963?"

"You don't mean . . . ?"

"That's right."

"But that song starts out with them dancing . . ."

He started swaying slightly from side to side, his eyes trained on hers.

The nerve of this man! "David, you're making me dizzy." Well, *something* was making her head spin.

"Belle, you've got a ten-second musical intro before the vocals. Do you want to sing the whole thing or just the hook?"

She groaned. "The hook is all you're gonna get, buster!"

The swaying stopped. "So . . . let's hear it."

This was harder than she'd expected. "I . . . can't!"

"C'mon, sweetheart. Just sing me the title, then."

She cleared her throat with a dramatic flourish, then lowered her voice to a tuneless whisper. "Uh . . . uh . . . 'Then He Kissed Me.'"

He slipped his glasses off, placing them carefully on the nightstand, never taking his gaze from hers. "Sorry, Belle, I didn't catch that."

Oh, those infernal eyes of his! They were looking straight at her, dangerously close.

"Sing it again for me, beautiful wife."

He meant it, she could see that. Had she really said *obey* in that ceremony today? *Humph.* She made herself whisper it again. "'Then He Kissed Me.'"

"That's better, Belle." He pulled her snugly against his chest, melting any resistance she'd ever thought about attempting. "Once more now, beloved. With feeling."

"Ohh, David!" Her lengthy sigh was the most musical thing she'd ever sung. "'And Then He Kissed Me.'"

And he did. For a very long time.

From the Kitchen of
Norah's Silver Spoon

Glazed Honeymoon Muffins

Muffins:

½	cup butter, softened
½	cup sugar
1	cup mashed ripe bananas
2	eggs, beaten
½	cup honey
2	cups flour
1	teaspoon baking soda
½	teaspoon salt
¾	cup roasted and salted peanuts, chopped

Glaze:

2	tablespoons butter, softened
2	tablespoons honey

Preheat oven to 325 degrees. Cream butter. Add sugar. Beat well. Stir in bananas, eggs, and honey. Blend. Sift flour, soda, and salt together in a separate bowl. Stir into banana mixture. Add peanuts and stir until just combined. Bake in greased muffin tins for 25 to 30 minutes or until muffins spring back when tested.

To make glaze, combine butter and honey in small bowl and stir until smooth. Brush warm muffins with glaze. Serve warm.

Dear One:

What a blessing it is to share this, my first novel, with you!

My path to fiction has been circuitous, to say the least. When I was ten years old, I wrote my first book, using a No. 2 pencil and a lined marble notebook. It was a mystery (yes, like Nancy Drew) and it was . . . uh, let's just say Carolyn Keene's job was quite secure. Even so, the fiction bug bit hard.

In school I did theatre. Nothing thrilled me more than climbing into another character's costume and persona, especially if she had the funniest lines! Ten years of radio — theatre without makeup — came next, then another dozen in professional speaking. Finally writing. Again. Still. Funny how the Lord takes us full circle, right back to where we belong. How faithful God is to wait while we "grow up!"

Radio is a funny business — literally. Listeners often conjure up hilariously off-the-mark ideas of what radio personalities look like. My own letter writers suggested I had olive skin, long dark hair, stood 5'2" and weighed 105 pounds. Well, almost . . .

It was fun to spin the hits again with the staff of WPER and share some crazy memories from my broadcasting years. If you've read any of my nonfiction books, you know

I married a wonderful radio engineer, but David isn't based on my dear Bill at all . . . honest!

David's story is his own, and probably my favorite one in the book. Most of us walk around feeling like we need to be forgiven for something. In truth, we do need that — it's called grace. Norah is the most grace-giving encourager I've ever "met." Perhaps because of her gifts of discernment and womanly wisdom (not to mention her wonderful way with muffins!), she was the hardest character for me to bid farewell at book's end. If you have a Norah in your life, give her a hug for me, will you?

And should you be considering a hot air balloon ride anytime soon, don't be dissuaded. I've been aloft ten times and it's very safe!

Thank you for coming to Abingdon, Virginia with me. I'm always honored to hear from my readers, and love to keep in touch twice a year through my free newsletter, *The Laughing Heart*. For the latest issue, plus laminated bookmarks and other free goodies, please write me directly at:

Liz Curtis Higgs PO Box 43577·Louisville, KY 40253-0577

Until next time . . . you are a blessing!
Liz Curtis Higgs

About the Author

Liz Curtis Higgs has written eleven previous books — six humorous books for women and five children's books. A conference speaker and columnist for *Today's Christian Woman*, Liz also spent a decade as a popular radio personality. She lives with her husband and two children in Kentucky.

The employees of Thorndike Press hope you have enjoyed this Large Print book. All our Thorndike and Wheeler Large Print titles are designed for easy reading, and all our books are made to last. Other Thorndike Press Large Print books are available at your library, through selected bookstores, or directly from us.

For information about titles, please call:

(800) 223-1244

or visit our Web site at:

www.thomson.com/thorndike
www.thomson.com/wheeler

To share your comments, please write:

Publisher
Thorndike Press
295 Kennedy Memorial Drive
Waterville, ME   04901